Haley Hill is a fresh new voice ~~in~~ an author, Haley launched and ~~ran a~~ agency – and is an expert in all th~~ings dating. She lives in South~~ London with her husband and twin daughters. *Love Is…* is her second book.

LOVE IS...

HALEY HILL

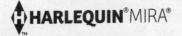
HARLEQUIN® MIRA®

Harlequin MIRA is a registered trademark of Harlequin Enterprises Limited, used under licence.

First Published in Great Britain 2016
By Harlequin Mira, an imprint of HarperCollins*Publishers*
1 London Bridge Street, London, SE1 9GF

Love Is… © 2016 Haley Hill

ISBN: 978-1-84845-474-3

0916

Our policy is to use papers that are natural, renewable and recyclable products and made from wood grown in sustainable forests.
The logging and manufacturing processes conform to the legal environmental regulations of the country of origin.

Printed and bound by
CPI Group (UK) Ltd, Croydon, CR0 4YY

To my grandmother, Grace, whose love life never quite measured up to the romance novels she read.

Keep flirting with the Elvis impersonator, nan, there's still time.

One of the greatest secrets to happiness is to curb your desires and to love what you already have.

Emilie du Chalet

Chapter 1

I sat on the toilet and stared at the packet.

After years spent bringing couples together, attending their weddings, then their offspring's christenings, spending more money on baby gifts than I did on my mortgage, surely I deserved my chance of happiness too. Wasn't that the way this karma thing was supposed to work? I thought Eros and I had a deal.

I glared up at the ceiling to register my protest, then ripped off the cellophane. It must have been about the hundredth pregnancy test I'd bought since our wedding day. I'd tried to restrict it to one per cycle, but invariably I ended up back at Superdrug, clearing the shelves in the family planning section, hoping that a different brand might provide a different result. And I'd tried them all, from the basic two-liners to the early-response super tests complete with digital screen to spell out the result in shouty capitals. And then of course there were the ovulation kits, the sight of which now triggered some kind of Pavlovian response in Nick, sending him on a desperate quest for alcohol before I presented myself wearing Ann Summers lingerie and a 'you know what that does to your sperm count' nod at his wine glass.

I continued to stare at the turquoise and pink branding until the colours merged like a Maldivian sunset and my thoughts wandered back to our honeymoon. At the time, I'd believed that all it took was a sandy beach, white linen sheets and a quick flick of the fertility fairy's wand. And after seven nights of consummating our marriage in a five-star beach hut, as I skipped into the chemist at the airport, I couldn't have been more certain that the tiny mound of a stomach I'd developed was the manifestation of Nick's and my future happiness, and entirely unrelated to the ten thousand calories I'd consumed each day at the hotel buffet. I glanced back down at the box and laughed out loud. If only I'd known, I thought.

My phone vibrated. I ignored it.

'Well, I know now,' I said to myself as I pulled out one of the tests, 'that even with the aid of a NASA-engineered ovulation detector, we had no hope of conceiving.'

Our first Harley Street consultation had been over a year ago, but since then, the doctor's words had been bouncing back and forth in my head like a ping-pong ball.

'Intra-cytoplasmic sperm injection is the only option,' he'd said.

He'd gone on to explain in medical terms that I had the follicles of a fifty-year-old heroin addict, my uterine lining was thinner than an Olsen sister, and my ovaries were about as useful as a snorkel in a tsunami.

My stomach churned. This round of treatment was our third and final chance. I took a deep breath and pulled out the test. My heart beat faster. I could feel the pulse in the tips of my fingers. I lost my grip for a second and it slipped from my grasp. I caught it swiftly with my other hand, as if it were the Olympic torch.

I'd learned from the fertility forums that it was better to wee into a container, to ensure the stick was properly immersed, rather than hold it under a stream of urine. The method was more accurate, 'Mum to Three Snow-babies' had advised. I rested the test, lid still on, on the cistern and spread the information leaflet open. I already knew it by heart. It didn't matter. I read it again. Just to be sure.

It is best to conduct the test in the morning after a night's sleep. The urine is more concentrated.

I couldn't recall sleeping, although my uncompromised pelvic floor muscles had at least managed to hold off any bladder evacuation.

My hands were trembling as I reached for an old lid from a toothpaste pump dispenser. It was the perfect size for collecting a sample, 'Here's Hoping' had explained on the Fertility Friends forum. I sat down on the toilet and held it under me until I felt warm urine overflowing from the top. Once I'd carefully submerged the test in the container, I closed my eyes, visualising the word 'pregnant' in my mind, hoping it might somehow instruct the test to comply. Moments later, when I found myself chanting and rubbing my womb, unwittingly re-enacting a hypno-spiritual video I'd seen on YouTube, I realised that I was in dire need of distraction. Instinctively, I went to call Nick, but then I remembered he had an important breakfast meeting, so instead I called Matthew.

He answered on the first ring.

'What?' he asked.

I could hear a child screaming in the background so I raised my voice.

'The two-minute wait,' I said.

I heard more wailing and then a noise that sounded like something choking. Matthew issued a reprimand and then came back on the line.

'OK, Ellie,' he said, retaining the disciplinarian tone for me too. 'Move away from the vision board. That photo of you and Nick cradling a Photoshopped baby isn't helping anyone.'

'It's worse than that,' I said. 'I was chanting.'

Matthew laughed. 'Look,' he said, 'two minutes is but a mere blip on the timeline of life. I've got another seventeen years to get through until these two are off my hands.'

I let out a deep sigh and flopped down onto my bed. 'It's not just the two minutes,' I said. 'It's all that came before it too. Surely you understand that?'

Matthew laughed again. 'Ah, but I do, my sweet.' He paused for a moment to intercept a further misdemeanour then continued. 'I remember precisely what preceded this current bout of neurosis.' He took a deep breath and then exhaled. 'This all began long before you started fretting about your inability to breed.'

I'd been hoping for distraction not ego annihilation. 'What did?' I asked.

'Well,' he said, in a manner that implied he was drumming his fingers on the table. 'Let's consider Eleanor Rigby's life journey so far, shall we? What were you doing before this all-consuming quest for conception?'

'I don't know, working?'

He sighed. 'Ellie, you spent five years planning your wedding.'

I went to speak but Matthew continued. 'Prior to that you spent four years aggressively soliciting a proposal from

Nick. Before that you engineered a career that enabled you to personally interview thousands of eligible men.'

'And women,' I said, 'as a matchmaker. I was trying to help people.'

He chuckled. 'This behaviour, although disturbing enough in isolation, was preceded by many other alarming antics: a shambolic engagement, two disastrous cohabitations, fours years cyberstalking Hugh Jackman, a stretch hyper-parenting a pet rat and six years fanatically coddling two Cabbage Patch dolls.' He paused and took a deep breath. 'Ellie, you've been looking for love since the day you were born.'

'No, I haven't,' I said, pulling myself up from the bed. 'And FYI, Bungle was a guinea pig. Not a rat.'

Matthew must've handed the phone over to his toddler, because all I could hear was the choking sound, then wailing, then manic laughter, then some salivary noises, then more wailing then Matthew coming back on the line.

'There you go,' he said. 'That's what your life will sound like if you get what you wish for.'

I rolled my eyes. 'It can't be all bad.'

'It's not all bad,' he replied, 'but it won't make you happy. Just like marriage won't make you happy. And kids certainly won't make your marriage happy.' He paused for a moment, seemingly to wipe a child's orifice, then continued. 'If you kept abreast of the latest research, as you should, you would know that a recent study showed a couple's happiness decreases proportionately with the birth of each child.'

I rolled my eyes. 'Who conducted that study?' I said. 'Was it you, interviewing yourself?'

He laughed. 'We're conditioned to think we need to have children in order to be content, when in fact, if we bother to look at the evidence, the opposite is true.' He let out a deep sigh. 'Why else do you think Lucy went back to work and left me looking after the little buggers?'

I giggled. 'You love it really.'

'No,' he said, 'I really don't. I love them, of course, but I don't especially enjoy sacrificing my every human right in the name of positive parenting.' He moved away from the phone to confiscate some crayons then continued. 'Freud said that our need to procreate is driven by a fear of death.' He went on to adopt a lady therapist voice. 'Do you fear death, Eleanor Rigby?'

I rolled my eyes. 'The only one who should fear death is you, if you don't shut up.'

He was still laughing when I hung up.

I checked the timer on my phone. Twenty seconds to go.

I flopped down on the bed again, feeling the weight of my body sink into the mattress. Nick said he would love me no matter what.

Would he really though? I wondered. Even if I could never give him the sandy-haired children he'd always wanted? The son he could hoist up onto his shoulders and teach what it means to be a man, or the little girl with pigtails reaching for his hand, eyes wide with adoration. What if it was just us? For the rest of our lives. Our union having no greater purpose than to provide comfort to each other in old age. We'd play bridge, grow vegetables and potter around the house. And then we'd die.

Ten seconds to go.

I burst back into the bathroom. Before I reached for the test, I stopped and looked up at the ceiling, retracting my earlier complaint to the Almighty and substituting it with a pledge to reinstate my monthly charitable donations.

I snatched the test from the pot and stared at the screen on the side. The words registered straight away.

Not pregnant.

I looked again, just in case I was hallucinating the 'Not'. I shook it and then held it up to the light. I knew there was nothing I could do to change it. I threw it in the bin along with the backup test and then went to get ready for work.

Chapter 2

I nudged the front door closed with my shoulder to force the lock into place. A flake of black paint fell onto the front path.

I turned to see Victoria, who was bouncing on the spot, clad head-to-toe in Lycra, ponytail swinging like a metronome.

'Morning, Ellie,' she said.

'Morning,' I mumbled, pulling my handbag onto my shoulder. I'd hoped I would be able to sneak out before she'd emerged from her five-thousand-square-foot double-fronted mansion for her morning showy-offy jog.

She continued to bounce but at the same time cocked her head. 'You didn't reply to my text.'

I sighed. Victoria had been charting my IVF process with the precision of a government agent. This, I suspected, was precisely the reason she'd been lurking by her front door since 7 a.m., jog-ready, to jump out and catch me on my way to work.

I glared at her. A glare that I hoped would say: *Do you think my face would look like this if I'd just discovered I was incubating a much-longed-for half-me-half-Nick bundle of cells? No, Victoria. Instead of expressing elation, relief and the warm glow of raised hCG, this face is more befitting an exhausted and dejected woman who has endured two years of invasive medical interventions comprising, yet not exclusive to, double-dose vaginal suppositories, self-administered stomach injections, daily internal scans performed with a dildo ultrasound device, leg-stirrup procedures with disturbing terms such as 'egg harvesting' and 'implantation', then topped off with a giant needle stuck between my eyes to release my chakra. And all that to be told once again that I have failed to do the very thing that women were made to do.*

Victoria screwed up her face. She'd been at the Botox again. 'Aw, Ellie, no luck?'

I shook my head and made a point of theatrically rubbing my barren uterus.

'Third time lucky maybe?'

'Victoria, this was the third time.'

'Oh yes, fourth then.' Her bouncing quickened. For a moment, there was a glimpse of empathy in her stretched smile.

I scowled at her. She knew there'd be no fourth attempt.

She sniffed, and started bouncing higher.

'You could always adopt,' she said, adjusting her heart rate monitor. And with that she sped off.

I stood on the street for a moment, not realising I was still holding my stomach, and looked up at Nick's and my house. Against the rows of magnificent Victorian villas, it looked like the neglected stepchild, stuck on the end like an ill-considered afterthought. While its siblings had been sent to Farrow and Ball finishing school, ours had been pebble-dashed and left to fend for itself against the elements. They say a pet chooses the owner and I wondered if that might be true for a house too. As much as I'd tried to fit in on this street, I was starting to doubt I ever would.

Up the road, mothers were bundling impeccably presented offspring into shiny cars. For them, life seemed so easy. Most had met their dashing eloquent husbands at top-tier universities, or later, working in some kind of glamorous grown-up profession. They'd gone on to marry in a grand French chateau or palatial Tuscan villa, then breed effort-lessly, popping out rosy-cheeked cherubs every year or so, sometimes two or three at a time, while also advancing their careers, renovating and interior-designing their houses and serving quail eggs as appetisers. They even found time to accessorise with chiffon scarves.

When Nick and I moved here, I wanted to be just like them, but in the past few weeks, the L.K.Bennett riding boots I'd bought on Northcote Road had started to pinch a little.

My thoughts were distracted by the sight of Victoria's three-year-old Boden-clad daughter marching out of their front gate, followed by an exhausted-looking woman who I presumed to be the latest au pair.

'Morning, Camille,' I said, grinning at the little girl a tad overzealously.

She looked me up and down and frowned. It was as though she could sense I wasn't biologically qualified to be communicating with her. Then she scooted off, her little ponytail swinging briskly. I watched her for a while, then made my way to the station, dodging stylishly swathed pregnant bellies and designer buggies.

I arrived at the Canary Wharf office with a large latte in hand. It felt good to be able to pollute my body again without the potential of embryo toxicity bearing down on my conscience. I pushed open the double doors to reception and took a deep breath. My role as CEO may have been usurped by the venture capitalist's grandson, Dominic, who'd apparently learned everything there was to know about romantic love at Harvard Business School, but what truly mattered was that the dating agency I had conceived seven years ago was now an international corporation. Matthew might believe my motives were questionable, but over the years I had helped thousands of people find love. I took another sip of coffee and smiled. If that wasn't a legacy worth leaving then what was?

'Afternoon, Eleanor,' Dominic said in his I'm-American-in-case-you-wondered accent. Then he slammed a file onto my desk. 'Meeting's in five.'

I gulped down the rest of my latte and leafed through the file, which contained the minutes and action points of the last investor meeting. My smile faded. I pushed it to one side and then switched on my computer, so I could at least reply to a few emails before the investors arrived.

Ten more franchise enquiries. One from Korea.

Matchmaking in Korea? I wondered. Surely they had more pressing things to worry about.

Then one from Victoria and her unnecessarily double-barrelled surname.

Subject title: FW: New hope for IVF-resistant couples.

I deleted it. Then I glanced at my phone. Nick had called five times. I dropped my phone back down on the desk. I knew it was cruel to extend his two-minute wait to an entire day, but I'd decided that a statement such as 'You have no hope of ever being a father, unless you substitute me for a fresh-follicled twenty-something or we find a psychologically unhinged surrogate on the internet' was probably best delivered in person.

Suddenly Mandi sped past, wearing an oversized neon pink kaftan.

'Meeting time, Ellie!' she shrilled, leaving the throb of luminous pink in my eyes. Dominic strutted ahead of her, clenching his buttocks as though he were harbouring a hamster in his colon. I screwed up my face, wondering if I had just cause to alert the animal authorities.

Then I looked back down and continued with my paperwork procrastination, flicking through the post. At the bottom of the pile was a gold envelope. It looked like a wedding invitation. My stomach flipped. The excitement had never waned. I ripped open the envelope, and pulled out a card. It had a watermarked image of a slim woman, grinning and holding a cocktail. *We've finally done it!* was the quote on the front. I flipped it over and read the back.

Dearest Ellie,
You are cordially invited to the Divorce Party of Cassandra Wheeler (formerly Stud-Wheeler).
Where: The Wheeler (formerly Stud-Wheeler) residence.
When: Friday 14th Feb
Dress to impress.
Please bring a bottle. Or five.

I let out a deep sigh as I slotted it into my divorce party file, which was getting fatter by the day. Then I pulled myself up from the chair to face the meeting and Dominic's ill-founded plans for my company.

Before I entered the meeting room, I saw Mandi through the glass walls and her latest assistant, sitting beside her, poised to take minutes as though she were at the G8 summit. The investor panel, which consisted of four heavy players in the tech and entertainment industry, were seated in a row opposite Dominic, who'd commandeered his side of the table as though he were hosting an episode of *The Apprentice.*

He stood up when I entered the room. 'Eleanor,' he said, gesturing for me to sit beside him in a smaller chair, 'so nice of you to join us.'

I forced a smile, then nodded at the investors.

Straight away, Mandi pulled her pink glittery laptop out of her bag, adjusted her headband and smoothed down her kaftan. I studied her ensemble. It was unlike her to wear anything that wasn't nipped in at the waist and tailored to her ribcage. She clapped her hands, and looked around, then clapped them again, as though she expected the lights to dim. When they didn't she leaned over and switched them off herself. Then she plugged her laptop into the projector, pressed a few buttons and a map identical in colour to her kaftan appeared on the wall.

'OK, everyone,' she began. 'Are we all ready?'

Dominic sighed.

I nodded and smiled. Mandi's assistant clapped.

Mandi clasped her hands together and grinned. 'I have fabulous news. Amazing! The best news ever!'

'You're leaving,' Dominic mumbled.

She ignored him, further dramatising with a drum roll to the table.

'As of this week,' she continued, 'we've finally done it. We have matchmakers stationed in every continent!' She pressed a key on her laptop and suddenly pink hearts popped up all over the globe, presumably identifying matchmaker infiltration hotspots.

She looked around the room and began clapping herself. Her assistant joined in.

'Yay, everyone!' Mandi said. 'Well done, us!'

Dominic raised both eyebrows. 'Every continent?' he said, leaning back in his chair. 'We have matchmakers in Antarctica?'

Mandi shook her head, as though she were about to reprimand a troublesome toddler. 'Antarctica is an iceberg, Dominic, not a continent.'

He rolled his eyes.

'Besides, it's melting,' she said. 'It's unwise to expand into an economy with diminishing returns. Didn't they teach you that at Harvard?'

One of the investors closed his eyes and sank into his chair.

Mandi glided over to the map like an air hostess pointing out the safety exits. 'Ten here…' she pointed to France '…ten here…' then Germany '…and here…' then Italy '…twelve here…' Sweden. She reached up and pointed to New York. 'Twenty matchmakers in New York…' her finger moved across America '…five in LA, seven in San Fransisco…' then down to Australia '…eight in Melbourne, five in Sydney…' The pointing continued, as did Mandi's list of countries.

Ten minutes later, when I was feeling somewhat dazed,

Mandi leaned forward and tapped on the keypad. Suddenly pink hearts started racing across the wall like some kind of customised disco ball. It felt as though they were throbbing in time to the pulse in my head. 'One hundred and one matchmakers,' Mandi concluded with a loud applause.

'We could make a coat out of them,' Dominic mumbled.

Mandi glared at him, her applause unfaltering. Her intern joined in.

'We did it,' Mandi said. 'It took ten years, but we did it. This is possibly the most exciting day of my life!'

I grinned at Mandi and high-fived her from across the table.

Dominic shook his head as though struggling to release himself from a disturbing dream. Then he stood up and disconnected Mandi's laptop as if disarming a nuclear bomb. He replaced it with his laptop and went on to present the previous year's accounts, taking personal responsibility for everything that was profitable and apportioning blame, mostly to me, for everything that wasn't. Then he concluded with his strategy for the coming year.

'Client retention,' he declared, as though he'd discovered the cure for cancer.

I frowned. One of the investors leaned forward.

Dominic continued. 'Currently we're retaining clients for an average of six months. If we could up that to twelve, we'd double our profits.'

The investor who was leaning forward, interrupted. 'Adjusting for client acquisition costs,' he said, 'we'd actually triple our profits.'

'Exactly,' said Dominic.

Mandi's hand shot up.

Dominic ignored it.

Mandi coughed loudly.

I gestured at Mandi to speak.

She turned to Dominic. 'But our job is to match people. To find them partners. We want them to find love and leave our agency. That's what they're paying us for.'

'Yes,' Mandi's assistant chipped in. 'The clients get upset if they've been with us for months without being presented with a life partner.'

Mandi glared at her.

Dominic ignored them both. Then he tapped the keys on his laptop.

He continued. 'You can see from my projections, if we delay matching our clients by a week or so each time, it will prolong the duration of the service, significantly increasing the revenue from monthly subscriptions.'

He pressed a key and a bar graph was projected onto the wall.

One of the investors made a note on a pad in front of him. Another one checked his mobile.

'Another significant change I propose,' Dominic said, leaning back expansively, 'is with technology.'

All four investors sat up straight. The one with the mobile in his hand quickly put it back in his pocket.

'Apps,' Dominic declared, this time as though he'd discovered a renewable energy source. He tapped on his laptop and then another graph appeared, seemingly demonstrating a considerable reduction in costs and an exponential growth in profits.

'Matchmaking apps.' He smiled a self-congratulatory smile, while pressing keys on his laptop, which projected an array of charts and screenshots onto the wall. 'If we convert our service to a digital interface, we'll cut staffing costs by ninety per cent.'

As Dominic continued babbling on about profit margins and shareholder dividends, I gripped the sides of my chair and starting counting back from a hundred, a technique Dr Phil had explored on a recent episode about anger management. I counted slowly and purposefully, breathing deeply as I did, but at fifty-six, I could no longer stand to listen to Dominic's attempts to brainwash the investors into agreeing to erode every value that the agency had been founded upon.

I stood up and glared at him. 'Enough,' I said.

Dominic stepped back. 'Excuse me?'

'You're excused,' I said, pushing past him and slamming shut his laptop, bar graph wilting as I did.

Mandi sat forward in her seat. An investor smirked.

Dominic glared back at me. 'What's the matter, Eleanor? Are you not concerned about profits?'

'Of course I am concerned about profits,' I said. 'My house is falling down, I'm thirty-six and still wearing Primark shoes. I had more disposable income when I was twenty than I do now. I would love nothing more than a nice fat dividend once in a while. But—' I turned to the investors '—that is not why I am here. That is not why I founded this company.' I turned back to Dominic. 'So yes, Dominic, I am concerned about profits. But what I'm more concerned about is our clients.'

Dominic rolled his eyes, as though I was about to suggest we pitch for government-funded matchmaking.

'This year,' I continued, 'we've had more divorces than marriages. Did you know that, Dominic?'

He straightened his tie.

'Last year alone, our clients reported 14,198 failed relationships and 1,239 broken engagements.'

Mandi's eyes widened.

I continued, 'Six hundred and seventy-five divorces.'

Mandi gasped.

I leaned forward and connected Mandi's laptop back to the projector. 'Mandi's presentation showed we're doing a great job. We have contributed to more marriages than any of the online agencies. However, we could do better. We're helping people find love. But I believe we should extend our service to help our couples maintain their relationships. They need our support.'

Mandi shook her fist in the air like a 'let 'em 'ave it' angry cartoon character.

Dominic tried to speak but I silenced him with a glare and continued.

'We offer a personal service. That's how we differentiate from all the other dating agencies. The superficial swipe-to-reject dating apps out there are feeding the narcissistic monster that is sabotaging the fundamental principles of marriage.' I narrowed my eyes at Dominic. 'Besides,' I added, 'if we dehumanise matchmakers, who's to say we won't dehumanise daters?'

Dominic shook his head. 'What does that even mean?'

I sighed, wishing Matthew was there to back me up by citing Freudian and Jungian papers.

Dominic rolled his eyes and began checking emails on his phone.

I whipped out the divorce party invitation and slid it across the table towards the investors.

'This is the tenth one I've received this month,' I said. 'We need to take action.'

'Hear, hear,' said Mandi.

One of the investors nodded.

I continued. 'No one gets married thinking they'll divorce.' I looked the investors in the eyes. 'No one falls in love thinking it won't last.'

Dominic glanced up from his phone.

I cleared my throat. 'We all hope for the best but few of us are equipped to deal with the worst.'

I noticed one of the investors was blinking rapidly and rubbing a tan line where his wedding ring used to be.

'And how do you propose we do that?' Dominic asked, as though I'd suggested we populate Pluto.

'Instead of cutting staff,' I said, 'we should recruit more, invest in their training. We should equip our matchmakers with the knowledge and the skills to support our clients.' I glared at Dominic. 'That is something even the most nifty app could never do.'

Dominic smirked. 'Nifty?' he said, his expression implying that the use of old-lady vocabulary could compromise the credibility of my argument.

I continued, keen to move on. 'We should train all of our matchmakers as dating psychologists.'

Dominic rolled his eyes again, and let out a why-don't-we-feed-the-starving-in-Africa-while-we're-at-it sigh.

I continued, pretending to ignore him. 'I want us to be pioneers in our field.'

Dominic threw up his hands. 'Oh, come on, Eleanor, that will cost a fortune.'

The investor with the tan line leaned forward and raised his hand to silence Dominic. Then he stared at me for a moment. 'OK,' he said. 'you've got my vote.'

Dominic went to speak but another investor cut him off. 'Me too,' he said.

The other two investors nodded in agreement. 'Let's do it,' one said.

The remaining investor, who was also Dominic's grandfather, turned to him. 'I'm with Ellie on this,' he said.

I smiled and, rather smugly, held out my hand to Dominic. He bypassed it, grabbed his laptop and then stormed out of the room, buttocks clenching as he did.

As soon as he'd left, Mandi jumped up from her seat and began clapping wildly.

'Yay, Ellie!' she shouted.

Her assistant followed her lead. 'Yay!' she said.

Perhaps it was because this was an unusual situation for them, or maybe they were genuinely moved by my proposal, but for whatever reason, the investors began to clap too. That was until one of them must have realised that it was a little odd and stopped. At which point the rest followed and then filed out of the room, checking their mobiles, seemingly trying to pretend it hadn't happened.

That evening, as I fought my way towards the underground, the wind battered my umbrella and rain swept under it and into my face. I squinted my eyes and pushed ahead. I may have won the case against Dominic—a victory for the relationships of others—but the jury was still out on how Nick would take the news that we had failed to conceive yet again.

The moment I reached our street, my umbrella finally

buckled under the elements and, as I waded through a giant puddle on our front path, I wondered if our marriage would survive this storm.

b... and under the aluminium and ... ...
... ...
... ...

Chapter 3

Before I opened the front door, I noticed the hall light was off. Nick wasn't home yet.

'Of course, out drinking,' I mumbled under my breath, although fully aware there was no one to hear me.

I ruffled my umbrella, drops of rain splattering up the walls, then I bent the spokes back into line and shoved it into the stand next to Nick's giant work-branded golf umbrella. It baffled me why corporations seemed so keen to advertise that they employed people who played golf in the rain.

After I'd shaken my coat and hung it over the radiator, I made my way into the kitchen. I looked around the empty room, then opened the fridge and grabbed a bottle of wine. It had been almost a year of not drinking, priming my body for reproduction, but now I was looking forward to drowning my non-compliant ovaries in Pinot Grigio.

I leaned against the counter and poured myself a glass. As soon as I took a gulp, my nerves settled and a warm sensation spread through my veins. I took another gulp and gazed up at the ceiling, then back down at our shabby kitchen. I squinted my eyes, trying to superimpose the building plans we'd had drawn up years ago onto the sixties-style laminate shambles in front of me. I knew exactly how it should look. I didn't have far to go for inspiration. Every house on the street had been knocked through into their side-return and extended out back to create the trademark South West London statement kitchen. I took another sip and wondered if the white gloss Poggenpohl dream would ever be mine.

'Cheers,' I said to the peeling work surface. 'Me and my kitchen, living the dream.'

I took another gulp and then checked my phone. It was 7 p.m. I called Nick. No answer. I took another gulp of wine and called Matthew to rant.

There a clattering noise in the background when he answered. 'Twice in one day,' he said, eventually. 'I'm honoured.'

'Can you talk?' I asked.

He sighed. 'I can talk, and I would love to talk. However, the real question is whether I will be allowed to talk.' There was the sound of something crashing to the floor, followed by wailing. 'Shit. I mean, sugar,' he said.

'Everything OK?' I asked.

There was silence, a muffled sound and then Matthew returned. 'Little sod keeps falling off his chair.' There was a faint sobbing in the background. 'It's this bloody booster seat. I'm sure it has an eject button. There you go, Zachary. Now eat your pasta.'

'Shall I call you back?'

'No, no. Are you OK?'

I took another gulp of wine. I knew he would know better than to ask me directly about 'the test'.

'Angelica, leave the vase.'

'I'm OK,' I said. 'It's just—'

Suddenly there was another crash followed by a scream. 'Fuck. I mean, fudge. Fiddlesticks.'

'Look, I'll call you back tomorrow,' I said.

'No, no.' Matthew's tone had an urgency to it. 'We can talk now.' He paused, then made a strange squealing noise. 'Angelica, sweetheart, please don't eat the broken glass.'

I grimaced. 'It sounds kind of hectic there?'

'Just another day in paradise,' he said. 'Zachary, *eat* the pasta, don't stick it up your nose.'

I thought for a moment about telling him the result, but I realised he'd probably guessed anyway. Besides, any mention would most likely provoke a diatribe about some study linking new parents to suicidal tendencies.

'Don't suppose you fancy coming to a divorce party with me next Friday night?' I asked.

'Angelica, I said no! Hang on, Ellie, I should really sweep up this glass.'

I continued, 'I need some company and Nick's entertaining clients. Again.'

His pitch suddenly increased. 'A party?' he said. 'One that doesn't involve soft play, chicken nuggets, or a balloon-wielding entertainer?'

I laughed. 'Yes,' I said.

'I'm in.'

'Don't you need to arrange a sitter or something?'

'Nope,' he said. 'It's about time their mother did some mothering.'

The bottle of Pinot Grigio was almost empty by the time I heard Nick's key in the lock. My throat dried up as I mouthed the words I would say to him. I downed the remainder of the wine, and mouthed them again. It was almost as if the act of saying them out loud would make them more final.

We will never have children.

I'd said it in my mind over and over all day: in the pauses between conversations with Mandi, in the lulls during the investor meeting, while Dominic sashayed around the office. Even wiping my bottom in the toilet had felt melancholic. Mine would be the only bottom I would ever wipe, I'd thought. I'd never change a nappy or lovingly slather Sudocrem on a rashy crack. Every thought seemed to extrapolate into a video projection of never-to-be-realised moments: the first steps, a tender kiss at bedtime, nursing a grazed knee, adjusting a school tie, a comforting cuddle when the world seemed cruel. Being a mother had so many facets. And I would know none of them.

I twirled my empty glass by its stem and looked out beyond our neighbour's roof at the tiny glimpse of sky. I liked to think my mother and father were up there somewhere, looking down, keeping tabs on the little three-year-old girl they left behind. Suddenly I found myself laughing. It seemed so unfair, almost deliberately orchestrated, to be denied a mother and then to be denied motherhood too. I dropped my head into my hands, knocking the glass to the floor.

Nick rushed into the kitchen. From his furrowed brow and teary eyes, I could tell he already knew. Maybe Victoria had told him, maybe he'd guessed. He smiled, but I knew it was for my benefit. He put his arms around me and pulled me into his damp coat. I hugged him tightly and buried my head in his chest.

After a while, he lifted my chin and looked into my eyes. 'It's OK, Ellie,' he said.

I knew he must be hurting as much as I was, and that now was the time we needed more than ever to love each other, but when I smelled whiskey on his breath, I felt my muscles tense. I pulled away.

'Well, it might be OK for you,' I said, with a sharp sigh.

Nick cocked his head, as though trying to make sense of my sudden change of tone.

'What's that supposed to mean?' he asked.

I shrugged my shoulders.

He leaned forward and stared at me. 'You're saying I'm glad it didn't work?'

'I'm saying,' I began, then paused just to be sure I wanted to continue, 'you didn't try as hard as I did.'

He stepped back, eyes wide. 'Seriously, Ellie? What is wrong with you?'

I glared at him. 'Wrong with me? You're the one who's spent the past year partying like the Wolf of bloody Wall Street. No wonder we couldn't conceive.'

He frowned. 'Partying?'

'You're out every night.'

'Working.'

'Drinking.'

He ran his hands through his hair. 'You know I hate entertaining. Drinking is the only way I can tolerate a night with those egotistical Neanderthals.'

I rolled my eyes. 'Oh, poor suffering you.'

'Besides,' he added, frown turning to a scowl, 'lately, it's been preferable to being at home.'

I jumped to my feet. 'Oh really?' I said.

'Yeah, you've totally lost it, Ellie.' He walked to the wine rack and grabbed a bottle of red. 'If it's not wheatgrass shots, it's acupuncture, then there's those ridiculous "hypnotise yourself into getting pregnant" bullshit podcasts you watch. And if you're not doing that, then you're on those barmy forums. You and the army of infertiles, inciting each other to drink five litres of milk or eat a kilogram of cashews, all charting each other's cycles like you're in some kind of crazy baby-making coven.' He paused to unscrew the top and pour himself a glass. 'Seriously, Ellie, you've been a nightmare to live with.'

I snatched the bottle from him. 'Well, at least I've been making an effort,' I said, pouring a glass. 'You, on the other hand, have been doing everything you possibly can to sabotage this whole process. You've pretty much done the opposite of everything the consultant told you to do.'

Nick grabbed back the bottle and slammed it on the counter. 'Ellie, I've done it all. I've had every test under the bloody sun. I've had sex on demand. I've taken all manner of weird supplements. I've even worn ventilated boxer shorts. I've tolerated your obsession with trying to control the uncontrollable and now, if I'm totally honest, I'm relieved.'

'Relieved?'

'Yes, relieved there's an end to it.' He paused. 'No more fawning over baby clothes, no more debates about buggy brands, or cots versus cot-beds. No more planning our weekends, holidays, furniture, house, careers, around the fact that you might or could potentially in the future be pregnant. No more pseudo maternity wear.' He gestured to the wrap-around jersey dress I was wearing, bought in anticipation that it might accommodate a small mound in the early summer.

I glared at him. 'I'm bloated from the hormones. Sorry I don't feel like prancing around in a pencil skirt.'

He glared back at me. 'And a sex life would be nice. At least one that isn't scheduled around the optimisation of sperm quality.'

I stepped back, hand on one hip, the other brandishing my wine glass. 'So that's it? Sex is more important to you than having a family.'

He rolled his eyes. 'If sex were more important to me, then I wouldn't have dedicated my most virile years to wanking into a plastic cup.'

'Oh—' I accidentally sloshed some wine onto the floor '—I forgot. I must remember to be grateful.' I gulped the wine down before I spilled any more. 'It's not as though I haven't made sacrifices too. I'm the one who's been injecting myself in the stomach every day. I'm the one who quit drinking for two whole years.'

'Making up for it now though, aren't you?' he said.

I continued. 'I'm the one who's had an entire medical team peering between my legs and extracting follicles from my ovaries.'

Nick screwed up his face.

'Oh, I forgot, that's not sexy, is it? Must remember to be sexy. Must remember to be grateful.'

Nick let out an elaborate sigh. 'You? Be grateful? That would be a first.'

I scowled at him. 'What's that supposed to mean?'

He sniffed. 'Come on, Ellie, you're never happy. You're always waiting for the next big thing. The wedding, then the house and now it's this obsession with having children. You can't keep waiting to live your life. This is it, Ellie. Look around you. This is your life. Just live it, will you.'

I raised my eyebrows and then waved my arms around. 'Great. A shitty kitchen and a drunken husband. What more could a woman want?'

Nick shook his head and smirked. 'There are plenty of women who would be more than happy with me.'

I stared at him. 'Ooh, had loads of offers then, have you?'

He shrugged. 'I have actually.'

Immediately, I envisaged pert-bottomed interns bending over Nick's filing cabinet and fluttering their eyelashes. 'Oh really?' I said, taking another glug of wine. 'And?'

Nick sighed, his expression softening. 'Ellie, I'm married. To you.'

He put his glass down and walked towards me. 'And I want you back.' He took my hands in his. 'I want us back.'

Chapter 4

Matthew stopped at Cassandra's front gate and scratched his head.

'I'm not sure balloons are entirely appropriate for a divorce party,' he said, gesturing to the bulging bunches tied to each post.

Dizzee Rascal's 'Dance Wiv Me' was blaring out through the open windows and, as we walked up the path, I could see silhouettes gyrating under a disco ball. The sunken roof of the Georgian townhouse looked as though it might collapse with the shame of it all.

I knocked on the door. There was no answer.

Matthew turned to me with raised eyebrows. 'We could always go for a quick bite to eat first?' he said.

I glared at him. 'No. We're here to support Cassandra.'

Matthew shifted his weight from foot to foot. 'You know how some people are terrified of clowns?'

I laughed. 'Not all divorced women are scary,' I said. 'Besides, Cassandra is a friend.'

He sculpted his quiff in his reflection from the polished knocker. 'She's not a friend, she's a client.'

'She's going through a rough time.'

Suddenly raucous laughter bubbled up from the hallway.

'Yes, sounds like it,' he said, adjusting his shirt collar. 'What if I'm the only man here? They might slice off my testicles or deep-fry my penis.'

I knocked again. I could hear Cassandra's high octave New York drawl approaching the door. 'Coming!' she screeched.

She greeted us with the determined smile of a TV presenter. 'Oh. My. Gaaaad. It's Ellie!' She flung her arms around me, nearly knocking Matthew over. 'It's so good to see you! Come in, come in. We have tequila.'

I grabbed Matthew's arm and pulled him in behind me.

Straight away we were thrust into the sitting room and towards the makeshift bar, which seemed sufficiently stocked to survive an apocalypse. Cassandra poured us each tumblers of tequila, then insisted we down them in unison. Afterwards, she leaned in towards me and pointed at Matthew.

'Is that Nick?' she asked in a stage whisper. 'Only I remember him being better-looking.'

Matthew stepped forward. 'Yes, I am—'

I blocked him with my arm. 'This is Matthew,' I said, interrupting whatever mischievous untruth he was about to present to Cassandra, 'my *friend*.'

Cassandra looked him up and down and then grinned. 'Not fair,' she said. 'I so want a gay buddy.' She turned to Matthew. 'Got one for me?'

Matthew, clearly, sensing an opportunity to avoid the

angry divorcees turning on him, suddenly ramped up his camp-o-meter and jutted his hip to one side.

'Sweetheart,' he said, flicking his wrist. 'If you can throw a party like this, I'll get you a gay boy quicker than you can say Liza Minnelli.' Then he skipped towards her and started stroking her dress. 'Is this Diane von Furstenberg? It's am-az-ing.'

I knocked his hand away after I noticed it edging towards the chest area.

'Let's mingle,' I said.

He poured two more tequilas, before air-kissing Cassandra and squeezing her bottom.

I rolled my eyes as we walked off. 'Behave,' I said.

He shrugged his shoulders.

I stopped and glared at him. 'You're a married father of two.'

He threw his arms in the air. 'I am what I am,' he shrilled, doing his best gayed-up interpretation of Gloria Gaynor, followed by an intricate sidestep across the dance floor. A pretty redhead laughed and joined in dancing with him.

I watched for a while and then pulled him to one side. 'Impersonating a homosexual in order to take advantage of vulnerable women is exploitative and a gross breach of our host's trust.'

He downed one of the tequilas. 'Ellie, a divorce party is hardly the ideal platform to preach moral standards.'

I snatched the other tequila, thought about putting it on the side, then downed it instead.

Matthew did a double eyebrow raise. 'I see you're drinking again?'

I nodded, wiping my mouth.

He stared at me for a moment, looking as though he were

about to offer something profound. Then, clearly thinking better of it, he put his arm around me and ruffled my hair.

'Come on, fag hag,' he said. 'Let's dance.'

A while later, once Cassandra had informed the DJ that we had a 'gay' guest, it was as though the playlist donned a pair of leather chaps and dropped an E. And despite Matthew's sterling efforts, which peaked at a rather gymnastic 'Vogue' pose, by the time we heard the intro to a remix of the Village People's 'In the Navy' we both agreed it was time for a tequila top-up. Matthew didn't bother with glasses this time; instead, he just grabbed the bottle. He took a swig and passed it to me.

I took a gulp and looked around the room. The furniture had been pushed to the side and the fireplace hidden behind the temporary DJ booth, but even through my now blurry vision, I could see that this was otherwise an elegant family room. I found myself imagining Cassandra and Dr Stud, or Stud-Wheeler, as they'd renamed themselves, snuggling on the sofa together, bottle of red in front of them, the latest HBO TV series on in the background. I held the image in my mind for a moment, before contrasting it with tonight's frenzied quest for oblivion and wondered when it was that they had stopped loving each other.

I snuck behind the bar and picked up a photo frame that had been placed face down on a radiator cover. Straight away I recognised the image. It was a photo I'd taken on our singles' trip to St Anton: the moment they'd jumped off the ski lift together, now freeze-framed forever. I smiled as I recalled the months I'd spent prior trying to persuade them to meet each other.

'No, he's too short,' Cassandra had said, when I'd shown her his profile.

'I usually date hotter girls,' Dr Stud had explained, before selecting the profile of a bikini-clad twenty-three-year-old nursing graduate.

I'd always known though that if I could just get them together on the ski trip then they would understand. And they did—well, for nine years at least. I glanced back down at the photo and took another swig. I would never forget the way they laughed together. It was as though they were the only two who knew the punchline. That kind of love couldn't simply fade to nothing. Could it?

I looked up to see the redhead giggling and then flashing her cleavage at Matthew. I glared at him. Just as I was about to intervene, Cassandra appeared beside me.

'Gimme some of that,' she slurred, snatching the tequila bottle from my grasp. I'd forgotten I was still holding it. She took a swig and then turned to me. Her mouth was smiling but her eyes looked vacant. She nodded to the photo. 'What goes up, must come down,' she said, surprisingly succinctly. Then she laughed. 'No one can defy Newton's theory of...' She rubbed her temples and swayed a little. 'Or was it Galileo?'

'Newton,' I said. 'Gravity. Are you OK?'

She took another swig and then wiped her chin. 'Never better,' she said, handing the bottle back to me. 'Right. Speech time.'

I was still gripping the photo frame as I watched Cassandra climbing onto a chair, microphone in hand. I should have intervened. It was clear to everyone that a public and drunken explanation as to why we should celebrate the breakdown of her marriage wasn't going to end well. However, as much as I wanted to preserve her dignity, part of me was desperate to hear what she had to say. I gripped the photo frame tighter and glanced over at Matthew, who was now cupping the redhead's breasts through her dress. In the past year the agency's divorce rate had doubled. Even my own relationship was in distress. I wanted to know why. Because if I knew what was wrong, then I was closer to finding a way to fix it.

Cassandra wobbled on the chair a little, then steadied herself and tapped the microphone. The DJ turned off the music.

'Hey, everyone!' Cassandra shouted.

The crowd cheered.

'It's great to see you all here tonight,' she said, looking around the room and holding out her hands. 'Some of you knew me before...' she pointed at a few people in the crowd '...and some of you knew me during...' she pointed out a few more '...but now, after nine forgettable years, Richard, or Dick, as I now prefer to call him, is finally out of my life...' She punched the air and the light from the disco ball caught a tear on her cheek. 'That bastard might have cost me £1.3 million in settlement and my last fertile years, and...' she pulled the skin tight on her face '...given me greater need for Botox, but now I'm rid of him.' She punched the air again like a motivational speaker.

The guests cheered and clapped and she gestured for me to bring her the tequila bottle.

'As I said,' she continued, having taken another swig, 'some of you knew me before, and some of you knew me during. But *everyone* will know me after! Let's get this party started!'

Cassandra jumped down from the chair and the music was replaced by synthesised siren. A group of faux policemen stormed into the room. They had sunbed tans, thick thighs and crew cuts.

Matthew caught my eye, with a 'can we please leave now?' expression.

I glanced back at Cassandra, who had begun to emit a noise not dissimilar to that of a mating tree frog.

Matthew immediately abandoned the redhead and shuffled up beside me nervously. The crowd, mostly comprising single women, parted and chanted as the dance troop ripped off their Velcro fastened trousers in one synchronised movement and went on to execute a choreographed 'stop and search' procedure, intermingled with an array of dance moves, which Matthew identified as the rear arrest, the handcuff hustle and the truncheon treadmill.

Once the routine had finished, and the only garments that remained were black satin pouches, Cassandra lifted up her skirt and called out to the dancer with the largest bulge. I did a double take. He looked disconcertingly like Nick.

'Officer,' she said, slapping her bottom, 'I've been a very naughty girl.'

After she'd manhandled his pouch, she whispered something in his ear and slipped him a fifty-pound note, followed by a cheeky wink in Matthew's direction.

A short while later, after Matthew had been the non-consensual recipient of an extended lap dance from PC Schlong, he asked me if we could leave. I led him out of the house and closed the door closed behind us. He glanced around skittishly and then sped down the front path to hail a passing taxi.

I giggled as we climbed in. 'You can't have the smooth without the rough,' I said.

He scowled at me. 'There was no need for him to dangle the bloody thing in my face,' he said.

I giggled some more.

'Stop laughing,' he said, folding his arms and staring out the window.

I leaned towards him and smirked. 'You've still got some whipped cream on your chin,' I said, still laughing.

His hand flew to his face until he realised I was winding him up. Then he glared at me. 'Speak about this to no one,' he said.

After I'd eventually managed to stifle my giggles, I shuffled up next to him.

'Cheer up,' I said. 'We had fun tonight.'

He sighed. 'Well, I'm glad *you* had fun while I was being lap-raped by PC Right Said Fred.'

I smirked. 'So you didn't have any fun at all? Not even squeezing Cassandra's bottom?'

He rolled his eyes.

'Or checking out that redhead's boob job?'

'She was asking my opinion.'

I sighed. 'Because she thought you were gay.'

'I can be objective.'

I shook my head.

He shrugged his shoulders. 'Lucy wouldn't care anyway.'

'Really?' I asked. 'You have a clause in your marriage contract stating that objective assessment of non-spousal secondary sexual characteristics is permissible?'

He shrugged his shoulders. 'Something like that.'

I raised an eyebrow. 'Is everything OK with you two?'

He folded his arms tightly across his chest. 'It's amazing. It really is.' He forced a smile. 'Since we chose to breed, our relationship has transcended that tiresome phase of animalistic passion and become a more spirit-centred union.'

I frowned. 'You mean spiritually centred?'

'No, spirit. She drinks gin, I prefer vodka.'

I slapped him on the arm. 'Can you be serious for just one minute?'

He sighed again and then gazed up to the roof of the taxi. 'What do you want me to say, Ellie? It's shit. My marriage is shit right now. It hasn't always been and I'm hoping that it won't always be, however, right now, it's shit.'

I turned to him with a scowl. 'You've got two beautiful children, a gorgeous home and a wife who loves you. You're so lucky, Matthew. You should be grateful.'

'Oh yes, because you think having a family is the key to your happiness. Ellie, you spent years thinking the perfect man was the key to happiness. When are you going to realise?'

'Realise what? That you like willies?'

He rolled his eyes. 'That there is no key...'

I stared at him.

He turned to me. 'You want to know the truth?'

'Go on then,' I said, half smiling.

'I enjoyed looking at that girl's boobs tonight, because I've forgotten what a normal pair looks like. In the past two years, Lucy's have been swollen, veiny and grotesque, if not leaking milk or infected. Her nipples have been cracked and furred with thrush. And now, when finally they've been handed back to me, empty sacks lined with stretch marks, she worries they don't turn me on. And, as much as I love her, as much as I want them to and as much as I reassure her otherwise, we both know deep down that she's right.' He turned to me. 'You think having babies will complete the you and Nick white-picket-fence happy-ever-after. Well, it won't.'

I smirked. 'You're just grumpy because you've had a ten-inch penis slapped in your face.'

He glared at me. 'Having kids changes everything, Ellie. I love Zach and Angelica, but Lucy's the one who wanted them. Then straight away she went back to work leaving me at home to wipe bottoms and boil pasta.' He looked down. 'She treats me like I'm staff. You should hear her: "Matthew, pick up the dry-cleaning. Matthew, clean the windows. Matthew, did you call the upholsterer? Matthew, are you listening to me? Matthew. Matthew!" She's lost all respect for me.'

'No, she hasn't.'

He rolled his eyes and let out a protracted sigh. 'Well, why else did she shag her boss then?'

For the rest of the taxi journey, we didn't speak. I knew there was nothing I could say that would lessen his pain. I squeezed his hand and we stared out the window.

'Not a word to anyone,' he said, as he climbed out the taxi.

I nodded.

'About PC Schlong, I mean. I have a reputation to uphold.'

I'd prefer to think it was because I was starting to feel like myself again, rather than a fear of ending up like Matthew and Lucy. Or worse, Cassandra and Richard. Either way, as I climbed into bed and snuggled up next to Nick, I felt something I hadn't felt in months. I leaned over and kissed him. I could tell he'd been drinking again but this time it didn't bother me. I kissed him again, and he kissed me back.

That night, making babies was the furthest thought from my mind.

Chapter 5

First thing on Monday morning, I noticed a voicemail from Cassandra. I waited until I was in the office and had finished my coffee before unleashing the assault on my eardrums. I put it on loudspeaker so I could temper the impact, and also so I could type some emails while I listened.

Unlike the usual mega-volume, her words were slurred and hard to decipher because she was sobbing and then sometimes laughing between them.

'I'm miserable, Ellie,' she said and then paused. 'It's not the same.' She sniffed. 'I want my Dick back.'

When I looked up, I saw Dominic leaning over my desk, hair coiffed, eyebrows raised. 'She wants her dick back?' he whispered, laughing. 'Just what we need: another "they matched me with a post-op" lawsuit.'

I rolled my eyes. 'It's not how it sounds,' I said. 'She's just got divorced.'

He rolled his eyes. 'And you want to counsel these freaks,'

he said, making an inverted comma gesture around the word 'counsel'.

I shook my head, tempted to prod him with the biro in my other hand.

'Cassandra isn't a freak,' I said, hand still firmly over the receiver. 'She's a client. And the Dick that she wants back is her ex-husband. Not male genitalia.'

Just as Dominic was processing what I had said, buttocks most likely twitching as he did, Mandi breezed over. She was wearing a patterned empire line smock, roomy enough to accommodate a sextuplet elephant gestation. I glanced down at her stomach and then back at her face. Despite the rumours circulating the office, I had yet to ask her the question formally. Dominic said it was a matter for HR and advised against it. Besides, once it was public knowledge, I feared Mandi might overload my inbox with a deluge of Pinterest nursery interiors.

Mandi leaned over my desk, eyes wide.

I decided it best to terminate the voicemail, before the entire office became involved.

Mandi leaned in further. 'Was that Cassandra?' she asked, holding her hands to her chest. 'How is she?' She looked to the floor. 'That poor, poor woman. Divorce has to be the worst experience for anyone.'

Dominic, who was still leaning on my desk, smirked. 'Worse than terminal cancer? Death of a child? Being de-capitated by ISIS?'

Mandi ignored him. 'And this is her second time. Simply awful. Is there anything I can do to help? And Richard, how is he? They were so in love, Ellie.' She wiped a tear from her cheek. 'So, so in love. How could we let this happen?'

Dominic interjected, with a dismissive flick of his wrist.

'If it was her second marriage, then statistically, they only had a twenty-five per cent chance of making it work. There is nothing you could have done.'

Mandi narrowed her eyes and poked Dominic in the chest. 'Would a doctor turn off a life support machine if a person had a twenty-five per cent chance of waking from a coma? No, they wouldn't.'

Dominic sighed. '*They* turned it off. Not us.'

Mandi scowled. 'This isn't Dignitas. We're a dating agency. We're supposed to help people.'

Dominic laughed. 'If only it was,' he said. 'There's a far greater chance of preserving dignity in death than in dating.'

Mandi tutted then turned to me. 'Ellie?'

I thought for a moment. 'Cassandra wants him back.'

Mandi held her hands to her chest again and nodded.

Dominic sniggered. 'Does she really though? Or is she just feeling sentimental after contracting pubic lice from a troop of strippers?'

I stared at him for a moment, wondering how he'd been privy to such classified information from the divorce party. Then I turned back to Mandi. 'She says she still loves him,' I said.

Dominic laughed. 'I thought I still loved an ex when I found an old photo of her topless.'

It was hard to imagine Dominic on a date, let alone in a relationship. I was almost certain he was a sociopath who fantasised about mutilating female body parts in the manner of Patrick Bateman from *American Psycho*.

Mandi scowled at him, then continued. 'They were so good together. Perfect for each other. You never saw them on the ski trip, Dominic. Or at their wedding. What would you know?' Mandi's chest was flushed now. She turned back to me. 'I have to help them, Ellie. I couldn't live with myself if I didn't.'

Dominic shook his head at Mandi. 'Get one of your matchmakers to deal with it. You're a manager now, you have more important things to do.'

'Nothing's more important than saving a marriage,' she said. 'And besides, Dominic, you should know by now, I'm a matchmaker first and a manager second.' And with that she stomped off.

Dominic glared at her as she walked away, then turned to me and pointed at his watch to remind me, as he did every Monday, that it was time for our weekly meeting.

'Another hour of my life I'll never get back,' I muttered, as I followed him into the meeting room.

'Sorry, what was that, Eleanor?' he asked, as he sat down in one of the executive orange leather seats he'd had commissioned for our meeting room.

I forced a smile. 'Another intellectually stimulating chat,' I said.

He looked at me and raised one eyebrow, then took a file from his briefcase.

'So,' he said, placing both hands on the table, 'this dating therapy thing you want to do.'

I stared at him. 'You mean the coaching programme, which has been formally approved by the investors?'

He nodded and smiled. 'Well, I believe it could generate more profit than our introductions service.'

I went to smile but Dominic's enthusiasm was concerning me.

He continued. 'So the investors and I have spoken and it was unanimously agreed that *you* should manage this project.'

I stared at him some more, wondering what point he was trying to make.

'In its entirety,' he added.

'I thought that had already been agreed.'

He leaned back and ran his hands through his hair. 'We expect you to write and deliver the programme.'

I shook my head from side to side. 'Well, the idea I had…'

'Yes?'

'…was to work with the top psychologists and researchers.'

Dominic clapped his hands together with the glee of a fisherman who had just felt a tug on his rod. 'Excellent, Eleanor. That's precisely what we were thinking too.' He glanced down at his file and began flicking through the pages. Then he nodded and pushed the file across the table towards me. 'You'll find a comprehensive list of experts in there.'

I opened it and glanced at the first page, which I immediately discovered was a fold-out world map.

Dominic continued. 'You'll start in New York; that's where most of the current research is being done. Using that as a base, you can travel to Long Island and Texas. Then, after that, you'll move on to Iceland, then Tokyo—there's some interesting research going on there—then Africa, and finally, you'll end up back in Europe.'

I leafed through the pages, noting every stop Dominic had listed on my protracted tour of the globe. I closed the file and shook my head.

'I'm not leaving London,' I said.

The beginnings of a smirk crept out from the corners of his mouth. 'But this is what you wanted, isn't it, Eleanor? To find a cure for heartbreak?'

I pushed the file back towards him.

'What about Skype? I could easily speak to the experts on the phone. I don't have to be there.'

Dominic shrugged his shoulders. 'Well, we think you do. That way you can witness and experience any interventions firsthand.'

I screwed up my face. 'I can't be the researcher and the recipient.'

Dominic grinned. 'The investors think you can.'

I stood up, ready to walk out. 'Well, I'll have to persuade them otherwise then, won't I?'

His smirk was at full capacity now. 'They've decided to channel all available resources into the project. So, good luck with that.'

That evening, I arrived home to find Nick in the kitchen, pan-frying tuna steaks. I could see he'd already prepared a salad and the table was set complete with a lit candle.

'Evening, my gorgeous girl,' he said, handing me a glass of wine.

I leaned in towards him and rested my head on his shoulder. I knew we'd have to have a conversation about our childless future at some point, but for the time being, I wanted it to just be Nick and I again. Without any complications.

Suddenly, my phone vibrated. It was a text from Victoria.

Hurry up. You're late

I scrunched up my face, remembering a vague acceptance of a dinner invitation last week.

'What is it?' Nick asked, sipping some wine.

I sighed. 'We're supposed to be having dinner at Victoria and Mike's tonight.'

Nick's smile faded. He glanced at the tuna steaks and then at the candle burning and then back at me. 'But I wanted a night with just us,' he said.

I leaned over and turned off the hob. 'So did I,' I said, 'but we promised.'

Nick let out a long sigh and then downed the rest of his wine.

'Come on,' I said, 'we'd better get a move on, you know what she gets like if her scallops are overdone.'

I leaned over and kissed him on the cheek and we made our way next door.

We rang the doorbell twice before anyone answered, which, given Victoria's domestic staffing levels, was quite unusual. There was a bit of a kerfuffle, some scratching at the door and what sounded like a tiny bird chirping, before eventually Olga, Victoria's housekeeper, opened the door. A bundle of grey fluff rolled out onto the flagstone step. I bent down to pick it up. At first I couldn't quite tell if the warm little body, with the fast-beating heart, was a cat or a rabbit or something else entirely, but when a pair of big blue eyes stared up at me, and the little tail started wagging, I realised it was…

'A puppy?' Nick asked, leaning in for a closer look.

Olga ushered us in. 'I take Rupert now,' she said.

'No, no, He's fine with me,' I said, looking down at his furry face and smiling.

'Careful, he's likely to pee all over you.' Victoria strode towards us, looking uncharacteristically flustered. 'At best.'

'Oooh, I don't mind,' I said, cradling him in my arms. I

nuzzled his fur with my face. He smelled like malt biscuits and freshly cut grass.

Nick leaned in closer and stroked him on the tummy. 'He's a cute little chap, isn't he?'

Victoria smoothed down her ponytail. 'We need to eat,' she said. 'Give the hound back to Olga. And make sure you wash your hands.'

Mike didn't join us until we were seated at the table and from his expression, he was as enthused about the dinner party as we were.

Once Victoria had formally chastised us for being late and thereby being solely responsible for the asparagus' limpness, she went on to explain Rupert's arrival.

'Camille's therapist suggested we get her a pet.' Victoria sniffed. 'She said that given the high turnover of au pairs, it would provide a constant in her life.' She flicked her ponytail and speared a piece of asparagus. 'Dr Osbourne has been harping on for months now about maternal attachment. Clearly trying to promote that book she wrote. She's been on the *Lorraine* show too.' She took a sip of wine, then shook her head quickly as if to disperse the alcohol. 'I was raised by sixteen different au pairs and it never did me any harm.'

Nick started coughing. It looked as though a bit of asparagus had gone down the wrong way.

Victoria glanced around for Olga, then tutted and topped up her own wine.

'I mean, seriously, what does Dr Osbourne expect me to do?' she continued, taking a sip. 'Give up my entire life to bring up my daughter?'

We all sat in silence. I swallowed the last mouthful of cold asparagus and then Mike stood up to pour us more wine.

'But I bet Camille must love Rupert,' I said, changing the subject. 'He's adorable.'

Victoria sighed. 'She's allergic. She's gone through two asthma inhalers since we collected him from the breeder.'

There was a scratching sound along the floorboards, and suddenly Rupert skidded into the dining room, hotly pursued by Olga.

'Rupert, Rupert, come!' Olga shouted.

Victoria scowled at Olga. 'Quiet,' she said, 'we are entertaining.'

'Sorry, Mrs Victoria,' Olga said, then tried to grab Rupert, but he bypassed her hand and scooted under my chair.

I bent down and picked him up. His eyes were wide, like a five-year-old who'd just arrived at Disney World. He jumped up and licked my face.

Victoria's ponytail began to swing violently. 'Olga, get that dog out of here right now. He's supposed to be napping.'

Olga held her hands up. 'I try, but he no want to nap. He want to play.'

Suddenly Rupert lunged forwards and swiped a Parmesan shaving from my plate.

Nick laughed.

Victoria tutted and marched towards me, snatching Rupert from my grasp. Then, arms outstretched, she handed him to Olga and waved them both out of the room.

'As if having a child isn't hard enough,' Victoria said, 'now I've got to train that bloody canine.'

Mike leaned back in his chair and laughed. 'You're not exactly training him though, are you, darling? Olga is.'

Victoria let out an extended sigh. 'She knows nothing about dogs. I think they eat them in her country.' She sipped some wine. 'I suppose I'll have to get a dog trainer. As if I haven't got enough to do already.'

Mike laughed again, though louder this time. 'Yes, whatever next, you might have to cancel a Pilates session or a lunch or, heaven forbid, a hair appointment,' he said, taking another gulp of wine.

Victoria swished her ponytail from side to side. 'Excuse me, Michael—' she'd taken to calling him Michael since they'd joined the Chelsea Harbour Club '—I didn't give up my career to manage household administration every day.'

Mike refilled his glass and leaned further back in his chair. 'So, tell us, Victoria. What precisely did you give up your career to do?'

Victoria's ponytail slowed to a stop and she glared at Mike.

Nick shot me a sideways glance.

I shifted in my seat, hoping Rupert would come skidding back into the room and divert the conversation.

Fortunately, Olga returned instead, with the main course. *'Filet de boeuf,'* she announced plonking the tray down on the table. 'And yes, Mrs Victoria, I wash my hands.'

We ate the beef in silence. Occasionally, I glanced at Nick but mostly I just chewed and gazed around the room. Whenever I visited Victoria's house, I felt as though I'd stepped into the centre spread of *Home and Garden* magazine. It seemed unfair that she could just swish her ponytail like a wand and get everything she'd ever wished for. My vision board was plastered with images of interiors like this, dotted around the doctored photo of Nick and I with a baby; however, so far all the universe had seen fit to deliver to me was up-cycled furniture from Gumtree. I huffed. Nick and I might not be worthy of parenthood, but surely the universe could spare a chesterfield sofa?

Rupert continued to yelp from the kitchen for the duration of two courses. I kept looking at Victoria, hoping she might soften her resolve and bring him in for a cuddle, but she was still glaring at Mike. Mike looked nonplussed.

'So, what breed is he?' I asked, in an eventual attempt to break the silence.

'Sporting Lucas,' Mike answered, matter-of-fact, between mouthfuls of crème brûlée. 'Apparently, the ability to hunt ground vermin is an essential skill for a family pet.'

Victoria shrugged her shoulders, still glaring at Mike. 'Well, you know what they say about living in London.'

We all looked at her expectantly.

She narrowed her eyes. 'You're only ever a metre away from a rat.'

Mike tutted, then scooped another mouthful of brûlée into his mouth.

Rupert was still yelping from the kitchen and now he'd added mournful pines into the mix. It took all my willpower not to run out and soothe him.

'Maybe he's trying to tell us something,' I said.

Victoria narrowed her eyes. 'What, that we have rats in our house? Don't be ridiculous. He's just being needy and probably wants more Parmesan.'

I turned to her. 'Or perhaps he's distressed? Having been dragged away from his mother and then locked in a huge kitchen by himself.'

Victoria flicked her wrist. 'He's nine weeks old; in dog years that makes him nearly one and a half. He'll get over it,' she said, pushing her untouched dessert to the side.

I glared at her.

She opened her mouth as if to say something and then closed it again, clearly thinking better of it, which was unusual for Victoria.

Mike stepped in instead, pushing his empty bowl to one side and turning to me and Nick. 'So, bad news about the IVF then, guys.'

Victoria sat upright in her chair and dabbed the sides of her mouth with a napkin.

'It's just not right,' she said, gesturing out the window. 'All those offensive-looking people breeding like there's no tomorrow, producing the most peculiar offspring.' She turned to me. 'And then there's you and Nick. You're an attractive, reasonably intelligent couple. Of course you're by no means thoroughbreds—' she took a sip of wine '—but certainly no reason to defy Darwin's theory, wouldn't you agree?'

I nodded, assuming I had been complimented in some obscure way.

Mike took another sip of wine. 'I read something in the *New Scientist*,' he said, 'about a man's virility dropping in highly populated areas. Like some sort of natural feedback mechanism.'

Victoria shook her head at Mike. 'Well, that's clearly not the case, my darling,' she said. 'Have you walked past Asda recently?'

Mike shook his head and continued, turning to me. 'So,' he said, 'reckon you'll go again?'

I glanced at Nick, who was now topping up his wine.

He took a big gulp. 'We can't afford it,' he said.

'Besides,' I added, 'our consultant said it's best I give my body a break from the hormones.'

Mike smirked. 'Yeah, and Nick a break too, I imagine.'

Victoria glared at Mike. Had she not been on the far side of a twenty-seater dining table, I imagine Mike would have received a stiletto heel to the testicles.

I glanced back at Nick, who was wriggling in his seat. I was tempted to ask him if he needed the toilet.

Victoria stared at him quizzically. 'Everything all right, Nick?'

He placed his now empty wine glass down on the table. 'I had some news today,' he said.

I scraped my empty crème brûlée ramekin, wondering where it had all gone.

'I've been offered a job,' he continued.

I sucked a tiny bit of brûlée off my spoon and awaited Nick's usual post–credit crunch story about a relentless head-hunter pitching a role with worthless share options, fourteen-hour working days and no bonus.

'It's a great role,' Nick said.

I nodded vaguely.

'Excellent prospects.'

Yeah, yeah, yeah, I said in my head.

'I'll be working with a talented team.'

Will *be working with?* I spun round on my seat.

'The only thing is…'

Ah, here we go.

'It's in New York.'

Suddenly, the spoon slipped from my grasp and spiralled through the air, before ricocheting between the marble fireplace and the mahogany table leg. I reached down to pick it up. By the time my head popped back up, the conversation was continuing without me.

'Well, I think you should go,' Mike said. 'There's no point

being childless in Clapham. It's like being poor in Paris, get out of here, mate.'

Victoria agreed. 'Yes, yes, and that ramshackle house of yours. I mean, let's face it, a renovation can only do so much.'

'Er, excuse me?' I raised my hand, partly because I felt like an invisible child with no right to a vote, but mostly because I wasn't quite sure what else to do. 'Am I allowed an opinion?'

Nick looked at me from across the table. He seemed so far away. 'Of course, sweetheart,' he said, in his high-pitched let's-placate-Ellie voice.

I wasn't falling for it. I folded my arms. 'I don't want to go.'

Everyone turned to me. Rupert's yelps had escalated and I could hear Olga in the background trying to soothe him.

'You aren't even going to consider it?' Nick said.

I shook my head. 'Nope. I love it here. I love our house. I love the parks. I love the people.'

Nick huffed. 'What do we need four bedrooms for? What are we going to fill them with? Pot plants?' He stared at me. 'The parks are full of scooting kids and dog turds. The people…' he glanced sideways at Victoria and then Mike '…well, they're a bit, you know, self-important, aren't they?'

'And they're so down to earth in Manhattan, aren't they?' I sneered at him.

Olga came back in the room with Rupert wrapped up in a blanket. 'He crying so much, he been sick,' she said, about to hand him to Victoria.

Victoria waved them away. 'Not near me. I'm wearing cashmere.'

I opened my arms and gestured for Olga to bring him to me. He scrambled out of the towel and onto my lap.

I looked down at him and the moment his bright blue eyes met mine, the pining stopped. I stroked his tiny head.

Nick coughed. Then I looked up to see Victoria staring at me, her expression had softened. She didn't need Botox, she just needed to lighten up.

Olga cleared the plates and Nick shuffled up next to me to stroke Rupert. Rupert wriggled out of my grasp and clambered onto Nick's lap. Nick ruffled Rupert's fur and smiled.

Victoria let out a sharp sigh. 'Oh, for heaven's sake,' she said.

I looked up. 'What?'

'Just take him, will you,' she said, her tone implying I might be more of a moron than she'd initially anticipated. 'The dog. Rupert. Have him.'

I frowned. 'Seriously?'

She glanced at Mike for confirmation. He shrugged his shoulders.

Victoria smiled and then turned to Nick.

'Well,' she said, smiled broadening. 'There's no way Ellie can go to New York now.'

Chapter 6

'Congratulations,' Matthew said, after I'd called him the following morning to share my news. 'You've just done what every other infertile couple does.' He paused to laugh. 'Seriously, the clinics should affiliate with an animal rescue centre. "Sorry, your embryos were useless but we have an adorable whippet called Wilbur who needs a home. He's very loving, great with kids. Not that that matters."'

I ignored him and continued. 'And Nick wants us to move to Manhattan.'

'Whoa, what's going on? First a dog and now emigration? Does he have a green card?'

'Nick?' I asked.

'No, Rupert,' he replied. 'Those Yanks are ruthless with their border control.'

'He's not a Border, he's a Sporting Lucas.'

He laughed some more. 'You're not allowed to go. Who else will entertain me with their ridiculous life?'

'I'm not going,' I said.

There was a pause on the end of the line. Initially, I thought this was because Matthew was taking time to consider the implications on my future happiness, however, the loud slurping noise revealed that, instead, he was just taking a moment to sip his coffee.

I sighed. 'Does anyone actually care?' Out of nowhere, Rupert jumped on my lap and gazed up at me.

Matthew sniggered down the line. 'Of course I care,' he said. 'I just care more after coffee.'

'So I was saying...'

'Yes, you're off to Yank land.'

'No, I'm not. I'm not going.'

'Why not?'

'I hate America.'

'You haven't even been.'

I rolled my eyes. 'Of course I have. The agency has an office in New York.'

He laughed. 'Yes, which you've visited once in three years, for, oh, what was it, all of six hours?'

'I've been twice actually. And I went to Disney World when I was twelve.'

'Aha,' Matthew said, in the manner of a psychotherapist who had just pinpointed the cause of a patient's neurosis. 'Florida in the eighties doesn't count. They were going through a difficult time: all visors and fanny packs.'

I chuckled. 'And there's no way I could join a nation who voted for a president who said: "most of our imports are foreign".'

Matthew sighed. 'They didn't vote him in. He voted himself in. And, besides, they have a new president now, only since 2008.'

'Yeah, one who sided with Argentina over the Falklands.'

'Ellie, you can't discount an entire nation based on political knowledge gleaned from a ten-year-old Michael Moore documentary and Perez Hilton's blog.'

'I can.'

He laughed. 'So when you leave, who's going to look after your clients?'

'I've told you I'm not going. Why isn't anyone taking me seriously?'

'I suppose you could work from New York too. At least then you'd be rid of old twatty-pants Dominic.'

'Are you listening to me?'

'And the Sporting Lucas. I suppose you can take him with you?'

'Matthew!'

He let out a deep sigh. 'Ellie, beautiful, gorgeous Ellie, platonic love of my life.' He sighed again. 'When you repeatedly say you're not doing something, usually it means you are.'

I paced around the hallway, ready to shout down the phone at Matthew that no matter what anyone said, I had no intention of moving to America, ever, when I noticed Victoria peering through the front window.

I attempted to 'sign' to her that I was on the phone, an act that I immediately realised could be no more explanatory than my actually holding a real phone to my ear.

She ignored me and started thudding on the door, by which point, Matthew had begun humming Frank Sinatra.

'Bm ber der der der, start spreading the news,' he sang, 'Ellie's leaving today. She wants to be a part of it...'

I rolled my eyes and hung up the phone.

Victoria bustled in, the moment I opened the door. Her arms were laden with Rupert-related paraphernalia.

'Morning,' she said. 'I forgot a few things.' She placed the items down onto a large pile in front of me, then smoothed down her ponytail. 'There's the mattress for Rupert's bed.' She pointed at a thick circular cushion. 'It's made from co-conut fibres so it's more breathable. Here's the pamphlet,' she said, reaching into her pocket and handing it to me. 'It's been clinically proven to reduce the incidence of Sudden Puppy Death Syndrome.'

I glanced at it and scratched my head.

She continued, plucking something else from the pile. 'This is his heartbeat cushion Olga found at Pets Are Our World. Apparently it settles him...' she pointed at something else '...along with his pheromone spray and plug-in. There's his brush, made from natural fibres...' she continued pointing '...his puppy shampoo—don't over-wash him, he's sensitive—toothbrush, toothpaste.' She turned to me. 'Dental hygiene is paramount to prevent future decay.' She turned back to the pile. 'There's one week's food. He's on Paula's Kitchen Puppy meals. They're grain-free, from ethically sourced meat, with no fillers, and also with added bergamot and dandelion for his liver and kidney. And there are some special grain-free treats in this bag.' Rupert jumped up, sniffing the packet and wagging his tail. She handed him one. Then reached in her other pocket and continued. 'I've printed off a list of human foods he must not have, under any circumstance, and also a list of garden plants that are poisonous to dogs. It's best to remove them from your garden just in case.' She glanced through the kitchen to the back door. 'Chances are you've got some of everything in that overgrown mass back there.' Then she handed me a bundle of papers. 'Here's his pedigree certificate and passport application forms. He can't go abroad until he's had his rabies vaccine. His vet's number is on the back...' she pointed out where '…just below the grooming salon. Also he has a few sessions with his nutritionalist plus a month's worth of canine psychology sessions to help him adjust to his new home.' She looked down at Rupert, then back at me. 'And just in case,' she added, her expression cooling, 'here's the number of a dog therapist in New York.' She looked me in the eye. 'If you were to go, it would be immensely traumatic for him and he would need extensive emotional support to adapt to such a change.'

'But I'm not going,' I said.

She took a deep breath and looked at me. 'You'll take care of him, won't you, Ellie?'

I nodded, bending down to pick him up. Victoria leaned in to stroke him.

Rupert wriggled, then jumped up into her arms.

Either he'd already been Stockholmed, or, I began to wonder, perhaps Victoria had been kinder to him than she'd let on.

'So,' she said, peeling him off her and placing him on the floor. 'Everything all right with you and Nick?'

I nodded, distracted by Rupert arching his back on my carpet.

Victoria squinted her eyes. 'Right, OK,' she said, before giving Rupert one final pat on the head. She shut the door quickly before he was able to follow her out.

Moments later, I caught sight of her running back up the front path. She posted a large envelope through my letter-box. Inside were multiple newspaper and magazine clippings highlighting various shocking facts about the US, including but not exclusive to terrorism threats, obesity crisis, gun crime, poor social welfare and the number of unresolved puppy abductions in New York City.

I stuffed the clippings back into the envelope and left it on the side, then took Rupert, along with the list of poisonous plants into our garden. I'd decided to stay home with him that day to settle him in and show him around.

I pushed open the old French doors and stepped out onto the patio, trying to recall the last time I had actually ventured into the mass of weeds and tangled shrubbery that was our ten-metres-square London garden. It must have been over a year ago when we'd just moved in. I placed Rupert down by my feet and watched him explore. To little Rupert, faced with dense foliage over twice his height, it must have seemed like a jungle. He stepped tentatively forward, then a crow squawked and he ran back between my legs. Moments later, he tried again, this time venturing a little further.

Just as I'd spotted a potentially toxic-looking weed, my phone rang again. It was Mandi.

'Ellie, where are you?'

Rupert bounded back between my legs. I shifted him away from the plant. 'At home,' I said.

Mandi paused for a moment as though she didn't quite know what to do with that information. 'Doing what?'

I bent down and tugged at the roots. 'Weeding.'

Mandi paused again. I imagined her twitching her nose. 'You need to come in.'

I threw the weed onto the patio. Rupert sniffed it then ran back between my legs. 'Can't it wait?' I said.

'No,' she replied, more sternly than Mandi usually spoke. 'It's important.'

When I arrived at the office, having transported an increasingly perplexed Rupert in his Louis Vuitton dog carry case, Mandi jumped out at me. She was wearing what looked like an Aztec-patterned tepee with a coordinated neck scarf.

'Ellie, you're late,' she said. 'Into the meeting room

quickly.' Then she stopped, turned and peered into the carry case. She held her hands to her chest and made a high-pitched squealing noise.

'Aw,' she said, 'a puppy! I absolutely love puppies. Did I tell you how much I love puppies? And kittens, of course. I love kittens. But not as much as puppies. Puppies I simply adore. He is just too cute. Can I cuddle him? Please can I?' She peered in closer. 'What's your name, little fellow?'

Rupert growled. I went to turn the carry case away, assuming Mandi's attire must have alarmed him, when I noticed Dominic standing behind her. Rupert growled again and then bared his tiny teeth.

Dominic sneered at the carry case. 'No animals in the office,' he said. 'Clause 13.5b on our lease. He'll need to be removed immediately.'

Mandi waved Dominic away. 'Oh, get a life,' she said. 'It's not as though he's running wild, chewing the table legs and weeing up your trousers. Besides, it's essential Ellie is present at this meeting.'

Dominic's jaw tensed before he followed Mandi, Rupert and I into the meeting room.

Once we were all seated, Mandi flipped open her laptop. I smiled at her, quietly hoping she was about to unveil an e-petition for which she had solicited a hundred thousand client signatures objecting to my relocation.

She stood up and cleared her throat. 'Eighty per cent of our matchmaking workforce is women,' she began.

Dominic sighed and checked his watch.

'Forty-three per cent of those are mothers,' she continued.

Dominic rolled his eyes.

'Our maternity package is grim.' She looked down and started rubbing her tummy. 'We offer little more than statutory pay, no child-care benefits and no additional support to mothers at all.'

Dominic sat back in his chair and stretched his arms above his head. He let out an extended sigh. 'Have you got something to tell us, Mandi?'

She ignored him. 'If our business is about bringing couples together, then surely our business should also be about preventing couples from separating.'

I leaned forward.

Mandi continued. 'If we don't support the family unit, then how can we say we are supporting the couple?'

Dominic sighed again. 'So let's cut to the chase, what do you propose?'

Mandi smoothed down her blonde flicks and pressed some keys on her laptop. 'I'll email you my full proposal, but, in short, I would like us to provide on-site childcare, flexi-working hours, extended holidays, extra sick pay when children are poorly, priority parking for pregnant women and breast-feeding stations in the office.'

He laughed again. 'How about prenatal yoga while we're at it? Or nappy bins in the meeting rooms. A jungle gym in the lobby?'

Mandi scowled at him.

'What about paternity rights too?' I interrupted. 'One of my closest friends is a house husband.'

Dominic rolled his eyes. 'Men shouldn't be looking after babies.'

Mandi and I both stared at him.

Dominic shrugged his shoulders. 'We're not built for it,' he said. 'We don't have the hormones or the attributes.' He nodded to my chest and raised his eyebrows. 'We were meant for world domination, not bottle feeding and nose wiping,' he said.

I glanced at Mandi, whose mouth was wide open, then back at Dominic.

Dominic smirked. 'Although the breast-feeding station sounds intriguing.'

I shook my head and stood up to leave.

Dominic followed me. 'Oh, by the way, Ellie,' he said, 'the investors rejected your request.'

I turned to face him. 'What request?'

'The request to conduct your research from the UK.'

I stepped back. 'I wasn't aware I had formally requested that yet. I didn't even know a meeting had been scheduled.'

He leaned forward and squeezed my shoulder. 'I sent you an email. The meeting was this morning,' he said. 'You missed it, while you were tending to—' he glanced down at Rupert, who was now sleeping in his carry case '—your *dependant.*'

That night Nick and I sat in bed together with Rupert nestled between us. Nick had insisted Rupert not be left alone with the weird heartbeat toy on his first night with us.

'Dogs are pack animals,' he'd said, seemingly trying to justify his sentimental side. 'They feel insecure unless the alpha dog is there to protect them.'

A lengthy debate as to whether Rupert would view me or Nick as his pack leader followed, before our conversation moved on to the topic of New York. It wasn't long until my arms were folded. 'How many times do I have to say this? I'm not leaving my clients,' I said.

Nick raised his eyebrows. 'You don't have any clients

any more. When was the last time you actually did any matchmaking?'

'The business needs me.'

'You can work from New York.'

'Well, I'm not leaving Rupert.'

'Oh, come on, Ellie. You're not going to let the perceived needs of a nine-week-old canine come between us and our future happiness.'

I stared at Nick. 'Sorry, whose future happiness?'

He stared back at me.

'Besides,' I continued, 'he's our responsibility now. There's no way I would consider rehoming him. He's been through enough turmoil in his little life already.'

Nick smirked. 'I wasn't suggesting that for a second. We would take him with us.'

I glanced at Rupert, then back at Nick. 'What sort of life would he have in Manhattan?'

Nick laughed. 'Ellie, we have a Brooklyn budget. I was thinking Park Slope.' He picked up his iPad and showed me an image on the screen. It looked nice enough, but there seemed to be lots of traffic.

'What about the pollution?' I asked.

'We live hundred metres from the South Circular. I suspect there is a higher concentration of sulphur dioxide on Battersea Rise than there is on Broadway.'

I glanced down at Rupert. 'I just want to give him the best life we can.'

Nick rolled his eyes. 'Are you going to fret about his schooling now? Or the cultural clash he might face when integrating with native American breeds?' He laughed again, though louder this time. 'Do you think the Brooklyn street dogs are going to back him into a corner, mug him of his grain-free puppy snacks, and say, "Hey, Stan, we've got us a Sporting Lucas here. He says he's from Engerland."'

I folded my arms more tightly across my chest. 'What about my friends?'

'You've seen Cordelia once in the past year.'

'It's not my fault she chose to move to Woldingham.'

Nick rolled his eyes. 'You hardly ever see Kat because she lives north of the river. And when was the last time you saw Matthew?'

'Last Friday actually.'

Nick turned to me with a frown.

'He came with me to Cassandra's divorce party.'

Nick raised both eyebrows. 'You went to a divorce party? Are you supporting a different cause now?'

'I'm not supporting divorce, I'm supporting Cassandra.'

He shook his head. 'She's a nut job, that one. I don't even want to imagine what went on at that party.'

I sighed. 'It was a divorce party, not a swingers party.'

He scowled at me. 'It's still weird. And not the sort of place I want my wife hanging out.'

'Hanging out? I haven't *hung out* anywhere since I was fifteen and wore Reebok Classics.'

He smirked.

'Besides,' I added, 'it's my job. You have to respect that.'

'No,' he replied. 'Your job is to run a business. You have matchmakers to do all the other stuff now.'

'Ah, thanks for telling my what my job is.'

'Well, at least I know what it is you do.'

I tutted. 'I know what you do.'

He raised an eyebrow. 'Go on then?'

I sat up in bed and lifted Rupert onto my lap. 'You work in finance.'

Nick rolled his eyes. 'Yes, me and the rest of the working population of London. What precisely do I do in finance?'

'You manage risk.'

'Manage? What does that mean?'

'It means you oversee risk algorithms.'

'Oversee?'

I huffed. 'Look, I don't follow you around all day taking notes. How am I supposed to understand the intricacies of financial technology?'

'You're not. But it would be nice if you cared enough to find out the intricacies of my life.'

I forced a laugh. 'Says he who didn't even know where his wife was on Friday night.'

'That's because I was too busy doing a job I hate.'

'Too busy entertaining. What a drag.'

'It is a drag spending time with a bunch of wide boys who think Chateaubriand is a type of wine.'

'If you hate it so much, why don't you leave?'

Nick sat back and glared at me. 'That's exactly what I'm trying to do.'

'But I don't want to move to New York,' I said.

'What about what I want?'

I glanced around the bedroom, then back at him. 'I can't believe you're so quick to give up on our dream.'

Nick sighed. 'What dream, Ellie? The dream you've been spoon-fed by your friends and those silly magazines you read. The dream that involves stripped floorboards, a herb garden, Petit Bateau-ed children and an ultimate migration to Surrey. The dream you've been trying to shoehorn your life into since the day we met.'

I looked down at Rupert. His shiny blue eyes stared back

up at me. It seemed as though he knew exactly what I was trying to say.

Nick's expression softened. He leaned towards me and squeezed my hand.

'We can't have children, Ellie,' he said. 'We have to accept that and move on with our lives.'

I snatched my hand back. 'I'm not going to leave my clients and I'm not going to leave Rupert.'

Nick pulled himself up in bed. 'You want to stay here instead? In a town with the highest birthrate in Europe, torturing yourself? And, what, try IVF another twenty times until you've bankrupted us or turned into even more of a mental case?'

'I'm not going to give up.'

'On what? You don't even know what it is you're holding out for.'

Nick pulled up the duvet, turned away from me and switched off the light. Rupert clambered off my lap, climbed onto Nick then back onto me until finally settling in the valley between us.

I lay there, listening to Rupert's gentle snores, watching the outline of his tiny ribcage rising and falling, and wondered what precisely it was that I was holding out for.

Chapter 7

I awoke to a damp duvet and a deep regret for co-sleeping with an eight-week-old puppy. Nick had already left for work. Usually he woke me to say goodbye so it was clear he was trying to make a point. I helped Rupert down from the bed, pulled on my dressing gown and went downstairs.

On the landing, I stopped and peered into the empty room across from our bedroom. The morning rays sliced through the centre of the room, directly across the space I'd planned to put the cot. I'd envisaged one of those old-fashioned bassinets, draped with a broderie anglaise blanket. I redirected my gaze to the walls, which were presently the dull grey of neglect. I'd planned to warm them with Dulux's Vanilla Sunrise, topped off with a frieze I'd seen in John Lewis which was covered with Beatrix Potter bunnies. My gaze finally settled in the dusty corner opposite me. It would have been the perfect place for a rocking horse. Rupert nudged my leg as if to guide me downstairs.

In the hallway, I stopped again and glanced around the

front room. It was still bare aside from a black leather sofa from Nick's old bachelor pad. It was going to be the play-room, filled with plump cushions and airy wooden trunks overspilling with brightly coloured toys. I took a deep breath and glanced back up the stairs. Nick was right: so many rooms, now with no purpose. I let out a deep sigh. It seemed neither the house nor I would have the chance to fulfil our potential.

A whimper from Rupert distracted me from my thoughts. He was looking up at me, head cocked as if to say: *I live here now too, you know.* Then he bounded over to the back door and started pining.

Once I'd opened the door, he sprang across the patio slab without hesitation and began rolling in the grass. The sheer delight in his eyes reminded me of a recent episode of *Dr Phil*, during which he'd iterated the importance of living in the moment. There was a yogi on the show who'd explained the art of mindfulness. At the time I'd found it hard to take the expert seriously; however, now, as I looked up to the sky and inhaled the fresh morning air, I wondered if perhaps Rupert could bring new meaning to my life.

'That's fox poo, you know.' Victoria's voice hit me from above. I swung round to see her standing on her stadium-sized roof terrace, swigging an isotonic drink from a flask. 'Hunting dogs love to roll in it. It masks their smell.'

I looked at her, then back at Rupert, who was still writh-ing in the grass, the orangey brown streaks along his fur now clearly visible.

'Rupert. No!' I shouted.

Rupert sprang to his feet and wagged his tail.

I looked back up at Victoria, who was now stretching her calves and smirking.

'You could have told me,' I said.

'What?' she said, lifting her leg up onto the glass wall around her terrace. 'That you have fox poo in your garden? It's been there for months. Along with the dead squirrel.' She leaned over to stretch. 'It's hardly surprising,' she continued, 'given that degree of neglect.' She placed her leg back down and then stared at me for a moment. 'Why are you still in your dressing gown? It's ten o'clock.'

I pulled the gown tighter around me. 'I didn't sleep so well last night.'

Victoria stared at me for a moment, then screwed up her face. 'Oh God,' she said, 'I hope you're not depressed. You know I can't abide depressed people.' She arched her back into a reverse downward dog, then sprang back up. 'Or fat people,' she added. 'So self-indulgent.'

I watched her shake her hair out of its ponytail and then roll her shoulders before walking back inside. Then I glanced back down at Rupert and the poo smudges around his neck and shoulder. He'd even managed to embed some in his diamanté collar. I scrunched up my nose and carried him at arm's length towards the bathroom.

According to a website dedicated to the behavioural tendencies of the Sporting Lucas, Rupert should have been delighted with his bath. Although not bred as a water dog, many Lucas-derived breeds were deeply fond of the water, the author of the website had explained, further evidenced by photos of Sporting Lucases enjoying an array of water-themed pursuits. Rupert, however, acted more like a kitten being plunged into concentrated hydrochloric acid, leaping out and desperately scrambling up the sides. I had to hold him down while applying a generous blob of his sulphite-free doggy shampoo.

Just as I was towelling him dry, the residual aroma of fox poo wafting towards me as I did, my phone started ringing. It was Matthew. I put him on loudspeaker and explained my situation.

He laughed loudly. 'I bet Nick is loving that. Three rounds of IVF and now a dog in the bed. He's probably wondering if you're ever going to have sex again.'

'Thanks, Matthew. That's really helpful.'

'You asked.'

'Er, no actually, I didn't.'

He continued. 'So, why aren't you at work? You're not leaving for New York already, are you?'

I sighed. 'No, Matthew. I'm not going. Remember?'

'Oh yes,' he said and then paused. 'So, in that case you've taken a day off work to show Dominic you're sulking.' He laughed again. 'Following which, he will undoubtedly issue you with a formal apology, cancel your travel itinerary and transfer his shares to you.'

I sighed. 'I'm not sulking. I told you, I've taken a day off to settle Rupert in.' Then I paused for a moment, wondering why there wasn't the usual foray in the background of Matthew's call. 'Where are your kids?'

Matthew laughed. 'I haven't killed them if that's what you're wondering.' There was a prolonged pause. 'Although,' he continued, 'on a particularly trying day I once masterminded an untraceable and painless way to do it.' He cleared his throat. 'You know, if the need ever arose.'

I sniffed Rupert and then towelled him some more. 'And when, precisely, might the need to murder your own children arise?'

'Oh, I don't know. Haven't really thought it through,' he said and then exhaled slowly. 'Perhaps if there was a nuclear war and the population of Barnes became zombified and started eating each other. Or there was a localised coup and gangs of machete-wielding rebels began slaughtering families whose children went to private school.'

I shook my head and picked up Rupert's brush. 'So, working from the theory that the village of Barnes is still at peace, rather than the set for a real-life depiction of a Will Smith movie, where are they?'

'Lucy's taken them on a playdate.'

'Isn't she supposed to be at work?'

There was a pause. 'She's taking a sabbatical. I'm on strike.'

'On strike? From what?' I asked.

'From domesticity. I still see the kids. Just not all day. And I'm refusing to perform any more household chores. This morning I went to the spa.'

I laughed.

He continued. 'And today I was going to come to your offices to meet you for lunch, but since you're sulking let's go to Barnes Bistro instead.'

I tutted. 'I'm not sulking.'

'One-thirty work for you?'

Then the line went dead. I glanced down at Rupert. He looked back at me with an expression that implied he might enjoy a trip to Barnes.

After I'd brushed him and sprayed a still pungent part of his neck with doggy deodorant, there were still two hours to spare before my lunch meet with Matthew. Rather than checking the inevitable emails laden with divorce and heartbreak or barked orders from Dominic, I decided a much more productive use of my time would be to clear the garden for Rupert. I didn't need Dr Phil to tell me that pulling up a few weeds was an infinitely simpler task than attempting to derail divorce for the masses.

Nick's unused garden gloves were in the shed, still in their packet. The garden rake and broom still had their tags on. Like most couples we'd had grand plans when we first moved in, but somehow life had taken over and the ideas we'd had, such as laying decking across the patio and packing tubs full with sage and rosemary, never quite came to fruition.

Rupert seemed to enjoy his playtime in the garden, chewing twigs, eating grass and sniffing spiders. Each time I scooped some leaves or weeds into a bag I squeezed it tight just to make sure he hadn't found his way into the pile. It wasn't long before I'd filled ten bags with dead plants, rotting leaves, the remainder of the fox poo and the dead squirrel.

Every so often, Victoria would appear on her roof terrace to offer direction. She seemed genuinely baffled as to why I hadn't arranged a 'professional' to do it for me.

Once I had finished, I hosed down the patio and brushed away the remaining mud and dust with the broom. Then I sat on the back step. I had two throbbing blisters on my hands but as I looked around at the courtyard with its high walls and creeping ivy—a pocket of tranquility in the busy streets of London—I couldn't help but let out a contented sigh. As I did, Rupert jumped into my lap and closed his eyes. My eyelids felt heavy and I was tempted to close mine too, but it was nearly one o'clock and, given the bizarre mood Matthew had been in of late, I knew it would be unwise to leave him unsupervised in a licensed premises for even the briefest amount of time.

After I'd quickly changed my clothes, I looked down

at the loose knit jumper and White Company trousers I'd selected, and wondered why I was dressing for the life I wanted rather than the one I had. I briefly considered digging out my old skinny jeans and Topshop T-shirts that I'd packed away in our spare wardrobe, but there was no time. I slathered on some lip gloss, tucked Rupert into his carry case, and set off to meet Matthew.

Just as I walked out of the house, my phone rang. I glanced at the screen, half expecting it to be Victoria complaining that a stray leaf had blown into her espaliered apple trees or else Matthew telling me to meet him at the nail bar instead.

As it turned out, it was an ex-client of mine, Harriet. She and Jeremy were the first couple I matched. But if I'd known seven years ago in the grounds of an eighteenth-century chateau in Versailles that I was committing to their relationship for a lifetime too, I might have reconsidered. Or at least insisted on some kind of matchmaker prenup.

Harriet was sobbing when I picked up. 'He's done it again, Ellie.'

I sighed. 'Oh dear.'

'I've just been through his receipts.'

'Are you OK?'

She sniffed. 'No.'

'So what is it this time?'

'Three grand.'

I'm not sure what was more disheartening. The fact that her husband Jeremy had spent three thousand pounds on strippers in one night. Or that Harriet, bred of Cheltenham Ladies' College, had begun using the term 'grand' like a character from a Martina Cole novel.

'Where?' I asked.

'The Windmill Club.'

I tutted.

'Can I see you, Ellie? I really need to talk this through.'

I glanced down at Rupert. He wagged his tail. 'Sure,' I said, trying to sound as upbeat as I could.

'I've got an hour or so before I have to pick the kids up. Where are you?' she asked.

'I'll be at Barnes Bistro in ten,' I said. 'I'll have a friend with me though if you don't mind him chipping in? He's a little eccentric but can be quite insightful sometimes.'

She took a moment to reply. 'That's fine. See you there. Thank you, Ellie.'

Matthew was seated at a table and talking to a waiter when I arrived.

'I want the biggest Brie and Parma ham baguette you have,' Matthew explained.

'I'm afraid we only have one size of baguette, sir.'

Matthew rolled his eyes. 'Well, how big is it?'

The waiter measured out a sizeable-looking baguette length with his hands. Matthew scrunched up his nose. 'I'll have two,' he said, 'and some fries. And a bottle of rosé.'

I held my hands up. 'I'm not drinking today.'

Matthew grinned. 'I wasn't ordering for you, sweet-cheeks.'

I ordered a mineral water and a seafood salad, then told Matthew that Harriet would be joining us.

'Excellent,' he said. 'My first attempt at "me time" is being sabotaged by a whiney housewife.'

I sat back in my chair and stared at him, trying to fathom what was going on under that bouffant quiff of his.

'Are you OK?' I asked.

He looked up to the sky as if to ask why he had been saddled with such an unintuitive friend.

I glared at him. 'Of course I know you're not OK. I'm just trying to decipher if you're having a bit of a wobble, or if you're about to totally go off the rails.'

He laughed. 'Don't stress. It's all manageable.' His grin widened. 'At least with a bottle of rosé.' Then he snatched the bottle from the waiter and began pouring himself a glass.

Once he'd finished his first baguette and most of the rosé, his mood seemed to settle. He even made a few jokes that weren't entirely at my or the waiter's expense. I speared the final prawn off my plate and looked around us. For once I hadn't even noticed the small children and babies dotted around me. I hadn't engaged a new mother in conversation, hoping her fertility might somehow rub off on me. I hadn't even remarked about how cute the kids' menu sounded. I glanced down at Rupert's carry case and smiled. His eyebrows twitched and he let out a tiny yelp. He was in a deep sleep. I imagined him dreaming about chasing leaves and bounding around the courtyard. What a sweet little world he lived in, full of exciting things to discover and adventures to be had.

My thoughts were interrupted by Matthew coughing violently, seemingly choking on some Brie. I jumped up and patted him on the back, slightly concerned I might be expected to perform the Heimlich manoeuvre.

He grabbed some more rosé and took a gulp, the colour quickly returning to his cheeks. When I realised he was no longer in danger of death, I gestured to his plate and sniggered.

'Want me to cut that up for you?' I said.

He rolled his eyes and wiped his mouth with a napkin, then pointed. 'It was that woman. Did you see her?'

I turned round to see Harriet walking towards us. Despite her husband's recent antics, it appeared she still had the oesophagus-blocking power of a Milanese runway model.

I removed the second baguette from Matthew's hand as she approached. Just in case.

'Harriet, hi,' I said, standing up to greet her.

She flung her arms around me. 'It's so good to see you, Ellie,' she said.

I hugged her in return but her ribcage felt so frail I was reluctant to squeeze too hard.

When we were all sitting down, I introduced her to Matthew, who had been silent since the choking incident.

She smiled at him. 'Nice to meet you, Matthew,' she said, sweeping her caramel-coloured hair from her face. He looked mesmerised, as though Woody Allen had met his latest muse. I kicked him under the table.

She turned to me. 'I'm so sorry, Ellie, I didn't mean to gatecrash your lunch.'

'It's fine, Harriet, honestly. Are you OK?'

The waiter brought another wine glass and Harriet quickly poured herself some rosé. Straight away Matthew ordered another bottle.

By the third bottle, Matthew had found his voice and Harriet seemed to be receptive to his advice.

'Dump him,' Mathew slurred. 'You shouldn't stand for that.'

Harriet nodded.

'Hang on,' I interrupted. 'She's married to him and they have two children.'

Matthew shrugged his shoulders.

'And she loves him,' I added.

Matthew poured himself and Harriet another glass. 'But does he love her? That's the question.'

'Of course he does,' I answered.

Matthew raised both eyebrows. 'If he loves her, why is he paying naked women thousands of pounds?'

I kicked Matthew under the table again then glanced over at Harriet.

She took a long gulp of wine. 'Precisely my point,' she said, then frowned. 'Although I don't think they're naked when he pays them.'

'Yes.' Matthew nodded. 'Excellent point.' He raised a finger in the air. 'There'd be no point paying them if they were already naked, would there?'

I tutted, feeling tempted to pour myself a glass of rosé too, but I resisted. 'And you, Matthew? Should Lucy leave you?'

He frowned. 'What for?'

I sat back in my chair. 'Well, restricting my point to the topic at hand. Weren't you the recipient of a lap dance the other day?'

He exhaled a laugh. 'It was unsolicited,' he said. 'I didn't pay. And it was a man, so it doesn't count.'

I narrowed my eyes. 'What about the boobs and bottoms you were groping?'

He smiled. 'I was in character.'

'What character? Pervy married guy?'

Matthew shot me a glare. 'No, long-suffering friend who was forced to adopt mock gay caricature in order to survive the wrath of dildo-wielding divorcees.'

Harriet laughed.

Matthew joined in.

I rolled my eyes, realising that the chance of any sensible conversation had been thwarted by their efforts to reach the combined blood alcohol level to floor a woolly mammoth.

Matthew sloshed some more wine into his glass. 'You should leave Jenemy—sorry, Jeremy—and marry me.' Then he jumped up from his seat and kneeled before her.

Harriet giggled as Matthew attempted to mould a ring out of Brie.

I sighed and checked my watch. 'Harriet,' I said, just as Matthew lurched forwards to kiss his bride, 'didn't you say you had to collect the kids from school?'

She pushed Matthew away, and stood up. Then she stopped, looked around her and sat back down.

'Fuck it,' she said, reaching for her phone. 'Jeremy can collect them for once.' She typed a text, then poured herself another glass. Straight away, her phone buzzed in reply. She glanced at the screen. 'He says it's fine,' she said, then tossed the phone into her bag. 'Wanker.'

I shook my head and poured some water into Rupert's travel dish. 'I'm sure Jeremy feels terrible, Harriet.'

'So he should,' Matthew chipped in. 'He sounds like a total twat.'

Harriet turned to me, her face scrunched up. 'Why aren't you on my side, Ellie?'

'You're a couple,' I said. 'I want you both to be happy.'

Matthew jumped up from his seat, waving a baguette around like a sword.

'Eleanor Rigby, warrior princess,' he said in his movie-trailer voice. 'fighting heartbreak wherever she goes.' He swiped the air with his baguette. 'She's on love's side.' He swished it from side to side as though slaying an invisible enemy. 'She may have lost the battle but she hasn't lost the war.'

Harriet laughed loudly and Matthew placed his baguette sword back into its imaginary holster and sat back down.

I looked at them both. 'Will you two just grow up?'

Matthew pulled his chin to his chest and made a silly 'ooooh,' noise. Harriet giggled.

'Right,' I said, picking up Rupert's carry case and glaring at them both. 'Clearly I care more about your relationships than you do.'

Then I stormed off, accidentally knocking over Rupert's water.

Matthew swished his baguette-sword again and shouted after me.

'Go forth, carry-cased crusader, and canine companion. Go forth and save us all!'

Back at home, I let Rupert scurry around the back garden while I made myself a cup of tea and leafed through the latest copy of *Grazia*. Since becoming a matchmaker, it seemed every waking hour had been dedicated to the needs of others. I'd been unable to detach myself from their loneliness, heartbreak or even their happiness. No matter what the time of day, there was always something I could have been doing to help them find, or more importantly, sustain love. However, since Dominic had ordered me to leave my post unmanned and embark on an elaborate jaunt around the globe, I realised that my clients and the agency would have to learn to survive without me. I laughed to myself. Given the result of today's intervention, though, they might be better off.

I flipped the page and began to read an article about a woman whose husband had spent the deposit they'd saved for a house on a blackjack table in Vegas. I read on. It appeared he was an undiagnosed manic-depressive. I glanced up from the magazine and stared out the window at the row of rooftops. If we were all forced to undertake a rigorous psychological assessment prior to marriage, I wondered how many of us would actually pass. I imagined even fewer would pass after.

Just as I read the part about how she'd filed for divorce the day he was sectioned, my phone began to vibrate on the kitchen counter. It was Jeremy.

'She's left me,' he said.

I pressed my ear closer to the phone, to check I'd heard right. 'What?'

'Harriet. She's abandoned the kids and left me.'

'Jeremy, slow down. What happened?'

Ten minutes later, after I, along with the guidance of a nurse from NHS Direct, coached Jeremy via the phone how to breathe into a paper bag to prevent further hyperventilation, he explained what had happened.

'She sent me a text,' he said, 'telling me to collect the kids from the pool. Which I thought was a bit weird, because they were supposed to be at school.'

'That might have been a typo?' I suggested.

He cleared his throat. 'Yes, after an hour at the leisure centre, followed by two hours filling out forms at the police station, it transpires that's precisely what it was.'

'Are the kids OK?'

'They're fine.'

'And Harriet?'

'She's left me, I told you.'

'No, she hasn't.'

He let out a deep sigh. 'Yes, she has. She texted me a picture of her and her new man. He was waving a baguette in the photo.'

'What?'

'The text said she never wanted to see me again, that she'd had enough and she deserved to be with someone who understood what commitment meant.'

I frowned. 'Someone like Matthew?'

'Who?'

'The man in the photo.'

'I suppose so.'

For a man who'd made tens of millions from scratch and then lost it all, who'd witnessed his childhood pet dog shot dead by his father, who'd lost the love of his life several times over, then finally found her again, this time Jeremy sounded as though he was ready to give up. I'd never heard defeat in his voice before.

'You can't blame her for being upset,' I said.

'Yeah, big deal. I stayed out a bit late the other night. Our clients were over from Singapore and they needed entertaining.'

My thoughts formed quickly. 'Where did you go?'

'The Windmill. I can't stand the place, but that's where they wanted to go. I sat upstairs all night at the bar, playing Angry Birds on my phone, while they racked up over three thousand on our expense account. Dodgy lot.'

'So you didn't even go downstairs?'

'No, not after last time on Mike's stag do when I ended up paying for a ton of dances I didn't have.'

'Why would you pay for dances you didn't have?'

'I didn't want to offend the girls.'

'What?'

'Most of them were studying, you know, trying to better their lives. It felt rude to turn them away without at least offering them something.'

I sighed. 'So you'd jeopardise your marriage to preserve the feelings of a stripper?'

'They're people too, you know. Anyway, I've done nothing wrong. Harriet's the one cavorting all over town with the bread guy.' He paused to sniff. 'If you speak to her, please tell her to come home.'

I tried to call Harriet and Matthew several times throughout the evening but it seemed Harriet's battery had run low or she'd switched off her phone. However, from Matthew's frequent tweets and Facebook updates, it appeared his phone was working fine; he was just ignoring my calls. Every half an hour or so, I and the rest of his social media network were treated to a selection of selfies and a location update.

18.07: with the driver on the 37 bus to Clapham High Street.
20.13: Matthew 'knighting' a pedestrian with his baguette.
23.03: Group hug with the doormen at Infernos nightclub

When they followed this up with a video of Matthew on the dance floor, sporting the baguette as willy substitute and with Harriet gripping it like Linda Lovelace, I switched off my phone and slumped down onto the sofa. Rupert jumped up next to me. It was becoming increasingly clear to me that I had spent the past ten years building a business around a concept that was flawed to the core. In a cruel twist to my idealistic plot, I'd been bringing people together only for them to, at best, drift apart, or, worse, destroy each other entirely.

I leaned forward and grabbed my iPad off the coffee table. With Rupert on my lap, tapping at the screen I searched the most recent emails from Dominic. I found the one I was searching for straight away.

Subject title: Eleanor's Itinerary.

I double clicked on the attached document and quickly scrolled down through the list of experts:

Susan Villecox, Head of Department, Social Anthropology, Columbia University
Elspeth and Ernest Kennedy, Co-founders, The Relationship Restoration Ranch
Professor Sheldon, Neurochemical Enhancement Theorist
Jed Tandy, Master of Neurolinguistic Programming and founder of Jed Tandy Inc.
Dr Gunnarsson, Dean of Social and Human Sciences, University of Iceland
Professor Takahashi, Founder, The Centre for Behavioural-Technological Advancement, Tokyo
Dr Menzi, Witch Doctor, YouTube broadcaster.

I thought about what Nick had said about not knowing what I was holding out for. Maybe my destiny wasn't to merge with the Aryan herd of Clapham. Ten years ago, I'd set out to find the answers, and now all I had were yet more questions. When another selfie of Matthew popped up on Facebook, this time revealing tequila shots and running-man dancing, I realised that all of us in our own way were trying to escape the truth.

'Maybe it is time for a change,' I said, and Rupert jumped up and licked my face.

Chapter 8

Matthew gripped my hand as we hurried to the station. It was cold enough to see my breath in the air.

'So let's get this straight,' he said. 'This is your last night out in London, the cultural capital of the world, and you're making us go to Blood Burger?'

'Blood's is cool.'

Matthew stopped, turned to me and took both my hands in his. 'Ellie, my darling. You are the sun on my cloudy day, you are the port in my storm, you are the song in my heart. But cool, you are not. So please don't call it Blood's. Next thing you'll be wearing Converse.'

I slapped his arm. 'Just because I'm not a sculpt-my-hair-into-an-ironic-quiff try-hard, doesn't mean I'm not cool,' I said, continuing ahead. 'Besides, they do the best blue cheese sauce.'

He laughed. 'The Yanks invented blue cheese sauce. You're going to drown in the stuff when you go.'

I sighed. 'Look, it's the only place I know in Shoreditch

and you know Kat's boyfriend won't come south of the river.'

Matthew stopped in his tracks again. 'Oh God no. You didn't invite Klive with a "K", did you?' He made his arms into a gangtsa-style 'K' when he spoke.

I rolled my eyes. 'You're lucky I invited *you*, considering your behaviour of late.'

'Fifty quid to eat a burger in a graffitied warehouse next to Mr Kunt with a "K". I'm starting to wish I hadn't been invited.'

I slapped him again. 'It's not graffiti, it's street art. Now hurry up. Our table's booked for eight o'clock.'

We arrived at Blood Burger just after eight-thirty. The entrance was via a backstreet, which seemed to double as a urinal. Straight away, I spotted Victoria's ponytail at the front of the queue. It was swinging from side to side while Victoria argued with a door woman who had a bolt through her nose. Matthew and I edged up to them to see what the problem was.

Victoria air-kissed us, then explained the situation.

'She wants to take my coat,' she said.

The door woman gestured towards the coat check and raised her eyebrows.

Matthew leaned in and stared at Victoria. 'How is that a problem?'

Victoria looked at me. 'I'm not leaving it here,' she whispered, leaning in towards us. 'It's Chanel.'

Matthew started laughing. 'The people of Shoreditch don't care much for haute couture,' he said.

Victoria glared at Matthew and then glanced around her. 'Shush,' she said. 'Or are you going to socialise the value of my jewellery while you're at it? Provide a full inventory for all the robbers within a one-mile radius.'

He smirked. 'This isn't *Oliver Twist*. East London has become gentrified since the eighteen hundreds. Didn't anyone tell you?'

It was nearing nine o'clock by the time we were seated at our table. Victoria had eventually been persuaded to hand over her coat after Matthew had promised to reimburse her its full market value should it be 'lifted' by a pierced staff member or unsavoury patron.

Straight away the waiter approached and handed us menus, along with a stern reminder that we would be expected to vacate the table by 10 p.m.

Matthew ordered several bottles of wine and then waved him away. I looked around the room and then around the table. Matthew fitted in well with his geek chic and Victoria, with her high ponytail and perma-haughty expression was intrinsically cool. But, no matter how hard I tried to convince myself that my high-street tea dress could perhaps be mistaken for Portobello vintage, deep down I knew I didn't belong here. Matthew clocked me readjusting the neckline and pulled my hand away.

'Ellie, no one gives a shit what you're wearing. Just chill out.' Then he leaned forward and squeezed my cheek. 'The Yanks will think you're adorable, whatever you wear.'

I looked at him, open-mouthed. 'Was that just a compliment from Matthew?'

He grinned. 'If you have any faith in their judgement, that is.'

I leaned forward and smacked him on the leg. He put me in a mock headlock.

'We're going to miss you, Ellie Rigby,' he said, ruffling my hair.

Victoria looked the other way. If I hadn't have known her better, I would've thought she was wiping away a tear.

Matthew suddenly freed me and then grabbed the open bottle of wine that the waiter had just placed in front of him.

'Let's drink,' he said, pouring each of us a glass.

We'd failed to order within the expected timeline so were forcibly supervised by the increasingly impatient waiter.

Victoria announced that she wasn't in the mood for a burger.

'Is there anything else on the menu?' she asked the waiter.

He sighed. 'There's the Blood Spud.'

She screwed up her face. 'You've really gone to town with the blood theme, haven't you?' she said. 'And what exactly is the Blood Spud?'

'A potato.'

'With?'

'Chilli mince.'

Her face contorted further. 'Anything vegetarian?'

The waiter checked his watch. 'Yes, the blood orange salad.'

'Fine. I'll have that then.' She let out a deep sigh as though she'd just forfeited generations of accumulated family wealth in one disastrous negotiation.

The waiter turned to Matthew. 'And for you, sir?'

Matthew, evidently amusing himself at the waiter's expense, insisted he consult with the chef on the gluten content of the entire menu, before eventually conceding that he was not in any way intolerant to gluten. He then ordered a

Double Blood Beaten Burger with a Big Daddy Bap. I could tell he enjoyed saying the word 'bap'.

'I'll have the Black and Blue,' I said, conscious time was passing. 'With extra blue cheese sauce, please.'

Suddenly, Matthew hid behind his menu. 'Fuck me,' he said.

I stared at him. 'It's only blue cheese sauce. I didn't order a ten-inch dildo.'

'No, not that.' Matthew pointed from behind the menu. 'Them.'

The waiter hurried off and I glanced behind me to see what Matthew was pointing at. I struggled to recognise them at first. Then I realised it was Kat and Klive coming down the stairs. Kat appeared to be wearing an orange sari and Klive was beside her looking like a Masai warrior after a Gok Wan makeover. I looked closer. Kat's hair was scraped back. No, wait a minute...

'She's shaved her head?' Matthew said, reappearing from behind the menu.

Kat waved. Klive puffed out his chest and glanced around the room, as though he were the guest on a prime-time talk show.

They approached the table and Klive pulled out a chair for Kat. Then he nodded at each of us, as though the matter of presenting our close friend with a freshly shaven head were an everyday occurrence.

Victoria broke the silence first.

'Please tell me this is fancy dress,' she said, pulling at Kat's robe. 'You've got a party to go to after, haven't you?'

Kat shook her head.

Klive took Kat's hand and looked at us solemnly.

'Katrina and I have chosen a new way of life,' he said.

Victoria rolled her eyes and Matthew started giggling.

In the years I'd known her, Kat had assumed all manner of religions and identities depending on whom she was dating. I looked her up and down, vaguely identifying her attire from a Louis Theroux documentary I'd seen recently.

'So, you're a Hare Krishna now?' I asked.

Kat nodded.

Matthew laughed again. 'You can talk, you know. It's only Buddhists who take a vow of silence. The Hare Krishnas are a noisy bunch. Always chanting. Are you sure you've fully researched this?'

Klive held up his hand to interrupt Matthew. 'Kat has been wrestling with demons for years and now she has found her path. As her friends you must respect that, shouldn't they, darling?'

Kat smiled vaguely.

'Yeah, the path to some hardcore pharmaceuticals, it looks like,' Matthew chipped in.

Klive puffed out his chest again. Next to his dark brown skin, the bright orange sarong looked almost luminous. I didn't recall anyone wearing that ensemble in the Louis Theroux documentary. It seemed less of an ego-transcending statement and more like a well-accessorised Westwood-esque interpretation of Hinduism.

Matthew was glaring at him. Just as he was about to say something, the waiter returned with a tray of cocktails. Matthew handed them out. Kat's smile faltered slightly.

The waiter turned to Klive. 'Can I get you anything, sir?'

Klive's chest seemed to expand further. 'Two empty glasses, please.'

The waiter stared at him for a moment. 'And?'

'That's all,' said Klive. 'We've brought our own water.'

The waiter shrugged his shoulders and walked off.

Kat cleared her throat and eventually broke her silence. 'Swami Peshwani says we shouldn't eat meat. Or drink alcohol,' she said.

Matthew laughed again. 'Swami Peshwari sounds like the subject of a *Watchdog* investigation.'

'*Peshwani,*' Klive corrected. 'Not Peshwari. He's a spiritual leader, not a coconut-filled naan.'

'So what else did Swami P. say?' Matthew downed his drink, then burped loudly. 'I hope you didn't give him any money.'

Klive's eyes narrowed and he leaned in, placing both hands on the table. 'He said those who live like you will be reincarnated as a lower being.'

Matthew laughed again. 'Those who live like me?' he said, reaching for another drink. 'I'd much rather be driven by instinct than bullshit my way through an unattainable set of standards.' He turned to Kat. 'I bet Klive didn't tell you that Hare Krishnas believe sex is for procreation only?'

Kat turned to Klive, eyebrows raised.

Klive shifted in his seat.

Matthew wagged his finger at Kat. 'If he puts his thing anywhere near you, call Swami P. immediately.'

The beginnings of a smirk appeared on Kat's face.

Just as Klive began to explain his seemingly selective interpretation of Swami Peshwani's gospel, the waiter reappeared with our food. Kat stared at Matthew's double blood beater and I saw a flash of longing in her eyes.

Matthew grabbed the burger with both hands and took a huge bite, letting the juices drip down his chin.

Klive stood up, muttering something about Matthew being an ignorant heathen who had no respect for another's beliefs.

'Oh, come on,' Matthew said, wiping his chin. 'You've just shoved your evangelical bullshit down my throat with that silly orange outfit, and your judgement on my life.'

'I'll let Krishna be the judge of you,' Klive said, smoothing down his sarong and placing his coordinating man bag over his shoulder. 'And it's saffron, not orange.'

A girl with pink hair sitting at the table next to us nodded in agreement.

Klive tugged on Kat's arm. 'Come on,' he said. 'We'll make the ten o'clock yoga class if we leave now.'

Kat looked at him, then at Matthew's burger and then at me. 'It's Ellie's leaving do,' she said. 'I'm going to stay.'

Klive's nostrils flared. He stared at Kat as though trying to summon her with his will. It wasn't working. 'Fine,' he said. 'But remember, sixteen chants per rosary.' He bent down to free one of his sandal straps, which had become tangled around a chair leg.

'Yes,' Matthew chipped in, 'or you might come back as a cockroach.' He leaned in towards Kat and whispered, 'One spelt with a "k" of course.'

Kat smirked. Then when Klive was out of sight, she swiped Matthew's burger and took a huge bite.

It was nearing ten o'clock when the waiter began hovering around us, insisting he clear our plates. However, Matthew, whose belligerence appeared to be escalating with each drink, had deliberately ordered more food and another round of cocktails in an attempt to delay our departure.

And Kat, who had been a teetotal fruitarian for the past three months, was now on her second burger and her fifth cocktail.

'Don't leave us, Ellie,' she said. 'What will become of me if you go?'

Matthew turned to her. 'You're wearing a saffron robe and have shaved your head. What else could go wrong?'

Kat burst out laughing. Then started slamming her hand on the table. 'Saffron,' she said, her laugh escalating, 'that's so funny. Peshwari naan. Hilarious. Can we have another burger?'

Victoria, who had been quietly consuming a Burgundian Chardonnay for the past few hours, sniffed and blinked repeatedly.

'I just don't understand why you're going to that ridiculous country,' she said. 'You have everything here.'

Matthew held his hand up to stop her. 'At least Ellie is trying to find happiness rather than just waiting to die in South West London, like you.'

Victoria sat up and poured herself a glass. 'I'm very happy thank you, Matthew. Just because I'm living a grown-up life, doesn't mean it's boring.'

He laughed. 'Your life is so boring, I can't even bring myself to describe it. It's all PTA and tennis club and: "how else can I spend my husband's money?" You want Ellie to have the same pointless life as you, just to validate your own uninspiring choices.'

I tried to interrupt but Matthew was in full flow.

'Ellie's miserable. Just look at her.'

I glared at him. 'No, I'm not.'

'She has a business that's failing.'

'It's not failing,' I interrupted.

'Oh, come on, Ellie. Record sales does not a successful business make. Your clients are deeply unhappy, they're all getting divorced.'

I put my hand up to speak but Matthew rattled on. 'Your house is falling into disrepair and your marriage is in crisis.'

'Hang on a second.' I put my hand up higher this time. 'You're the one with the crisis of a marriage. Not me.'

Victoria and Kat turned to Matthew.

He closed his mouth and his shoulders slumped.

The waiter, who had resumed his hovering, leaned in. 'Excuse me, sir, we need the table. The next guests are waiting.'

Matthew looked up at him, gripping his steak knife. His knuckles whitened.

Immediately, I imagined the scene culminating in a *Peaky Blinders*–style bar brawl and a 'Bloodbath at Blood Burger' morning headline, with a caption under Matthew's mugshot: 'Red meat binge sends patron into murderous rage'. There might even be a comment from Klive along with a link to the enrolment form on Swami P.'s website.

'If they want the table so badly,' Matthew said, jaw tensed, 'tell them to come and get it.'

The waiter raised his eyebrows and then wandered off muttering something about another five minutes not being a problem.

I leaned back in my chair. 'This is the reason I'm going away,' I said.

Kat frowned. 'Because there's only a two-hour sitting for restaurants in London?'

I looked at her and then around at the diners in the restaurant. I couldn't see a genuine, non-alcohol-induced smile in the room.

'Because none of us have really figured it out,' I said, downing the last of my cocktail. 'I still need answers.'

Victoria nodded her head from side to side.

Kat leaned forward. 'What answers do you really hope to find, Ellie? The cure for disillusionment?'

Matthew, who until then had been holding his head in his hands, looked up. 'No,' he said, 'she expects to find the cure for a broken heart.' Then he started laughing.

I shook my head. 'I'm not looking for a cure,' I said. 'Simply a way to reduce our risk.'

Matthew stopped laughing. 'Ellie, love is not a medical condition. It doesn't have a prognosis.'

I stared at him. 'If love isn't something we can enhance, prolong or modify then what is it?'

He ran his hands through his hair. 'Best you ask the experts that one,' he said.

I leaned forward and looked him in the eye. 'That's precisely what I intend to do.'

Kat leaned towards me and draped her arm around my neck. 'Just don't ask anyone who's named after an Indian flatbread,' she said.

Matthew didn't even crack a smile. He sat in silence, staring ahead.

Kat shuffled up next to him. 'Come on, you,' she said, squeezing his knee, 'it could always be worse. At least you're not bald.'

Matthew looked up and stared at her for a moment. Then he cocked his head.

'It quite suits you,' he said. 'Very *Alien* chic.' Then they both laughed.

When he had stopped laughing, he looked at us each in turn.

'I'm sorry,' he said. 'I've been a bit of an arse tonight.'

'Tonight?' Kat replied.

He laughed again. 'OK, I've been a total arse since I

found out my wife was shagging a fifty-year-old with a comb-over.' He dropped his head in his hands again. 'He wears Moss Bros. suits, for fuck's sake.'

Kat and Victoria looked at each other. I went to speak but quickly realised I had nothing to say.

Suddenly Matthew threw down his knife and fork and jumped up onto the table, grinning like a serial killer.

'This is your last night with us, Eleanor Rigby,' he said, striking a pose and knocking over the condiments. 'And I'm in the mood for dancing.'

We arrived at Shoreditch House a short while later. Matthew and Kat insisted we bypass the queue and walk straight in the entrance. Kat had a company account, but I suspected the main reason we were waved through by the burly doorman was because he fancied Matthew.

'I'll happily tolerate a hair ruffle and a bum squeeze for my girls,' Matthew said when we were at the bar.

'And a willy up the bottom too, I suspect,' Kat said, with a wink.

Matthew's eyes widened.

Kat flung her arms around his neck. 'Come on, you loved it,' she said. 'Isn't it about time you came out?' she said with a wink. 'You know we won't judge you.'

Matthew rolled his eyes. 'What would Krishna Klive say if he found out you were inciting homosexual acts?' He fluttered his eyelashes and flicked his wrist. 'Besides, honeybundle, I am so not gay.'

'You so are,' Kat replied.

Matthew lurched forward and squeezed Kat's boobs together, nuzzling her cleavage through her sari and making strange primal noises.

'I'm as red-blooded as the rest of them,' he said.

She laughed. 'You're all talk.'

'Er, yes. And all married. With kids,' I interrupted, pulling him off her.

I glanced around for Victoria to back me up, but I couldn't see her. Eventually, I located her wobbling against the bar. I dragged Matthew and Kat over to where she was standing.

'I've been sick,' she said, gesturing to neat pile of vomit by her feet. The people around her began to disperse.

She leaned against Matthew and started to cry.

'I think Mike's going to leave me,' she said.

Matthew shrugged his shoulders. 'I'm not surprised,' he said. 'It's probably because you bore him.'

Victoria's eyes narrowed and she swished her ponytail, seemingly angered into sobriety.

Matthew continued. 'You don't do anything interesting. If you are not leading an interesting life, then how can you interest him?'

'And you? Mr House Husband? What do you do that's so interesting?'

'Nothing,' he said. 'That's precisely my point. And most likely why my wife chose to have sex with a man who has hairy ears and halitosis.' He looked down at the floor and then back at Victoria. 'Because I was too busy buying wipes in Costco.'

I arrived home to find Nick angrily shooting aliens on his Xbox. Rupert was sitting on his lap, eyes wide.

I leaned down to stroke Rupert but Nick pulled back, shielding him from me as if I was foaming at the mouth and coming at them with a screwdriver.

'You're drunk,' Nick said. 'Where have you been?'

I steadied myself against the door frame and slurred a few sentences, which I believed contained adequate information as to my evening's activities; however, Nick just glared at me and I think actually fired a shot in my direction from the controller.

I slumped down next to them and mumbled something about the standard of Rupert's care under Nick's watch.

Nick scowled at me.

I continued. 'He's up way past his bedtime and clearly overstimulated,' I said, then I pointed in the general direction of the screen. 'Not to mention being exposed to X-rated material.'

Nick tutted. 'I think you'll find a present yet neglectful parent is preferable to an absent one.' Then he muttered something under his breath about responsibilities and maturity.

'Typical,' I said. 'I have one night out.' I held up one finger in front of Nick's face. 'One,' I said again, to enhance the impact. 'You're out all the time and I go out once—' my one finger was still raised '—to say goodbye to my friends and goodbye to my home—' I took a breath, realising I had an excellent argument '—which incidentally, you're making me leave.'

Nick dropped the controller and sat up. 'No, no,' he said. 'Don't start that. You agreed it was a good idea to go to New York. We made the decision together.'

I stared at him, arms folded until my frown gradually softened. 'Sorry,' I said, 'I'm just feeling a bit sad. I'm going to miss it here.'

Nick put his arm around my shoulder and pulled me to him. Rupert spread himself across both our laps.

'I'm sorry too,' Nick said. 'I suppose I was just a bit

peeved that I couldn't come out with you tonight and was left looking after Rupert.'

I rested my head on Nick's shoulder.

'We'll have plenty of nights out together in New York,' I said, squeezing his hand.

He looked down at me and smiled.

I went to smile back but suddenly my eyelids felt heavy.

Chapter 9

It might have been because I was the recipient of an Ibiza-grade hangover, or perhaps because Mandi was wearing an especially acidic version of lime green that morning, but for whatever reason my stomach started churning the moment I arrived at the office. I walked into the meeting room, coffee curdling in the remnants of Grey Goose cocktails.

Mandi was alone, sitting at the head of the table. She grinned and then rushed over to pull out a chair for me. Even though her baby bump was still officially non-declarable she moved around with caution, judging spaces as though she had a meteor-sized appendage protruding from her girth.

She sat back down and clasped her hands together.

'Ellie,' she said, 'you won't believe how excited I am about this trip of yours.' She put her hand to her chest. 'It's going to be so amazing. I just know you're going to find the answers for all of us.' She let out a deep sigh. 'We are all depending on you, Ellie. I know you won't let us down. I have so much faith in you.' Then she leaned in and whispered, 'Dominic is running late, so let's get started without him.'

Straight away she handed me an enhanced version of Dominic's original list of experts, complete with copies and critiques of any published findings. She went on to explain the supplementary forms that she had also included.

'Here is a list of all the bookings I've made on your behalf,' she said, pulling out a wodge of papers. 'I've added a few that Dominic overlooked. Some have questionnaires you need to fill out prior to your appointments.'

I read through the list and then looked up at her. 'You know I'm not the subject of this study, don't you?'

She nodded and then smoothed down her blonde flicks. 'You have to lead by example though, Ellie.'

I pointed to the first on the list. 'You've booked Nick and I into a couples' counselling retreat?'

She nodded. 'It's preventative. Like Botox.'

She waved a brochure at me. On the cover, there was a nearly naked elderly couple doing yoga.

I looked back down at the brochure, then back up at Mandi. 'This wasn't quite what I had in mind.'

Mandi sighed. 'Come on, Ellie, it can't all be academic.' She pointed to the brochure. 'It says here we shouldn't intellectualise our problems.' She picked up the brochure and read. '"Ernest and Elspeth have been helping couples like you for over thirty years"—' she glanced up at me and then back down '—"through a series of relationship-transforming practical exercises."'

Suddenly Dominic swept in, buttocks tight, as though they were gripping the detonator to a bomb that could wipe out London. He snatched the brochure from Mandi's hand. Then he looked at the cover and screwed up his face.

'The investors aren't funding a swingers holiday,' he said, before lobbing the brochure in the bin.

Mandi's face crumpled.

'They want results,' he said and then turned to me. 'The only way this project of yours is going to be deemed a success is if the divorce rate of our clients drops significantly. And by significantly, I mean from fifty per cent to twenty per cent at least.'

Mandi gasped.

Dominic flicked through her list and began crossing out the experts she'd added, in thick black marker. 'What good will it do for Ellie to meet mail-order brides in Ukraine?' he said.

Mandi cleared her throat. 'I thought she'd learn a different perspective on marriage.'

Dominic shook his head and tutted. 'And a bloody pygmy tribe in the Congo. Seriously, Mandi, what were you thinking? This isn't *Eat, Pray, Love*. Our clients want happiness. They don't want some sob story about poverty in Russia or polygamy in pygmies. They want a Hollywood happy-ever-after, for fuck's sake. They want fulfilment, they want it now, and they want it to last. And it's our job to give it to them. That's what they're paying us for.'

Mandi and I stared at him.

He continued. 'When Mickey Rourke requests another facelift, his surgeon doesn't send him on a weekend retreat to work through his motives. Or steer him towards a decade of psychotherapy. He simply says, "Yes, certainly, sir. That will be twenty thousand dollars."'

Mandi scowled. 'How can you compare a spiritual union between two souls to something as crude as a rhytidectomy?'

Dominic let out a sigh as though he were a teacher forced to provide extra tuition to a particularly gormless pupil. 'Because the client expects the same result from both: to be happy.'

Mandi shook her head. 'But a facelift won't make anyone happy.'

Dominic smacked his hands on the table. 'And there we go. First prize to the pregnant lady with the neon green dress.' Then he quickly glanced at me. 'Are we allowed to acknowledge the pregnancy yet?'

Mandi looked up at the ceiling, breathed in slowly and then looked back down at Dominic. 'So you're saying there are no answers for Ellie to find?'

He smirked and grabbed the black marker again. 'I couldn't possibly comment. All I'm saying is that Ellie needs to find a way to slash our divorce rate.' He started ripping out pages and crossing through entire paragraphs. 'Or she might find herself out of a job.'

Mandi snatched the pen from his grasp. 'You can't fire Ellie from her own company,' she said, pointing the nib at his face.

Dominic smiled. 'Now she's no longer the majority shareholder, yes, I can,' he said, before sliding his doctored version of Mandi's report across the table towards me.

I glanced down at the report, which was now sporting more marker pen than a pre-surgery Kardashian, and I sat silent for a moment, my hangover momentarily clearing. I thought about Matthew's insecurities, Harriet's heartbreak, Victoria's fear of abandonment, mine and Nick's bickering. What did make a happy marriage? Was it simply a case of benign compatibility? Or could we take control of our destiny? My eyes scanned the list of advisors and I suddenly realised there was no point looking for a cure. At least not until we had an accurate diagnosis.

'Divorce lawyer,' I suddenly blurted out.

Mandi and Dominic stared at me.

'I need to meet with a divorce lawyer,' I said, though louder this time.

Mandi put her hand to her chest. 'Ellie, don't be hasty. Not every marriage is doomed. You and Nick can work things out.'

I frowned at her. 'No, Mandi,' I said. 'I need to find out why people are getting divorced before I can even begin to consider a way to prevent it. I need to meet with the world's most experienced divorce lawyer.'

I grabbed Dominic's pen and began to write. 'And I'll need a report from all of our matchmakers. I need them to interview each of their clients who have been divorced or separated. I want to know precisely why they chose to divorce. I want to know if they are happier now. I want to know why they thought it couldn't be fixed. I want to know *everything.*'

Dominic sat back and let out another deep sigh. 'We already know why people divorce, Ellie.' He sighed again, as though forcing out his very last breath. 'Infidelity, irreconcilable differences, growing apart. People just fall out of love.'

I narrowed my eyes at him. 'Infidelity isn't a cause, it's a symptom. Growing apart and irreconcilable differences are too vague. Besides, no serious study would rely on anecdotal evidence. I don't want a one-word answer or a box that people ticked on a divorce petition. I want the truth. Then and only then can I begin to find a way to help people.'

Mandi clapped.

Dominic leaned back in his seat and threaded his fingers together. 'Yeah, good luck getting the truth out of anyone. Most of all a lawyer.' Then he began to laugh.

Mandi clasped her hands together and let out a squeal.

'Wait, Ellie, we have forgotten something really important,' she said.

Dominic stopped laughing and turned to her, seemingly keen enough for a solution to entertain Mandi's suggestion.

She sat up straight and readjusted her headband. 'You know when scientists conduct studies into HIV and things like that?' she began.

Dominic nodded as though hoping it might speed her up.

'Well, instead of focusing on the sick people, they tend to look at the groups who are immune.' She looked at us both and nodded. 'Such as those who have the virus but don't go on to develop the full infection. Like apes and a small group of prostitutes in South Africa.'

Dominic shook his head as though trying to dislodge a fly in his ear.

She continued. 'So, shouldn't we be studying the happily married people instead then? To see how they do it.'

I screwed up my mouth and considered her argument. I glanced at Dominic, who had ceased shaking his head.

'Great idea,' he said. 'Now all you have to do is find a happily married couple who are actually happy.' Then he laughed again, although this time it was more of a snort.

I put my hand up to stop him. 'Mandi has a very valid point, Dominic.'

Dominic resumed his laughter and then stood up as though he'd just awarded himself centre stage.

'Eleanor, you have to remember, our clients don't want the truth, they want hope. Hope that they will be different, that they will transcend the limitations of humanity and attain a higher state of fulfilment.' He looked at me, a smirk fixed on his face.

I immediately wondered if he'd been liaising with Matthew on some kind of secret chat room for philosophers against humanity.

I shook my head slowly. Was it that Dominic was grossly underestimating our clients? Or, I wondered, as the door swung shut behind him, perhaps just himself?

After he'd left, I turned to Mandi. Her eureka expression had faded and she began to cradle her head in her hands and cry. At first it was just little snuffles, but it soon escalated to full-on sobs intermitted with desperate wails. After a while, she looked up at me, mascara tramlines down her cheeks.

'Five of my clients divorced this week,' she said, wiping the tears away with her sleeve. 'I can't take any more of this heartbreak. You have to find the truth, Ellie. Find it. And prove him wrong.'

I leaned forward and squeezed her shoulder.

'Don't worry,' I said. 'I will.'

Chapter 10

It was early evening when I walked home, past the seemingly endless rows of terrace houses. As I shielded my face from the low winter sun, I began to wonder what truth existed beyond the glossy front doors. I'd always assumed the couples who resided in them were happier than me, rationalising that if they were effective enough to produce four offspring, hold down two careers and still have time to commission bespoke mosaic floor tiles for their front path, then perhaps they had the answers I was looking for.

I looked up at an especially grand entrance porch and sighed. I knew now that heartbreak didn't discriminate. The divorce rate, which had been creeping up year on year, was like poison ivy, cracking the jet-washed bricks of happy homes just like this.

And it wasn't as though divorce was the only indicator of heartache. There were plenty of other relationships limping on, hoping to reach the finish line, to the imaginary fanfare of a revered anniversary. As I strode ahead, I began to think about my own marriage. There was no doubt I loved Nick more than I had ever loved anyone before. However, at the same time, petty irritations had begun to fester, and I was beginning to realise that his behaviour wasn't infallible and neither was mine.

The sun was setting by the time I reached our house. The last glow of the day sent an eerie shimmer across the cracked concrete of our front path. Just as I was considering how I would spend the evening before Nick came home, I noticed a flash of blonde in the corner of my eye. I looked up to see a slim lady and a small boy peering into our front window.

She jumped back when she saw me.

'Oh gosh, I'm so sorry,' she said, pulling her son away from the window to stop him from pressing his nose against the glass. 'You must be the owner.' She wiped her hand on her skirt and then held it out to me. 'I'm Kerri. We're moving in next week. I hope you don't mind us nosing in your window. It's just—' she looked down at the boy '—Freddie, he was dying to see the place and we were just heading back after his swimming club and he'd done so well tonight, so I thought it would be nice to show him where we'll be living. I'm so sorry. I hope you don't mind.'

I laughed. 'Of course not.' Her petite features and pretty blue eyes looked disconcertingly familiar. She reminded me of someone from the past. 'Why don't you come in?' I turned to Freddie. 'You like dogs?'

He grinned and nodded.

His mother smiled. 'Freddie loves dogs. Thank you so much.' Then she stared at me for a moment and her eyes suddenly widened. 'Ellie?'

I studied her more closely. She looked so familiar but I

just couldn't place her. Then I looked into her eyes again and my mind immediately flashed back to a time when they were framed by three sets of false lashes.

'Kerri?' I said.

She jumped up and down, then ran towards me and flung her arms around my neck.

Five minutes later, after she'd attempted to verbally download the past seven years of her life, Freddie began to huff and puff.

'Can we see the dog now, Mum?' he asked. 'Please?'

'Oh yes, of course,' I said, reaching for my keys. 'I should've invited you in straight away.' I turned to Kerri. 'You will stay for a drink, won't you? We still have so much to catch up on.'

She nodded and then shrugged her shoulders. 'It's not like we have anything to go home to anyway.'

When I opened the door, Rupert leaped out and into my arms as though he'd been abandoned for months. Freddie's grin faded and he looked up at me through knitted brows.

'Has he been home by himself all day?' he asked.

I nodded, feeling my stomach knot as I did.

Freddie looked back at Rupert's full-body wags and then at me.

I bent down to Freddie's level. 'I'm so busy at work at the moment,' I said, 'and Rupert's not allowed in the office.'

Freddie scowled at me.

'But I walked him earlier though,' I added, as though a seven-year-old boy could comprehend, or even care about, the justifications adults make to appease their consciences.

In the manner of a determined social worker, Freddie carefully extracted Rupert from my grasp and then took him inside. Without invitation, he made his way to the kitchen and filled Rupert's bowl with fresh water. Then he started opening cupboards presumably in search of Rupert's dinner.

'In the fridge,' I said, following them into the kitchen. 'Brown label. Campfire stew, there's half a tin left.'

While Freddie spooned Rupert's food lovingly into his bowl, Kerri and I sat at the kitchen table drinking wine.

By our second glass, Kerri still hadn't mentioned him, so I felt a little reluctant to ask the question. But after a further gulp of wine, I eventually mustered the courage. 'So, how is David?'

Freddie glanced up and then back down at Rupert, who was quietly munching on his stew, tolerating increasingly enthusiastic strokes.

Kerri stared into space, and took a sip of wine. Immediately, I regretted questioning her. Perhaps they'd just separated. It might still be raw.

'He's dead,' she said.

My muscles tensed. I'd had a response all ready to come out. I'd had countless conversations like this with clients before. I was good at this. This was my profession. I said nothing.

'Please don't go all weird on me, Ellie,' she said, taking another gulp of wine. 'I don't need to be protected. I just need to be able to talk about it.'

I looked at her, at the creases in her forehead and the frown lines between her eyebrows. There was the reason I hadn't recognised her straight away.

'When did it happen?' I asked.

'Five months ago,' she said.

'How?'

'Cancer.'

'Bloody hell,' I said.

She sighed. 'Yep. We found the lump in January and he was dead five weeks later. The night before our sixth wedding anniversary.'

I looked at her and then at Freddie. He had the same kind smile as his father, the same purposeful stance, the same green eyes.

'How do you even begin to cope?' I asked.

She forced a laugh. 'You don't.' She took another gulp of wine. 'It's like one day your world is full of colour, then the next it's black and white, like a thick cloud of dust has settled and you know it will never go. I can see my old life but it's in the distance, somewhere unreachable. I keep having dreams that he's still alive.' She looked out through our back doors as though searching for something. She wiped her eyes. 'And then I wake up and it all starts again.' She looked down at the floor. 'Or I'll see Freddie's school bag in the hallway and think it's David's briefcase. I used to nag him about leaving it there. I was always saying: "One of us will trip over it and get hurt."' She took another sip of wine. 'I was prepared for the pain. I was prepared for the endless torturous nights. It's the little things though.'

I reached across and squeezed her hand.

'I've lost his mini screwdriver. The one he always used to tighten the door hinges and to change the batteries in Freddie's toys. I've looked everywhere and I can't find it.' She held her head in her hands, her body shaking. 'It has a black and yellow handle.'

'I'm sure we've got one you can borrow.'

She looked up at me, tears streaming down her cheeks. 'But I have to find it. It's in the house, I know it is. I can't lose it.' She started sobbing. 'I can feel him slipping away from me, Ellie, and there's nothing I can do to stop it.'

Freddie was standing in the doorway. 'He's gone, Mummy,' he said. 'Daddy's gone.'

Kerri hurriedly wiped her cheeks, sat up, then sniffed and smiled. 'Freddie, sweetheart. I thought you were playing with Rupert?'

Freddie held Rupert in the air. 'He did a wee on the carpet.'

Kerri smiled and jumped down off the stool. 'Oh, don't worry, sweetheart. Where is it? We'll clean it up.'

I watched as Kerri donned the mask of upbeat mum, suppressing her despair to reassure her son. Freddie watched closely, mirroring her convincing smile with his own. Love and its endurance had so many layers, many of which I had yet to experience, let alone comprehend.

Rupert jumped up and licked Freddie's face. I watched Freddie squirm and laugh. Rupert's tail was wagging. I looked at Kerri and then back at Freddie. No matter how besotted Nick and I had become with Rupert, I knew deep down that I couldn't justify taking him with us to New York. This was his home now.

I took a breath and then swallowed. I said the words quickly, just in case I changed my mind midway.

'Do you think Freddie might like a dog?' I asked.

Kerri nodded, nonchalantly.

'One like Rupert?' I added, my voice wavering a little.

Kerri turned to me, her eyes widening.

I smiled and nodded.

She jumped up and hugged me. 'Yes, yes, yes!' she said. 'Thank you.'

'It's the least I could do,' I replied, trying to ignore the enormous lump in my throat.

* * *

We drank the rest of our wine in silence, watching Rupert bounding after Freddie around the sofa. Rupert kept jumping up and licking his face. Each time, Freddie laughed loudly.

A tear trickled down my cheek. 'He's such a precious little fellow,' I said, gazing at Rupert.

She squeezed my hand, then looked back at Freddie.

'Yes, he is,' she said.

Chapter 11

Nick and I spent most of the flight to New York exploiting the airline's offer of complimentary mini bottles of wine and excitedly toasting our future together. But it wasn't until we landed at JFK airport, and were herded through passport control as though we were new arrivals at Guantanamo Bay, that I felt the first pangs of regret.

'Behind the line, ma'am,' a female official shouted, when my toes inadvertently compromised the boundary line.

I'd visited New York twice before, but as Matthew had so readily pointed out, it was only really for a few days, just to help with the new office set-up and to train matchmakers. Back then I'd found the caricatured patriotism and deep suspicion for anyone without a US passport entertaining. However, having left Rupert, my friends and my memories behind to start a new life, right then—albeit with Blossom Hill–enhanced emotions—I needed to feel welcome.

I huffed. 'Sorry,' I said, stepping back just behind the line, like a petulant teenager. The official stared at me and then at my toes. I noticed she had a taser in her front pocket. For a moment I was almost tempted to jump over the line and do a little victory dance just to see if she'd actually use it. Nick, seemingly sensing my unconscious attempts at deportation, took my arm and pulled me back to where he was standing, a compliant fifty centimetres behind the boundary.

She eyeballed me further when I switched on my phone and it virtually exploded with texts:

Have a cowfeee. Then come home. Matthew

Where is Rupert's shampoo? Kerri

Did you know there's a single mother now living in your house? I hope she's not DSS. Victoria

I think I'm in love. Kat

I want Jeremy back. Harriet

I've emailed you the report. Mandi x
PS Dominic is sitting at your desk.

When I'd covertly read my texts and Nick and I had eventually reassured the security staff that there were no possible terrorism threats from my nail polish remover, we were released and left to navigate our way towards Brooklyn.

Nick burst out laughing when we arrived at the property.

'When it comes to houses,' he said, 'you certainly have a type.'

I stepped back and looked it over.

Now we no longer had Rupert in tow, it seemed a little

odd to be renting a family home in Park Slope, which was, in effect, New York's version of Clapham. But we'd signed a six-month lease so there was no option of switching it for a pad with a roof terrace on the Upper East Side. That and, Nick pointed out, a twenty-thousand-dollar-a-month budget deficit.

Once Nick had managed to prise the keys off our shiny-smiled realtor, reassuring him that we would most definitely distribute his business cards amongst our friends, family, neighbours and colleagues, and endorse him on the exhaustive list of websites he'd listed, we made our way inside. Our boxes had already been delivered and were stacked up in the hallway.

At first I'd thought it odd that Dominic had offered to arrange my entire relocation, then I reasoned that he must have felt bad for ousting me, but when I looked at the pile of belongings in front of me, I realised it was most likely because he wanted to make sure I actually left. I imagined him back in London, gleefully removing any remaining items from my desk and putting up a photo of himself, before calling a meeting to inform any staff who had failed to read the hourly email bulletins that they now reported directly to him.

Nick slipped his arms around my waist and kissed my neck.

'Welcome to our new life, Mrs Rigby,' he said.

I turned to him and smiled.

From the website link Mandi had sent me, I had learned that Montgomery, Baustein and Associates was the largest law firm in NYC practising family law. I arrived at the offices precisely one minute ahead of time, slightly concerned that I might be billed by the hour. From Mandi's notes I'd gleaned that they handled five hundred thousand divorce petitions per year and they also had offices in London, Frankfurt and Brussels.

Presumably touched by the video Mandi had sent of her singing a doctored version of Toni Braxton's 'Unbreak My Heart', along with her personal plea to Montgomery, Baustein and Associates to help mend the broken hearts of the world, the founding partner, Clifford Montgomery, had agreed to meet with me.

I walked into the foyer and gazed up at the vast glass atrium and the shiny white walls. It seemed inconceivable that the blood money from pain and heartbreak could have built such an astounding empire.

Mr Montgomery's PA was waiting from me at a private reception desk for his clients. She had eyes like a fawn and lips like a Maybelline model but she retained a professional poise, almost as if to reassure her peers: *I'm here to work, not shag the boss.* She handed me a pass and led me to the private lift.

On the way up, she politely reported the company's stats.

'This month we have processed nearly forty-nine thousand divorce petitions,' she began.

I raised my eyebrows.

'February is generally our busiest month.'

I smirked. 'What with Valentine's Day and everything.'

She looked at me, seemingly unsure as to whether I was being serious. 'Our clients include movie stars, sports personalities, businessmen and even congressmen.'

'I thought politicians weren't allowed to get divorced?'

This time she cocked her head as though trying to ascertain if I was simply being weird and English or if I was actually a simpleton.

Eventually, she continued. 'We won a case this week where our client was awarded a thirty-million dollar settlement.'

I raised my eyebrows again.

There was a moment's silence as the lift kept climbing. I noticed a wedding band on her left hand.

'So what do you think is the key to a happy marriage?' I asked.

She leaned over to the lift buttons and pressed one that was already lit. 'My husband and I go to therapy regularly,' she said, 'we keep ourselves in shape, we try to communicate without blame and—' she looked up to the ceiling '—we never flirt with other people.'

I nodded, wondering if she hadn't misunderstood the question as to how to prevent divorce.

The lift doors opened directly into the penthouse office, which at first glance seemed to comprise the collective square footage of our London offices, Victoria's mansion and Clapham Common.

I was greeted by a soft English accent. 'You must be the wonderful matchmaker Mandi has told me so much about.'

I turned around to see a small, portly man wearing pinstriped trousers, a blue striped shirt and red braces. His face was round, with a grey beard. He looked not unlike an extremely wealthy Father Christmas.

'Mr Montgomery?' I asked.

He gestured for me to sit down on an enormous leather office chair.

'Yes,' he chuckled. I half expected him to pull out a present from a sack and for an elf to appear and take a Polaroid of us. 'You've come all the way over the pond to meet a fellow Londoner.'

I pulled out a pen and paper. 'Doesn't matter,' I said, although I'd been secretly hoping the world's top divorce attorney might be more like Will Gardner from *The Good Wife*.

'Thank you so much for agreeing to meet with me,' I added.

'The pleasure is all mine.' He threaded his fingers together. 'Off you go, my dear, please fire away.'

'Right,' I said, clicking my pen. 'So, what I'd really like to know is why couples divorce.'

He sat back and rubbed his beard, presumably to conceal the wry smile that was creeping out the corners of his mouth.

I felt obliged to provide further information. 'I'm looking into why marriages fail so I can try to find a way to prevent it.'

By now the smile had stretched across his face. 'That's very noble of you, Ellie.'

I wrote: 'Why marriages fail' on my notepad and then underlined it.

'So,' he continued, 'you want to know why marriages fail, or why people divorce?'

I nodded.

'Which one?' he asked.

'They are the same thing, aren't they?'

He chuckled and shook his head. 'Failure is subjective,' he said. 'Most divorces occur because one or both parties failed to deliver what was perceived to be their part in the marriage contract.'

'What does that even mean?'

He chuckled again. 'Law,' he said, rubbing his beard, 'much like love, is largely governed by interpretation.'

I looked up. 'So, is marriage about law or about love?'

He laughed again. 'Marriage,' he said, 'for most, is about love. Divorce, however, tends to be more about law.'

I looked down at my pad and considered what to write. Then I looked back up again. 'The marriage contract,' I said. 'What precisely is that?'

He chuckled again and looked down at my wedding band. 'What is it to you?'

I opened my mouth to speak and then closed it again, realising that I couldn't recall any of the written information on the marriage certificate Nick and I had signed. It had seemed so irrelevant at the time.

Mr Montgomery continued. 'Love means different things to each person. Just because you love or think you love your husband, doesn't mean that he sees love the same way.'

I glanced down at my notepad again.

'Look,' he said, leaning forward in his chair. 'When a man says to a woman, "I love you", then immediately there are expectations, an unspoken unwritten contract. For her, being loved might mean having a foot rub every day, a Gucci handbag for her birthday. She might think if a man loves her then he will pre-empt her every emotional need, keep her financially secure, or put up shelves, or look after their children while she pursues her career. For a marriage to be deemed happy in modern times, both parties expect to have their needs fulfilled. Without sacrifice or selflessness. And you see, Eleanor, that can only go one way.'

He leaned forward and handed me a file. 'Here is a report of all the divorces we've handled in the past year.'

I heaved the file onto my lap and began leafing through the pages.

Mr Montgomery continued. 'All personal details have been deleted, aside from the reason. The laws in the US are different from those in the UK. Here, we have what is called a "no fault" divorce, which simplifies the process a little. However, in the UK for a quickie divorce the client must cite "unreasonable behaviour", which is often not the case, so aside from those, you will see that very few divorces are due to any truly unsavoury activities like drug taking, or abuse. Most of the causes—' he pointed to the UK listings '—are because of irreconcilable differences.'

I continued to leaf through the report. The figures seemed interesting but I wasn't entirely sure what to do with them. They gave me the reasons but no insight into the motives.

I glanced back up at him. 'And in your opinion, could some of the irreconcilable differences have been reconciled?'

He chuckled again. 'Most,' he said, leaning back and swivelling on his chair. 'In answer to your original question, I believe the reason most couples divorce is because they don't see the true value of marriage until it's too late.'

'Are you married?' I asked.

'Divorced,' he answered, 'three times.'

I left the offices with a lump in my throat and a fifty-page report detailing the demise of nearly six hundred thousand marriages. During the lift ride back down to the foyer, I thought about the forces at work, sucking the love from these marriages and then spitting it back out into a divorce attorney's shredder, and I wondered how to combat them.

Strangely, an image of Matthew brandishing a baguette

flashed through my mind, along with his mocking plea for me to 'save us all'. I sighed. Perhaps it had been naive of me to believe I could have any impact at all. I glanced down at the wad of paper in my arms. If we truly had brainwashed ourselves into believing we were entitled to fulfilment, then how could we ever begin to rectify that?

My phone rang as I walked out onto Park Avenue. Just as I answered it, an Armani-clad woman barged past me, knocking the phone out of my hand.

I fumbled on the ground, trying to retrieve it.

'Jesus Christ, look where you're going,' she shouted back at me.

I heard Matthew giggling when I put the phone to my ear. 'Jesus Christ is in New York?' he asked.

'No,' I said, laughing. 'Lucky for him, his resurrection came long before Bergdorf and Goodman.'

'Not sure Jesus would see himself as lucky, Ellie,' Matthew replied. 'So, aside from enraging the locals, what the devil have you been up to?'

I sidestepped into what seemed to be the slow lane on the sidewalk. 'I just met with a divorce lawyer.'

'Wow,' Matthew gasped. 'I didn't realise it had got that bad.'

I sighed. 'Why does everyone think Nick and I are splitting up?'

'Er, perhaps it's because you're telling them you've met with a divorce lawyer.'

'It's for my research.'

'Ah, yes, of course. Research. Found the answers yet, Super Ellie?'

I stopped outside a pizza shop. 'Not yet,' I said, eyeing

up a slice. It was only eleven o'clock but I hadn't had any breakfast.

'One plain slice, please,' I said, handing the vendor ten dollars.

'You're eating pizza without me?' Matthew asked.

'Sorry,' I said, grabbing the slice.

He tutted. 'I feel so betrayed.'

I took a big bite. 'Sorry,' I said again, with my mouth full. 'I'll save you some. So where are you today? Having your legs waxed?'

'Nope,' he said. 'Seaweed wrap.'

I wiped my mouth with the napkin. 'You're still on strike?'

'Yep.'

'And Lucy's OK with that?'

'Of course not, she's going nuts. Her boss said he'd fire her if she isn't back in the office next week. Or he might have said, "finger her", I can't quite remember.'

I sighed. 'You don't really want her to get fired, do you?'

'The further away she is from that smarmy twat, the better chance we have of saving our marriage.'

I shook my head. 'So by abandoning your kids, and forcing your wife out of a job, you're actually helping your marriage?'

'Yes,' he said, 'or, worst-case scenario, I'll lose two inches off my thighs, which will benefit me when I'm single.'

'Seriously, Matthew. There has to be a better way.' I took another mouthful of pizza.

He laughed. 'My way is working just fine,' he said, clearly keen to terminate the topic. 'So,' he continued, 'who's the next expert on your hit list?'

I wiped my mouth again. It appeared I had lost the ability to eat and walk at the same time. 'An anthropologist. Susan Villecox,' I said.

'Willy cocks?'

'No, *Villecox*,' I corrected.

He giggled.

I rolled my eyes. 'You're such a child.'

He carried on laughing. 'It's not my fault all relationship experts sound like sexual deviants.'

I ignored him and continued. 'She's spent the past twenty years studying romantic pairing amongst humans and primates.'

He sniggered. 'I bet she lives in Long Island.'

I glanced down at the remainder of the pizza and then shoved it into my mouth.

Matthew was still laughing. 'She does, doesn't she? Please tell me I'm right.'

I swallowed. 'Just because you guessed where she lives, which is hardly surprising considering it's in the state of New York, doesn't make her research any less credible.'

Eventually, he stopped laughing.

'Make sure you do save me some pizza,' he said. 'I might be out sooner than you think.'

Chapter 12

On the train to Long Island, I downloaded Mandi's report onto my phone. She'd listed hers and all the other match-makers' interview results in various tables and charts and carefully highlighted why each of our clients had chosen to divorce or separate.

Quickly realising that there was enough reading material to last an entire train trip around China, I jumped straight to the summary and scan-read it. It was the final paragraph that shocked me the most, which stated that over seventy per cent of the women and over eighty per cent of the men interviewed said they wished that they could have saved their relationship.

I called Mandi straight away.

'Hey, Ellie! It's so great to hear from you! How are you? How are the Americans? How is Nick? How was the divorce attorney? Have you read the report?'

'Yes, I've just read it.'

'It's so depressing, isn't it, Ellie? We are supposed to

be helping our clients. We're supposed to be making them happy. Helping them find love. And instead all we're doing is making them miserable. Setting them up for heartbreak.' She paused. 'I'm so depressed, Ellie. This is so depressing.' She let out a long deep sigh. 'And yet another divorce notification yesterday.' She paused. 'Harriet and Jeremy. Can you believe it? I nearly cried.'

My stomach flipped. 'What? No way. You mean the other Harriet and her husband Julian surely? Not Harriet and Jeremy?'

She sighed. 'No, Harriet and Jeremy. He called me yesterday. He's filing for divorce. He sounded gutted. I tried to talk him out of it but he wasn't interested. He mentioned something about a man called Matthew who keeps taking Harriet to spas. I never thought she was the type to cheat, did you? And they make such a beautiful couple. I can remember the day he proposed like it was yesterday. The poem he wrote her. They were so happy. Oh, Ellie, this is beyond depressing. If Jeremy and Harriet can't make it, then what hope do the rest of us have? What are we going to do?'

I watched Manhattan fading away into the distance.

'Mandi, take a deep breath,' I said. 'Divorce isn't an airborne virus.'

She sighed. 'At least if it was, we could quarantine those infected.'

I laughed, imagining Mandi erecting makeshift Ebola-style isolation units in our offices.

'We don't need to inform the World Health Organisation just yet,' I said. 'As far as I'm aware no one has died from divorce.'

Mandi sighed again. 'But, Ellie, divorcees are dead. They are dead from the soul down. Their spirit has gone.'

I frowned, wondering where in the body Mandi imagined the soul to be located. Somewhere at the top, I reasoned, for her comment to make any sense.

'There is life after divorce, Mandi,' I said.

'I know, I just can't bear to think about it. All those poor people, heartbroken and lonely. If Steve ever left me, I would simply die.'

I smirked, recalling her drunken sharing last month when she detailed Steve's most irritating habits.

'You wouldn't miss the lip smacking when he eats though, would you? Or the slurping noise he makes when he drinks his tea.'

She giggled. 'Or the way he scratches his balls through his jogging pants.'

'Or the fact that he calls them "jogging pants".'

She laughed. 'OK, so no marriage is perfect, but still, the report showed that most of our clients were happier married than they were divorced, so how do we fix this?'

'That's precisely what I plan to figure out.'

She paused for a moment. 'I have every faith in you, Ellie.' Then she quickly added, 'Oh, by the way, did you know Dominic is hacking into your email?'

I laughed. 'Of course he is. I wouldn't expect anything less.'

Sexual deviant or not, Susan Villecox had an impressive Long-Island residence. The wrap-around glass sliding doors and porcelain tiled floors were more befitting a Hollywood movie star than an academic famed for her introversion. She greeted me wearing a Donna Karan trouser suit and a Cartier diamond choker. Her grey hair was swept up off her face into an elegant chignon.

'Such a pleasure to meet you,' she said, smiling as she took my hand. 'What a beautiful girl you are. A quintessential English rose.'

I smiled back at her, wondering if she had mislaid her glasses.

'Do sit down, my darling.' She gestured for me to take a seat on a sleek white sofa. 'Let me fix you a drink.'

She returned with two drinks and handed me one. Then she sat down, kicked off her shoes to reveal a perfect pedicure and lifted her legs up onto the sofa.

'So, tell me, Ellie, what would you like to know?'

I took a sip of my drink. It tasted like gin, only stronger. 'I'm trying to understand more about the reasons we divorce.'

She nodded.

'I've seen so many of my clients suffer, and I want to help them.'

She regarded me for a moment. 'And you? Are you suffering?'

I took another sip. 'Not right now,' I said.

She laughed. 'To love is to suffer,' she said.

I reached for the notepad and pen in my bag.

'Woody Allen said that,' she said. 'You don't need to write it down.'

I put my bag back down and felt my cheeks flush.

'He was right though,' she continued. 'It's in our nature to suffer, or to anticipate suffering when we are not.' She took another sip of her drink.' More often the anticipation of suffering is more painful than the suffering itself.'

I stared at her for a moment trying to make sense of her words.

She laughed to herself. 'Humans have been falling in

and out of love for centuries. This kind of suffering is nothing new.'

'But we're supposed to be evolving, aren't we?'

'Indeed, that is part of the problem.'

I took another sip, hoping that the gin might help decode her riddles.

She continued. 'We are complex creatures, hard-wired for a world that no longer exists. We have drives that have been embedded in our brains for hundreds of generations. Yet we expect to conform to a fixed set of values that have been determined by society.'

Immediately, I imagined Matthew sitting next to me, topping up his drink and nodding.

Susan placed her glass onto a side table.

'Our drives and values are at odds,' she continued. 'And where there is tension, there is suffering.'

'So how do we stop our drives and values being at odds?'

She raised her eyebrows and stared at me. 'How do you think?'

I looked down at the floor, then back at her. 'Change them?'

She smiled. 'Precisely, Ellie.'

I took another sip. 'But we can't adapt our drives, so we have to adapt our values?'

Her smile dropped. 'You want to tell our idealistic society to tolerate infidelity?'

I shrugged my shoulders.

She laughed. 'Besides,' she said, 'sexual jealousy is just as strong as the drive to stray, so the tension would still be in place. Try again?'

I wrapped my fingers on the side of my glass. 'So if we can't adjust our values, then we have to adapt our drives.' I took another sip. 'But our drives are an intrinsic part of us. We can't alter them.'

Susan smiled. 'Ah, but we can, Ellie.'

I scrunched up my mouth. 'Drugs?'

She smiled and then nodded at my glass. 'Intimacy is enhanced every day by socially acceptable drugs such as alcohol, prescription medications like Viagra and illegal drugs such as cocaine and ecstasy. Neurochemical enhancement is probably the closest to a solution for adapting our drives to suit our values.' She leaned over to the table and then handed me a business card. 'Professor Sheldon is at the forefront of research in this area. Give him a call.'

I smiled and tucked the card into the side pocket of my handbag.

Once I'd finished my drink, Susan was quick to show me out. Just as she was about to close the door, I turned back to her.

'Is there any other advice you could offer me?' I asked.

She smiled and regarded me for a moment. 'You want everyone to be happy and in love. That is an admiral endeavour.' She looked out beyond me and up at the sky. 'However, if we lived in a world where all our wishes were granted without any effort or pain, how would we ever learn to grow, as an individual or as a species?'

Nick arrived home soon after me, but not before I'd laid the table and popped a bottle of Chardonnay in the fridge. He rushed into the kitchen, then grabbed me round the waist and kissed me on the lips.

'Evening, my gorgeous, gorgeous girl,' he said. 'I missed you today.' Then he stepped back and tasted his lips. 'Have you been drinking already?'

I smiled. 'You know what the academics are like. They love a tipple.'

Nick shook his head. 'Just don't make a habit of it. Daytime drinking is a slippery slope.'

I laughed. 'Yes, it's much better for the liver if you concentrate your fifty unit consumption to between the hours of 6 p.m. and midnight like you do.'

He smirked and then checked his watch. 'One minute past six,' he said, before opening the fridge and nosing around. Straight away, he spotted the bottle I'd bought and grinned.

I pointed back at the fridge. 'I got us fillet steaks too, spent a month's rent at Lobel's.'

He looked at me, then back at the fridge and cocked his head. 'Are you feeling guilty about something?'

I shook my head and laughed. 'I thought it would be nice for us to celebrate the first day in your new job.'

He grabbed the wine and turned to me. 'Have I told you how much I love you, Mrs Rigby?'

When we sat down to eat, I asked Nick how his first day had gone.

He took a sip of wine. 'I just know I'm going to love it. My team is super-intelligent and dynamic. I've already learned so much just working with them for a day.'

I took a sip too. 'That's great,' I said. 'And how many of you are in the team?'

He chewed his steak and then swallowed. 'Just three of us: Jenna, Amy and me.'

I took another sip.

He continued. 'You'd love them. Jenna has a first from Harvard, she's only twenty-eight and she's already a Director. Amy has an MBA from Princeton. They are both so funny too. Jenna had me in stitches today when she was telling me about this creepy guy on the floor above. Apparently, he's got the biggest crush on her. She said that he—'

I cleared my throat. I'd heard enough about crush-inducing Jenna and super-brain Amy. 'And the offices, are they nice?' I asked.

Nick took a gulp of wine. 'They are so cool. You can order a latte on an iPad. There are fridges stocked with drinks and snacks, you can just help yourself. And there are fresh doughnuts delivered every afternoon. Jenna says that when—'

'I'll have to pop by one day,' I interrupted, 'and try a doughnut?'

Nick speared another chunk of steak. 'I'd rather settle in a bit first,' he said. 'Wouldn't want people to think I've got a needy wife to contend with.'

I went to speak but accidentally breathed in some wine and started coughing.

'You all right?' he asked, shoving the steak into his mouth.

I coughed one more time to clear my throat. 'Fine,' I said.

After he'd gone on to list the multiple team-building social occasions he'd diarised, he eventually got around to asking how my day had been.

'What was her name, the anthropologist?'

'Susan Villecox.'

'Willy cocks?'

'Oh, don't you start. I had enough of that from Matthew.'

Nick rolled his eyes. 'I thought we'd left him in London?'

I sighed. 'We did. I mean, we didn't leave him there. But I didn't pack him in my suitcase either, if that's what you're worried about.'

'Wouldn't be surprised.'

'What's that supposed to mean?'

He shrugged his shoulders. 'Well, you don't do much without him right beside you, do you? Sometimes I wonder if I haven't married you both.'

I screwed up my face. 'What? I hardly see him any more, remember.'

Nick refilled his glass and let out a deep sigh. 'Anyway, moving on, so did you learn anything from this willy cocks lady?'

I shook my head from side to side. 'She said that we can't avoid suffering. And that our values are at odds with our drives.'

Nick frowned. 'Whose values? Yours and mine?'

'No, humankind's.'

Nick nodded and chewed some more.

I continued. 'Ancient males and females pair-bonded to raise children.'

He raised his eyebrows. 'What, no effeminate male BFF hanging around too?'

I continued, ignoring him. 'However, according to her research, during that time the couples were routinely unfaithful.'

Nick took another mouthful of steak. 'I thought it was just the men who were hard-wired to stray?'

I laughed. 'Nope, the women were at it too. Having a romp in the bushes with a genetically superior male and then fooling her partner into raising his children. It was for the better of the species, Susan Villecox told me.'

He chuckled. 'Lucky for me there are no genetically superior males then.'

I smirked. 'Whereas I need to keep a close eye on any girls younger and more fertile-looking than me.'

Nick looked down. It was as though the word 'fertile' had sucked us back to London, back to the unfilled nest that we had left behind.

I reached across the table and squeezed his hand.

'Look,' I said, 'we don't have anything to worry about. If we keep loving each other, then that's all that matters.'

Nick sat back and laughed. 'If you believe that, Ellie, then what's this mission all about?'

I looked down at my plate and closed my knife and fork together. 'To stop people falling out of love.'

Nick shook his head, smiling like one might at a three-year-old who had just declared she wants to be a princess when she grows up.

'And what experts have you got lined up for tomorrow?' he asked.

I leaned back and stretched my arms above my head. 'None. I've had enough information for today, I need to let it all settle. I'll probably take a stroll around Central Park and make a plan.'

Nick smirked again.

'What? Why are you laughing?'

He stood up to clear the plates. 'Nothing. It's just nice to see you wind down a bit and take some time for yourself.'

I sat up and folded my arms. 'I'm not taking time for myself,' I said. 'I'm contemplating the future happiness of society, which incidentally,' I added with a smirk, 'is far more constructive than eating doughnuts and gossiping with Jenna and Amy.'

He leaned over and tickled me until I opened my arms again. 'Stop it,' I said. 'I'm serious.'

He bent down and kissed me on the forehead. 'You know I could never fall out of love with you.'

I looked up at him and smiled. Then I refilled our glasses, realising that this might be an opportune time to introduce Mandi's weekend plans for us.

When Nick sat back down, I shuffled up next to him.

'Are you up for some fun this weekend?' I asked.

He looked at me and frowned. 'Sounds ominous. What sort of fun?'

'Something new,' I said.

His eyes widened. 'If there are surgical gloves and paddle whips involved, then it'll have to be a "no".'

I laughed. 'It's more of a cultural experience.'

'The Burning Man? Aren't we a bit old to be dropping pills and dancing with our tops off?'

I laughed. 'It's in Texas.'

He smiled. 'Rodeo?'

I shook my head.

'I'll need more details before I can commit.'

I took a gulp of wine and then leaned over and pulled the brochure from my file.

He glanced at the cover and then back at me. 'What is this?'

'Read it,' I said.

'"Enhance your intimacy,"' he read out, then turned to me. 'You said no paddle whips.'

'Read on,' I said, nodding back down at the brochure.

He continued. '"Strengthen your bond. Group counselling sessions."' He pushed the brochure away. 'No fucking way are we doing that.'

I topped up his wine. 'Come on. Mandi booked us in. We should give a shot.'

He pointed back to the brochure. 'It says for distressed couples, or marriages in crisis.'

I snatched it off him. 'Yes, but look here, it also says for couples who want to take their relationship to the next level.'

'Sounds like some saggy couple pushing tantric sex.' He flipped through the brochure to the end. '"Love is like a bonsai tree, it needs constant care and attention." Seriously, Ellie?'

I glared at him.

He glared back.

'We have to go,' I said. 'The future of humanity is at stake.'

He raised his eyebrows.

'If you don't, then I'll stalk you at your new office, ordering lattes on an iPad while acting up like a needy wife.'

He narrowed his eyes, then sighed. 'Fine,' he said. 'I'll come.' He rolled up the brochure and pretended to spank me on the bottom. 'But you owe me, Mrs Rigby. Big time.'

Chapter 13

By 11 a.m. on Saturday morning, Nick and I were sat cross-legged in a tepee in Texas. The founder of the retreat, a thin lady named Elspeth Kennedy, was standing before us. She was wearing an embroidered kaftan and dangly earrings which tinkled every time she moved, like tiny wind chimes. She addressed us along with the three other couples in the group.

'Welcome,' she said, clasping her hands together. 'Welcome, all.' She then opened her arms to the group. 'Before we begin I would like to explain the rules.' She paused to take a breath. 'During your stay there will be no communication with the outside world. No phones, no iPads, no laptops. No electronic devices whatsoever. There will be no Instagram, no Twitter, no Facebook and no texts. While you are here, you will reserve all your attention for each other. You will remind your bodies how to watch and how to listen. You will learn how to engage and how to connect.' She handed around a basket. 'Place your devices in here, please. They will be locked in our safe.'

Once she had collected our phones plus Nick's iPad, Mac Air, Kindle and headphones, she continued. 'Rule two: no alcohol. Rule three: no inter- or intra-couple sex. That means no sex with your partner or anyone else's partner.'

One of the men raised his hand to question whether solo sex was permissible. Elspeth glared at him.

'Sex or the expectation of sex,' she said, still glaring at him, 'disrupts the process. Alcohol clouds our senses. Rule four: follow all instructions. You have to trust the process to benefit from it. Does anyone have a problem with the rules?'

Nick went to put his hand up, then obviously thought better of it.

Elspeth clapped her hands. 'Right,' she said, 'everyone, on your feet and into a circle.'

Nick smirked and seemed to deliberately take his time getting up.

Elspeth continued. 'Now we're going to go round the group introducing ourselves. Tell us your name and why you're here.' She squeezed my shoulder. 'You start.'

Everyone turned to me and smiled, including Nick, who seemed quite amused by the situation.

'My name is Ellie and I am here because...' I paused to consider what to say.

'Take a breath and be as honest as you can,' Elspeth said, stroking my back.

'Because I want to learn how to prevent divorce.'

Elspeth's eyes widened momentarily and then she nodded.

'Thank you for sharing,' she said, then moved along. 'Next,' she said, poking Nick.

'Hi, everyone,' he said looking around, 'I'm Nick. And I'm here because Ellie made me come.'

I could sense a fleeting frown from Elspeth but she tempered it and smiled instead. 'Excellent,' she said. 'Very honest, Nick. Well done.'

Next was a gay couple, Malcolm and Doug. Malcolm explained that Doug had been unfaithful and they were trying to rebuild trust. Doug seemed desperately repentant. The third couple was Maureen and Walter, who'd asked about solo sex. They must have been in their late sixties. Maureen explained that since retirement Walter had developed an unhealthy obsession with dirty magazines. And that he had suddenly quite out of character begun flirting with her friends at the bridge club.

The fourth couple, Chloe and Tom, were newly married and starry-eyed. Their parents had paid for the retreat as a wedding present. Neither of them had any idea why they were there.

Elspeth continued. 'Now hold hands, everyone.'

I held Nick's and Walter's hand. Walter winked at me.

Elspeth looked at us each in turn. 'Two out of the four couples here today will divorce,' she began. 'Counselling won't make you immune. Forty per cent of couples relapse within six months of the cessation of counselling or therapy.' She nodded her head and her earrings jangled like percussion to her speech.

She pointed to me. 'Are you happy?' she asked.

I glanced sideways at Nick and then back at her. 'Yes,' I said.

She narrowed her eyes. 'It is widely accepted that self-reported happiness, especially from women, is rarely reliable.'

She turned to Walter, who was sitting a little too close to Chloe. 'Are you happy?' she asked.

He looked sideways at Chloe, then back at Elspeth. 'Yes,' he answered.

Elspeth raised her eyebrows and stared at him.

He cleared his throat. 'OK, most of the time, I am,' he replied.

Elspeth smiled. 'Excellent honesty,' she said.

'And you?' She pointed to Malcolm.

Malcolm looked down. Doug reached across and squeezed his hand.

Malcolm shook his head. 'No,' he said. 'I'm not happy at all.'

Doug snatched back his hand and shuffled away from him.

Elspeth turned to Doug with a kind smile. 'The truth is often painful to hear, isn't it, Doug?' Then she turned to the rest of us. 'That's why we lie, to protect others and ourselves.'

Doug and Malcolm glanced at each other; both of them had tears in their eyes.

Elspeth continued. 'This weekend, we are going to find the truth in ourselves. Then in a blameless safe environment we are going to learn to communicate it to our partner.' She nodded again and her earrings jangled. 'But first you must adjust to your surroundings and enjoy some free time. This is a beautiful ranch and you must treasure your time here. Go for a swim in the lake, take a walk, there's a buffet lunch laid out in the hall. You can do whatever you like. But you must stay in your couple. Please be back by 2 p.m.'

She then handed out some truth beads, which she instructed us to wear around our necks throughout our stay.

After a few polite nods, the couples dispersed, although Walter lingered until Elspeth ushered him out.

Nick took my hand as we made our way out of the tepee. 'This isn't so bad,' he said, looking up at the sun shining and then across the vast grassy planes. 'No droopy downward dogs in sight. And a buffet to tuck into.'

I sniffed the air. 'I smell ribs,' I said, licking my lips. 'Let's get there first before anyone else gets a look in.'

Nick laughed. 'That's my girl,' he said, patting me on the bottom.

By 2 p.m., after Nick and I had scoffed a giant rack of ribs, a twelve-ounce steak and a vat of BBQ sauce, and taken a long walk around the ranch, we dashed back to the oversized tepee that was the counselling centre.

We were the last couple to return. It wasn't until we sat down that I realised Elspeth had been replaced by her 'spiritual life partner', Ernest. I immediately recognised him from the brochure, although with his drainpipe leather trousers and shaggy dyed hair he looked more like a displaced Rolling Stone than a revered professor of psychology.

He sat cross-legged and addressed us all as though he were about to present story time at nursery school.

'You've probably all heard of the psychologist John Gottman,' he said.

I nodded but everyone else looked back at him blankly.

Ernest laughed to himself. 'He claims he can predict divorce with ninety-six per cent certainty.'

More blank expressions.

Ernest ran his hands through his hair. 'What many people don't realize—' he rolled his eyes and mumbled '—because I'm not whoring myself around every chat show that'll have

me—' he blinked and then looked up '—is that I can predict which couples will divorce with ninety-nine per cent
certainty.'

Maureen gasped.

Ernest rubbed his hands on his thighs. 'Data collected
from twenty years of research has given me the power to
see into your future.'

He jumped to his feet. 'During your free time, my team
and I monitored your interactions via the microphones on
your truth beads.'

Nick sat up. 'What?' he said. 'Is that even legal?'

Ernest turned to Nick with a wry smile. 'It's in the terms
and conditions on your booking form. Besides,' he added.
'In the state of Texas, on private property virtually anything goes.'

Nick turned to me and raised his eyebrows.

Ernest continued. 'So, if you would like to hear my findings, put your hand up.'

My hand shot up. Nick glared at me.

Maureen's hand went up too, as did Chloe's and Tom's.

Ernest looked at me and then at the others. 'Before we
continue,' he said, 'let's take a moment to consider our mo-
tivation for wanting to know the results.' He readjusted the
crotch area of his leather trousers. 'It's the same reason we
have our palms read, or look at the arrangement of the stars
or into crystal balls.'

I took my hand back down.

'It's for reassurance,' he said. 'Reassurance that everything will be OK without us actually having to do anything.
A need that is fuelled by fear and insecurity. And laziness.'

I glanced at Nick, who was tracing a shape in the sand
on the ground.

Then Ernest looked at Chloe and Tom. 'Or a false certainty that the news will be good.'

He rubbed his hands together. 'Still want to know my findings?'

I nodded.

He shook his hair, as though auditioning for a shampoo ad. 'OK, you two,' he said, gesturing towards me and Nick. My stomach tightened. 'You have a good relationship.'

I glanced at Nick.

'However, there is some contempt there,' he said with the beginnings of a smile. 'It's early stages and just creeping in. But disdain is like tooth decay—' he shook his hair again '—if you don't address it, there will be problems and you will almost certainly divorce.'

Nick looked at me, eyes wide.

My heart was pounding. 'You can't possibly tell from overhearing us eating ribs, surely?'

Ernest shrugged his shoulders. 'We can.'

Nick grimaced.

'Don't worry,' Ernest added. 'It isn't critical yet. We can help you.'

I sighed, feeling as though someone had just amputated my legs and then presented me with a wheelchair as a solution.

Ernest turned to Malcolm and Doug. 'There is a lot of love between you two,' he said, then shook his head. 'But Malcolm's resentment is too deep for your relationship to survive. Without intensive therapy, you will almost certainly separate within two years.'

Malcolm burst into tears and Doug sprang forward to comfort him.

Then Ernest turned to Chloe and to Tom and scrunched

up his face. 'This is not what you want to hear,' he said hitching up the waistband of his trousers, 'but your relationship is unlikely to survive marriage. Tom, you have narcissistic personality disorder. It's unlikely you'll ever be able to sustain a happy relationship.'

Chloe immediately burst into tears. Tom frowned and then went to comfort Chloe, but Ernest jumped forward, beating him to it.

After he'd soothed Chloe, by rubbing her shoulders and then giving her a tight embrace, Ernest addressed Maureen and Walter.

'It is clear there is some tension between you,' he said, before turning to Walter. 'And some unfulfilled desires.' He raised his eyebrows twice in quick succession. 'However, overall, you have a great regard for each other and I predict you will stay married.'

For a while, we all sat silent, seemingly stunned by our predicted outcomes, then Ernest forced us into a seated circle and made us all hold hands. He stood at the centre, arms out like he was offering his soul to the heavens. He began to chant. As his off-key murmurs floated up and out of the tepee, my line of sight was drawn to his crotch, where the leather trousers bunched and bulged with a faded sheen. The shiny skull on his belt buckle made me wonder if he saw himself more as an anarchist biker than scrawny scholar.

'Now, my children,' he said, between chants, 'we are here to heal.' He began to rub his hands over his body, lingering at the groin and then back to his chest. 'To heal the decay in our hearts.'

Nick tugged on my hand, stifling a snigger.

Ernest opened one eye. 'Silence,' he said.

Nick raised his hand.

Ernest ignored him.

'Hey,' said Nick, half smiling, 'Ernie.'

Ernest scowled briefly, then forced a smile. 'Yes, Nicholas.'

'Can you please explain what the fu—' He paused and then glanced at Maureen. 'Sorry. I'd like to know, how is this chanting helping anyone?'

Ernest closed his eyes for a moment and then opened them again as though preparing to address a wayward toddler.

'Nicholas, my son,' he said, peering down his nose at Nick, who seemed to be growing less tolerant by the second, 'it's essential our minds are connected with our bodies before we can be receptive to change.'

Nick rolled his eyes. 'As far as I'm aware, my mind is already connected to my body by a central nervous system. Can we move on now, please?'

Tom and Walter sniggered.

Ernest shrugged. 'OK, if you think you're ready.' He looked around the group. 'But this is a challenging exercise. Pain and suffering must be exposed before they can be exorcised.'

Nick rolled his eyes and then continued tracing a shape in the sand. It looked like a man. There was a large bulge in the groin area. Ernest must have noticed it too because he walked past Nick, kicking his sand sketch as he went.

'Right then,' Ernest said, readjusting his crotch area in a way which made me wonder what was going on under there. 'We need you in couples for this exercise. Sit opposite each other and hold hands, with as many body parts touching as you can.'

Nick sniggered.

Ernest spun round. 'For those of you who can't take this seriously, there is the door.' He pointed to the tepee entrance.

Nick sniggered again. 'It's more of a flap though, isn't it?'

Ernest's frown subsided. He stared at Nick and rubbed his chin and nodded. 'Ah, I see. Now I understand.'

Nick frowned. 'Understand what?'

He nodded again, though more slowly this time. 'To you, the door to the tepee represents a vagina.' He continued nodding and then turned to the rest of the group, then back to Nick. 'The door to your healing is a vagina. The tepee is the womb. I understand your resistance now. You are fearful of the womb. You are fearful of women.' He began to rub Nick's shoulders, his groin almost touching Nick's ear. 'It's all right, Nicholas. You are safe here.'

Nick jumped away. 'I'm not safe while you're thrusting that thing in my face.'

Ernest patted Nick on the shoulder, then addressed the rest of the group. 'When a man is fearful, he tries to dominate.' Then he turned back to Nick with a false smile. 'You don't have to feel threatened by my manhood, Nicholas.'

Nick took a deep breath, looked up to the roof of the tepee and then back down at the sand again. I could tell he was fighting the urge to either punch Ernest on the nose or rip the tepee from the ground.

Eventually, he looked up at me.

'You owe me,' he mouthed.

Chapter 14

The focus of the afternoon's sessions, or so Ernest told us, was to enhance intimacy within each couple. With each session though, I grew ever more fearful that we would be asked to strip off and fellate our master. And there were a few moments when it looked as though Nick might bolt out through the tepee flaps like an induced foetus. However, despite how alarming we were finding the experience, for whatever reason, we both stayed.

The final session, Ernest explained to his exhausted audience, was the crucial one. We were to write down our three biggest relationship fears and then share them with each other, and then the group.

I stared at my piece of paper for a while, then shifted from my cross-legged position because my leg was numb and started rubbing my calf. Ernest rushed over and began rubbing my leg vigorously. Just as I was about to explain to Ernest that there was nothing wrong with my inner thigh, Nick stood up and glared at him.

'Nicholas, I am no threat to your relationship,' Ernest said, sitting down and putting my leg on his lap. 'Just relax, Ellie. Sometimes our bodies try to sabotage our healing. You are trying to move forward but your subconscious is holding you back.'

I stared at him. 'My subconscious gave me pins and needles?' Suddenly I realised my toes had made contact with his crotch. I scrunched them up in an attempt to recoil but in doing so I inadvertently gripped his package with my toes. Ernest smiled and thrust himself further onto my foot. I glanced at Nick, who was now shaking his head, trying not to laugh.

After I'd pretended my pins and needles had passed, I sat back on the ground and stared at the paper again. I picked up the pencil Ernest had provided and studied it. It was thick and long, and had the texture of a tree trunk. It led me to wonder how Ernest might psychoanalyse himself. Soon he was lingering behind me.

'Are we struggling, Ellie?' He began rubbing his chin again. 'It seems you have a blockage when it comes to your fears. Why do you think that is?'

I scrunched up my face.

'Perhaps if we take a look at what Nick has written then it might help you.' He leaned over and snatched the paper from Nick. Aside from a large vaginal opening, which Nick had doodled on the side, there were three sentences scrawled on the paper.

Ernest read them out.

'Fear number one,' Ernest began. 'Our relationship will get boring.' He turned to Nick. 'So, Nick, you fear that your relationship with Ellie might get boring?'

Nick nodded. 'That's what I wrote.'

Ernest looked at me. 'And how do you feel about that, Ellie?'

My stomach had clenched a little when he read it out, but it was a reasonable fear so I wasn't too concerned. 'Slightly worried that Nick thinks I'm boring,' I said.

Nick interrupted. 'That's not what I meant, though.'

Ernest silenced him with a hand gesture. 'I hear insecurity. Let's move on to the next on the list.' He looked down at the paper. 'Fear two: I worry that Ellie will be disappointed in me.'

My mind started whirring. 'Why would I be disappointed in you? Are you going to disappoint me?'

Nick rolled his eyes. 'That's not what I meant.'

Ernest interrupted with a silencing hand gesture. 'And the final one...' he squinted his eyes at the paper '...I worry that Ellie will grow to hate me.'

Ernest looked at me, then back at Nick.

'Why would I hate you?' I asked.

Nick uncrossed his legs and then crossed them again. 'Because you always seem unhappy with me. You say I drink too much, I work too much, I don't listen to every word that comes out of your mouth. You even got angry at me because my colleague is hot. How can I help that?'

I huffed. 'I knew it. So you think she's hot?' *And funny and clever*, I thought but didn't say.

'Just because she's hot doesn't mean I want to be with her. You know our relationship is so much more than that, Ellie.'

I scowled at him.

Ernest chipped in. 'Ellie, I think we've stumbled across your biggest fear. One which Nick seems to be fuelling.'

Nick and I both turned to him.

'Abandonment,' Ernest said, with a nod. 'Ellie, your biggest fear is abandonment. That's why you're insecure. And Nick's not helping with his fraternisation with sexually desirable women.' Ernest stared ahead for a moment. 'These women, I suppose they have large breasts, Nicholas?' His gaze drifted to Chloe's cleavage, as though nuzzling it with his eyes. 'Full bouncy breasts. A symbol of the nurturing you lacked.'

Nick burst out laughing. 'I don't know. I'm not perving when I'm at work. I'm working.'

Ernest took both Nick's hands in his. 'Freud himself identified the common urge to suckle a bountiful bosom.'

Nick was almost belly laughing by this point. 'I don't want to suckle anyone's bosom. Apart from Ellie's.'

I screwed my face up. 'You want to *suckle* me?'

Nick laughed again. 'No, that's not what I meant. Bloody hell, good job we're not on *Oprah*.'

Ernest gipped Nick's hands again. 'No need to feel shame, my son. These are natural drives. You should embrace them.' Ernest looked at me, then back at Nick. 'You just need to reassure Ellie that if you copulate with another, it doesn't mean you will love her any less, or leave her.'

'What?' I couldn't help but interrupt. 'You're telling Nick to have an affair.'

Ernest let out a deep sigh. 'Not of the heart but just of the body. He needs it. He's a man.'

Nick chipped in. 'I don't want an affair of the body or the mind.'

Ernest smiled and nodded slowly as though he knew better. 'The societal constraints we have inflicted upon our relationships only lead to resentment and shame.'

I tutted and went to stand up. 'This is bullshit. Elspeth might let you *copulate* with whoever you like, but that's not how I choose to live my life. Love is the only pure thing left in this world. I came to you to find out how to keep it that way. Not for you to sodomise it with phallic pencils and bulging leather trousers.' I stopped and took a breath, realising that my argument had ceased to make any sense.

Ernest took my hand. 'Resistance is fear, Ellie. Fear will kill your marriage.'

I snatched my hand away. 'You might have your wife fooled, but you're not fooling me.' Then I grabbed Nick's hand and dragged him from the tepee womb.

We marched off hand in hand and laughing, until we realised we were on a remote ranch, with no means of transport and that our flight wasn't until the next morning. Elspeth was at the ranch exit when we approached. It was hard to tell whether she'd heard the commotion, or if she'd had truth beads wired up to the tepee, or if she was just familiar with such an occurrence, but she seemed to understand.

'Don't go tonight,' she said. 'Stay, have a good meal and a decent night's sleep, then you can head off in the morning. The transport will be here at 10 a.m.' Her eyes were almost pleading with us. 'Ernest won't bother you, I promise.'

Immediately, I envisaged Ernest sneaking into our tent and prodding us with a paddle whip in the middle of the night.

Nick and I looked at each other. Nick shrugged his shoulders.

'All right,' he said. 'What's for dinner?'

The dinner bell sounded at 7 p.m. and Nick and I darted into the dining hall with our heads down and our eyes fixed on the buffet. After an afternoon spent discovering my deepest fears, which I now knew to be Ernest determining the future of romantic love, I was ravenous again. It seemed Nick and I had consumed our ration of ranch meat at lunch, and instead of endless racks of ribs and giant slabs of steak, we were offered couscous, quinoa and chargrilled Mediterranean vegetables. I found something resembling chicken tagine so I heaped some spoonfuls onto my plate, grabbed some bread and then followed Nick out into the ranch grounds.

The sun was setting so he suggested we salvage some romance from our weekend with a picnic under the stars. He'd laid out a blanket on a grassy mound overlooking the paddocks and the fields beyond. The horizon seemed so far away. From such a perspective, it was easy to understand how people had once so readily believed the earth was flat.

Nick rummaged in his bag. I heard a familiar clink and then he revealed two bottles of wine. 'Ta-da,' he said.

I laughed. 'Banned substances. Naughty you.'

He grinned. 'Thought you might need something to forget that leg rub you had earlier.'

I screwed up my face, recalling the moment my toes had accidentally gripped Ernest's genitals.

'Pour me a glass now,' I said, grabbing a plastic tumbler from his hand.

A few glasses in and I was already starting to feel better. Nick and I were lying on the blanket and looking up at the stars. I could hear the group's post-prandial sing-song in the distance. Ernest had a guitar and for the past hour had been keenly demonstrating his repertoire of country and westerns. Although, perhaps Dolly Parton's 'Jolene' wasn't the ideal choice for his vocal range.

During a brief interval, I sat up and refilled my glass. I

took a long sip and then stared up at the sky. 'Maybe *wine* is the answer to a lasting marriage?' I mused out loud.

Nick chuckled. 'Of course,' he said, sitting up and mimicking Ernest. 'The extensive research I've conducted...' he paused to fondle his groin '...proves that drinking alcohol...' he rubbed his hands over his body '...is the best intimacy-enhancing activity a couple can undertake.' He shuffled closer to me, then unzipped his trousers and pulled out his willy. 'Don't be scared, Eleanor. Don't be fearful of the penis. Embrace it.' He moved closer, grinning and then shook his hair and let out an orgasmic sigh.

I laughed. 'Put it away,' I said. Then I thought for a moment. 'So, if we get drunk together, it will enhance our intimacy and we'll stay together. If you get drunk without me, you might end up running off with that hotty you work with.'

Nick zipped up his trousers and then sighed. 'I'm not running off with anyone, Ellie. I don't want a supermodel with a Harvard degree. I want you.'

I took another sip of wine. 'Good job I'm not that then, isn't it?'

Nick rolled his eyes. 'That's not what I meant.' He leaned across and took my hand. 'You are so much more to me, Ellie, and you always will be. Even when you're old and wrinkly, with a colostomy bag.'

I slapped him on the chest. 'Who says I'll be the one with the colostomy bag?'

'All that white bread you eat. It's not good for you.'

'Oh, shut up. You'll be the one in line for a liver transplant, looking like a corn-fed chicken and pooing on the care-home carpet.'

He laughed, went to take another sip but then stopped.

'How about we stop fretting about the future and enjoy now?' He held his glass up towards mine.

I chinked his glass.

Nick leaned forward and kissed me. Then he suddenly pulled back, with a mischievous glint in his eye.

'You up for a bit of naughtiness?'

I smiled. 'What, out here on the blanket?'

He laughed. 'No, not that.' Then he paused for a moment and looked me up and down. 'Later though, hold that thought. Definitely later.' He glanced back towards the ranch house, then back at me. I could tell he was hatching a plan.

'You know *The Italian Job*,' he said.

I sighed. 'Yes, of course I do. You've made me watch it a hundred thousand times since we met.'

He looked up at the stars and then back down at me. 'I've made you watch *The Italian Job* thirty times a day? Really?'

I rolled my eyes. 'Why do you always do that?'

He grinned. 'Why do you always exaggerate for effect? Anyway, if they can steal thirty-five million dollars' worth of gold bullion from a group of Italian gangsters, then surely we can retrieve our confiscated phones from Elspeth's safe?'

'I'm not sure a couples' retreat in Texas is an appropriate setting for a heist,' I said. 'Besides, surely it's simpler to just ask for our phones back instead.'

Nick puffed out his chest, assuming his desired leading character, which seemed more Vinnie Jones than Michael Caine. 'Those motherfuckers stole my phone. I want it back,' he said.

I laughed.

He sat up, looked at the ranch house and then back at me. 'OK, here's the plan.'

Once Nick had described a sophisticated safe-cracking

technique he'd seen in a recent Jason Statham movie, I thought for a moment. Elspeth seemed to be the kind of woman who would have a procedure documented for everything, maybe including how to open the safe.

'I think there might be another way,' I said.

Nick frowned, looking slightly concerned that my plan might not involve a balaclava and a zip cord.

Once we had agreed our strategy, we quickly finished off the second bottle of wine, rolled up our blanket and then made our way back to our tent. The flaps had been rolled back, as though inviting entry. I immediately envisaged Ernest taking care of this personally, caressing them as though they were labia. Inside, the bed had been turned down for the night, and some honesty beads had been left on the pillow.

Nick saw them and put his hand over my mouth and looked at me.

'I'm sure tired,' he said, adopting a bizarre faux American accent. 'Let's get a good night's sleep before we head back tomorrow.'

I stifled my giggles. 'Yes, Nicholas, I'm sure tired too. Sleep tight.'

Nick grabbed the beads and threw them out the tent opening. Then we snuck out and stealthily made our way to the ranch house. It was dark now and the campfire sing-song had died down. There were just a few guests—Walter, Doug and Tom—still sitting around the dwindling fire. Ernest and Elspeth were nowhere to be seen.

Nick and I snuck around to the side entrance. The door was still open so we crept into the kitchen. We could hear people talking a few rooms away. Nick told me to wait as he went ahead to locate the office. He returned a few moments later and ushered me towards him.

'This way,' he whispered.

We crept down a corridor, passing a door which was ajar. I peered through the crack to see Ernest with his arm around someone. I looked closer. It was Chloe. She looked as though she had been crying.

'There, there,' I heard him say, 'you'll find someone to love you, don't worry, my angel.'

He was stroking her arm, his fingertips brushing her breast. She leaned in towards him and sobbed. He squeezed her tight, his other hand edging down her back. The bulge in his leather trousers looked bigger than earlier.

Nick tugged my arm. 'Come on,' he mouthed.

I followed Nick into the office and began scan-reading the names of the files lined up neatly on a shelf above the computer.

'"Procedures", that's it,' I said, a little too excitedly.

Nick put his finger to my lips.

We flicked through the file. There seemed to be a procedure for everything: to greet guests, retune honesty beads, even how to turn down beds. As I'd suspected, Ernest's name was written next to that job. Soon we came to a procedure entitled 'Contraband'. I quickly read through it, while Nick peered around the door to make sure no one was coming.

'Found it!' I said.

Nick swung round and glared at me. 'Shhh,' he said.

'I've got the safe code,' I whispered. 'Now, where's the safe?'

Nick glanced around the room.

'Doesn't it say in there?' He gestured to the file.

I looked back down to check I hadn't missed anything. 'Nope,' I said.

Nick looked around the room again, then focused on an oil painting on the wall. It was of a naked lady sprawled across a sofa. She had a large crop of pubic hair and looked a lot like Elspeth.

'I bet it's behind here,' Nick whispered, smirking. He pushed the painting to one side, revealing a safe behind it.

Nick punched in the code and I checked no one was coming. I could still hear Chloe's faint sobs coming from the other room.

Nick handed me my phone and pocketed his. He then rubbed his hands on his jeans as though he'd touched something nasty.

'What else is in there?' I asked, switching my phone on.

He shook his head. 'You don't want to know,' he said. Then he pushed the tip of something pink and rubbery back into the safe.

We crept back down the corridor and my phone began to buzz. I glanced at the screen to see text message after text message coming through. It was Matthew.

Where are you?

Ellie CALL me.

CALL ME NOW

Nick snatched my phone and switched it off. 'You'll get us caught,' he said, in not so much of a whisper.

'It's Matthew,' I mouthed.

He glared at me. 'Let's get out of here first,' he said, dragging me down the corridor.

I pulled him back and pointed to the door that was ajar. I could still hear voices. I peered in. Now Ernest was almost on top of Chloe. Her jumper was pulled up and he had his hand between her legs.

Nick tugged my arm again.

'Wait,' I said pulling him back towards the door. 'Look.'

Nick peered in. His eyes narrowed and his jaw tensed. He glanced back at me as if to glean permission.

I nodded.

Then Nick kicked open the door. Ernest jumped up, looking startled. Chloe, still sobbing, pulled down her jumper.

'What are you doing?' Nick said, pulling Ernest up from the sofa, by his belt.

Ernest's eyes widened. 'She was upset,' he stammered.

Nick threw him back down on the sofa.

I stepped forward. 'Upset because you ruined her relationship. She came here happy and newly married and you've messed it all up.'

Ernest stared at me.

'You're supposed to be helping people—' I looked at Chloe, who was wiping the tears from her cheeks '—not destroying their relationships and taking advantage of them.'

For a moment Ernest was silent, then he cleared his throat. 'She's in a stage of healing. She'll be stronger for it.'

'What's going on?' Elspeth said, entering the room. She looked at me and Nick, then back at Ernest. 'Are these guests trespassing in our ranch house?'

Ernest nodded.

I stared at her. 'We are saving a young girl from being penetrated by your priapic husband.'

Elspeth narrowed her eyes at me. 'Defensiveness will not prevent your fears from being realised, my dear.'

I frowned. 'What's that supposed to mean?'

Elspeth looked at Chloe. 'She's a young, desirable girl. Men cannot and should not resist their urges.' Then she turned to Nick. 'And the reason Nick's so angry is because he would like to do the same.'

Nick laughed. 'Seriously? I don't think so.'

She reached out and squeezed Nick's arm. 'You can't deny your drives, Nicholas. You'll end up angry and re-pressed.'

Nick laughed again. Then looked at Chloe. 'No offence, Chloe, but I have no interest in having sex with you.' He looked back at Ernest. 'What's wrong with you?'

Ernest stood up to meet Nick's height, the enhanced bulge still present in his trousers. 'You're the one who came here for my help. Perhaps that question should be redirected to you?'

Nick stopped laughing, then winked at me before swing-ing a punch up towards Ernest's jaw.

Elspeth gasped and Chloe grinned as Ernest's eyes rolled back and he crumpled to the ground, limp and flaccid.

Outside the ranch house, while Nick and I were deciding our best means of escape, I heard the rumbling of an engine in the distance. It sounded like one of those sit-on lawnmow-ers, or a turbo hedge-trimmer. While I was wondering why a landscape gardener would choose to conduct his work at midnight on a Saturday, the noise became increasingly louder. It appeared to be coming up the driveway. I squinted my eyes as a cloud of orange dust, seemingly emanating from a large motorised sweetcorn, sped towards the ranch.

Nick stepped forwards for a closer look.

Suddenly the horn sounded. It was quite high-pitched, like a mallard's mating call, and quickly followed by someone shouting and waving their arm frantically out the window.

'Ellie! Ellie!'

Nick frowned. 'Is that…?'

'Matthew!' I shouted, as a figure flung open the door and then ran towards me waving its arms.

'Ellie! Ellie! I found you!' Matthew jumped into my arms like a puppy reunited with its owner. He reminded me of Rupert.

'What are you doing here?' I asked, trying to prise him off me while at the same time realising we now had a means to exit the ranch hastily.

'I'm coming to New York. Didn't you get my messages? I need some space from Lucy. I need a few weeks to think. I've cashed in my Apple shares. I have money to burn. I miss you, Ellie. I miss my life. I miss me. I miss having fun. I miss the way it used to be.' He was talking at a million miles an hour.

'Hang on, hang on,' I said, making slow down gestures with my hands, and glancing around me. 'Where are your kids?'

Matthew waved the question away. 'They're with their mother.' He paused. 'Anyway, it's so great to be here. I've been calling you every five minutes, Ellie. Why didn't you answer your phone? I needed to talk. I couldn't get hold of you. Is it OK if I stay with you for a bit? In New York, I mean. Not here on a ranch. Not really the ranch-worker type. Although I do have a great pair of cowboy boots from that shop on the King's Road.' He glanced down at his Converse. 'Oh fuck, I forgot to pack them.'

Nick was frowning. 'Are you on something, mate?' he asked, cocking his head.

Matthew patted down his quiff. 'I might have had a few of those energy drinks. It was a long drive.'

Suddenly a voice interjected. 'He's in a state of mania.'

We all turned to see Ernest. He was standing behind us, still wearing his leather trousers, but now with the addition of a waistcoat and a Stetson. He had a lasso in one hand and a rifle in the other.

Ernest continued. 'He's bipolar, and most likely following a long period of depression, he's now in a manic phase. Which means he's acting rashly and making ill-considered decisions and believes himself to be indestructible. I suggest you take him to the nearest hospital for medication.' Then he paused. 'Either way, I want you all off my ranch now.' He threw our bags at us, then fired two shots in the air.

Matthew jumped upwards like a Masai warrior, then began patting his torso looking for puncture wounds. I grabbed his arm and led him towards the car.

'I'll drive,' Nick said, glancing back and glaring at Ernest.

Matthew and I climbed into the back seat of the car, kicking the empty Red Bull cans aside.

Nick climbed into the driver's seat, looked around and frowned. 'Why did you rent a Cinquecento in Texas?' he asked.

'It's all they had left,' Matthew said. 'Besides, I wasn't really anticipating its use as a getaway vehicle from an armed psychotic ranch owner.' He glanced back out the window. 'It's surprisingly fuel efficient, though,' he added, 'and it has heated seats.' As he went to switch them on by means of demonstration, Nick knocked his hand away, so he could unlock the handbrake.

As we drove off, Ernest was circling his lasso in the air. Nick gave him the finger out the window.

It was a three-hour drive back to the airport, during which Matthew entertained us by reliving the entire series of *Dallas*, complete with uncannily realistic JR Ewing and Sue Ellen impersonations. It wasn't until the effects of his caffeine binge began to subside that we were able to engage him in a sensible conversation.

'That Ernest dude was a case, wasn't he?' Matthew said, tipping up one of the cans of Red Bull to confirm that it was officially empty.

I laughed. 'He's supposed to be one of the leading psychoanalysts in the world.'

I went on to explain the tepee vagina, the bulging leather trousers and the Chloe molestation.

'Blimey,' said Matthew once I'd finished. 'It certainly beats Clapham, doesn't it?'

At the airport, thanks to a quick flash of my corporate credit card, we were able to fly back to JFK that night. There was only a slight delay, when airport security discovered a half-empty can of Red Bull stashed down Matthews' trousers. However, he managed to charm the security guard by complimenting him on his mullet hairdo. The guard looked genuinely flattered.

We arrived back at Park Slope in the early hours of the morning, at which point both the streets and Matthew were eerily quiet. I settled Matthew to sleep in the spare room while Nick made coffee.

When I walked into the kitchen, Nick had his back to me. I stopped and stared. Over the years it was as though I'd forgotten to notice him: his broad shoulders, the gentle curve of the muscles under his T-shirt and the soft frown he has when he's concentrating. I walked towards him, wrapped my arms around his waist and nuzzled his neck. He smelled of Dunhill cologne and warm skin.

He turned to me and smiled. 'Remember that thought I asked you to hold earlier?' he asked.

I smiled.

That night, I knew it wasn't the dubious couples counselling that had brought us closer, but instead it was the adventure we'd had. And for a short while, the questions I'd been asking about love were silenced.

Chapter 15

I rang the doorbell yet again. It was one of those hefty or-
nate designs with a long metal handle like the old-style
toilet flushers. After I'd expended a vast amount of kinetic
energy pulling the bloody thing, the result was the faint
tinkling of a bell, which one might imagine attached to a
tiny fairy's slipper.

Matthew stood next to me shuffling from foot to foot.

'Maybe he's out?' Mathew said, sculpting his quiff. 'Let's
go and get some brunch instead. I saw a diner up the highway.'

I glared at him. 'You didn't have to come,' I said. 'I was
happy to leave you festering on the sofa.' I hammered on
the door this time. 'You were the one who decided it was
imperative I have a chaperone on visits from now on.'

He patted down his quiff. 'I said *assistant*, not chaperone. While I'm here, I will be your research assistant. And
your security guard too. To protect you from any leather-
clad molesters.'

I shook my head. 'You are not going to be my assistant. What's actually going to happen is: you will come to your senses, preferably in the next twenty-four hours, and then go back to London to be with your family.'

He tutted. '*Research* assistant,' he repeated. 'Anyway, it's clear you need help considering you're struggling to enter a house.' Then he leaned forward and peered through the letterbox.

'Yoo-hoo!' he shouted. 'Anyone home?'

Moments later a small lady opened the door. 'Yes, sir, can I help you?' she asked in a clipped Spanish accent.

Mathew stepped forward. 'My colleague and I have an appointment with Professor Sheldon,' he explained, hamming up his British accent.

She nodded, then ushered us in. We walked through the expansive hallway, my heels clipping on the tiled floor. There were marble busts displayed on pillars and oil paintings of long dead earls and counts. I wondered for a moment if Professor Sheldon hadn't had his house airlifted from a Hampshire estate to the suburbs of New York.

We were presented to him in the library, which was a long, narrow room at the back of the house. It had moss-green carpets and rows of deeply varnished bookshelves. Professor Sheldon was seated at an expansive bay window that overlooked the grounds. He wore mustard-coloured cords, red socks and a tweed hunting jacket. At his feet were two sleepy wolfhounds.

He clicked his fingers. 'Socrates. Plato,' he said.

Straight away, the dogs stood up, stretched a bit and then sauntered out the room. 'So, Miss Rigby,' he said, pulling out a pipe from his inside pocket, 'how may I help you?'

I stepped forward, feeling unsure about what to do with

my hands. 'I'd like to find out more about your research,' I said, shoving them deep into my pockets.

He rolled his eyes. 'Well, obviously you're not here for my thoughts on *The Only Way is Essex*. Why are you so nervous, girl? Stop fidgeting and sit down.' He reached for a small sliver tray, at the centre of which was a cluster of tiny blue tablets. 'Have one of these,' he said. 'That'll sort you out.'

Matthew pushed past me and went to grab a tablet. Professor Sheldon pulled the tray back. 'And who might you be, young squire?'

Matthew grinned and held out his hand. 'Matthew Willoby-Warbuton, Ellie's research assistant.'

Professor Sheldon smirked. 'Ah, yes, the Willoby-Warbutons,' he said, leaning back and rubbing his chin, 'I know them well. Excellent grouse shooters. How is your father?'

Matthew glanced at me, eyes wide.

Professor Sheldon laughed. 'Don't panic, boy. I'm just pulling your leg.' He handed the tray to Matthew. 'You certainly deserve a Valium for dreaming up that ludicrous identity.' Then he went to light his pipe. 'Although I suggest you temper the accent. It's coming across more Basil Fawlty than Hugh Grant.'

Matthew took a tablet off the tray, looking more relieved than amused.

Professor Sheldon offered the tray to me again. 'Are you sure you wouldn't like one, Miss Rigby?'

I shook my head. 'No, thank you.'

'Can I offer you a cup of tea instead?' He arched his neck towards the door. 'Rosa,' he shouted. 'Tea, please.'

Matthew and I took our tea on a weathered brown leather sofa adjacent to Professor Sheldon's window seat.

'Drugs,' he said suddenly, after a period of prolonged silence, and then paused to look out the window.

'Drugs?' Matthew asked, clearly emboldened by the Valium.

Professor Sheldon turned back to us. 'Yes, my dear boy. Drugs.' He took a sip of tea. 'They might just be the answer.'

I took a sip too. 'Drugs to prevent divorce?' I said, leaning forward. 'But if you look at the evidence, drug use actually—'

Professor Sheldon lifted his hand to stop me. 'Hush,' he said. 'And listen. I haven't finished yet.' He looked out the window again and then back at me. 'You said you were familiar with my research.'

I nodded, although I quickly remembered that I hadn't actually read any of it. Mandi had sent me his details and I'd meant to read up on it at the couples retreat but I'd had my phone confiscated and then Matthew had arrived and then—

'Miss Rigby, please pay attention.' Professor Sheldon clicked his fingers. One of the wolfhounds walked back into the room and sat at my feet. 'Stroke him,' he said.

I looked down at his amber eyes and handsome face. He reminded me of a larger, more distinguished-looking Rupert.

'Go on, he won't bite.'

I stroked him.

Professor Sheldon checked his watch. 'Carry on stroking him,' he said. 'I'll tell you when to stop.'

I stroked his head and twirled his ears while Professor Sheldon went on to describe the neurochemical basis of love.

'It's common knowledge that dopamine, phenylethylamine and oxytocin set the foundations of love,' he began.

I nodded, glancing down at the dog, who then shuffled closer.

Professor Sheldon continued. 'We have raised levels of each during the early stages of love.'

The wolfhound put his head on my lap. I continued stroking him.

'Oxytocin is the bonding hormone.'

'Yes,' I murmured. He wasn't telling me anything I didn't already know.

'It's released in both baby and mother during breastfeeding.'

I nodded, glancing back down at the wolfhound. His eyelids were heavy. I twirled his ears again and he sighed.

'It's released during orgasm, during prolonged physical contact.' He placed his tea on the side. 'And when you stroke a dog, oxytocin is released in both dog and human.' He checked his watch and then looked at the wolfhound, then at me. 'You can stop now if you want to.'

I put my hand back on my lap and the wolfhound pined. I went to stroke him again.

Professor Sheldon smiled. 'Like I said it's the bonding hormone.'

I stared at him for a moment. 'I'm still not sure what you're saying.'

He looked me in the eye. 'It takes twelve seconds of uninterrupted physical contact between humans for oxytocin to be released.'

I glanced down at the dog and then back at Professor Sheldon. 'The reason couples divorce is because they don't have time to cuddle?'

'They don't have the time or the inclination. Attraction wanes, we all know that. Attraction drives couples to have sex and solicit physical contact, and that in turn will keep them together. Oxytocin, you see, is the answer.' He went on to describe a case of a man who fell in love with a porn star. 'He'd never met her, you see, he'd just watched her movies. And because of the oxytocin released during his orgasm, he'd developed a deep emotional bond with her.'

I gazed out of the window while he went on to explain that the man in question would wear a dinner jacket before watching her movie and masturbating. Professor Sheldon explained that this response was perfectly logical.

I glanced beside me at Matthew, who looked as if he had fallen asleep. I poked him in the ribs and he jolted back to life.

'Sorry,' I said. 'I'm not sure my research assistant got all that.'

'Something about porn and stroking?' Matthew said, rubbing his eyes. 'What did I miss?'

Professor Sheldon smirked. Then he reached down under the window seat and pulled out a large cardboard box. He pushed it with his foot towards me.

'Take a look,' he said.

I leaned forward and peered inside. 'Inhalers?' I asked.

He shook his head. 'Nasal sprays. Take one.'

Matthew jumped up from his seat and grabbed two. He passed one to me.

I inspected mine. There were no instructions, only a basic label.

'Oxytocin nasal spray,' Professor Sheldon said.

I stared at the nasal spray and then back at Professor Sheldon, suddenly realising what he was suggesting.

'Try it,' he said. 'Two sprays per day, at a time when you see your partner.'

'Or your dog,' Matthew added.

Professor Sheldon ignored him. 'It changed my and my

wife's life. She couldn't bear me near her but now she gives me a back rub every night.'

Matthew giggled. 'Have you considered upping the dose?'

Professor Sheldon smirked. 'It isn't a sex tool, my boy. It's a bonding hormone and it should be used sparingly.' He glanced back out at the grounds again. 'A natural release of oxytocin is preferable, of course, but this is for more resistant cases.' Then he stood up and summoned the wolfhounds. 'The phase-three trial results are excellent. We imagine it will be FDA-approved by March next year,' he said, reaching for a full-length waxed coat, hanging on a hook by the door.

'Time for a stroll now,' he said, tipping an imaginary hat. 'Good day to you, Miss Rigby, and also to you, Master Willoby-Warbuton.' Then he shouted to Rosa, 'Get the boy an espresso before he leaves, can't handle his Valium.' And with that he was gone.

On the way home, Matthew was still quite heavily tranquillised, so while driving I took the time to contemplate the ethics of a neurochemical intervention in love. Logically it made sense. Scientific and technological advancements had enabled us to modify our bodies, our homes, our food and even our moods, so why not modify love? Why shouldn't we save millions of couples and their families the pain of divorce? I hadn't thought twice about injecting myself with hormones to increase my chances of conceiving, so why wouldn't I do the same to increase the longevity of my marriage?

I drove on, looking out at the tree-lined streets and the American-dream houses, with their basketball hoops fixed to the walls in the front yards. I'd always imagined such homes to be bursting with joyous chaos, pancake breakfasts and freshly squeezed orange juice. However, Mr Montgomery's statistics didn't correlate with that image. Perhaps we shouldn't be so quick to employ Professor Sheldon's nasal spray? I fixed my eyes on the road ahead, readjusting my jean pocket every once in a while to stop the spray from digging in my leg.

Once we were back on the main highway, Matthew sprung to life, as though the Valium had been booted off its receptors leaving caffeine to head up the party.

'Waffles!' he said, like the drunkard from *Father Ted*.

I checked my watch.

'It's brunch o'clock,' he said. 'There's a diner up here I'm sure.' He began pointing. 'Look. There!'

I glanced up at the sign and frowned. 'It's a Hooters.'

He ruffled his quiff. 'Yeah, so what? They sell food and I'm hungry.'

I tutted. 'I'm not eating my lunch surrounded by a bunch of oversexed rednecks. Besides, there's no way I could explain that one on my expense submission.'

Matthew leaned towards me and winked. 'Not even for Key lime pie?'

My tummy began to rumble. 'Oh all right,' I said. 'But as soon as we've eaten we're out of there.'

Chapter 16

Our Hooters waitress was called Sandy. She skipped over to our booth in a teeny-tiny vest and hot pants. My immediate thought was that her implants were both large and sturdy enough for her to be able to deliver meals on them.

'Hi, guys, and welcome to Hooters,' she gushed, flashing large white teeth. 'I'm Sandy, your waitress for today.' She paused to smile again. 'Have you been to Hooters before?'

First she looked at Matthew. He nodded. I could tell he was making the effort to focus on her face. Then she looked at me. 'Ma'am?'

'No, this is my first time at Hooters,' I said.

She scrunched up her face, then smiled again. 'Well, let's hope we'll make you wanna come back! Would you like me to explain the menu to you?'

I frowned. 'Is it in Latin?'

She shook her head.

'Well, no then, I think I'll be OK.'

She grinned. 'Amazing, can I get you some Hooterstizers to start?'

Matthew ordered some chicken strips and naked buffalo wings and the Double 'D' Burger for his main course.

I decided to play it safe and have the Cobb salad. It seemed to be the only item on the menu that hadn't been trademarked.

'Can I get you any drinks?' She grinned again. 'We have an amazing offer on the cocktails.'

Matthew picked up the drinks menu. 'One Orange Shorts Margarita for me, please.'

I glanced down at the menu and then rolled my eyes. 'Go on then,' I said. 'One for me too.'

Sandy clapped. 'If you order a third you get the *Hooters Girl* glass for free.'

'Excellent,' I said, 'I was wondering what Nick might like for his birthday.'

Sandy's smile wavered but she blinked a few times, then ramped it up again. 'Amazing,' she said. 'I'll get those for you now.'

Matthew leaned back and lifted his arms above his head. 'Victory!' he said. 'Let's get Ellie smashed at lunchtime on a weekday.'

I sighed, thinking about all the distraught clients left to navigate their way through the treacherous waters of divorce while I, their only chance of salvation, was happily ordering cocktails in Hooters.

I looked across at Matthew, hoping he might offer some insight into my dilemma, but he was reading the paper placemat.

Suddenly he laughed, then showed me the photo on it. 'Sandy, our waitress, is Miss Hooters International,' he said, then looked back at the photo. 'If I was ten years younger this would have been my defining moment.'

I laughed.

'Listen to this,' he said and went on reading from the placemat. '"Sandy believes that working at Hooters gives her a valuable opportunity every day…"' He paused and smirked. 'To do what? Any ideas?'

I laughed. 'To meet new people?'

He shook his head. '"To make people *smile*",' he said, clearing his throat. '"When Sandy isn't volunteering to help sick children or serving up a relaxed dinner to Hooters customers, she enjoys boating and fishing."'

I laughed. 'Fishing?' I said. 'She doesn't look the type.'

Matthew giggled. 'Because she's not the type. She's a *Weird Science* kind of Hooters fantasy, created to appeal to the customers. I'm surprised they haven't said: "And Sandy especially enjoys anal sex and pairing men's socks."'

I sucked some margarita through my straw, wondering if perhaps the company shouldn't diversify and instead of serving cocktails, the waitresses could present each client with an oxytocin nasal spray and a firm word to go back home to their wives. If I hadn't have seen such despair in Matthew's eyes, I would have offered him the same advice too.

Following the combined consumption of buffalo wings, chicken strips, a Cobb salad and a Double 'D' Burger, a side of curly fries, two Key lime pies and four further cocktails, Matthew and I were feeling quite at home in Hooters. Sandy's shift had ended and after I'd explained my mission to cure divorce, she, along with an even larger-breasted colleague, Debbie, had joined us in our booth.

'So, ladies,' I slurred. 'What do you think is the secret to lasting love?'

Matthew drum-rolled his hands on the table.

Sandy was the first to answer. 'Compromise,' she said, sitting up straight as though she were at the front of the class.

Matthew did a mock yawn. 'Bor-ing. Try again.'

Sandy screwed up her mouth and thought for a moment. 'Denial,' she said eventually. Then she covered her mouth as though she'd surprised herself.

Matthew sat back. 'That's more like it,' he said.

'Denial for whom?' I asked.

She scratched her nose and looked around at the customers. 'Well, the men have to be in denial to be happy. They need to believe that they are eternally desirable to young attractive women.' She interrupted herself with a high-pitched giggle. 'And women are in denial because they need to believe their husband is only attracted to them.'

Matthew clapped his hands and laughed.

'But what about loyalty?' I asked. 'A person might be attracted to another but be loyal to their partner.'

'Yes, but,' Debbie piped up, 'how do we define loyalty? Is it the same as fidelity?'

Matthew sucked the dregs of his cocktail through a straw. 'We don't need to define fidelity. It's simple. Not shagging anyone else.'

Debbie nodded slowly. It turns out she was studying a PhD in philosophy. 'How about oral sex?' she asked.

Matthew smirked. 'Yes please,' he said.

I rolled my eyes and then answered for him. 'Oral sex is clearly infidelity too. So let's just say, no sexual contact with anyone else then.'

Matthew raised his eyebrows. 'What's sexual contact?

Brushing up against a Hooters waitress and then getting a hard-on?'

'What's a hard-on?' Debbie asked.

'A boner,' Sandy replied, 'and that's not infidelity, that's sexual harassment.'

'Ah,' said Matthew. 'But if the harasser is in a relationship then technically that's infidelity too?'

I nodded.

Matthew raised a finger. 'But if the waitress accidentally brushed up against him, then I'm not sure that's infidelity, because men can't control their physical reaction to that.'

Debbie laughed. 'They can. Apparently ninety per cent of arousal is in the brain.'

Matthew sniggered. 'For men, up until the age of twenty-three there is no brain involvement whatsoever. Even after that it's debatable.'

'OK,' Sandy said. 'So we're agreed that for it to be infidelity it has to be intentional sexual contact.'

Matthew smiled. 'This conversation is oddly arousing.'

'What about imagined sexual encounters?' Debbie asked.

'Fantasies, you mean?' Sandy asked.

Debbie glanced across at a group of men, then back at us. 'The other day, I read about some new porn gaming goggles that are in development. Men can put them on, attach electrodes to their bodies and have any type of virtual sex with any avatar they select from the programme. Or several at once if they'd prefer. What if a husband did that every night instead of sleeping with his wife? Is that infidelity?'

We all sat in silence for a moment.

Sandy scrunched up her face.

Matthew shrugged his shoulders. 'Sounds fun,' he said.

I sighed.

Matthew turned to me. 'So, if Nick was out one night, and you had a virtual Hugh Jackman to shag you senseless for an hour or two, you'd say no, would you?'

I thought for a moment. 'It would feel a bit wrong,' I said, then paused. 'How would you feel if Lucy—?' I stopped myself as soon as my brain caught up with my mouth. 'Oh bugger. Sorry.'

Matthew's shoulders slumped.

I leaned forward and squeezed his arm. 'I'm sorry,' I said. Then I turned to the girls and whispered, 'It's a bit of a sensitive subject for him.'

Sandy nodded. Debbie raised an eyebrow.

I was about to continue, but Matthew threw his arms in the air.

'Thank you, Ellie,' he said. 'Acting like I have special emotional needs or something.' He turned to Sandy and Debbie. 'Yes, my wife shagged her boss.' His voice increased a decibel. 'She shagged her troll-faced wanker of a boss, in a bloody Travelodge, while I was at home with our kids—' he sank his head in his hands '—making penne arrabbiata.' He looked up between his fingers. 'How could she do that? My life is over.'

I took his hand. 'No, it's not,' I said. 'You're just going through a shitty time right now, that's all.'

Sandy wiped a tear from her cheek. 'Poor baby,' she said, shuffling up next to him.

Matthew quietened down for a second. Then he opened one eye and closed it again and made a whimpering sound.

'I loved her so much,' he sobbed.

Debbie shuffled up on the other side and squeezed his hand.

Matthew managed to force out a tear. 'I feel so betrayed,' he said and his chest began to heave.

Sandy pulled him towards her and soon he was nuzzling her cleavage, while Debbie was stroking his hair.

I stared for a moment in disbelief, momentarily reconsidering Freud's observations about a man's urge to suckle.

I cleared my throat. The advice that had been grumbling was now ready to erupt. 'Yes, it is a tricky time for him. However, abandoning his kids and running off to Hooters is probably not the best way to deal with it.'

Matthew raised his head. 'Thanks for your one minute of empathy, Ellie,' he said.

I shrugged my shoulders. 'I just think, when there are children involved, you should put your own feelings aside.'

Matthew sat up straight and scowled. 'So you're saying I should have stayed with her?'

I shook my head. 'Of course not,' I said. Then I prodded the table. 'What I'm saying is you shouldn't be here.'

He looked around as if to remind himself of the location. 'Oh, come on, she had sex with her boss and you're telling me I can't admire a few girls in hot pants.'

I rolled my eyes. 'No, not Hooters. I'm saying you shouldn't have come here. To America.'

He sighed.

'You should be in London, with your kids. They won't understand why you've just vanished without explanation.'

'I told them why I was going.'

I frowned.

'I told them Mummy had been mean to me so I was going to see Mickey Mouse to cheer me up.'

'Great. Yes, that sounds like a perfectly measured and considered explanation. That won't make them insecure at all. Besides, does any child even know who Mickey Mouse is any more? Surely Olaf from *Frozen* would have been a better choice?'

Matthew slammed his hands down on the table. 'You're right, oh pious Ellie. I shouldn't have abandoned my kids. And I should've selected a more current Disney figurehead to justify my paternal failings. I just had the crazy notion that instead of admitting myself to a psychiatric unit for suicidal and homicidal urges following a deep depression, that I would be better placed visiting my best friend for a few weeks to see if she could offer me some support in my time of need. But no, I get lambasted by the one person I was hoping would be on my side. It's no surprise I ended up in Hooters.'

He looked to either side of him but Sandy and Debbie had shuffled away not long after the mention of a psychiatric unit.

I stared at Matthew. His hands were trembling and his eyes were teary. I'd grown so used to him deflecting every negative emotion with humour that I'd forgotten he had them. I stared at him some more, quickly realising he didn't need Ellie the Matchmaker wagging her finger and telling him how to fix his mistakes. What he needed right now was a friend.

'Another drink?' I asked.

He smiled, albeit briefly. 'I think I want to go home,' he said.

Chapter 17

By the time we reached Brooklyn, the March evening sun had set and the roads were darkening. A street lamp lit up the moment I stepped out of the taxi. Matthew stumbled out, with his shoulders hunched and his head stooped. He looked as though he'd undergone some sort of accelerated ageing programme.

I took him inside and put him straight to bed in the spare room. For a fleeting moment, I considered tucking him in like an older sister might her younger brother, but then I realised that if I did, once he rallied, he'd never let me forget it. I listened outside for a few minutes until I heard him snoring, then I went downstairs to open a bottle of wine and wait for Nick.

Wine glass in hand, I kicked off my shoes and collapsed onto the sofa, wondering how I would explain to the car hire company that the new pickup address was a Hooters parking lot.

I felt something digging in my pocket and remembered

the nasal spray. I pulled it out and studied it again, instantly recalling the intensity in Professor Sheldon's eyes.

'Try it,' he'd said. 'Two sprays per day. At a time when you see your partner.'

I took a sip of wine and wondered about oxytocin. If it occurred naturally in our bodies, then what harm could really come from boosting the levels a little? I glanced back down at the nasal spray. It looked like anything you could buy off the shelf at Boots.

I'd meant to consider it further. In fact, I think I'd actually meant to have another sip of wine. However, for some reason, before I could stop myself, I'd shoved the nozzle up my nose and administered two sprays in quick succession. I took a strong sniff and then sank back into the sofa, half anticipating some kind of *Trainspotting*-like oblivion. I waited a few more minutes and nothing came.

I grabbed the spray again and reread the label, supposing it might indicate it was actually a placebo saline solution. Before I could reconsider, I'd pumped another two sprays up my other nostril. Then I looked around the room fearful that paramedics might whisk me away for emergency clearance of the nasal passages followed by enforced enrolment in an 'oxytocin abusers support group'. I sank back into the sofa and closed my eyes, waiting for Nick to return.

Soon after, I heard footsteps coming up the front path. I sat up, poised and ready to greet Nick. At first, I found myself adopting a centrefold like pose on the sofa, but quickly realised that such behaviour would most likely spark concern, so I swung my legs back down and rested my hands on my lap.

However, instead of opening the door, he rang the bell. I huffed as I pulled myself up from the sofa, envisaging a drunken Nick patting down his suit, searching for his keys, while they were being swept along a gutter somewhere, or thrashing around the footwell of a taxi. I took another deep sniff, to maximise any residual nasal spray and offset any lost-key-related annoyance, then opened the door.

At first I assumed I was hallucinating, and that somehow, in addition to being a pivotal bonding hormone, oxytocin, when delivered via the nasal passages also had visual-perceptual-altering properties, transforming the love of my life into someone I despised.

I blinked twice and then stared at him for a moment. It was clear to me it was Dominic but he looked different.

'Hello, Ellie,' he said, before walking past me and into the lounge.

His walk seemed to have mellowed and was now more of a saunter than a gluteal-constricting strut. I turned and followed him in.

'Take a seat,' I said, wondering at what point he planned to explain his presence.

He eyed the wine, then leaned across to pour us both a glass. 'Going to need some of this,' he said.

I sat down opposite him and scowled.

'Why are you here?' I asked, once it became apparent he had no plans to volunteer an explanation.

He leaned back and took a sip of wine. 'The investors asked me to come.'

I raised my eyebrows. 'You were sent here to check on me?'

He laughed. 'No one sends me anywhere, Ellie. I'm the CEO.'

I narrowed my eyes. 'Oh, come on, Dominic, we both

know the investors call the shots. They sent you here to check on me, didn't they?'

He leaned back and smirked. Instead of its usual I-win-you-lose tightness, his smirk had more of a cheeky edge to it. 'You have nothing to worry about,' he said. 'The investors know you'll do anything it takes to find the answers.' He took another sip of wine. 'As do I.'

I stared at him. Maybe it was the way the light from the table lamp caught his face but his features seemed softer, less pinched and his hair looked less slick than usual and shorter than before.

'You've changed your hair,' I blurted out.

He smiled and then patted it with his hand. 'Er, yes,' he said, almost bashfully.

I found myself smiling too. 'It suits you,' I said.

I looked down at his shoes. I'd never been much of a fan of buckled brogues but his looked smart.

'New shoes?' I asked.

Dominic looked up and frowned. It was more a concerned frown than his usual patronising one. 'You're being quite odd, Ellie.'

I laughed. '*I'm* being odd? You're the one who just appeared on my doorstep with no explanation.'

He took a gulp of wine. 'I told you. I've come to see how your research is going.'

'You just thought you'd travel over three thousand miles across the globe to check up on the research that you tried to block funding for.'

He put his glass down and stared at me. 'I arranged your trip. Why would I do that if I was trying to block it?'

'Because you wanted to get rid of me, so you could install your CEO profit-maximising customer-fleecing strategy without my interference.'

He laughed. 'Install? You make it sound like a regime.'

I stared at him again. I'd never noticed how perfectly aligned his teeth were. He stopped laughing and then looked back at me. I stared at him some more, at his intense hazel eyes and his slightly furrowed brow. I found myself imagining how he must have looked as a child.

'So,' Dominic said, leaning forward and lacing his fingers together, 'how is it going?'

'What?' His question jolted me from my trance. 'Me and Nick?'

He smirked. 'No, the research.'

I felt my cheeks redden. 'Oh yes, that, great.' I took a sip of wine. 'It's going really well. Thanks.'

Dominic nodded and then picked up his glass. 'I read the report you sent and your findings interest me, and, well—' he paused and took a sip of wine '—I think it would be a good idea for me to work with you on this and accompany you on your next trip.'

I frowned.

'The investors want the research wrapped up by the end of April with a view to launch in early May. They believe couples counselling will become the most profitable arm of the business. They want to focus their prime resources on this research.'

I sat back and smirked. 'And you're their prime resource, are you?'

'Seems so,' he said, taking another sip of wine. 'Besides,' he added. 'I'm quite interested in the outcome.' Then he held my gaze a little too long. 'From a profit perspective, I mean.'

* * *

Suddenly I heard the key in the lock. I put down my glass and sat up straight. Then I turned to see Nick in the doorway. Nick looked at Dominic, then at the wine and then at me.

Dominic stood up and held out his hand. He was several inches taller than Nick.

'I'm Dominic,' he said. 'Ellie's colleague.'

Nick shook his hand. 'Nice to meet you, *Dominic*,' he said, pronouncing his name more like Domi-dick. 'Would you like a drink?' Nick added, with a nod at the empty glasses. 'Oh, looks like you've already had one.' Nick examined the bottle. 'My 2002 Margaux. Good choice.'

Dominic checked his watch. 'Better be heading off now,' he said.

Nick held the door open for him.

Dominic walked out, then glanced back at me. 'I'm staying at the Waldorf,' he said. 'I'll call you tomorrow.'

I nodded. 'Sure, bye!' I said, suddenly realising I was waving like a child's entertainer.

Once the door had closed, Nick turned to me.

'What was that all about?' he asked.

I began to clear up the glasses. 'Oh, I don't know,' I said. 'All very weird. He's come out to check up on my research.'

'No. What's up with you? You were giggling like a One Direction fan when I walked in.' Nick began fluttering his eyelashes and put on a high-pitched girly voice. 'Ooh, Dominic, you're such a twat. I really hate you.'

I glared at him. 'No, I wasn't.'

He glared back. 'Yes, you were. Seriously, Ellie, I haven't seen you flirt like that since...' he sighed '...I don't know. And I thought you loathed him.'

Suddenly the nasal spray caught my eye, on the sofa.

Nick followed my gaze and then frowned. He looked back at me and then walked towards it and picked it up.

'What's this?' he said, examining the container. 'And why are you staring at it like it's incriminating evidence in a first-degree murder trial?'

I looked down, busily trying to concoct a tree-pollen-allergy themed excuse in my mind.

Nick held it up in my face. 'So, somehow this is linked to Dominic?'

My eyes widened. 'It was meant to be for you.'

He looked back at the bottle and read the label.

'Oxytocin,' he said, before looking up at the ceiling. I noticed the vein in his neck was pulsing. 'You went to see that love drug professor today.'

I nodded, and scrunched up my face.

He grabbed his phone and typed something in. Then he read from his screen.

'"Oxytocin is a mammalian hormone that also acts as a neurotransmitter in the brain. In women, it is released mainly after distension of the cervix and vagina during labour, and after stimulation of the nipples, facilitating birth and breastfeeding, respectively."' He paused, stared at me, and then read on. '"Oxytocin is released during orgasm in both sexes. In the brain, it is involved in social recognition and bonding, and might be involved in the formation of trust between people."' He looked back at me, and held up the screen. 'Tell me you didn't, Ellie?'

A nervous laugh suddenly spilled out of my mouth. 'I only had a couple of sprays.'

Nick sighed. 'How many precisely?'

'Four.'

'And what's the recommended dose?'

'Two.'

Nick's eyes narrowed. 'Great. So you've just had the equivalent of a mind-blowing, life-altering orgasm with Dominic and now you're all loved up. Brilliant. Fucking brilliant.'

Nick threw the nasal spray to the floor. Then he swooped down and picked it up again. 'Actually,' he said, 'I might take this to work with me and give myself a couple of sprays before my meeting with Jenna.'

I snatched it back. 'It was an accident. I meant it to be for you. You were supposed to come home first. I wasn't expecting Dominic to come before you.'

Nick glared at me. 'Bad choice of words, Ellie.' He shook his head. 'It's always the way with you. You're always getting yourself into these predicaments.'

I frowned. 'I'm always having neurochemical orgasms with men I loathe?'

He huffed. 'Why did you even think to spray with me? I thought we were good.'

I leaned forward to take his hand but he knocked it away.

'You're still trying to make us perfect, Ellie, aren't you? We will never be perfect. We're just us. So please leave us alone and stop meddling.' And with that, he stormed off, lobbing the nasal spray in the bin as he did.

Chapter 18

That night Nick sulked off to the spare room, only to discover Matthew sound asleep in the foetal position with his face wedged between two plump pillows. He returned to our room with the apparent caveat that he would sleep as far over the other side of the bed from me as possible.

When I woke the following morning, his side was empty.

'Ellie!' Matthew's cheery voice wafted up the stairs, along with the heady aroma of pancakes. 'Breakfast.'

I pulled a sweatshirt over my nightdress and made my way downstairs. Matthew was at the hob frying eggs and whistling.

'Good morning, USA,' he said, opening his arms wide and waving a spatula as though conducting an orchestra.

I poured myself some orange juice and sat down at the kitchen table. Nick was reading the *New York Times* and refusing to make eye contact with me.

'And how is my sweet English rose today?' Matthew asked with a smile.

'I'm fine,' I said. 'Are you OK?'

He looked up at the ceiling. 'I have pancakes, I have maple syrup and I have my friends. What more could anyone ask for?' he said.

I raised my eyebrows and glanced at Nick, who quickly looked back down at his paper.

Following a few more episodes of shimmying and sizzling, Matthew spun round with the frying pan and plopped two eggs onto each of our plates. He then stood back and clasped his hands together, before proceeding to direct our attention to the rest of the foodstuffs laid out on the table.

'Here is the bacon. Here are the sausages. The pancakes are here and the maple syrup...' he picked up the syrup, drizzled some on his plate and then placed it back down on the table '...is here,' he said, and then clapped his hands.

I sat down next to Nick and forked some pancakes onto my plate.

'I've been thinking,' began Matthew, between mouthfuls.

I poured the coffee. 'That sounds good,' I said tentatively.

Matthew put his knife and fork back down on the table. 'I've made a decision,' he said, then he paused to chew, and then swallowed. 'I'm going back home,' he said eventually.

Nick looked up from his paper.

I leaned across the table and squeezed Matthew's hand. 'Back to Barnes? That's such great news.'

Matthew sprang up from his seat. 'No,' he said, 'I'm going back to Lucy.'

Nick raised his gaze again.

Matthew continued. 'I've been a fool, Ellie.' He jumped up and pranced around the room as though auditioning for an amateur dramatic production.

I put my knife and fork down. 'Have you even spoken to her?'

'Not yet,' he said, before lunging over the kitchen island and grabbing the spatula. 'I'm going to take a leaf out of Ellie's book. I'm going fight for her. I'm going to fight for love.' He began thrusting the spatula as though it were a fencing foil. 'I'm going to fight for my wife. I'm going to fight for happiness, I'm going to fight for my right...'

'...to party?' Nick interjected, while Matthew jumped around the room, nimbly tackling his invisible enemy.

I glanced at Nick and smirked. He smiled back.

'So what do you think?' Matthew said, concluding his performance with what looked like some kind of elaborate jeté.

I scooped up some egg. 'It's a bit soon, isn't it?'

Matthew dropped down onto the chair next to me and let the spatula fall to the floor. 'You said I should go back.'

I chewed while I considered my response. 'That's not quite what I said.'

Matthew was nodding. 'At Hooters, you said I should go back to my kids.'

'Hooters?' Nick interrupted. 'What were you doing at Hooters?'

I waved the question away.

Nick looked to Matthew for an answer.

Matthew shrugged his shoulders. 'I was hungry,' he said.

Nick rolled his eyes, shook the paper and then continued reading.

I turned back to Matthew. 'I told you to go back to your kids. Not to *her*. You can't just forgive her. She hasn't even apologised yet.'

Matthew poured more maple syrup over his pancakes. 'I

still love her,' he said, the syrup drowning the pancake, 'so I will forgive her.' He began to cover a sausage on his plate with syrup too, and then a slice of toast and then an egg. 'Besides, I haven't apologised to her yet either.'

I leaned forward and snatched the syrup from him and placed it back on the table. 'Apologised for what? What do you need to apologise for? Devoting your life to your children and the home you shared with her, so she could pursue her pointless career and shag her rancid boss?'

Matthew took a bite of syrupy sausage. 'I was to blame too. It was my decision to look after the kids. Then I started moping about, bitching and whining about how hard my life was, half sozzled on Waitrose wine. No wonder she didn't want to come home at night.'

I narrowed my eyes. 'I don't think you're being fair on yourself.'

He shrugged his shoulders and then shoved the remainder of the sausage into his mouth.

'We were happy once,' he said.

I looked at Matthew more closely, wondering if he was advancing up the mountain of mental illness or if instead he'd already reached the summit and was now tumbling down the other side. He rolled up a syrup-sodden pancake and carefully folded it into his mouth. I watched him clear his plate, devouring every syrupy morsel. If only it were as simple as defiantly waving a spatula to make the hurt go away.

After Matthew had gone upstairs to pack, Nick was still avoiding eye contact and now feigning interest in the sports pages.

I stopped tidying for a moment and stood and stared at him until he couldn't ignore me any longer.

'What?' he said, glancing up, eyes narrowed.

I threw the dishcloth at him and grinned.

He peeled the dishcloth off his shirt and glared at me.

I sighed. 'Look,' I said. 'It was accident. I never meant to oxytocin myself for Dominic.'

He shook his head. 'That's not the point, Ellie.' He folded the paper onto his lap. 'It's just—'

Suddenly my phone vibrated on the table. Nick grabbed the phone and glanced at the screen. He handed it to me.

'A text from lover boy,' he said with a sneer.

I rolled my eyes. 'Hardly,' I said.

Nick stared at me while I read the text, as though searching for any outward signs of arousal.

'So what does he want?' he asked.

'He's decided he wants to supervise my research from now on. Like he gives a shit about helping people. Or attending a Love Language seminar headed up by a guy named Jed Tandy.'

Nick raised his eyebrows. 'That's where you're going today?'

I nodded. 'Mandi booked it. She's obsessed with NLP.'

Nick screwed up his face. 'NL what?'

'Neuro-Linguistic Programming,' I said glancing back at my phone. 'It's a life-coaching technique. I just don't get why Dominic would want to come.'

Nick tutted. 'It's obvious, isn't it?'

'Is it?' I asked reaching for my mug of cold coffee and taking a sip.

He rolled his eyes and sighed. 'He fancies you. You must know that.'

I laughed, snorting the coffee out my nose. 'I appreciate your faith in my universal appeal,' I said, 'but seriously? You think Dominic, who I've worked with for nearly five years and who has taken every opportunity to push me out of the company that I founded, and who has gone against pretty much every value I stand for, actually secretly wants me?'

Nick nodded.

I laughed again, though louder this time. 'Oh, come on. I know you're legally obliged to think I'm the most gorgeous girl in the world—' I glanced at him for confirmation '—but I don't think Dominic is really lusting after a married woman in her thirties.'

Nick's frown deepened further. 'I saw the way he looked at you. Trust me, a man knows these things.'

I shook my head and sat down next to him. 'Even if you are right, it would take a vat of intravenous oxytocin for me to bear even envisaging such a scenario.'

Nick finally let go of the paper he'd been clinging to and looked at me. 'I just want you to be aware, that's all.'

I checked my watch. 'I doubt Dominic has any plans to slip a roofie in my coffee in front of three thousand Jed Tandy disciples,' I said, leaning forward to kiss him on the forehead. 'Love you,' I said, before charging upstairs to get ready.

'Love you too,' said Matthew, charging down the stairs with his suitcase.

I stopped and spun around on the stair. 'You're going now?'

'Yes, I'm on the 10 a.m. flight, thanks for having me!' Matthew was shouting but his voice quickly tailed off as he grew further away from me.

'I'll call you!' he hollered from the street outside. He blew kisses and then waved in the general direction behind him.

They were about to close the doors by the time Dominic and I arrived at the conference centre, but Dominic jostled through the crowd and grabbed my hand so I could follow. At first I flinched, then I reminded myself that it was perfectly normal for two colleagues to link hands in a potentially dangerous crowd-crush-type situation.

Once inside, we were issued with name badges, but because Dominic had booked at the last minute, and because several people were involved with the booking process, there'd been some confusion and Dominic's badge had Mandi's name on it instead. There was no time to dispute. We were ushered in by a man dressed in black who was talking urgently into a walkie-talkie. He hurried us to our seats three rows from the front, glancing around the room as though searching for Islamic insurgents.

The lights dimmed and the crowd hushed. I turned around to see hundreds of eager faces, seemingly desperate to get a glimpse of their saviour.

A booming movie trailer voice suddenly shook the room. 'Ladies and gentlemen,' it said.

The recording paused and the crowd was silent. Then it continued: 'Will you all please welcome…' It paused again, then continued: 'America's most revered Master of Neurolinguistic Programming. Mr Jed Tandy!'

Flames shot up from the side of the stage and Jed appeared at the centre of a revolving circle, wearing an earpiece and a million-dollar smile.

The audience cheered, hollered and clapped. The woman next to Dominic spontaneously burst into tears. Jed lifted his hand to the crowd in mock modesty as if to say: *Me? A revered Master of Neurolinguistics? Well, only if you say so.*

The audience continued to clap and cheer throughout the ten-minute duration of the stage flames. When the flames died down, Jed held out his arms to the audience.

'Hello, New Jersey,' he said, ramping up the grin.

Then the audience and the flames began to roar again.

I glanced at Dominic and then looked around the room, wondering where all these people had come from, and why they believed Jed could solve their problems.

Eventually the audience quietened down again.

Jed pointed one finger in the air. 'What's the most widely spoken language in the world?' he asked the audience.

The man with the walkie-talkie was now clutching a microphone and darting around the crowd. He finally settled on a middle-aged man with his hand up.

'American,' the man said, puffing out his chest.

I heard Dominic tut.

'Uh, uh,' said Jed theatrically shaking his head. 'Good try though. Anyone else?'

The man with the microphone dashed through the rows of seats to reach a young woman with curly red hair.

'It's Spanish,' she said eagerly.

Jed wagged his finger. 'Good guess, but no. Try again.'

The man with the microphone appeared beside the woman next to Dominic, who'd burst into tears earlier.

'Chinese,' she said, almost squirming with victory.

Jed shook his head. 'Great guess,' he said and she slumped back in her chair.

Dominic exhaled loudly. 'That's not a great guess,' he said. 'Chinese isn't even a fucking language. Neither is American. This is painful.'

Jed continued. 'The most widely spoken language in the world…' he opened his arms to the audience again '…is a language which is spoken by each and every one of you.' He began pointing to each member individually in the audience. 'You, you, you, you, you.'

Just as walkie-talkie man made his way towards another audience member who had his hand up, Dominic snatched the microphone from him.

'It's the language of love,' Dominic said, with an expression usually reserved for the acutely constipated.

Jed began to clap and also look relieved. 'Yes, ladies and gentlemen, this young man has identified the correct answer. So today, at the seminar entitled "The Language of Love", we will be indeed discussing that very language. Not Chinese, I'm afraid, ma'am.'

Dominic turned to me with a tight smile. 'Chinese isn't a language,' he said, under his breath.

Two hours into the audience participation ordeal, we were granted a coffee break. While the majority of the audience queued to ask Jed a question or to share their experiences, Dominic and I made our way to the refreshments.

'This is hell,' he said handing me a grey-looking beverage, which could have been either coffee or tea.

'It is what it is,' I said reaching for a digestive biscuit. I took a bite and regretted not opting for the ginger nut instead. 'I have to say, I was surprised you wanted to come.'

He laughed. 'He's got great reviews.'

I smirked. 'Probably written by his staff and brainwashed clients.'

'And Mandi,' Dominic added.

I laughed. 'She said Jed changed her life.'

Dominic raised his eyebrows. 'Was that the "I can change your life" seminar?'

I giggled. 'Think so.'

'My brother rates him too,' he said, offering me a ginger nut. 'He attended a few business seminars, said Jed transformed his business.'

I sniggered. 'Was that the "I can transform your business" seminar?'

Dominic grinned. 'OK, we've killed that joke now.'

I took a few gulps of what I'd now identified as coffee. 'So why are you here?' I asked.

Dominic looked around the room as though searching for an answer. 'I don't know,' he said. 'I suppose I just wanted to find out more about the product we're selling to our clients.'

I laughed. 'Love isn't a product.'

He shrugged his shoulders. 'It is really.'

I shook my head.

Dominic continued. 'People buy a product to solve a problem, right?'

I frowned. 'Do they?'

He nodded. 'Yes, of course. Think about it. What was the last thing you bought?'

I blurted the answer out before I had a chance to think. 'A cocktail at Hooters.'

Dominic blinked. 'Not what I was expecting, but let's go with it. So what problem did it solve?'

I looked to the ceiling. 'I was thirsty.'

Dominic raised his eyebrows.

I took another sip of coffee. 'OK, my friend was feeling bad. He'd recently separated from his wife and he needed cheering up.'

'Why didn't you just buy *him* a cocktail then? Why did you need one?'

I looked up to the ceiling again. 'Because I'm feeling the pressure at the moment.'

'What pressure?'

'To make everyone's relationship happy.'

'Whose relationships?'

'I don't know, my clients', my friends' and my own, I suppose.'

'Your relationship?'

'No, I mean, yes, my relationship is happy. I love Nick very much.' I looked down at the ginger nut in my hand. Then shoved it in my mouth before I could say anything else.

Dominic stared at me.

'Ladies and gentlemen,' the movie trailer voiceover began, 'please make your way back into the hall. The Love Language workshops will commence in two minutes.'

Dominic carried on drinking his coffee.

'So,' I said when my mouth was empty. 'Do you really believe love is a product?'

He shrugged his shoulders. 'It is for us, Ellie. We sell love. Our business is a product, not a service. Our clients don't want a process, they want the finished product: a life partner who will solve all their problems.'

I shook my head. 'I don't expect Nick to solve all my problems,' I said, reaching for another biscuit, 'only the ones he's created.'

Dominic laughed.

'Ladies and gentlemen,' the movie trailer voiceover began again. 'This is your final call. Please make your way back into the hall. The Love Language workshops will commence in one minute.'

I put my coffee cup down on the table. The man with the walkie-talkie ushered us in with a glare. Jed was already centre stage, but the rows of chairs had been reconfigured into pairs facing each other. The attendees were lined up, two by two, as though ready to board Jed's ark.

Just as we were led to the back of the queue, Jed leaped off the stage like a frog off a lily pad and made his way towards us.

He held his hands out. 'OK, guys,' he said loudly into his mic so everyone could hear, 'I'm sensing some resistance with this couple.'

Dominic and I looked at each other. I felt the urge to giggle but I managed to suppress it.

Jed glanced back at the attendees. 'And we all know the cause of resistance?' Some arms shot up. But clearly tired of audience participation, Jed decided to answer his own question. 'Fear,' he shouted. 'Fear,' he said again, approaching Dominic.

Dominic drew himself up to full height, which easily dwarfed Jed. Jed jumped on one of the chairs to compensate. 'Fear,' he said, 'is all in here.' He poked Dominic in the forehead.

Dominic looked as though he were about to head butt him.

'Tell us what you're afraid of?' Jed asked, leaning in to read Dominic's name tag. 'Mandi.'

Dominic turned to me. I looked at Jed.

'Go on,' Jed said, throwing his arm around Dominic's neck. 'Share with us. What is your biggest fear?'

Dominic looked at him and then took a deep breath. 'Becoming so self-obsessed that I spend four thousand dollars on a life-improvement seminar, lining the pockets of a self-appointed Master of a practice with no evidence-based outcomes and further contributing to the exploitation of stupid people who think Chinese is a language.'

Jed forced a smile and nodded. 'Behind fear there is always pain. We have a lot of work to do. But we're all here for you, Mandi, we're here to support you. Aren't we?' Then, after leading the audience into a clap, he dragged Dominic and I to the first two chairs.

'Thanks for volunteering, guys. We really want to help you find your love languages. Give a big hand to the lovely couple.' Jed leaned forward and read my name tag. 'Ellie,' he said, 'and Mandi.'

I went to put my hand up, to explain that we weren't a couple, and that Dominic wasn't really called Mandi, but I quickly realised it would be fruitless. Jed bounced around between us, explaining the rules of the exercise.

'This workshop is called "Harnessing Your Voice",' he said. 'OK, Ellie, you go first. Finish this sentence.' He grabbed my head turned it to face Dominic. 'Repeat after me, Ellie,' Jed said. 'I feel angry when you...'

I looked at Dominic, who was smirking, then at Jed and then back at the audience.

'Go on,' said Jed.

I took a deep breath and looked Dominic in the eye. 'I feel angry when...you say I'm wrong.'

Jed clapped. 'Excellent, Ellie. Now, can you explain why that makes you angry?'

I laughed. 'It makes me angry because I know I'm right.'

Jed nodded again. 'Well done. And why do you like people to know you're right?'

I looked back at Dominic, who now had his finger on his

chin and was leaning forward with his legs crossed, like a college professor.

'Go on,' said Jed.

I scratched my head. 'Because it means they will listen to me.'

Jed nodded his head slowly. 'And why do you like it when people listen to you?'

I drummed my fingers on my leg. 'Because then I can help them.'

A frown flickered across Jed's face. 'Excellent. And why do you like to help people?'

'So they will be happy.'

'Why do you like people to be happy?'

'Because sadness is terrible.'

'Wow,' said Jed, taking in a sharp breath and thumping his heart. 'This is powerful.' He turned to the audience and then back to Dominic. 'Do you see here? When you say Ellie is right, she feels she can make the world happy. When you disagree with her, she feels powerless as though the world will spiral into sadness. Can you understand now why Ellie might react so emotionally when you don't agree with her?'

Dominic nodded, his expression almost sincere.

Then Jed turned back to me. 'Do you think you can save everyone from sadness, Ellie?'

I thought for a moment, then nodded.

'And if I questioned that assumption, how would you feel?'

I stared at him, then glanced around the room, feeling like an ill-prepared prime minister at question time. 'Well, you'd be wrong,' I said.

Jed raised his eyebrows. 'Defensiveness is just another form of resistance,' he said, leaning forward to touch my

shoulder. Then he turned to the audience. 'And what is resistance fuelled by?' he asked.

'Fear,' they chanted, like a pack of newly converted cult
members.

I glared out at the crowd. 'I'm not fearful,' I said, loudly
enough for them to all hear me, including a guy at the back
in an AC/DC T-shirt who appeared to be recording the entire workshop on his mobile phone.

Jed stepped forward and squeezed my shoulder again. 'So
I'll ask you once more. What if people couldn't be saved
from sadness? How would you feel?'

My stomach flipped. I turned to Dominic.

'But they can,' I said.

'What if they can't?' he asked again, his face moving
closer to mine. 'What if sadness is a natural and inevitable
emotional state for all of us?'

I narrowed my eyes. 'But it isn't,' I said.

'What if it was?' he asked again, his face so close I could
feel his breath.

I looked down. 'Then I'd be redundant.'

'Redundant?' he asked.

'Of purpose,' I said.

He nodded slowly, then lifted his head to the crowd. 'Redundant or free?'

I frowned. 'Free?'

'Of the burden you've placed on your shoulders.' He
leaned forward and rubbed my shoulders while looking
into my eyes. 'World happiness is a heavy load to bear,' he
said with the hint of a smirk.

I brushed him off and went to stand up.

He pushed me back down again. 'As you can see, ladies
and gentlemen, when we get to the root of the issue, the re-

sistance increases. We have to keep going. It's like an exorcism.'

I heard Dominic giggling.

Jed spun round to face him, then readdressed the audience. 'And often,' Jed said, 'the partner may try to sabotage their lover's emotional growth, fearful that it may lead to abandonment.'

I glanced at Dominic, who was rolling his eyes.

Jed turned back to me. 'Are you ready now?'

I flinched. 'Ready for what?'

'To question your assumption?'

I sighed. 'Go on then.'

He sprang towards his flip chart and grabbed a marker. He read the words out as he wrote them.

'I believe I can save the world from sadness,' he said, then turned to me.

'Is this true?'

I nodded. 'Sort of. But it does make me sound like I think I'm some kind of messiah.'

Jed nodded. I immediately imagined Ernest chipping in via satellite link to Texas, diagnosing delusions of grandeur.

'So would you like to amend it?' Jed asked.

I scrunched up my mouth and stared at the words. 'OK,' I said eventually. 'I believe that *sometimes*, I may be able to help *some* people avoid *some* sadness.'

Jed nodded slowly. 'And the reverse of that is?'

I shrugged my shoulders.

He sighed. 'You believe that some of the time you *can't* help some people avoid some sadness?'

I repeated the sentence in my head before agreeing. 'Yes,' I said.

'Which means?'

I looked at him, wondering what it was I needed to say to conclude this torturous exercise. 'I'm free?' I said.

Jed jumped in the air and clapped. 'Breakthrough!' he shouted. Suddenly the audience began clapping.

Jed raised his arms to the ceiling. 'Breakthrough!' he shouted again, before pulling me up from the chair and holding my arm aloft. 'She's free,' he shouted.

Dominic suddenly jumped up beside me, grinning. 'You're free, Ellie! You're free!' he shouted, mimicking Jed's accent, before grabbing me round the waist and pulling me away from Jed and towards him.

The audience became more frenzied, clapping wildly, while loudly chanting: 'Breakthrough. Breakthrough.' The man with the AC/DC T-shirt began to sob.

When the crowd eventually calmed, Dominic leaned into me and squeezed me around the waist. I flinched. It was the exact same way Nick used to hold me when we first met.

'This guy is mental,' he whispered in my ear. 'Let's get out of here.'

I glanced around and saw Jed watching us.

Jed lifted his arms in the air again but this time his face was serious. 'OK,' he said. 'Quiet, please. Our work is not yet done.' Then he walked towards Dominic and gestured firmly for him to sit down. 'Your turn now,' he said.

Dominic looked around him and then up at me as if searching for intervention. I shrugged my shoulders and offered an apologetic smile.

Jed stood facing Dominic, then asked his opening question.

'Finish this statement,' he began, nodding at Dominic and then turning to me. 'Ellie, I feel angry when you...'

Dominic rolled his eyes and sat down. 'Ellie, I feel angry when you...' he paused, then laced his fingers together and smirked '...when you exclude me.'

'From what?' I asked.

Jed glared at me. 'Let Mandi speak, please, Ellie.' Then he turned back to Dominic, who had now adopted a sad, victim-like repose.

'Go on, Mandi,' Jed said, nodding at him encouragingly. 'What is it that Ellie does that makes you feel excluded?'

Dominic glanced up at him. 'Excludes me,' he said as though Jed were a bit simple.

'Yes,' Jed said, looking more irritated now than encouraging. 'From what do you feel excluded?'

Dominic glanced down at his hands. 'Oh, I don't know, decisions, I suppose.'

Now Jed nodded. 'And how does that make you feel?'

I secretly willed Dominic to say 'excluded', but it was as though he forgot to be disdainful of the process for a moment.

'Unwanted,' he said, before closing his mouth quickly.

Jed looked to the audience, many of whom were nodding their heads, or murmuring concern. 'Abandonment again,' Jed said, addressing the audience.

Dominic shuffled in his seat. 'I meant my opinions are unwanted.' He scratched his nose and then glanced up at me. I smiled.

Jed observed our interaction before proceeding. 'So how do you feel when you think your opinions are unwanted?'

'Pissed off,' Dominic replied.

'Anger is fear remember, Mandi.'

Dominic rolled his eyes.

Jed continued. 'Why do you want your opinions to be wanted?'

'So I feel included.'

Jed sighed and then glanced sideways at the clock. 'And when you're included you feel?'

'Good,' Dominic replied.

'Because?'

'Oh, I don't know. Because I feel needed, I suppose.'

Jed cocked his head. 'And if you don't feel needed, you feel?'

Dominic looked at me and then at the crowd and then glared at Jed. 'Rejected. There, I said it. I have a fear of abandonment. You were right. Probably something to do with the fact that my mother died when I was two and my fiancée was killed in a car crash.'

Jed stood motionless for a moment. Then he stepped back and turned to the audience. 'Breakthrough,' he said softly, before tentatively raising his arms. 'Breakthrough,' he said louder this time. The audience followed his lead, most with expressions as bewildered as Jed's. 'Breakthrough!' he screamed and began clapping louder, before completing his victory lap of the hall, which this time seemed less of a lap and more of a direct sprint away from me and Dominic.

As the audience's eyes followed Jed, Dominic jumped up and took my hand.

'Let's go,' he said, leading me away.

When we reached the doors, they were locked. Dominic tried to force the handle but it wouldn't budge. Moments later, the man with the walkie-talkie appeared beside us.

'Can I help you?' he asked in a way that implied he regularly rehearsed the question in front of a mirror.

Dominic glared at him. 'We'd like to leave,' he said.

Walkie-talkie man shook his head. 'No,' he said. 'Mr Tandy insists that all delegates complete the workshops.'

Dominic squared up to him. 'We would like to leave,' he repeated. 'Now please open the door.'

Suddenly Jed was beside us, looking a little flushed. 'Don't worry, Geoff, these two can go. They've both had breakthroughs.'

Geoff's eyes widened. He looked at Jed, then back at us. 'Didn't you say resistance is fear, Jed?'

Jed shuffled from foot to foot.

Geoff stared at him some more. 'What is it you fear about these two, Jed?' he asked, hooking his walkie-talkie to his belt and then resting his arms on Jed's shoulders.

Jed forced a smile. 'Nothing,' he said, a bead of sweat dripping from his top lip. 'Geoff is right,' Jed said, holding his arms out to us. 'You should stay for "Love Languages" part two.'

I looked at Dominic and shrugged my shoulders. I was here to learn after all. Dominic looked back at me and let out a deep sigh.

Following a horrendous buffet lunch, during which Dominic and I were bombarded with well wishes from fellow delegates regarding our breakthroughs, we were summoned by Geoff to reconvene back in the hall. I hadn't even had the chance to ask Dominic about what he'd said about his mother and fiancée.

The chairs had been rearranged theatre style, so we were all facing the stage. Jed was reintroduced by the movie voiceover and the stage effect flames reignited. The audience began clapping wildly, their enthusiasm clearly untempered by lukewarm coffee and stale sandwiches.

While Jed began loudly defining the different love languages and explaining what makes one of us feel loved might not do the same for another, I glanced to my side to see Dominic about to drift off. I nudged him in the ribs with my elbow.

'The key to a happy relationship,' Jed said, while pacing back and forth on the stage, 'is to discover *your* love language and that of your spouse.'

'Did he just say "spouse"?' Dominic asked, rubbing his eyes.

I jabbed him again. 'Listen. This is important.'

Soon after, we were instructed to pair off for a session entitled 'Finding *Your* Love Language'.

Dominic sat opposite me and then grinned. 'So what makes you feel loved, Ellie?' he asked with a double eyebrow raise.

I bit my lip and thought for a moment.

'Time,' I said. 'Someone spending time with me, wanting to be with me.'

'Someone?' Dominic asked, with another eyebrow raise. 'Or Nick?'

I tutted. 'Nick, of course.'

He crossed his legs and smirked. 'Well, you said "someone".'

'Well, it's obvious I meant Nick.'

He shrugged his shoulders. 'What else makes you feel loved? Flowers? Chocolates?'

I scrunched up my mouth. 'I suppose I like presents, but it's more the gesture, the token, to show that he's thinking about me.'

Dominic smirked. 'Who? Someone? Or Nick?'

I rolled my eyes. 'And you, what makes you feel loved, Dominic?'

'Blow jobs,' he said.

I tutted. 'Anything else?'

He let out a sharp sigh. 'I don't know. I haven't really thought about it.'

'Isn't now the time to think about it?'

He looked down at the floor, then back up at me, a fleeting sadness preceding his smile. 'What's the point?' he asked.

I cocked my head and stared at him for a while. 'What you said earlier, about your mother and your—'

He interrupted me with a laugh. 'I was just winding him up,' he said, then he laughed some more.

I continued staring at him, realising that the conversation had now reached a dead end.

'So,' I said, gripping my workshop notebook and pen and adopting a Jed Tandy–style demeanour. 'Do you have a *spouse*?' I asked, emphasising the word to make him laugh.

He grinned. 'Why? Are you interested?'

I rolled my eyes again. 'I'm married, Dominic. Did I forget to tell you that?'

He sat back. 'No, Ellie, you didn't forget to tell me that.' He lifted his arms up behind his head. 'In fact, if I recall correctly, you told me approximately thirty seconds after we were introduced.'

I felt my neck flush. 'No, I didn't.'

He smirked. 'Yes, you did. You said: "Hi, I'm Ellie, I'm married and I've been a matchmaker for five years."'

I frowned. 'That was a weird way to introduce myself.'

He laughed. 'Yes, I thought so. I found it odd that you

chose to prioritise your marital status over your profession too.'

I frowned.

Dominic laughed. 'I just assumed it was an unconscious reaction to my good looks. "Wow, he's super hot. I'm married. Must not have these thoughts. I'm married. God I want him. I'm married. I bet he has a huge…"'

I smirked. 'You're not funny.'

He grinned. 'Then why are you smiling?'

I sighed. 'You want to know what I really thought?'

He nodded.

'I thought you were a privileged little prick who walked like he had a stick up his arse.'

Dominic sat back and laughed. 'Blow me,' he said. 'Eleanor Rigby swears. I never thought I'd see the day.' He laughed some more and then his expression suddenly shifted. 'Just for the record,' he said, leaning forward, 'I wasn't asking you to blow me.'

I giggled.

'Although any offers would be gratefully received,' he added.

I raised my eyebrows. 'So you don't have a girlfriend then?'

'You so want me, don't you?'

I sighed.

He was still grinning. 'No, I don't have a girlfriend. I'm saving myself for you.'

I sat back and stared at him for a while.

He rolled his eyes. 'Oh, don't even try to analyse me, Ellie. Poor Dominic had his heart broken and now he deflects any questions about love with crude innuendo and requests for oral sex.'

I laughed. 'Dominic, I've been matchmaking for ten years. I don't have to analyse anything. I can read you like a book.'

His eyes widened momentarily, then he sat back with his arms folded. 'You know every good book has a killer twist, don't you?'

I smiled and then nodded.

Once a now jaded Jed had concluded the afternoon sessions of the Love Languages conference, we took our goody bags, which comprised Jed Tandy branded materials and a signed copy of his *Master the Language of Love* handbook complete with DVD series, Dominic and I made our way outside.

The air was icy and I pulled my coat in around me.

'Fancy a bite to eat?' Dominic asked. I could tell he was trying to be casual but there was an underlying awkwardness.

I shook my head. 'Nick and I are having a night in tonight.'

Dominic nodded. 'No worries,' he said. 'I'll probably just head back to the hotel now anyway.'

I grabbed my phone as Dominic walked away and dialled Nick's number. It took twelve rings before he picked up.

'Hey, babe,' he said. I could hear music pumping in the background and squealing female voices.

'Where are you?' I asked.

'Vodka Fusion. Work drinks.'

'Oh right. Sounds like fun,' I said, realising he'd clearly forgotten our planned night in. Or chosen to forget it because he was still annoyed.

I held out for an invite, then the line began to crackle.

'It will probably be a late one,' he said between crackles. 'Don't wait up!'

* * *

I stood on the cold stone steps and watched my breath clouding into the evening air. Since we'd arrived in New York, not once had Nick and I even so much as gone out for dinner together. So much for our fresh new start.

I looked across the street and saw Dominic about to turn a corner.

'Hey!' I shouted. 'Wait for me!'

Chapter 19

'I don't mean to criticise your husband,' Dominic said, as he took my hand and led me to the front of the queue, 'but I can't believe he hasn't taken you to Sushisamba yet. What's wrong with the man?'

I shrugged my shoulders. 'Who's to say I couldn't have brought Nick here instead?'

He scrunched up his face. 'A woman taking a man out for dinner?' Then he shook his head. 'That's just wrong.'

Dominic dragged me to the front of the queue and straight through the doorway. We were greeted by the front of house, who was six feet of Russian supermodel.

'Table for two,' Dominic said.

She glanced at the queue, then back at Dominic. 'You have a reservation?' she asked in a tone generally reserved for gathering military intelligence.

Dominic leaned forward and whispered something in her ear.

She nodded and smiled. 'My apologies, sir. Come with me, please,' she said before walking ahead.

As we weaved our way through the glitzy crowd, I leaned into Dominic. 'What did you say to her?' I asked.

He smirked as we sat down. 'I told her she could have my number.'

I frowned and then laughed. 'More like you told her your grandfather is the chief investor in the restaurant.'

Dominic laughed.

'I told you I could read you like a book.'

'Maybe,' he said and then smirked.

Straight away and without ordering we were presented with cocktails. I took a sip of mine and looked around, suddenly feeling conspicuous in my dull grey work suit, which was creased from sitting all day. I glanced down and noticed there was a stain on the inside of my trouser leg: the result of an overzealous embrace from an empathetic delegate with an egg mayonnaise sandwich.

Dominic must have noticed me trying to rub off the stain with my napkin because he reached for my hand and lifted it back towards my drink.

'Relax,' he said, with a soft smile. 'It's not like you've got anyone to impress, is it?' He winked. 'After all you're married, don't forget.'

I smiled. 'Marriage doesn't save anyone from the humiliation of a greasy crotch stain,' I said, and then took another sip of my cocktail. It tasted like chilled lychee heaven.

The head of house, seemingly having abandoned her post as door monitor, placed menus in front of us. She leaned in extra close to Dominic so he had an uninterrupted view of her sculpted cleavage.

Dominic did a double eyebrow raise as she walked away. 'She's really angling for my number, isn't she?'

I laughed. 'So what did you really say to her?'

He shrugged his shoulders. 'It was as you said, I reminded her my grandfather paid her salary, of course.' Then he grinned at me.

I looked at him for a moment, trying to read his expression but I failed to glean anything other than genuine amusement.

'Right,' he said, suddenly breaking eye contact and picking up his phone. 'This trip we're going on.'

He began scrolling through his phone. 'OK, here it is. The travel plans.' He looked at the screen, mumbling the destinations as he read. 'Texas, Long Island, Iceland...' Then he paused.

'Why on earth has Mandi booked a retreat in Bali for a week?' He glanced at me as though demanding an explanation. 'We're not here to find ourselves. We need to get results.' He scowled at me. 'What happened to the list I sent you?'

I glanced to the ceiling and then back at him. 'Mandi said it was too Western-centred. She insisted we balance it with some Eastern philosophies.'

Dominic rolled his eyes. 'Most Western practices are based on Eastern principles anyway. It's not as though we've managed to come up with anything new.' He sighed and then scratched his head. 'Us Westerners just choose to evidence our research rather than rely on generations of inherited assumptions.' He continued to read. 'Ayahuasca,' he said facing the phone to me. 'What is that?'

I squinted at the screen. 'Oh yes,' I said. 'Mandi said it's a therapeutic tea that the Peruvians drink. Apparently, you get to see inside yourself and it makes you a better person.'

Dominic tapped on his phone. He frowned at the screen. 'Ayahuasca is a hallucinogen, one which is illegal in most countries, it seems.' He looked up at me. 'Mandi wants us to take some crazy trip so we can hallucinate the answers on how to prevent divorce? What is wrong with her?'

I narrowed my eyes. 'Her? What's up with you? How come this is all suddenly *us*?'

Dominic shifted in his seat and then took a gulp of his cocktail.

'You clearly need some supervision,' he said.

I frowned, wondering why everyone seemed to think I was incapable of conducting this research alone.

The supermodel reappeared at our table.

'I take your order?' she purred at Dominic.

Dominic glanced at me, then back at her. 'We'll have the fifteen-piece sashimi, lobster rolls, rock shrimp tempura and the pork belly lettuce wraps.' He handed her the menus. 'Oh, and the Moqueca Mista.'

She nodded, her gaze lingering on Dominic, almost implying the threat of suffocation between her thighs if he didn't reciprocate.

He waved her away and then turned back to me. 'I'm quite surprised you've been so passive in this whole process,' he said. 'You've got such strong opinions about everything else.'

I frowned. 'It's not my fault I'm unfamiliar with the menu.'

Dominic laughed. 'I'm talking about the research. You were the one who was all gung-ho about finding a cure for divorce and developing advanced training for matchmakers.

And now it's come to it, it's as though you're delegating the process to everyone else.'

'Oh I am, am I?'

He nodded. 'Why else would you let me and Mandi arrange your trip?'

I took a breath. 'I didn't let you and Mandi arrange my trip. You foisted it upon me.'

He leaned back. 'Oh, come on, Ellie. You're hardly the sort of person who lets things be foisted upon them.' He paused for a moment. 'If you were that way inclined I would've ordered the sea urchin.'

I sighed.

'Look,' he said, 'it's common knowledge that you and I haven't seen eye to eye.'

I raised my eyebrows.

'OK,' he said smiling, 'it's common knowledge that you hate me.' He leaned back and smoothed down his shirt. 'Although I stand by my hypothesis that you're deeply attracted to me and you're unconsciously attempting to drive temptation away.'

I rolled my eyes.

He continued. 'And you're letting me and Mandi...' he paused '...who's a raving loon at the best of times...' he paused again '...and now fuelled by hormones...' He looked down at his plate. 'She's positively mental. You should've seen the outfit she was wearing last week. My God.'

I slurped the last of my cocktail and then gestured for the waiter to bring me some more.

Dominic raised his eyebrows. 'Thirsty, are we?'

I smiled. 'I need something to tide me over while I'm waiting for you to get to the point.'

He laughed, then waved at the waiter too. 'Wine list,

please,' he said. Immediately, the Russian supermodel breezed past and handed it to him, lingering gaze intensifying.

Dominic glanced at it, then ordered an expensive-sounding Chablis. He turned back to me.

'The point I am trying to make, Miss Rigby, is that you have spent the best part of a decade trying to find the secret to everlasting love, and now you've reached the final point, you are deferring responsibility.' He folded his arms across his chest and looked at me. 'Don't you think that is a little odd?'

I glared at him. 'How can you accuse me of trying to defer responsibility when I'm the only one who's done any research? I didn't see you and Mandi in the bloody couples' counselling vagina tent in Texas.'

Dominic double blinked. 'Well, firstly, Mandi and I are not a couple, so that would've been odd.'

I nodded. 'Odd like the couples' coaching you and I just had with Jed?'

Dominic laughed. 'Yes, precisely. And secondly, what is a vagina tent?'

'It's a metaphor,' I said, waving my hand dismissively.

The waiter interrupted us by announcing the arrival of the food, and introducing each dish as though they were guests at a society ball.

Dominic took his chopsticks and pointed them at me. 'A metaphor that you deliberately used to distract me from my line of questioning.'

I smiled. 'I was simply making the point that I could not be accused of deferring responsibility when it is I who has conducted the research thus far.'

Dominic dunked a piece of salmon sashimi into the soy

sauce. 'You may have conducted the research—' he popped it into his mouth and chewed for a moment before swallowing '—however, you're just meeting all the experts that Mandi and I lined up for you.'

'That's not true,' I said, spearing some tempura. 'The divorce lawyer wasn't on your list.'

Dominic took a long slow glug of wine. 'We won't find the right answers if we don't ask the right people.'

'We? What's with all the we's?' I stared at him. 'What I don't get is why you suddenly give a shit.'

Dominic sat back, looking a little startled.

I continued. 'The moment you joined the company, all you've cared about is the bottom line.' I smeared some wasabi on a lobster roll, realising that perhaps the oxytocin might be wearing off. 'You've repeatedly discounted any areas of the business that focus on customer well-being or long-term satisfaction. And now, out of nowhere, you appear with a new-found, and quite frankly dubious, concern for our clients.' I shoved the roll into my mouth and glared at him.

He took another sip of wine, this time quick and fast. 'Look, I understand it must appear like a complete turnaround—'

'Yes, it does.'

'This new service has the potential to be immensely profitable. Not only one-to-one coaching but also weekend retreats, even trips around the world for clients to find the answers themselves. We could treble our turnover in one year.'

I rolled my eyes.

Dominic continued. 'Look, Ellie, I was brought into the business to make money for the shareholders, not to wrap the clients in cotton wool.'

I sighed. 'For a man with an MBA, it's odd that you can't see the connection between the two.'

'The two what?'

'Happy clients and healthy profits.'

Dominic leaned forward and squeezed my hand. 'I'm hesitant to blight your utopian view of the world, Ellie. But have you considered for a moment that perhaps by trying to prevent your clients from experiencing any heartbreak, you are in actuality stifling their growth?'

I sat straight up. 'You think heartbreak is a good thing?'

He downed the rest of his wine. 'Well, it's certainly the best thing that ever happened to me.'

I arrived home, unsure of two things: the whereabouts of my keys and the rationale behind us ordering a third bottle of wine. I rummaged in my bag, locating all manner of lost objects, not one of which could be used to access my house. After a while Nick came thundering down the staircase and opened the door.

'Where the hell have you been?' he asked, eyes squinting at the light.

'Out,' I said stumbling into the hallway. 'I thought you were out tonight too?'

He went to check his watch, only to realise he was wearing nothing but his boxers and a pair of socks. 'Yes. I was out this evening. But not all bloody night. Ellie, it must be 4 a.m. Where have you been?'

'Dominic and—'

He sighed. 'I might have known old slimy pants would be involved. Fabulous.'

'Fabulous what? That your wife is no longer the teetotal

bore who stays in every night, waiting for you to rock up stinking of whiskey?'

He laughed, although his eyes remained pinched. 'Fabulous that my wife is oblivious to the fact her twat of a colleague is trying to shag her.'

I sighed. 'We just went for dinner.'

'Oh, Dominic and I just went for dinner.' He cocked his hand and starting parading around the room with clenched buttocks.

'Well, that's all it was.'

He paused his show for a moment. 'Even in New York, restaurants don't stay open to...' he craned his neck to see the clock on the wall '...4.37 a.m. You must have gone somewhere else.'

'A bar.'

'Well, that's bloody obvious. Which one?'

I screwed up my face. 'I don't know. We got a taxi there. I think it was a jazz bar.'

'Ooh, Dominic took me to a jazz bar.' He recommenced his silly walk around the room, his boxer and sock combo doing nothing for him. 'My "colleague" and I went to a jazz bar. How wonderful.'

I was starting to get irritated. 'And you?' I asked. 'Were you mentoring Jenna this evening?'

'Mentoring?'

'It's a polite way of saying flirting.'

'I don't flirt.'

'No, of course not. You're just discriminately friendly to pretty girls.'

He scowled at me. 'Don't turn this around onto me, Ellie. You're in the wrong and you know it.'

'How am I wrong?'

'You fancy that guy. I can tell. And you're still hanging out with him. Worse still, you're now going on holiday together.'

'It's a work trip,' I said. 'Besides, I told you, I'll come back for a few weekends. And you can come visit me too?'

Nick shook his head. 'Jenna and I are swamped at work right now, it will be almost impossible.'

I let out a long slow breath, as though trying to exhale any thoughts of Jenna, and then walked towards him and put my arms around his neck. 'I love you,' I said. 'That will never change. You have nothing to worry about.'

He stepped back and stared at me. 'I wish I could believe you, Ellie.'

'You can,' I said.

He looked me in the eye. 'You of all people know that we shouldn't be complacent.'

I took a deep breath. 'We'll be fine,' I said. 'Now come on, let's go to bed.'

He pulled me back, his eyes pleading. 'I don't want you to go with him.'

I frowned.

'On the trip,' he said. 'I don't want you to go with him.'

I looked back at him and, for a brief moment, considered relenting. But then I realised that our marriage wasn't just about Nick's wants, it was about my needs too. And I needed to find the answers I'd been searching for. Not only for us, but for my clients too.

Chapter 20

It was only our second month in New York, but as I watched Nick heave my suitcase into the back of a yellow taxi, it felt as though I were leaving home all over again. I'd left my hopes for a family in London, but now part of me worried that I might be leaving something greater here.

Nick had offered to accompany me to the airport, an act which I would have liked to consider romantic, although I suspected was more of a final attempt to persuade me to stay or failing that, at the very least, an opportunity to take the piss out of Dominic.

Dominic was standing in the check-in queue when we arrived. He was wearing dark blue jeans and a Paul Smith shirt. I immediately sensed Nick tense.

'Ooh look, Dominic has got his best shirt on,' he said.

I glared at Nick. 'Is it really necessary to start every sentence about Dominic with an effeminate "ooh"?'

Nick laughed. 'Yes. It is.'

I turned to him and wagged my finger. 'And you need to stop with the bottom-clenching walk too. He'll notice.'

Nick chuckled. 'That is the point.'

When we reached the check-in queue, Dominic stepped forward to greet us. He addressed Nick first.

'All right, mate?' he said to Nick.

Nick broadened his shoulders and shook Dominic's hand. 'All right.'

Then Dominic turned to me with a smile. 'So, Ellie, are you ready for Reykjavik?'

I laughed. 'Yes, although I still don't fully understand why we wiped Bali off the list.'

Dominic turned to Nick and raised an eyebrow. 'You know what women are like unsupervised with a travel budget.'

Nick smirked.

'Have you ever been to Reykjavik, mate?' Dominic asked Nick.

Nick nodded. 'Yes, mate,' he said, enunciating the 'mate' as if to mock Dominic's attempts at British colloquialisms.

'He went there for a stag do,' I added.

Dominic chuckled. 'Ah,' he said, 'any recommendations?'

Nick smirked. 'Yeah, keep out of the whorehouses, they're a rip-off.'

I rolled my eyes. 'He's joking,' I said, noticing Dominic looking a little annoyed. I nudged Nick in the ribs.

Nick laughed. 'Seriously, *mate*, it's a beautiful country.' He squeezed my hand. 'I'd always promised Ellie I'd take her one day.'

Dominic glanced up at the departure board and then gestured to the check-in desk. 'We'd better get a move on,' he said, turning to me. 'Let me take your case, Ellie.'

Nick swooped in and snatched it off him. 'I've got it,' he said.

I rolled my eyes. 'Thanks, but it has wheels. I'm really OK by myself.'

Once we'd reclaimed a place in the queue, Dominic manned the cases while Nick and I said goodbye.

Nick slipped his hands around my waist and glanced over my shoulder.

'I'm finding it hard to be sincere with old beady eyes over there watching us,' he said.

I looked behind me to see Dominic pretending to be busy on his phone.

'Oh ignore him,' I said. 'I want to say goodbye properly.'

Nick swallowed. 'You'll be back at the end of May, right?'

'Or before,' I said. 'Maybe I could pop back next weekend? Or the one after?'

Nick rolled his eyes. 'Pop back? You're not nipping out to the corner shop. You're travelling across four different time zones.'

I scowled at him. 'Millions of people manage long-distance relationships, Nick.'

'Millions?' he said, laughing. Then he kissed me. 'I'm going to miss you,' he said.

I took a sharp breath. 'Me too,' I said.

He held my waist tighter and looked me in the eye. 'Don't go,' he said.

'I have to.'

He sighed. 'It's not as if the matchmaking Mafia are holding you to ransom. You don't have to.'

'It's something I need to do,' I said. 'Are you sure you can't take a few weeks' holiday and join me for a bit?'

Nick sighed. 'I told you, I'm swamped.' He looked down. Then he looked back up at me, eyes teary. 'I love you, Ellie Rigby.'

I leaned forward and rested my forehead against his. 'I love you too,' I said.

He wiped his eyes and then took my hands in his. 'Promise me one thing,' he said.

I smiled. 'Yes,' I said.

'Two months is a long time,' he began. 'The world is full of temptations.'

I nodded.

'You have to promise me...' his gaze intensified '...promise me that no matter what happens, in the time you're away, you won't...' He paused again. 'Promise me you won't...'

'Won't what?'

Suddenly a smiled edged out from the corners of his mouth. 'Get fat,' he said and then burst out laughing.

I slapped him on the chest. 'You're not funny,' I said.

He pulled me into his arms. 'Oh, and don't shag that twat either, you know it would kill me.'

The next morning, my phone alerted me to the fact that Reykjavik was four hours ahead of my body clock. In two hours, Dominic and I were due to meet Dr Gunnarsson, a sociologist, who, according to Mandi's notes, was going to explain why Iceland's inhabitants report the highest levels of happiness while at the same time suffering one of the highest divorce rates in the world. I jumped out of bed and shivered, briefly contemplating showering in my thermals.

I was still shivering at breakfast with Dominic.

'It's so bloody cold here,' I said. 'Maybe people are happier divorced because it means they can keep their clothes on in bed.' I craned my neck to see if there was a coffee pot anywhere on the hotel breakfast counter.

Dominic, seemingly in tune with my needs, jumped up and grabbed a pot. I watched him while he poured me a cup. He was rocking the Iceland chic, broad shoulders insulated in a stylish cable-knit jumper, while I was layered in several old hiking fleeces. Once he'd poured the coffee, he picked up a hunk of rye bread and studied it.

'Do married people have sex? I thought they didn't,' he said, taking a bite.

I rolled my eyes. 'Of course we do.'

He raised his eyebrows and reached for the jam. 'No need to be defensive. I wasn't necessarily referring to you.'

'Necessarily?'

'Well, you are married, so you would have a better idea than me.'

'Nick and I have sex.'

He nodded and slathered some butter on the bread. 'As gorgeous as you are, Ellie, I doubt you have as much sex as you did when you first met.'

I eyed a boiled egg that was on the table. 'Is this really a breakfast conversation?'

'Maybe not,' he said, spooning on the jam, 'but it's a valid question.'

I picked up the egg and put it on my plate. 'Well, it sounds like more of a judgement than a question.'

'I apologise,' he said. 'I was just wondering, that's all. I read something about how sex is essential to maintain a couple's bond. There's a hormone that is released during sex and that is how a couple bonds and stays bonded.'

I couldn't help but laugh. 'Oxytocin,' I said.

Dominic looked back up at me. 'You really have done your research, haven't you?'

I nodded.

'So how does it work?'

'It's released when you stroke your dog or have sex.'

Dominic coughed. 'With your dog?'

I frowned. 'Of course not. Also when breastfeeding. Both the baby and the mother release it. It's basically physical contact or orgasm which causes it to be released.'

Dominic smirked.

I continued. 'So if a couple stop having sex, or have cuddles which last less than ten to twelve seconds, apparently the levels drop.'

Dominic hooted with laughter. 'Cuddles? Do grown-up people actually have cuddles?'

I sighed. 'You know what I mean.'

He stared at his bread for a while and then back up at me. 'And friendship?' he said. 'You and I talking right now. We're bonding, aren't we?'

I laughed.

'But we haven't had any cuddles, have we?' he said, smirking. 'Or orgasms.' Then he leaned back in his seat. 'Unless, of course, you count that dream I had about you last night.'

I felt my cheeks flushing. 'Stop it.'

He grinned. 'I'm joking,' he said, his smile widening. Then he took a quick slurp of coffee. 'Come on, eat up, I'm dying to meet this guy.'

The taxi ride to Dr Gunnarsson's office took us through the quaint streets of Reykjavik. I stared out the window as we passed the rows of Lego houses. I envisaged their architect to be a four-year-old child armed with crayons and a naive vision of how a town should look. I sat back ready to take in more scenery but was distracted by my phone, which kept vibrating.

Dominic leaned over, glancing at the screen. 'Someone missing their cuddles?'

I batted him away, and scrolled through my messages. I hadn't checked any since we'd landed. Three were from Nick.

7pm: Hope you had a good flight x

11pm: Miss you xx

1am: Remind buttock twat you're married xxx

I laughed out loud at the last one.

'What?' Dominic asked. I wouldn't tell him, so he huffed and pretended to look out the window.

Then I noticed there were three voicemails and a strange text from Matthew. I called him straight away.

He answered on the third ring. 'Ellie, where have you been?' He was almost shouting. 'I've been trying to get hold of you for days!'

'Days?' I asked.

He let out a sharp sigh. 'Well, since yesterday. And now it's today, so technically, that's two days I've been trying to reach you.'

'I'm in Iceland. Are you OK?'

'No, I'm not.' His voice sounded pained, like he was being held up at gunpoint. 'Iceland the country?'

I laughed. 'No, Iceland the frozen food store. I thought Sara Lee might help combat the rising divorce rate.'

Matthew sighed. 'This is no time to joke, Ellie.'

'I'm sorry,' I said, leaning across to slap Dominic, who was now laughing loudly at my joke.

'Is that Nick?' Matthew asked.

'No,' I said. 'It's Dominic, my colleague. He's helping me with the research.'

'The CEO guy?' Matthew asked.

I nodded, although fully aware Matthew couldn't see me.

'The one you hate?'

'Yes,' I said, glancing at Dominic to make sure he hadn't heard. 'But I thought we were supposed to be talking about you.'

Matthew took in a deep breath and then exhaled slowly. 'She's left me, Ellie.'

My stomach lurched. 'Oh,' I said. 'What happened?'

'I don't want to talk about it on the phone.'

I sighed. 'Please not another Smart car Red Bull road trip,' I said. 'You can't leave your kids again.'

Matthew huffed. '*She* left me. And *she* took the kids. None of this was my choice. And it wasn't a Smart car. It was a Cinquecento.'

'Whatever,' I said. 'I thought you two were sorting things out.'

'We were.'

'What happened?'

'I told you, I don't want to talk about it on the phone.'

I sighed. 'Well, you're going to have to. I'm in Iceland and you're in London.'

'I don't want the buttock clencher to overhear.'

'He won't, don't worry.'

'No. I can't. I have to go. I'll call you later.'

Then the line went dead. I tried to call back but it went straight to voicemail. I left a garbled message promising that next time the buttock clencher would be out of earshot. As soon as I said the words, I realised that just because Matthew couldn't hear me, it didn't mean that Dominic couldn't.

Dominic turned to me with raised eyebrows. 'Buttock clencher?'

I winced and then offered a smile. 'His words, not mine,' I said.

Dominic frowned. 'But he hasn't met me,' he said.

I shrugged my shoulders. 'I'm sure he did one time.'

'Hmmm,' Dominic murmured, eyeing me suspiciously.

It turned out that Dr Gunnarsson's office was based off campus on the outskirts of town. The taxi driver dropped us off in the car park, which was deserted apart from a man wearing a pair of micro shorts and a fleece. He had wild blond hair and a beaded necklace and looked like a hybrid of Boris Johnson and Bon Jovi.

He greeted us. '*Góðan daginn*,' he said.

Dominic and I looked at each other. The eccentric caretaker, or whoever he was, picked up a tatty-looking rucksack and gestured for us to follow him.

We took a small grassy path up beside a cluster of buildings, which led to another path along the side of a hill.

'Is Dr Gunnarsson's office up here?' I eventually asked, slightly concerned we'd been duped by a serial killer.

The man stopped and laughed heartily. Then he turned to me. 'Bore,' he said, holding out his hand. 'Bore Gunnarsson.'

I felt my face flush. 'Sorry,' I said, taking his hand. 'I'm Ellie, lovely to meet you.'

Dominic laughed and stepped forward. 'Good to meet you, Dr Gunnarsson,' he said, giving me a sly wink. 'I've been following your research for some time now.'

'Bore, please call me Bore,' he said, continuing up the path. 'And as you've been following my research, as you say, you'll know precisely where we are going.'

Dominic glanced at me.

I shrugged my shoulders.

The path followed a river. Its grassy banks and misty turquoise water made me think that it too had been the brainchild of the four-year-old with the crayons.

Dr Gunnarsson stopped and turned to us.

'This is known as Steam Valley,' he said, raising one arm out in front of him. 'Iceland lies in the middle of the continental rift, the point where the tectonic plates of North America and Europe join.' He pointed at the ground. 'The country was created by magma seeping out between the joining of the two plates. The plates continuously shift,' he continued, 'creating a weak point where energy can be easily released.' He paused and scratched his chin. 'Rather like a marriage,' he added. Then he unzipped his fleece and threw it to the ground. 'This results in what is known as a hot spring.' He whipped off his micro shorts and underpants, then ran and jumped into the steaming pool beside us. 'Come on,' he said, before dunking his head under the water.

I glanced sideways at Dominic.

'I'm game,' Dominic said, pulling off his jumper. I stood silent and watched. His chest was broad, tanned and toned and his stomach flat and taut.

He looked at me and smiled. 'You coming?' he said, un-zipping his jeans.

I quickly turned the other way, placing my hands over my eyes. 'No, I think I'll sit this one out.'

Bore laughed. 'You have to be at peace with your body to be at peace with your soul.'

'My body is at peace. Thank you very much. It's just nice and warm in its fleece right now.'

I heard a splash.

'You can look, I'm in now,' Dominic said.

I glanced down at him, leaning against the side of the spring, steam rising off his chest.

Bore turned to me, brow furrowed. 'My secretary in-formed you I conduct all my meetings here, didn't she?'

I shook my head.

'It opens my mind,' he said, leaning back and closing his eyes.

'Great,' I said. 'I'll just perch on the edge and ask you questions from here.'

Bore opened his eyes again. 'Iceland is an equal coun-try. To engage in an equal debate, we must all be equal. Be-sides,' he added, 'to understand us, you must live like us.' Then he dunked his head back into the water.

Dominic was grinning. 'If it makes you feel any better, Bore and I will turn the other way when you get in.' Dom-inic flipped himself over. 'There you go,' he said. 'Can't see anything.'

Bore did the same, after reminding me that it was my soul he was keen to discover, not my body.

'OK,' I said. 'So long as you promise no peeking, Dom-inic.'

He laughed. 'Of course not. I'm a gentleman.'

I quickly removed my shoes, socks and both of my fleeces. Then my T-shirt.

'You done yet?' Dominic asked.

'No,' I said, quickly covering myself in case he turned around. Then I wriggled out of my jeans. I wrapped a fleece around my body and quickly whipped off my bra and knickers. Then. as quick as I could. I dropped the fleece and slid into the water.

'I'm in,' I said, instantly feeling the warmth spread around me.

Dominic flipped over and smiled. 'Welcome,' he said, moving towards me.

It was cloudy but I could see the outline of his body through the water. I couldn't help but glance down.

Dominic caught me looking and grinned.

Bore turned to face us. 'Now,' he said, leaning back against the side. 'Make yourself comfortable and look up at the sky. When a question for me comes, don't filter it, just let it out.' His body was rising up and his penis began bobbing up on the surface. I screwed up my face and Dominic laughed.

Dominic leaned over and whispered in my ear, 'Is there an eel in the water or is he just pleased to see us?'

Bore looked up and frowned. 'Let's just get the silly toilet humour out of the way first. Any more comments to mask your deep-rooted body insecurities and suppressed sexuality?'

Dominic leaned back and dipped his hair in the water. 'You said no filtering.'

'I did indeed.'

Dominic sat up and ran a hand through his wet hair. I wondered if he was deliberately acting out an aftershave advert. 'So my question to you, Bore,' Dominic said, 'is, with all the goodwill in the world, how do we ignore the fact we're naked in a spring?'

I giggled.

'You don't ignore it,' Bore said. 'You face it. Remove the barriers to intimacy to allow free-flowing communication. By being naked, I am making myself vulnerable to you and to nature.'

I lay back and stared into the sky, letting my thoughts flow around my head. I glanced up to see Dominic watching me. He quickly looked away.

I sat up to ask Bore a question. 'So Icelandic people,' I said, 'are the happiest in the world?'

'Well, as far as it is reported,' Bore replied.

'Yet they have the highest divorce rate?' I asked.

'Yes,' said Bore.

I stared at him for a moment and waited for an explanation.

'Why?' I asked, when it was apparent one wasn't coming.

Bore took a deep breath. 'We are yet to discover a universal measure for happiness, so we must rely on self-reported data,' he began. 'That being said, Iceland does have the highest reported levels of happiness. The divorce rate is high. Yet there is no proven link between the two. It's not cause or effect. And if it was, does happiness cause divorce? Or does divorce cause happiness?'

'Well,' I said, 'in my experience, divorce certainly doesn't cause happiness.'

Bore raised a finger. 'Marriage promises happiness. Have you considered, Ellie, that it is only unhappy people who pursue happiness? And therefore in turn, unhappy people get married, because they think it will make them happy?

And when it doesn't they get divorced and blame their un-happiness on a failed marriage?'

I looked down into the spring, while my mind processed what he had said. Then I turned to Dominic.

He was looking down thoughtfully too. Then he looked up and cleared his throat.

'So you're saying,' he said, 'that just as happiness and divorce are not causal, neither is happiness and marriage.'

'Precisely,' Bore said, sinking his shoulders into the water.

I did the same and then tipped my head back. I looked back up at the sky and watched a wispy cloud float past.

'It's beautiful here,' I said.

Bore smiled. 'I'm glad you've finally noticed.'

Dominic looked me up and down in the water. 'Quite spectacular,' he said.

Bore glanced at Dominic and then at me and smiled.

'The Icelandic people,' he continued, 'believe in freedom and independence. We place a high degree of importance on self-sufficiency. This lack of dependence enables us to leave a marriage we no longer want to be in.'

I shook my head from side to side. 'Women too?' I asked.

Dominic looked to Bore.

Bore lay back, his manhood bobbing to the surface again. 'We also place a high degree of importance on gender equal-ity. If you look at the countries with the lowest divorce rate, you'll find the women don't have the rights or the freedom to divorce. Or they would be socially and economically ex-cluded if they did.'

Dominic dunked his head under the water, then popped back up again. 'But having the freedom and the means to divorce is an enabler, not a cause. A lower divorce rate in other societies does not indicate a greater success at marriage, does it?'

Bore nodded. 'So what does?' he asked us.

'How would I know? I'm not married,' Dominic said, before submerging himself in the water again.

Bore looked at me.

I thought for a moment. 'I suppose success is measured by goals. It depends what a couple hopes to achieve from a marriage. If they achieved what they wanted then it is a success.'

Bore sunk back down into the water. 'That's an interesting perspective,' he said.

'What's your perspective?' Dominic asked him.

Bore looked up to the sky and tapped his hand on the side of the spring. 'Marriage is no more than a collection of moments in time. The past is sentiment and the future is fantasy.'

I looked blankly at him. 'So you don't agree with marriage?'

He shook his head. 'I have no opinion either way. If marriage can't make you happy then it can't make you sad. So what is there to lose or gain?'

Dominic stared at him. 'There's a lot to lose,' he said.

Bore glanced round at him.

Dominic splashed steamy water over his shoulders. I found myself gazing at his collarbones.

'Marriage forces us to live by a set of rules,' Dominic said.

Bore smiled. 'We all live by our own moral and social codes, either way,' he said. 'The majority of married people just lie, or split up, if their true desires conflict with their marriage vows.'

I went to stand up in protest, momentarily forgetting I was naked. Dominic raised his eyebrows before I quickly sank down into the water again.

'I disagree,' I said, my conviction disarmed by the grin on Dominic's face.

'Go on,' Bore said, arching his back and rolling his shoulders.

'I stand by my vows,' I said. 'Even through the bad times.'

Dominic's brow furrowed.

'But that's your moral code,' Bore said. 'Not one that marriage enforced on you.'

'Why would I get married if I didn't believe in the vows?'

'Why indeed?' Bore said. 'A very interesting question. But it seems that many people do.'

'It's simple,' said Dominic. 'People get married because they believe in the vows at that precise moment. They don't understand that circumstances may change and in time they might feel differently.'

I turned to him. 'I disagree.'

Dominic glared at me, his nostrils were flaring. 'How can you be so sure, Ellie? What if something happens and your whole life and future changes? How could you possibly predict how you might react?'

I looked to Bore, who raised his eyebrows. 'With the best will in the world, humans are fallible,' he said.

I lay back in the water and, despite the heavy weight in my core, I felt myself floating.

We all floated together in silence until suddenly Bore jumped up and pulled himself out of the spring to get dressed. Then he glanced down at the mound in his shorts. 'Apologies,' he said. 'These kinds of debates get me quite excited.'

I grimaced and Dominic looked the other way.

Bore smiled at Dominic. 'You have nothing to be intimidated by, my friend. You're mightily endowed yourself.'

Dominic glanced at me and then back at Bore.

'I must go now,' Bore said, pulling some towels out of his rucksack. He wrapped a tiny one around himself and then threw another two on the side of the spring.

'One last question,' I said, raising my arm out of the water, 'before you go.'

He nodded. 'Of course.'

'How can I help people who want to stay married?'

He looked at me and then over at the other springs bubbling up across the valley.

'Remind them to enjoy their time together,' he said, 'whichever moral code they live by, because as I said, love is nothing but a collection of moments in time.'

I watched him walk away, micro towel now replacing micro shorts and I wondered what I was expected to do with this information.

Dominic moved next to me and squeezed my shoulder. 'You can't save the world, Ellie,' he said.

I quickly backed away to the other side of the spring. 'I know,' I said. 'I can't.'

Chapter 21

That evening I was feeling contemplative and fancied staying in my hotel room to process the day's learnings. Also, I'd promised Matthew a Skype call, and I had an inbox rammed with emails from Mandi that I had yet to address. However, just as I snuggled into bed with my laptop, mini-bar wine and a giant bag of crisps, there was a hammering on my door. It was Dominic.

'Open up,' he said. 'We're going out.'

I tried to ignore him, hoping he'd assume I was asleep, but after his repeated threats to force the door open if I continued to pass up on a night exploring Reykjavik in favour of 'moping' in my room, it became apparent he wasn't going to give up. I dragged myself out of bed and opened the door, wearing one of Nick's old T-shirts.

Dominic looked me up and down.

He frowned and then smiled. 'I've booked us a table at The Gallery,' he said, pushing past me. 'You've got five minutes.' He flipped up the lid of my suitcase, rummaged for a bit, then pulled out a red dress.

'Wear this,' he said, throwing it at me. I stood there, silent. Then he checked his watch and stared at me. 'Would you like me to pick your underwear for you too?'

I handed the dress back to him. 'I've told you, I'm not going out.'

Dominic shook his head. 'You can't stay in. We're only here for one night. It's the best fine-dining restaurant in Iceland. Besides,' he added with a smile, 'we owe it to our clients. We need to find answers, remember?'

I rolled my eyes. 'I'm not sure we're going to find the answers in a restaurant.'

He handed back the dress. 'We came here for an Icelandic perspective on love and that's what we're going to get. So hurry up. Meet me downstairs in five.'

When I walked into the foyer, Dominic's eyes widened.

'That's more like it,' he said, jumping up and taking my hand. 'You look nearly as good dressed as you do naked,' he added with a smile.

I pulled my hand away. 'Firstly,' I said, 'you're my colleague, so you shouldn't notice how I look and, secondly, you haven't seen me naked.'

He smirked. 'Didn't anyone tell you water is transparent?'

I rolled my eyes. 'It was murky.'

'Not that murky,' he said. 'And don't pretend you weren't checking me out either. I saw you.'

'I wasn't checking you out.'

He laughed. 'You so were.' Then he grabbed my hand again. 'Come on,' he said, 'let's eat.'

* * *

According to the digital thermometer behind the hotel desk it was minus thirteen degrees outside, and although I felt my fingertips numb as we walked through the streets, I noticed the chill inside was beginning to thaw. Dominic kept trying to take my hand, and although it was something I would routinely do with Matthew, with Dominic I knew it was wrong.

After dinner, we sat outside a bar with blankets on our laps and the infrared heaters blazing down on us.

Dominic downed his shot straight away and wiped his mouth. 'Do you think it's wrong for a married person to be attracted to someone else?' he asked.

I went to nod. The idea of Nick being attracted to another woman had always filled me with fear. I paused before I replied.

'I'm not sure,' I said. Then I looked up at the sky. The stars twinkled, almost as if to say, *We have the answers but we're not telling you.*

Dominic looked up at the sky too. 'Does it make me a bad person for desperately desiring a married woman?'

I laughed. '"Desperately desiring"? Are we in a Barbara Cartland novel all of a sudden?'

He shuffled in his seat. 'Is it so wrong?' he asked.

I nodded. 'I suppose it depends how people act on their desires.' I took a tentative sip from the shot glass in front of me and grimaced. 'We are supposed to be a civilised species. We have rules in place.'

'And if those rules weren't there?'

I laughed. 'If we acted purely on impulse? Men would be mounting any girl they fancied on the way to work. We'd never get anything done.'

Dominic looked at me. 'You always say men, as though we are the only ones with desires. What about you?'

I laughed. 'What about me? I don't want to mount anyone on the way to work.'

He leaned forward and took the shot glass from me, his hand brushing mine as he did. 'You don't stop being a sexual person just because you're married, Ellie.'

His gaze seemed to intensify in the infrared light. I felt his fingers curl around mine and he leaned in closer, his lips parting.

'Ellie! Is that you?'

I recognised his voice immediately and jumped up out of my seat.

'Matthew?' I said, squinting across the street.

He ran towards me with open arms. 'I'm here!' he said. 'I'm in Iceland. I'm here!'

He flung his arms around me and twirled me around.

'I'm here,' he said again, dropping me to the ground and staring at Dominic. Then he looked back at me and then at Dominic again.

'If I didn't know you better, Eleanor Rigby,' Matthew said, one eyebrow raised, 'I'd have thought I was interrupting something.' Then he let out an exaggerated laugh.

Dominic stepped forward. 'I'm Dominic,' he said, stretching his hand out to Matthew, 'Ellie's colleague.'

'That's reassuring,' Matthew said, looking him up and down. 'For a moment, I thought Ellie had forgotten she was married and had taken an Icelandic lover with a bizarre penchant for cable knit.' He stepped forward with his hand out. 'I'm Matthew, Ellie's best friend,' he said.

They shook hands.

'That's equally reassuring,' Dominic said. 'For a moment, I thought Ellie had a gay stalker who dressed like Kate Moss.'

Matthew glanced down at his fur gilet and opened it as though he were selling wares. 'This,' Matthew explained, 'is Helmut Lang. A collection inspired by primal man.'

Dominic laughed. 'I didn't know cavemen wore skinny jeans.'

Matthew scowled and mumbled something about cable knit and Dale Winton.

'OK, boys,' I interrupted. 'Let's not forget why we are here.'

Matthew looked at me with narrowed eyes. 'Yes, why are we here, Ellie?'

I raised my eyebrows. 'I know why I'm here. To help my clients find lasting love. Why are *you* here?'

Matthew shifted his weight. 'Because my wife's left me and her wanky boss has taken her and my kids to Center Parcs for the weekend to celebrate.'

'Center Parcs?' I asked.

Dominic's expression softened. 'Shit, mate. That's bad.'

Matthew eyed our empty shot glasses. 'You've been drinking Brennivín without me?' he asked, shoulders slumping. Then he put on his puppy dog eyes. 'Can we get some more? Please, Ellie, please,' he said. 'I need to get wasted.'

Dominic looked at me and shrugged his shoulders.

I sighed. 'Oh OK then,' I said, putting my arm around Matthew and realising this night was about to take an interesting turn.

'Bloody Center Parcs. Can you believe it?' Matthew slurred, leaning against the chrome pillar of the student nightclub we had stumbled into. 'Not Barbados or the Maldives, but instead my wife would rather bob up and down in a giant pool with a wave machine than save our marriage. And to take my kids too. The bloody cheek of it.'

Dominic patted Matthew on the back, with an expression that suggested he understood his pain.

Matthew hung his head. 'I keep imagining his lardy belly rubbing up against her.' He shook his head. 'I can't shake the image.' He shook his head again. 'Nope, still there.'

Dominic leaned forward and topped up Matthew's shot glass. 'That's tough, mate.'

Matthew downed it and turned to Dominic. 'I mean, it's not as if she's run off with someone like you.' He punched Dominic in the stomach. Dominic didn't flinch. 'You know, all chiselled and gladiator like. I could sort of understand it.'

Dominic laughed.

'But,' Matthew said, reaching for the Brennivín bottle, 'instead she'd rather be with a hairy arse called Nigel. It makes me want to heave.' Matthew tipped up his glass and waited until a tiny drop weaved its way down into his mouth.

'I'll get another round,' Dominic said, patting him on the back again.

I shuffled up next to Matthew and watched Dominic walk towards the bar. Matthew turned to me. 'So what's going on, Ellie?'

I frowned. 'What do you mean?'

He narrowed his eyes. 'You know exactly what I mean.' He pointed towards Dominic, who was now at the bar talking to a busty blonde who had just approached him.

I sighed. 'Nothing is going on.'

Matthew rolled his eyes. 'Nothing you're going to admit to yourself, it seems. By the way, how is Nick?'

The blonde said something to Dominic and giggled. 'Nick?' I asked.

Matthew let out a deep sigh. 'Your husband?'

I rolled my eyes. 'He's fine,' I said. 'Busy with work.'

Matthew stared at me for a moment, then shook his head slowly.

I looked down, then back up at him. I hadn't noticed how deep the lines in his face had become. 'What about you?' I said. 'I'm worried about you, you know.'

Matthew laughed. 'I'm worried about me too,' he said.

I reached across and squeezed his hand. 'So what's happened? I thought the reconciliation was going well.'

'It was,' he said.

'What went wrong?'

He looked down. 'I don't want to talk about it.'

I frowned. 'You said you didn't want to talk about it on the phone. We're not on the phone any more.'

'You're right, Ellie, a tacky hovel of a nightclub is the perfect setting to discuss my issues with impotence.'

I stood upright. 'What?'

He raised his hand. 'My name is Matthew and I'm impotent.'

I shook my head. 'Since when?'

'Since I haven't been able to have sex with my wife.'

'Just her?'

Matthew sighed. 'Yeah, her, along with fifteen hookers, four exes and a Shetland pony.' He stared at me. 'Of course just my wife, Ellie. I'm not some kind of soulless manwhore.'

I took a breath. 'She can't really blame you. It's pretty obvious what the cause is.'

Matthew nodded. 'I know. Every time we tried, you know, all I could think about was sweaty Nigel pumping away at her.'

I squeezed his hand tighter. 'She should understand that surely?'

He shrugged his shoulders. 'Nope. She just cried and said that I didn't find her sexy any more.'

I tutted. 'That's not really fair, is it?'

He shrugged his shoulders again. 'Doesn't matter if it's fair or not. It is what it is. She shagged her boss, so I can't shag her any more even though I want to, so she's now shagging her boss again because I can't shag her because she shagged her boss. There's some bloody irony for you there.'

Dominic laid a tray of drinks down on the table next to us. 'If a double Jägerbomb doesn't wipe that smarmy cunt from your mind, then I don't know what will, mate,' he said, handing Matthew a glass.

Matthew downed his straight away, then rubbed his temples. 'Must pace myself,' he mumbled, 'so I can chaperone you two.' Then he fell backwards and passed out on a nearby sofa.

Chapter 22

The next morning, I poked my head out from the duvet and the icy air sent me straight back under again. I reached an arm out to grab my phone and felt the duvet move on the other side of the bed. I peered over my shoulder and saw a shock of dark brown hair on the pillow next to me. My stomach flipped and I hid back under the duvet, scenes from a steamy spring flashing through my mind.

Just as I was trying to wipe the images from my mind, my phone began to vibrate in my hand. It was Nick. Before I could decide otherwise, I'd answered.

'Hi,' I whispered.

'Hi, gorgeous,' Nick said. 'How are you?'

'All good, thanks,' I said. 'You?'

Nick laughed. 'I'm fine,' he said and then paused. 'Apart from the fact my errant wife hasn't been returning my calls.' He paused again. 'Not to mention the slurred voicemail I received last night from her best friend Matthew telling me

I needed to come to Iceland. Something about an emergent tree? Or an emergency, I couldn't quite decipher.'

I felt the mattress bounce so I glanced over my shoulder.

'Ellie? Are you there?' Nick asked.

I heard a muffled yawn.

'Yes, I'm here.'

'Are you going to tell me what the hell is going on?'

'Nothing,' I said, an image of Dominic's glistening chest returning to my mind. 'I'm in bed. Can I call you later?'

Nick huffed. 'Sure, but Jenna and I are heading out to a conference in Washington later.'

I reached out and put my phone back on the side, before catching a glimpse of a fur gilet hanging over a chair in the corner of the room. Instantly, my panic lifted. It was only Matthew.

I rolled over and slowly peeled the duvet off him.

He was curled in the foetal position, and wearing two layers of thermals. The vivid images of Dominic and I in the spring began to fade as my consciousness sharpened and I began to accurately recall the previous night's events.

I leaned forward and prodded Matthew. 'Wake up,' I said.

Matthew rubbed his eyes, and then smiled. 'You're here,' he said, stretching his arms above his head.

'I am.'

'Phew,' he said, pulling himself up against the headboard. 'I had a dream that my chaperoning skills had been compromised by Jägerbombs.'

I laughed. 'You were useless before the Jägerbombs. Lucky, I'm not as morally repugnant as you first thought.' Then I jumped out of bed. My head throbbed with the sudden movement. I shook it, hoping to clear my conscience too. I may not have physically shared a bed with Dominic, but that night, in my dreams, I'd done just about everything else.

At breakfast, even though Matthew was positioned between us, I could barely make eye contact with Dominic. When he spoke, I had intense flashbacks of him kissing my neck in my dream, which if I didn't quickly redirect my focus to Matthew's fur gilet, would progress to him kissing the rest of my body.

Feeling my cheeks redden, I poured myself a coffee and focused my attention on Matthew. 'So you're really flying back today?' I asked him, recalling snippets of a Brennivín-blurred conversation from the night before.

He nodded, staring down into his coffee cup.

Dominic turned to him. 'What are you going to do, mate?'

Immediately, I envisaged Nick sitting with us, rolling his eyes and mimicking the term 'mate'.

Matthew sighed. 'I don't know.'

Dominic leaned back in his chair. My thoughts continued to wander. I hadn't called Nick back yet. However, I reasoned he was probably on a plane with Jenna now anyway. In business class no doubt, drinking gin and tonics while intelligently debating a feature in the *New York Times*. Dominic lifted his arms up behind his head and I found myself staring at the strip of stomach exposed.

Matthew leaned in and waved his hand in front of my face. 'Ellie, are you with us?'

I glanced up and nodded.

Matthew continued to stare at me, as though demanding further explanation. Eventually, he gave up and turned back to Dominic.

'So, what would you do if you were me?' Matthew asked him.

Dominic leaned back a little further, exposing another inch of stomach.

'You really want to know what I would do?'

Matthew nodded.

Dominic leaned forward, placing his hands on the table. 'I'd knock back some super-strength Viagra, storm into Center Parcs and bang all traces of that smarmy git out of her.' He paused and then sniffed. 'This should never have been allowed to happen in the first place. She's your wife.'

I stared at Dominic open-mouthed.

'I'd lose the furry waistcoat first though,' Dominic added.

Matthew examined his gilet as though looking for clues.

I shook my head at Dominic. 'Seriously? That's your advice?'

Dominic shrugged. 'He didn't ask for my advice. He asked me what I would do.'

I raised my eyebrows. 'OK then. Clearly you're the expert.'

Dominic reached under the table. He reappeared with a stack of napkins and handed them to me. They had scribbles all over them.

'Talking of experts,' Dominic said. 'Here are my notes from last night.'

I frowned. 'What notes?'

'Your interviews,' he said. 'You asked me to take notes.'

I frowned again. 'What interviews?'

He laughed. 'Don't you remember? Before you let us go home, you insisted on interviewing all the couples in the club to ask them about their views on marriage and lasting love. You kept saying, "Dominic, are you getting all this? Dominic, write it down."' He chuckled. 'You were very focused.'

'What was I doing?' Matthew chipped in.

'Sleeping. On the sofa,' Dominic said. 'You passed out after the first Jägerbomb.'

Matthew mumbled a suggestion that his drink must have been spiked.

Dominic laughed loudly. 'By who? A sexual predator with a thing for rabbit fur?'

I flicked through the napkins and read what Dominic had written. There was impressive clarity considering his likely blood alcohol levels and the low lighting in the bar. He'd even collated the results and put them into a pie chart on the final napkin. Directly below an Icelandic name and a phone number.

I held up the napkin to Dominic and pointed at the number. 'I assume this is the blonde from the bar?' I asked.

He leaned forward to look and then laughed. 'Could be,' he said, looking up at me and grinning. 'You're not jealous, are you?'

I tutted. 'Of course not,' I said, screwing the napkin into a ball. 'I just don't think she's your type, that's all.'

Matthew glared at me.

'What?' I said. 'I just think he could do better.'

Matthew shook his head. 'My work here is done,' he said. He stood up and shook Dominic's hand. 'Nice to meet you,' he said, before turning to me. 'Eleanor Rigby,' he said, throwing his arms around my neck. 'A pleasure as always.'

When he pulled away, he looked me in the eye as though he were about to say something profound, but instead he just patted my back and then left, snakeskin suitcase trundling behind him.

It wasn't until after a protracted debate with the hotel manager regarding the minibar bill that Dominic and I were free to head off to the airport. Our flight to Tokyo was in two hours and Professor Takahashi's secretary had already called us several times to ensure I was on schedule. She seemed greatly offended that we hadn't agreed to use the personalised Takahashi Diary App, with inbuilt geolocator and algorithms, to predict our likelihood of punctuality.

In the taxi, Dominic rubbed his eyes and yawned.

'So this guy is a robot designer?' he asked.

I flicked through the file on my lap and reread the entry Mandi had written about Professor Takahashi's research.

'He's a human behaviourist who is building technology to enhance romantic relationships,' I said and then put the file down.

Dominic rubbed his eyes again. 'What does that mean? He makes high-tech dildos?'

I glared at him. 'Why do you have to be so crude? Not everything is about sex, you know.'

Dominic laughed. 'Yes, it is.'

I flipped open the file again and reread the entry. 'Look,' I said pointing at the page. 'It says here, the majority of his research is into the non-verbal cues that are vital to human communication.'

Dominic snorted. 'Well,' he said, suddenly waving his phone at me, 'according to Wikipedia, Professor Takahashi has developed an advanced virtual intercourse experience.'

I shook my head. 'It means verbal intercourse, obviously.'

Dominic laughed again. 'Really? What's with the naked girl in the picture then? And the guy with electrodes on his cock?'

I snatched the phone off him and scrolled through the images. Next to the video image of a spreadeagled woman, there was a man wearing a headset, with electrodes on his privates and a smile on his face. I realised that this must have been the researcher that Debbie from Hooters had been referring to.

I handed the phone back to Dominic and shook my head.

'What?' he asked. 'How can you not think this is totally awesome? I seriously can't wait to meet this guy.'

I stared at him, wondering for a moment what precisely it was that the Y chromosome was meant to offer the population.

'How can I not think this is awesome?' I said. 'This man is trying to cleave apart real human relationships, substituting people with avatars. Do you have any understanding of what this means?'

Dominic slapped his hand to his forehead. 'The apocalypse is here. Robots rule the world, while humans deteriorate into pasty, shrivelled beings, living underground in isolated pods and communicating via screens.' He turned to me and grabbed my hand. 'We have to stop this, Ellie.' He took a deep breath. 'Before it's too late.'

I brushed him off. 'You're such a twat.'

He grinned. 'Oh, come on, Ellie. How many times do you need to be told: you can't control the world. Change is going to happen with or without you. Don't be so fearful. Just go with it.'

I looked out the taxi window at the Icelandic mountains fading into the distance and wondered if it was really possible for technology to meaningfully enhance romantic relationships. If synthetic oxytocin could help us stay in love, and we could outsource our partner's fantasies to technology, then maybe marriage would prevail after all?

I glanced up to see a puffin soaring through the sky, its

bright orange feet stretched out and its beak jutting forwards and I smiled. We still had a long way to go to out-
class nature.

Dominic and I didn't sit together during the flight. At check-
in, I was informed that someone had upgraded me to business class. They couldn't disclose the lady's name, although
they were happy to divulge that she had a double-barrel
surname and a haughty attitude. Dominic tried to upgrade
himself but they refused, stating that my upgrade was con-
tingent on him staying in economy.

Dominic stropped off down the aisle with his Kindle
and I sat down to summarise the research findings so far.

Initially I read through all my notes, then I made a few
notes on my notes and wrote the heading 'Summary'. After
I'd stared at a blank page for twenty minutes, I decided to
refresh my thoughts with a glass of champagne. Three mini
bottles later, after I'd befriended all the passengers in my
vicinity and solicited their opinions on lasting love, I fell
asleep watching a movie about a mountain dog on a skate-
board.

At baggage retrieval, Dominic gazed up at the vast suspended ceiling.

'This airport is amazing,' he said.

I scowled at the empty conveyor. 'I wish it was amazing enough to deliver me my suitcase,' I said, arms folded.

Dominic glanced down and shrugged his shoulders. 'It's
been twenty minutes since we last saw a suitcase. Maybe
we should just leave your details and head off.'

I sighed and then checked the time on my phone. There
were three text messages from Professor Takahashi's sec-

retary, asking us to confirm our whereabouts and also a missed call from Victoria.

'OK then,' I said, shoving my phone into my pocket. 'I'll guess Japan will have to learn to love my skanky old fleece.'

Dominic laughed. 'It's Nick I feel sorry for, marrying a hottie and ending up with a hiker.'

I slapped him on the arm, then sent him off to register my lost suitcase with the relevant personnel.

While he was gone, I called Victoria to quiz her about the upgrade.

'Darling!' she said. 'So lovely of you to finally call me back.'

'Sorry,' I said. 'I've just been so busy with this research.'

'I know,' she said. 'Nick told me you were in Iceland, of all places.'

'Nick?' I asked.

'Yes,' she said. 'I spoke to him last night.'

'Last night?'

'Are you going to repeat everything I say?'

'Only if it doesn't make any sense. Why are you speaking to Nick? And why did you upgrade my flight?'

She let out a sharp sigh. 'I've been speaking to Nick because you weren't answering my calls. Which is beyond rude, given the predicament you've left me in. As for the upgrade, I thought you might need some time away from your travelling companion to reflect.'

'What are you on about?' I shook my head. 'And what predicament have I left you in?'

She let out a sharp sigh. 'Renting out your house to that trollop.'

'Who?' I asked, briefly distracted by the sight of Dominic waving his arms around at a staff member.

'Can't remember her name: short, big boobs.'

'Kerry?' I asked, one eye on the staff member, who was now nodding at Dominic.

'Yes. Her.' She let out another sigh. 'It appears Mike has fallen for her pathetic "my husband died I'm lost and all alone" bullshit act.'

'It's not an act. Her husband did die.'

'Yes, well, she can't have been too devastated.' Victoria then put on a little girl voice. '"I'm all sad and grieving but still, I have big breasts and I like to fuck."'

'No. She wouldn't do that.'

Victoria swallowed, then cleared her throat. 'She came around asking to borrow a screwdriver. Such a cliché.' She huffed. 'Anyway, now Mike's under the impression he's some sort of DIY superhero, saving a damsel from the distress of unaligned shelves. Every night he's over there with his spirit level, claiming he's building a kennel for the hound or a tree house for her son, but I'm not an idiot.' She paused. 'You have no choice but to evict her.'

I rolled my eyes. 'Maybe you should have a chat with Mike first,' I said, 'and find out what's really going on?'

She laughed. 'Well, maybe you should have a chat with Nick, find out what's really going on there,' she said, 'unless you're planning on leaving him for this guy, Donald.'

'Dominic,' I said. 'And no, I'm not leaving Nick for him. He's my colleague and we're conducting research.'

I noticed Dominic walking back towards me.

'Oh.' Victoria sniffed. 'I was starting to think you and Nick must be on a break. Research on what?'

'What makes love last.'

'Ah,' she said. 'Now it all makes sense. You're both sleep-

ing with other people to test the concept of an open marriage, I see.'

'I'm not sleeping with Dominic.'

Dominic, who was now beside me, raised his eyebrows.

Then my stomach tightened. 'What makes you think Nick
is sleeping with someone else?'

Dominic leaned in closer.

'Oh, nothing,' she said. 'I must be mistaken.'

'Who?' I asked. 'Tell me.'

She let out a high-pitched laugh but it tailed off quickly.
'Oh, it's just that girl he works with, the pretty one, Jenna
something? Haven't you seen them both on Facebook? She's
been tagging them together all over Manhattan. And all
over your house in Park Slope too, it would seem. Looks
as though she stayed over last night.' She paused. 'Anyway,
must go. Mike's home.'

I went to speak but before I could form the next question
in my mind, she'd hung up the phone.

I stood motionless while my mind tried to process Victoria's words: 'Jenna'; 'the pretty one'; 'stayed over last night'.
Then I looked down at my phone. My fingers twitched,
previously indifferent, now desperate to dial Nick's number. I wondered what he would he say. It was unlikely he'd
confess infidelity over the phone. Then my thumb hovered
over the Facebook app, envisaging photos of Jenna with her
shiny hair and her perky bottom, undoubtedly dressed in
gym gear while stretching out her glutes.

Adrenaline shot through my veins and my hands began
to tremor. I slid my phone back in my pocket. I didn't need
Facebook. Images were already racing through my mind,
merging together to create my own movie of Nick and
Jenna's romance. Them, chinking wine glasses at some

glamorous client party, running side by side in Central Park, buying fancy cheese at a farmers' market, snuggled up on our sofa watching a documentary. Then arm in arm outside a jeweller's, debating the kindest way to break the news to Nick's neglectful wife. I imagined Jenna's voice to be brimming with cheerleader wholesomeness as she reassured Nick that with her it would be different.

Tears began to well. Dominic put his arm around my shoulder and wiped them from my eyes. I looked up and he pulled me to his chest. The instinct to push away was gone. It felt warm and safe. I leaned into him and he kissed me on the forehead.

'I'm sure it'll all be fine,' he said, brushing a strand of hair from my face. 'He's an idiot to risk losing you.'

He pulled me in for another hug, then cracked a huge smile. 'Even with this skanky old fleece.'

Then he took my hand and led me out of the airport.

Chapter 23

When we arrived at Professor Takahashi's Centre for Behavioural-Technological Advancement, his secretary smiled politely, although her eyes betrayed her deep dissatisfaction at our two-minute-late arrival.

'We are honoured to have you,' she said. 'Fortunately, he is still able to see you now.' She pointed to a digital clock which counted in seconds.

I wasn't sure what I was expecting when we walked into his office—I suppose a small middle-aged man, wearing a suit and glasses, and sitting at a desk. Instead, Dominic and I were greeted by a man almost as tall as Dominic, with broad shoulders and a young, kind face. He was wearing a white T-shirt and light grey trousers.

'Good afternoon,' he said.

I offered my hand to shake but he dismissed it. 'No formalities here,' he said. 'Now please take a seat.'

I glanced around the room for a chair. There weren't any. I turned to Dominic for assistance. He also looked baffled.

The office looked nothing like an office at all. It was stark white with a square hole the size of a large table in the middle. The walls were smothered in digital screens and there was no furniture.

Professor Takahashi sat down at the edge of the hole, dangling his feet in it.

'Come,' he said, 'please sit down.'

I tentatively stepped towards the edge to see that the room was suspended above another floor which had been intricately landscaped and looked to be entirely uninhabited. There were small polished pebbles, beautiful trees with teardrop leaves and tiny twisting branches. In the centre was a water fountain bubbling away like a doll's house Icelandic spring.

Dominic looked up and around. 'Wow,' he said, 'this is one serious office.'

Professor Takahashi nodded. 'For our minds to be inspired,' he said, 'our environments must enrich.'

Professor Takahashi's secretary came in and handed us each a glass of green tea. She left as efficiently as she had arrived.

'So where do you keep all your stuff?' Dominic asked.

Professor Takahashi took a sip and then picked up his phone. 'This,' he said holding it aloft, 'is my calculator, my filing cabinet, my pen, my brain, my business partner, my confidant, my personal shopper, my friend, and,' he said, tapping on the screen, 'my lover.'

Dominic sniggered.

Professor Takahashi pointed to the screens on the walls around us. 'Technology,' he said, 'can be all things to all men.'

I put my tea down. Some sloshed over the side and onto the white floor. 'I disagree,' I said.

He turned to me. 'Of course you do. Because your brain is limited.'

Dominic scowled at him. 'Ellie is highly intelligent actually.'

Professor Takahashi smirked. 'And you would say that because your brain is limited too.' He looked around and then down at the garden. 'Our brains are all limited. We cannot redesign them. However, technology, we can redesign over and over until it is capable of delivering what we want.'

I put my hand up. Professor Takahashi waved dismissively. 'No formalities,' he said.

'OK,' I said. 'I still don't agree. How can a limited brain build technology that is superior to it? That doesn't make sense.'

He smirked again. 'We cannot run faster than a Ferrari. The designer is always the master,' he said.

I took a breath, still unconvinced. 'So how does your research equate to love? Do you really believe that love can be technologically enhanced?'

Professor Takahashi nodded. 'Of course.'

Dominic swung his legs back and forth over the ledge. 'Or do you mean sex can be enhanced?'

'No,' Professor Takahashi said, tapping on his phone again. 'I mean love.' He pointed to a screen on the wall adjacent to us, then to a row of sci-fi like headphones that were hanging next to it.

'Put them on,' he said.

Dominic grabbed me a set of headphones along with his, and helped me pull down the visor over my eyes. A 3D image of Professor Takahashi's head suddenly appeared in front of us, and began explaining his most recent experiment. The video demonstrated that he and his team had

monitored a thousand couples in love, measuring neurochemical, behavioural and physiological changes, over a
five-year period. For the duration, half the groups received
Professor Takahashi's technological interventions and the
other half received nothing. The results shot onto the screen
in 3D glory. The group with the interventions had only a
five per cent divorce rate five years later. The placebo group
had a thirty per cent divorce rate.

I pulled off the headgear and turned to Professor Takahashi, desperately trying to find fault with his research, to
prove that there was more to love than its component parts,
but as I let all the information sink in, I knew I would strug-
gle to dispute the evidence.

I nodded my head. 'This is groundbreaking stuff,' I said.

Then I turned to Dominic, who was removing his head-
gear.

'Did you see that?' I asked him. 'A five per cent divorce
rate?'

Dominic ruffled his hair and smirked. 'I was looking for
the naked woman.'

I rolled my eyes and then quickly turned back to Professor Takahashi. My heart was racing. 'Tell me about the
interventions. How do they work? Can I do them? Am I
qualified?'

Professor Takahashi tapped on his phone and then looked
up at me. 'They are still in development.'

'But what are they? Can you explain them? How does
the technology work? Can we license it?'

He took in a slow deep breath. 'Before you ask a question,
you must understand why you want the answers.'

'I do understand,' I said.

He clasped his hands together. 'You already have love.'

I frowned. 'Yes, but I want the answers for my clients. That's why I'm here.' I glanced at Dominic, then back at Professor Takahashi. 'How do you know I have love?'

He smiled and held his arms open. 'The headsets measure everything. The screen was watching you closer than you were watching it.'

Dominic stopped swinging his legs.

Professor Takahashi continued. 'Digital communication is a two-way process. The software learns about you as you use it. It's intuitive.'

I shot a sideways glance at the screen. 'So what did it learn from me?'

Professor Takahashi looked at Dominic and then at me. He tapped on his phone and the screen lit up.

'Measurements were taken from your eyes, skin, heart, sweat glands and brain waves. Then a series of algorithms can use this information to provide an early warning system for waning love. The technology can then prompt the subject to undertake a specific activity which will trigger vital neurochemicals and physiological processes to maintain the relationship, such as sustained physical contact, therapeutic intervention or even something as simple as a date night.'

He tapped on his phone again and then smiled. 'The early warning system kicks in at around a number five on the scale.'

I stared at the screen.

Professor Takahashi turned to me. 'You are very safely at a number nine.'

He pointed to Dominic. 'Your reading was virtually identical, although you were closer to a ten.'

Dominic glanced at me and his eyes darted down to the water fountain.

Professor Takahashi continued. 'These are common readings for the early stages of love.'

I sat back. 'Is ten years early stages?'

Professor Takahashi's eyes dropped down. Suddenly, he seemed as fascinated by the water fountain as Dominic was. Then he looked up. 'Of course, if these measures are taken in the absence of your partner then you would be in the high-risk category. Naturally, for the subjects of Takahashi technology, the early warning systems would have been triggered in advance, as a preventative measure. Therefore in our study such a situation would have never occurred.'

I sipped some more tea, trying again to find fault with his reasoning. 'But these measures, they can't be that accurate. Love is more than just a bit of sweat and a few fast heartbeats.'

Professor Takahashi looked me in the eye. 'The software can easily differentiate between sexual attraction and other emotions and drives.' He looked back at me and Dominic, then tapped on his phone. 'If we further refine the findings to sexual attraction, here are your results.'

The number ten and a graph appeared on the screen. Professor Takahashi gestured to me. 'Your sexual markers were sky-high, which indicate you have had intense sexual thoughts about a person you are with within the last twenty-four hours.'

My eyes widened. 'But you can't tell who that person is?'

He nodded. 'We can tell that it is a person in this room.' He raised his eyebrows. 'And I doubt it's me.'

Dominic looked at me, barely able to contain his smile.

Professor Takahashi tapped his phone again. 'And you,' he said turning to Dominic, 'were having intense sexual thoughts at the time the measurements were taken.'

Dominic's neck vein twitched and he looked back down at the water fountain.

I took another sip of tea.

'So what intervention would be appropriate for the high risk category?' I asked, quietly between sips.

Professor Takahashi pursed his lips. 'It depends what anomalies the algorithms detected.'

I coughed to clear my throat, which seemed to be growing dryer by the second. 'Um, how about one part of the couple having intense sexual thoughts about another person?'

Professor Takahashi scratched his nose. 'If the urges have been untempered by our early warning system, then our studies have shown that suppression of such desires can lead to resentment and anger in the relationship. To prevent this, in extreme cases, we might look at controlled consent.'

'Controlled?' Dominic asked.

Professor Takahashi nodded. 'The potential damage of extra-marital sex can be limited if it is consensual and conducted in a controlled environment.' Then he tapped on his phone again. 'We have developed a "safe sex" technology that allows users the opportunity to live out their sexual fantasies within the agreed boundaries of marriage.'

Dominic leaned in closer.

Professor Takahashi continued. 'Users can select their preferred sexual activity and preferred sexual partner. The experience is virtual yet the technology is so advanced that to the brain it is real. To preserve a primary bond while indulging our fantasies, the headgear emits synthesised pheromones identical to those of our partner, so our brain is confused into thinking the sexual act is with them and our bond is enhanced. Many users will model their sex-partner avatar on their life partner.'

Professor Takahashi jumped up. 'Follow me,' he said.

He led us through a set of double doors and into a corridor. He pointed to the doors as we passed. 'Chambers One and Two are in use,' he said. 'Chambers Three and Four are vacant.' Then he turned to us. 'Would you like to try?'

Dominic glanced at me as if to glean permission and then back at Professor Takahashi. 'Sure,' he said, 'why not?'

Professor Takahashi turned to me and raised his eyebrows.

I shook my head. 'No thanks.'

He narrowed his eyes as though I'd just rejected his first-born.

'At least come and see how it works,' Professor Takahashi said, gesturing for me to follow him and Dominic into the room of Chamber Three.

Once inside, Professor Takahashi pulled open the door to the chamber. It looked like a high-tech tanning booth. He pressed a button and the booth lit up. Then he tapped a password onto the screen and explained how it all worked.

'First,' he said tapping at the screen, 'select your preferred avatar from these images. Then,' he continued, reaching for a strange rubber ensemble, which looked like a well-endowed alien had shed its skin, 'put this on and the head-gear too.'

Dominic's eyes widened.

Professor Takahashi continued. 'If you don't like any of the suggested avatars, then imagine the person you would like in your mind and the headset will interpret it.'

Once the headset was in position, a face closely resembling mine appeared on the screen.

Dominic turned to me and grimaced. 'Sorry,' he said, then he smiled. 'Do you mind?'

'I'd rather you didn't,' I said.

Professor Takahashi looked at me. 'I'm afraid you can't censor fantasies, it's not healthy for the subject.'

'Subject? He's a subject now is he?'

Professor Takahashi continued. 'You can select location—' he tapped on the keyboard '—see here: shower, office, bed. And these,' he said, picking up a tangle of wires, 'are electrodes. They simulate pressure and touch: all the normal sensations you'd experience throughout your body during sexual intercourse.' He pointed to the screen. 'Remove all your clothes and place the electrodes on the bodysuit here, here, here and here. You see?'

Dominic nodded.

Professor Takahashi scratched his head. 'One problem,' he said to Dominic, 'we don't have your partner here to take a pheromone sample.'

Dominic laughed. 'That's really not an issue,' he said.

Professor Takahashi stared at him for a moment and then continued. 'The chamber will know when you're ready to start. You can have as many turns as you want. Just press this button when you're done.'

After Professor Takahashi had left the room, Dominic turned to me and winked.

'Sure you don't want to join me?' he asked.

'No thanks,' I said, 'but knock yourself out.'

Outside in the corridor, I stood with Professor Takahashi and stared at the floor.

'Are you certain you don't want a turn?' he asked.

I shook my head.

'I think it could be highly beneficial for your dilemma.'

I looked up. 'What do you mean "dilemma"?'

'To re-bond with your primary partner.'

I sighed. 'He's in New York. You won't be able to get his pheromones.' *He's too busy depositing them all over his twenty-five-year-old colleague*, I thought, continuing the sentence in my head.

Professor Takahashi looked to the ceiling. 'We have something else we could use. It's a hormone called oxytocin, which is—'

'I know what that is.'

Professor Takahashi continued, seemingly oblivious to my glare. 'If we release it in the booth at the time of climax, your bond will be re-strengthened.'

I thought for a moment, then took a deep breath, realising that perhaps my marriage could do with some strengthening.

'OK then,' I said. I walked into Chamber Four, feeling oddly like I was ending my time on death row.

Afterwards, I flung open the door to the booth, stepped out and then slammed it shut, before marching down the corridor searching for Professor Takahashi. I found him in his office, legs dangling over the side of his ridiculous floating bench. Dominic was sitting next to him.

Professor Takahashi removed the headphones he was wearing and looked up at me.

I glared at him, hands on hips. 'You didn't tell me the avatar could change,' I said, feeling my jugular twitching. 'At the last bloody minute!'

Dominic leaned back, resting on his arms. 'So you had a go, did you? Good for you.'

'No. Not good for me,' I said, temporarily redirecting my glare to Dominic, then back to Professor Takahashi. 'Thanks to that bullshit booth, I got a dose of oxytocin for the wrong bloody person. Again.' My head throbbed. 'How is that supposed to strengthen my primary bond, Professor Takahashi?'

Professor Takahashi jumped to his feet and tapped on his phone. 'This is interesting,' he said, seemingly more focused on digitally documenting my experience than actually helping me. 'In some resistant cases, the unconscious desires can override the conscious. I should have explained that was a risk. My apologies.'

I tutted loudly. 'So what do I do now?'

Professor Takahashi glanced at the digital clock on the screen beside him. 'The effect of the oxytocin will pass,' he said. 'It needs to be topped up regularly to form a lasting bond, so—' he glanced at Dominic and then back at me '—I suggest you return to New York to spend time with your primary partner.'

I sighed. 'Why do you keep saying "primary partner"? Like I have a secondary, or tertiary bonds all over the globe?'

Professor Takahashi raised his eyebrows. 'It was your unconscious that sabotaged your treatment, Ellie, not my booth.'

'Treatment?' My hands were back on my hips. 'For what?'

Professor Takahashi looked me in the eye. 'A marriage in crisis,' he said.

Every muscle in my body tensed. I wanted to leap across the hole in the floor and swipe my foot into Professor Takahashi's face like a character from *The Matrix*. But instead I stood there scowling like a huffy child.

'Come on, Dominic,' I eventually mustered, 'we're going.'

Professor Takahashi nodded at our exit, then glanced back down at his phone.

Outside the centre, Dominic hailed a taxi.

'Come on, grumps,' he said, opening the taxi door for me. 'You need cheering up.'

'I'm not grumpy,' I said, getting in. 'I'm justifiably enraged for being duped by a hyper-sexed tanning booth.'

He climbed in after me, leaned across and dug me in the ribs. 'It's not your time of the month, is it?' He started laughing loudly.

I glared at him until he stopped. 'My primary relationship is in crisis. My husband is most likely shagging his Mensa-grade, knockout colleague, and now, nearly halfway through my research, I still have no bloody clue how to make love last. I think I have a very plausible and non-hormonal reason for my mood change.'

Dominic looked at me for a moment, then smiled again. 'So you admit to being grumpy. A full confession. Excellent. Now we can commence your "treatment".'

He looked out the window and pointed.

'We're in Tokyo,' he said and started waving the expense card around. 'Let's do what the Japanese do best. Let's buy stuff.' Then he turned to me and nodded at my fleece. 'Besides,' he added, 'you might need something less thermal to wear tonight.'

I zipped up my fleece defensively and shuffled away from Dominic. Professor Takahashi's words were still darting around in my head. Surely the feelings within us were more than a collection of variables to be measured and monitored by technology? And was my marriage really in crisis? I wondered. I gazed out the window and thought about Clapham, about Rupert, about our romantic old house. What was it about that life that had made Nick want to escape? We'd been apart only for a few weeks, but he seemed such a distant figure in my mind. I needed to be reminded of him, reminded that we hadn't lost what we'd once had. I turned further away from Dominic, then reached for my phone and dialled Nick's number.

The international ringtone pulsed into my ear as I considered what I might say.

Nick: 'Hi, sweetheart. How's Japan?'

Me: 'Great, thanks. I just went into a booth to have virtual sex with you but instead I got another shot of oxytocin at the moment of orgasm when my subconscious flipped your face and body for Dominic's. Because really, I'd much rather have sex with him. So how are you? All OK there? How's Jenna? Still sleeping with her?'

Fortunately it went to voicemail. I left a garbled message asking him if he'd like me to pick up anything from the Japanese shops, as though international commerce were an unrealised notion.

When he saw my expression, Dominic snatched my phone and threw it into my bag.

'Come on, fleecy,' he said. 'Last one to Prada is a rotten *tamagoyaki*.'

Inside Prada, we wandered around looking at the chicly dressed mannequins.

'Remind me why we're here again?' I said, fondling a

pink fur scarf. 'Not sure Prada holds the secret to lasting love.'

Dominic picked up a man's shirt and unfolded it. 'Thoughts on navy?' he asked, holding it up under his chin.

I was about to say something scathing or sarcastic but when I looked at him, at the deep blue against his tanned skin and hazel eyes, I found myself smiling.

'Looks good,' I said, quickly realising I was once again under the spell of oxytocin.

He smiled and then handed it to a sales assistant.

'I'll take it,' he said. Then he walked over to me and linked arms. 'Your turn now.'

I walked alongside the rails, eyeing the sheer fabrics draped over heavy wooden hangers. I stopped to look more closely at a tailored white shirt. Nick loved the classic look on women. I held it up. It was the kind of shirt Jenna probably wore to work, with just a hint of pert, tanned cleavage.

'No,' said Dominic, removing it from my hand. 'Try this on instead.' He handed me a bright orange silk garment. I held it up against me, trying to ascertain whether it was a dress or a top.

I snatched back the shirt. 'I'll try on both,' I said.

Dominic looked at the shirt and then cocked his head. 'OK,' he said, grabbing a grey leather miniskirt. He checked the size, then handed it to me, 'but pair it with this.'

'Yes, sir,' I said, attempting a salute.

The staff tried to block Dominic from entering the fitting room, but he barged past them claiming he was my stylist and his presence was vital.

I pulled the curtain shut and unzipped my fleece. I had a white vest on underneath and my chest seemed to burst right out.

'Ooh, hello,' Dominic said, peering through the crack at the side.

'Sod off,' I said, closing the curtain tighter and covering myself with my arms. I knew I'd been eating like a pig and drinking like a German but I hadn't realised just how much weight I must have gained without twice-weekly trips to my Virgin gym. I pulled off my vest and noticed that my stomach had that well-fed curve to it too.

'I hope we're having sushi tonight,' I said, mostly to myself.

'If you wear that orange dress, I'll eat gorilla testicles.' Dominic sniggered. 'You done yet?'

'No,' I said, stepping into the dress. As I slid it on, I remembered how different I looked with a few curves. Until now, the strain of the business expansion and the seemingly endless rounds of fertility treatment had left me flat bottomed and flat chested.

I readjusted the straps and looked in the mirror.

Dominic peered around the curtain.

'Bloody hell, Ellie,' he said and then swallowed.

I looked at him, then back at my reflection.

'You don't think it's a bit Kardashian?' I said, turning round and assessing the impact of the weight gain on my rear.

Dominic laughed, then shook his head. 'I always knew you had a great body,' he said, 'and I had a good eyeful in Iceland, but, well, all I can say is wow.'

I turned back to the mirror. 'Maybe I should get the white shirt instead. I'm not sure I'm comfortable parading around Tokyo dressed like a Pussycat Doll.'

Dominic narrowed his eyes. 'Ellie, this is Prada. It's classy. Besides, you couldn't look tarty if you wore pink

PVC hot pants.' He paused and then rubbed his temples. 'Is it wrong for that image to give me a hard-on?'

I rolled my eyes and then pulled the curtain shut.

'You're getting that dress,' he said. 'And the shirt too, along with a few pairs of jeans so you look less like a homeless hobo for the remainder of our time here.'

Chapter 24

That night we dined at Dazzle, a restaurant Dominic said was famed not only for its Michelin-starred food but also for its award-winning interior. He claimed it was the only venue worthy of my new dress.

By my second glass of champagne, I began to feel less exposed in the four square inches of satin.

'Did you know Tokyo has more Michelin star restaurants than any other city?' Dominic said, taking a sip. 'It would have been criminal not to come to one.'

'Yes,' I said, taking a sip myself, 'and it's vital to our research that we thoroughly immerse ourselves in a different culture.'

Dominic laughed. 'Not sure we can fully justify expensing those Louboutins as well as the dress.' He gazed down at my shoes, pausing en route to glance at my cleavage.

Then he looked up at me and smiled.

My stomach tightened.

He leaned forward and placed his hand on top of mine. 'I'm sorry,' he said.

'For what?'

His smile softened. 'Sorry about Jenna and Nick. That's a shitty thing to find out.'

'I know,' I said, and then paused. 'But it's not as though I've been entirely innocent, is it?'

Dominic laughed. 'Oh, but you have, Ellie.' He squeezed my hand and then glanced back at my chest. 'I wish you hadn't, but you have.'

I took another sip of champagne.

Dominic leaned forward and swept a strand of hair from my face. 'You have to admit you've been tempted though, haven't you?'

I stared at him and then took another sip.

He grinned. 'I'll take that as a yes.' He topped up my glass. 'If I get you completely drunk, might I be able to tempt you a little bit more?'

I forced a laugh and then shook my head.

Dominic snatched the glass away. 'Actually, on second thoughts, this might take longer than anticipated so best you pace yourself.'

I laughed.

He took my hand again and stared at me. 'You know I'd be with you in a heartbeat, Ellie Rigby, don't you?'

I laughed again. 'Didn't that booth sex get it out of your system?'

'I mean *be* with you. Not just have sex. Besides,' he said, 'that booth just made me hornier.'

I grabbed my glass back and took a gulp. 'So what did you think of it?'

He screwed up his mouth. 'A brilliant concept, but something not quite right about the whole thing.'

I nodded. 'Me too.'

Dominic downed his champagne and then leaned forward. 'I have to ask you,' he said. 'The female bodysuit, did it have, you know, something attached to it?'

My face flushed.

Dominic closed his eyes and took a deep breath. 'I never need porn ever again.'

I laughed.

He continued. 'So are you going to tell me who it was?'

'Who what was?'

'The person your avatar turned into in the end, you know, at the crucial moment?'

I stared at him. His mouth was curled at the edges, ready to spread into a huge grin. He knew it was him.

'Hugh Jackman,' I said, taking another sip. 'Can you believe it? Like my bond with him needed strengthening at all.'

Dominic scrunched up his face. 'You're joking, aren't you?'

I shook my head, laughing.

'You seriously like him? I mean, he was OK as Wolverine but isn't he a chorus singer too? Don't you find that a bit camp?'

I laughed. 'Not jealous, are you?'

He huffed and then refilled his glass.

I stared at him until he met my gaze. 'So you're not threatened by my actual real relationship with my husband. You don't see that as a barrier at all? However, you are threatened by a Hollywood star who I have zero chance of ever meeting, let alone actually embarking on a relationship with?'

He laughed. 'I like you, Ellie. I can't help my feelings.'

He took another sip. 'And of course I'm aware that your real-life "colleague-shagging" husband is a barrier to our relationship.'

I took a deep breath. 'We don't have a relationship, Dominic.'

He put his glass down and stared at me, his expression suddenly shifting. I noticed his jaw tense. 'Then what is this, Ellie?' he said, pointing at us both. 'What is it?'

I glanced down at the empty plate in front of me and tried desperately to think of something to say.

'For fuck's sake, Ellie,' he said, loudly enough for the people on the table beside us to glance over. He stared at me, imploring me to speak. I could see his lips trembling.

I said nothing.

He stared at me some more, then eventually stood up, knocking over his champagne glass as he did, then stormed out of the restaurant.

I looked back at the glass, still spinning around on the table top. It fell to the floor and shattered instantly.

The waiter hurried over, and began clearing up the glass and dabbing the spill. I looked up to see the other diners staring at me in silence. I glared back at them, hurried after Dominic.

Outside, the air was heavy and hot, noises bombarded my eardrums: engines roaring, music booming, people shrieking, sirens blaring. It felt as though the city itself were trying to warn me.

I found Dominic hailing a taxi and felt a sudden surge of fury.

I reached for his arm. 'So you were just going to leave me here in the street, were you?'

He turned round, eyes narrowed. 'You can't have it all ways, Ellie,' he said. 'You can't pretend not to care and then act like you do.'

I stared back at him. 'I can't care,' I said. 'I vowed not to care.'

He waved the taxi on and then walked towards me.

'This is madness,' he said. 'How can you pretend there's nothing there?'

'Because I have to,' I said, my gaze dropping down to the pavement.

He came closer and gripped my arms. 'Well, *I* don't have to,' he said, pulling me towards him. 'And I don't want to.'

I looked up at him, at the intensity in his stare.

'He doesn't deserve you,' he said, then pulled me closer. I could feel his muscles pressing against me. I tried to wriggle free but his grasp was firm.

Another siren came blaring down the street and it felt as though my senses shut down to the city around me. When his lips met mine, all I could hear was silence.

Moments later, Dominic lurched backwards. I opened my eyes to see that someone had him by the scruff. It took a few seconds for my brain to register what was happening, but when I saw Nick's wide eyes, staring back at me in disbelief, the realisation of what I had done bore down like a jackhammer to the cranium.

Without saying a word, Nick turned to Dominic and punched him in the face.

Dominic fell backwards, then quickly regained his balance. 'Whoa, easy, mate,' Dominic said, rubbing his cheek.

'Easy?' Nick said, grabbing him by the arms.

I stepped forward.

Nick looked at me again, before kneeing Dominic in the stomach.

Dominic staggered backwards, then when he'd caught his breath he held up his hands. 'OK, OK,' he said. 'Fair enough, I deserve it.' He walked towards Nick with his hand out as though he intended to make peace. 'But,' he added, quickly retracting it, 'you deserve this.' Then he punched Nick in the stomach.

Nick doubled over and then coughed several times before charging at Dominic.

'Enough!' I shouted, waving my arms in the air.

They both turned to me.

'This is my fault,' I said. 'Be angry with me. Not each other.'

Nick glared at me. 'Yes, it is your fault.' Then he glared at Dominic. 'But this creep has been after you from the beginning.'

Dominic laughed. 'Creep?' he said, tucking his shirt back in. 'I'm the guy who's been here for Ellie while you've been shagging the office slapper.'

Nick's face contorted and he squared up to Dominic. 'You know fuck all about me or my life, so why don't you just fuck off.'

Dominic shrugged his shoulders. 'I know that you're a bloody idiot for neglecting Ellie.'

Nick pushed Dominic away and then turned to me. 'Oh great, so you've been crying on this twat's shoulder, have you? Telling him I'm neglecting you. You're the one who wanted to go on this ridiculous trip.'

'Well, you're the one who wanted to drag me away from my friends and my life to go to New York.'

Nick glared at me.

I glared back at him. 'I never wanted to go,' I said.

Nick stepped forward. 'Well, I never wanted to live in a dusty old house with carpets in the bathroom.'

I narrowed my eyes. 'It was a beautiful house.'

'It was a shithole. And we didn't have the money to renovate it.'

'I loved it.'

Nick continued to glare at me. 'Well, I didn't.'

'But you said you were happy there.'

Nick sighed. 'I never said that, Ellie. You were so busy making plans for the both of us, you forgot to ask.'

I scowled at him. 'You should've told me you weren't happy.'

Nick raised his eyebrows. 'I did but you never listened. You were too preoccupied trying to create the perfect life for us.'

'Great, so it's all my fault.'

'Yes, it is,' Nick answered.

'What about your part in all this?'

Nick threw up his arms. 'My part? So now you're going to tell me I drove you into this bellend's arms?' He gestured at Dominic. Then glanced back at me. 'Nice dress, by the way,' he said. 'Can't remember the last time you wore something like that with me.'

Dominic stepped forwards. 'Don't blame Ellie,' he said. 'It was mostly me.'

'Mostly?' Nick said turning to me, eyebrows raised.

I raised mine back at him. 'What did you expect?'

'What did I expect? I expected my wife to be faithful to me.'

'Really? While you had Jenna in our bed every night.'

Nick laughed loudly. 'That's what you think, is it?'

I folded my arms. 'That's what I know. Victoria told me.'

Nick nodded slowly. 'And you believe everything she says, do you?'

I shrugged my shoulders. 'I do actually.'

Nick forced another laugh. 'You wanted to believe it, didn't you? It gave you the perfect excuse to jump into bed with this idiot.'

Dominic stepped between me and Nick.

Nick backed away, shaking his head slowly. 'I think we're done here,' he said.

I went to follow him but he turned to me and shook his head again. 'We're done, Ellie,' he said. 'We're done.'

I looked at Dominic and then I looked at the place where Nick had been standing. I could hear my heart beating, feel it pounding into my ribs and squashing my lungs. I tried to breathe but only mustered a thin gasp of air. More sirens came blaring down the road. I looked around. I wanted to go home, but I had no idea where home was any more. Dominic slipped his arm around my waist and pulled me towards him.

'It's OK, Ellie,' he said. 'Everything will be OK.'

Chapter 25

That night I slept alone. I dreamed I was on a bridge between two continents. They drifted further and further
apart, stretching the bridge until it grew so narrow it eventually split and I plunged into the ocean. Then I woke, rushed
to the bathroom and vomited.

It felt good to purge, although I was unsure whether it
was guilt, anger or Michelin-star dining that I was trying to
expel. Afterwards, I drew back the curtains and slid open
the door to the balcony. It was nearing 1 a.m. but the sounds
of the city hadn't waned at all. I looked out at the buildings
and bright lights sprawling to the horizon and I wondered
where Nick was, or if he would even stay in Tokyo. I glanced
down at my phone, hoping for a clue. There were three new
messages from Dominic.

Can't sleep

Are you awake?

Can I see you?

I felt a throb in my chest as I deleted each one. Then I sent a message to Nick.

Where are you? We need to talk.

I wasn't expecting a reply but my phone buzzed thirty seconds later.

I'll be there in five. Room number?

When I heard him knock on the door, my stomach flipped. My hands were trembling as I pulled the hotel robe over my negligee. Although he'd seen me naked more times than my mother, given the circumstances, it felt inappropriate to greet him dressed like Belle du Jour.

His eyes were bloodshot and teary. I ushered him in.

'Drink?' I said, gesturing to the minibar.

He shook his head and sat down on the sofa.

I sat down beside him and he turned to me, fingers laced together.

'Why?' he asked. 'I need to know why?'

I glanced down at the carpet.

'Why did you do it?' he asked again, leaning forward.

I looked up at him. 'It was nothing,' I said, though the words came out as more of a squeak.

He stared at me and then sighed. 'Oh, come on, Ellie. I saw you with your tongue down his throat.'

'It was just one kiss.'

Nick took a long deep breath and ran his hands through his hair. 'Do you know how hard it is for me to hear this?'

'I'm sorry,' I said. 'It was really only one kiss. I didn't mean for it to happen.'

He laughed and shook his head. 'Ellie, I know you. As much as I don't want to believe it, I know there's more to it.'

I glanced out the window and watched the white lights flashing on the wings of a plane in the distance. 'I don't know,' I said.

'You don't know what?'

I looked out again but now the plane was gone. 'I don't know how I feel.'

Nick took a sharp breath. 'Do you love him?'

'No,' I answered quickly.

'He loves you. I can tell.'

I looked into his eyes. They looked like Rupert's: desperate, pleading, loyal. 'I love you,' I said. 'I'm just a little bit lost at the moment.'

Nick forced a laugh. 'It sounds like you're trying to convince yourself more than me.'

I pulled my robe tighter around me and Nick glanced down.

I found myself wondering if he was comparing my body to Jenna's.

I forced a smile. 'Why did you come?'

He rolled his eyes. 'Sorry,' he said. 'I didn't mean to cramp your style.'

I sighed. 'I'd hardly heard from you in days. You never responded to the voicemails I left about scheduling a weekend for me to come back. And then you show up without any warning. In Tokyo.'

Nick sighed. 'You'd hardly heard from me? You never answered my calls either. And when we do talk, you always seem so grumpy with me.'

'Yes, perhaps because I suggested you take some leave and join me in Africa, and you said no.'

'It clashes with a conference Jenna and I have to attend.'

I sneered at him. 'But you found time to come now?'

He raised his eyebrows. 'Because Victoria said I should come.'

I frowned.

He nodded. 'And Matthew too.'

I sat back, still frowning.

'They both warned me about him. They've been saying it for weeks.'

I screwed up my face. 'So why did you leave it until now to care?'

'I have a job, Ellie. A grown-up job, with proper working hours.'

I glared at him.

He continued. 'And I trusted you. I was certain you'd never do that to me.'

My stomach tightened. 'So when did you stop trusting me?'

He looked down at the floor and then back at me. 'When I stopped trusting myself.'

I stood up straight away. 'What do you mean?' I said, staring at him, my eyes wide. 'I was right about you and Jenna?'

He stared at the carpet. 'Nothing really happened.'

I raised my eyebrows. 'Nothing really?'

He looked up and into my eyes. 'I was lonely, Ellie, and I missed you.'

I paced around the room. 'Well, you're a fucking hypocrite then, aren't you?'

He held up his hands. 'Come on. You have no right to be angry.'

'I have every bloody right to be angry! While I've been working my arse off, trying to find a cure for divorce and save our marriage, you've been doing God-knows-what with that tarty-tits home-wrecker.'

'She's not a home-wrecker.'

'Oh, I am sorry,' I said, folding my arms. 'Didn't mean to insult your beloved. As well as having a super bloody brain and thirty-six inch legs, I know she also runs marathons and does charity work for Syrian orphans.'

Nick sighed. 'You're not being very mature about this.'

I laughed. 'You're the one who punched Dominic in the face.'

Nick scowled. 'Oh, you're on his side now, are you? Don't mess up Dominic's pretty face or smudge his make-up.'

'He doesn't wear make-up.'

'Oh, he's just naturally tanned like that then, is he?'

'He has Mediterranean genes.'

Nick clapped his hands. 'Of course,' he said. 'I bet he's got a huge cock too?'

I opened my mouth to speak and then closed it again.

Nick raised his eyebrows. 'Oh, he has then, hasn't he?'

I glared at him.

His eyes narrowed. 'I'm amazed you can tell that from just one kiss.'

I shook my head. 'And you seriously expect me to believe "nothing really happened" with Jenna?' I marched towards the hotel door. 'Go,' I said, opening it and glaring at him. 'Just go.'

Nick looked at me for a moment and then swallowed. 'I'm gone,' he said, before storming off down the corridor.

My phone buzzed. Nick stopped and turned back, scowling at me, then he glanced down at my gown, which had fallen open.

'Big cock booty call?' he asked, nodding at my phone.

I wrapped the gown around me again.

Nick lowered his head and then kicked the wall. A chunk of plaster fell to the floor. He glanced back up at me. 'Make sure he knows I bought that negligee for you,' he said, 'for our anniversary.' Then he turned and walked away.

After he'd gone, I closed the door and slid down onto the floor, holding my head in my hands. Only a month ago, Nick and I were settled in London and planning a family. Tears began to stream down my cheeks as I wondered if he'd ever really been settled with me. Or if I had been truly settled with him. I wasn't sure what the term 'settled' even meant any more. Did it mean content? Or did it mean unchanging? I picked up my phone. Along with five more texts from Dominic, there was a text from Victoria.

Hi Darling, Everything OK?

I deleted it, then threw my phone to the floor. I glanced at the minibar, and wondered why Matthew couldn't coordinate his impromptu appearances with the times I needed a friend the most. I grabbed my phone from the floor and a bottle of Prosecco from the minibar. Matthew's mental state might have been precarious of late but I was in dire need of advice so I called him.

'You awake?' I asked, pulling out the cork with my teeth.

Matthew sighed. 'No, I'm answering my phone in my sleep.'

'What time is it there?'

'It's 6 p.m. I'm also cooking dinner in my sleep.'

'It's 3 a.m. in Tokyo.'

He sighed again. 'Ellie, is there a point to this call?'

I took a swig from the bottle. 'I hope so,' I said.

'Are you drunk?'

I took another gulp. The fizz tingled on my tongue. 'No, but I plan to be very soon.'

'Oh dear,' he said. 'What's up?'

'You want the short version?'

'Please. My stir-fry is wilting.'

I took another long swig, then a deep breath. 'Well, to summarise,' I began, 'Victoria told me Nick had been sleeping with Jenna so I kissed Dominic. Nick saw. But he said nothing *really* happened with Jenna, whatever that is supposed to mean. Anyway, now he thinks we're even, but I don't. Then we just had a talk and it ended badly, he's left and Dominic keeps texting me and I don't know what to do.'

'Oh,' said Matthew.

'Oh? Don't you have anything better than that?'

He paused for a moment. 'I knew this would happen.'

'That's not very helpful.'

'What do you want me to say?'

I tipped more champagne down my throat. 'I think my marriage is over.'

Matthew took a breath. 'Let's not be hasty.'

I grabbed another bottle. This time Merlot. 'I'm not being hasty. I think it's what Nick wants.'

'Has he said that?'

I unscrewed the cap. 'Not exactly.'

'Sounds like you want him to say it.'

I took a glug. 'What?' I asked, nearly spitting it out.

'Sounds like you want Nick to say it's over so you can be with Dominic.'

'Are you serious?'

'Yes I am, Ellie.' He paused for a moment. 'You have a long history of trying to create perfection. You and Nick are not perfect. Nor is your marriage. You won't find perfection with Dominic either.'

I swirled the wine around in my mouth and then swallowed.

'I know that,' I said.

Matthew sighed. 'I don't think you do, Ellie.'

After Matthew had ended the call complaining that his prawns had turned rubbery, I took another swig of wine, then dropped back onto the sofa. I wondered what advice I would offer a client in my predicament. I took another gulp. There was no doubt what I would say. I would remind her that it took her years to find Nick and that marriage is a precious entity that must be nurtured and respected. I would then tell her to grow the fuck up, stop drinking like a Geordie, stand by her vows, and go save her marriage.

I heard a knock at the door. I shook my head to clear my thoughts, but my vision blurred and I began to feel queasy. I pulled myself up off the sofa and rubbed my forehead.

I opened the door. It was Dominic.

'Room service,' he said brushing past me. He looked around and then peered into the open minibar. 'Looks like you need a restock,' he said, pulling a bottle of champagne from a paper bag.

I pulled my gown tight around me. 'Now is not really a time to celebrate, is it?' I said.

Dominic raised his eyebrows. 'Oh, I don't know,' he said,

glancing at the empty bottles. 'You seem to be having your own little party for one in here.'

I collapsed down onto the sofa and hung my head.

He sat down next to me and reached for the two glasses on top of the minibar. 'No matter how shitty you're feeling, there is never an excuse for drinking from the bottle. You're better than that,' he said, handing me a glass.

He twisted off the cork and then poured.

'So,' he said, eventually.

I sat up and took a big sip. 'So?'

He looked down at the floor, then back at me. 'So,' he said, 'it turns out I love you.'

I scanned his expression, searching for any signs of insincerity but all I could see were his eyes, all wide and vulnerable. 'No, you don't,' I said.

He shrugged his shoulders. 'Yes, I'm afraid I do.'

I dropped back down. 'Oh,' I said.

He turned to me, brow furrowed. 'That's not quite the response I was hoping for.'

I went to speak but nothing came out. I noticed a vein in his temple had started to pulse.

'Is there a chance you could feel the same?' he asked, eventually.

I closed my eyes and sighed.

'Ellie?'

I opened them again. 'Yes, Dominic, there is every chance I could feel the same way.'

A smile quickly spread across his face, then he leaned over and slipped his arms around my waist.

I pulled back. 'But I can't be with you,' I said. 'I'm married and I love Nick.'

He fell back against the sofa and stared up at the ceiling. 'Fuck,' he said. 'Fuck fuck, fuck.'

I leaned back and looked up at the ceiling too.

After a few minutes' silence, he turned to me. 'Will you at least acknowledge that he doesn't deserve you?'

I turned to him. 'Maybe I don't deserve him either? Maybe we don't deserve each other?' I grabbed my glass and took another sip. 'We've only been apart for a few weeks and already he's lusting after his colleague and I'm...'

Dominic leaned in closer. 'And you're what?'

'I'm here with you.'

His smile widened. 'Lusting after me? Come on. Just say it.' He started jokingly unbuttoning his shirt. 'You know you want some of this.'

I laughed. My head felt woozy. Even though I was struggling to focus, I couldn't drag my gaze from his chest. Before I could talk myself out of it, I'd reached for my glass and downed the contents. Matthew was right. I wanted an excuse. I needed to not be responsible for my actions. I leaned in towards Dominic. He grabbed me and lifted me astride his lap.

His gaze moved from my chest to my face. 'In the booth, at the end, you thought of me, didn't you?' he asked.

I nodded and then hung my head.

'I knew it,' he said, laughing. Then he paused. 'I never went through with it though.'

I looked up. 'What?'

'The booth. I couldn't do it.' He brushed the hair from my face and looked into my eyes. 'I wanted my first time with you to mean something.'

He stared at me for a moment, then pushed the robe from my shoulders. I closed my eyes as his hands slid up from my waist. Just as he leaned in to kiss my neck, I suddenly flinched. He pulled back and studied my face.

'You do want this, don't you?' he asked.

I looked at him and then at the champagne bottle. I was tempted to down the remainder, to silence the voices in my mind. I was tired of being the sensible one, trying to control everything and preserve the world's feelings. For now I just wanted to be.

I pressed my finger to his lips.

He shook his head. 'I have to know,' he said. 'This has to be more than a drunken fling.'

I stared back at him. 'And what if it can't be any more than that?'

He let out a sharp sigh. 'You're not going to give me the "if only we'd met in another lifetime" bullshit, are you?'

I shook my head.

He dropped his gaze and then sighed. When he looked up, the vulnerability in his eyes had vanished. He kissed my forehead and jumped to his feet.

He said nothing as he buttoned up his shirt, but when he caught me staring at the bulge in his trousers, he smirked.

'I don't want you using me for my big willy,' he said, readjusting himself.

I looked away.

He kneeled down in front of me and turned my face back towards him. 'Seriously though, Ellie, you need to decide.'

I looked up at him and into his eyes. 'I thought I just had,' I said.

Chapter 26

The next morning, I awoke on the sofa in my hotel room. Someone had tucked up my legs and draped a blanket over me. I sat up and peeled off the hair that was stuck to the side of my face and glanced at the empty bottles on the table beside me. The champagne bottle had been turned upside down in the bucket and beside it was a folded note.

I grabbed the note and stared at it. I recognised Dominic's writing straight away. I rubbed my eyes and unfolded it.

Dear Ellie,
I've gone back to London. You need to decide.
Dominic

My temples throbbed as I tried to piece together the mosaic-like memories of the previous night. I reread the note several times as though expecting a crucial clue to jump out at me. When no such inspiration arrived, I walked out onto the terrace. I took a deep breath and gazed out across Tokyo's skyline. Years ago I'd set out to help people, to help myself. Back then I'd believed that by finding my clients love, I was bringing happiness to their lives. Now I realised that I'd probably spread as much misery as I had joy. I pulled my phone from my gown pocket and dialled Nick's number. It went straight to voicemail. I took another deep breath and looked up. There were two planes crossing each other's paths in the sky. I wondered for a moment if Nick and Dominic might be passengers in each, jetting five hundred miles an hour away from each other and away from me. I glanced back into the room, at the suitcase which had eventually found its way back to me, and I suddenly realised that the rest of this journey I would be taking alone.

I showered and dressed with startling proficiency. It was as though, free from the turmoil of indecision, I was able to see my objective more plainly. Afterwards, I stared at myself in the hotel room mirror, wondering who exactly was looking back at me. The jeans Dominic had bought me added a roundness to my hips, and the shirt he'd bought made my chest look perkier. I breathed in and turned sideways. I'd have to tackle that muffin top at some point but, I quickly reasoned, a little weight gain from eating in hotels and restaurants every night was a small price to pay when the well-being of humanity was at stake.

I leaned in further to examine my skin. In the last few years, it'd always seemed to be dry or blotchy or some other way problematic, but in recent weeks it could almost have been described as dewy. When I found myself imagining Professor Sheldon describing the beneficial effects of oxytocin on the skin and hair, I turned away from the mirror, the icy chill of guilt washing through my veins like an anaesthetic.

How can nature be so cruel as to reward amoral behaviour? I stared at my reflection some more. Why did marriage feel like an endurance while new love more like a trip to the spa? Perhaps, I wondered, my thinking had been flawed and the best for humankind wasn't prolonging the inevitable demise of long-term love. Maybe instead we should embrace temptation? Society as we knew it might break down as a result, but at least we'd all have good skin.

Mandi called when I was packing so I shared my thoughts with her.

'No, no, no, Ellie,' she said her voice becoming progressively more high-pitched with each syllable.

'It was just an idea,' I said. 'I haven't formulated any concrete conclusions yet, but maybe we weren't meant to pair for life—'

'Ellie, stop,' she interrupted.

I paused.

She sighed. 'You have to come home.'

'I'm going to Africa today and then—'

'No,' she said.

'What?'

'The investors are pulling the funding.'

My stomach lurched. 'Why?'

She sighed again. 'They've been disappointed with your lack of communication. They think you're struggling to get results. They mentioned something about Louboutins on the expense card.' She paused and then took a sharp breath. 'Besides, it's carnage here, Ellie. Our clients keep getting divorced. We need you.'

I screwed up my face. 'I've told you before, Mandi, divorce isn't contagious.'

'You have to come home,' she said.

I collapsed down on the bed and looked out at the sky. 'I need to find the answers first, or I'm no good to you,' I said. 'I'm no good to anyone.'

'They've cancelled the corporate credit card. We've got you on a flight to Heathrow today.'

I took the phone away from my ear and stared at it. There was no way I was going to let anyone stop me from finding the truth. I felt closer than ever. My hand twitched and then before I could consider the ramifications of what I was about to do, I screamed 'No!' at the top of my voice, then swung my arm back and hurled the phone out through the open terrace doors.

I watched it curve up and over the balcony. Then it seemed to pause in mid-air, like a panicked cartoon character, before plummeting towards the street below. I flopped back down on the bed and then lay there for a moment, flinching at the likely time it would have hit the pavement, and hoping it hadn't struck a passer-by.

I was going to Africa and no one was going to stop me.

Two hours later, it seemed a man named Bob on the HSBC customer support line was going to stop me. However, after repeatedly stating that emergency overdraft extensions could no longer be approved via the telephone, he eventually relented and handed me over to his supervisor. Following a series of lengthy conversations involving said supervisor and three others, along with extensive input from several other departments, I persuaded a lady called Rita to give me another credit card, albeit with a twenty per cent interest rate.

The following day, I arrived at a Amboseli lodge in the Laikipia plains of Northern Kenya.

The host, Hasina, greeted me with an open smile. She had deep lines running from her nose to her mouth, which made me wonder if she'd been smiling like that since birth.

'Welcome,' she said, taking my hand and squeezing it. 'Did you have a good journey?'

Instead of relaxing and looking out at the vast dusty landscape on the drive from the airport, I'd spent most of the time patting my pocket, unconsciously searching for my phone. I felt like I'd taken a digital vow of silence.

I nodded. 'Yes, thank you,' I said.

She leaned forward and took my suitcase. 'Come,' she said. 'Your friend is waiting for you by the pool.'

I glanced around urgently. 'The witch doctor's here already?'

She chuckled, then wheeled the suitcase ahead. 'Follow me,' she said.

I followed her up the stone steps to an elegant thatched room with open sides. I glanced around at the rustic four-poster bed and rose-petal-lined bath and took in a sharp breath.

'This is beautiful,' I said, 'but I don't think it's my room.'

She laughed. 'It is the only room available. Your friend has the other.'

I glanced around again. 'There must be some mistake,' I said. 'I don't have a friend to meet.'

She shrugged her shoulders.

I glanced across the plains, then back at the cottage, suddenly realising there was nothing to stop a local hippopotamus from sharing my bath. Or bed for that matter.

'Where are the walls?' I asked.

She smiled and held up her hands. 'Walls are a barrier to the view,' she said.

I studied the short path between the watering hole and my bed. 'Are you sure it's safe?' I asked.

She looked at the watering hole, then back at me and smiled. 'Every wonder has its price,' she said. 'I'll leave you to settle now,' she added, backing away.

I collapsed down on the bed and let the ceiling fan blow warm air on my face. For a moment, I imagined Dominic lying next to me, pulling me towards him. Just as I went on to imagine him springing out of bed to deter an inquisitive hippo, I heard the sound of high heels clacking on the stones. When the sound ceased, I glanced up to see Victoria standing at the foot of my bed, wearing a bandeau designer swimsuit and a sheer white wrap. She lifted up her oversized Pucci sunglasses onto her forehead and screwed up her face.

'For heaven's sake, Ellie,' she said, flicking her ponytail. 'This isn't a time for moping.' She leaned forward and prodded me. 'Get up,' she said.

I pulled myself up and glared at her. 'What are you doing here?' I asked, shielding my eyes against the sun. 'And where is Camille?'

She pushed my arms aside and stared at my shirt. 'I'm here to save you from yourself. Camille is with her father.' She cocked her head. 'Is that Prada?' she asked, looking pained.

I nodded, batting her hand away.

She shook her head and tutted. 'Something so precious deserves more respect,' she said. 'It'll ruin if you don't take good care of it.'

I stared at her, wondering if it was really the shirt she was referring to. 'If you have something to say, then please say it,' I said, jumping off the bed. I heaved my suitcase onto the mattress and unzipped it.

She leaned over and met my eyes. 'I have plenty to say, my darling,' she said. 'There's no rush though. We have three days together.' She glanced at her watch. 'Dinner's at eight.' Then she looked me up and down and sniffed. 'I suggest you have a shower. Don't want to attract any more wild dogs now, do we?' Then she strode off, swishing her wrap behind her as though it were a cape.

I sat back down on the bed and looked around. In any other circumstance this place would have been heavenly. Everything about it, albeit marginally polluted by the presence of Victoria, should have induced tranquillity. However, instead I felt misplaced, as though I was the subject of a nature documentary: a domesticated creature being released back into the wild.

I showered and dressed methodically, letting the thoughts buzz around in my head like flies. At any moment when they seemed to settle, and I'd begin to feel at peace, it was as though the wiry tail of self-doubt would swipe them back into disarray. I kept reaching for my phone, craving the connection, the reassurance of others. Without digital distraction, though, I was forced to face my thoughts. Thoughts I'd tried to bury to the back of my mind. One thought kept racing around, banging into the sides of my head, seemingly desperate to escape.

You made a vow.

And with that thought, came many others.

He's your husband.

How can you be so selfish?

What is wrong with you?

At dinner, I decided to silence the voices with alcohol. I ordered a neat rum. Victoria scrunched up her nose and turned to Hasina.

'You have a Petit Chablis?' Victoria asked.

Hasina nodded, although I suspected that this was almost certainly not what Victoria would be given.

Once we'd ordered, I laid down my menu and looked out across the plains. Beyond our candlelit lodge, I could see nothing but black. Darkness stretched from the edge of the lodge to the horizon. For a moment, I imagined hundreds of glowing eyes staring back at me, waiting for me to justify my failings. Suddenly a little rock rabbit ran under my chair, quickly followed by her three babies. She stopped for a moment and looked up at me. Then looked back at her babies and ran on ahead.

Victoria grimaced and lifted her feet from the ground.

'Ugh, rodents,' she said. 'This place would be perfect if it wasn't for the animals.' She looked around to ensure the ground was clear and then put her feet back down. 'I mean, we're the superior species, they should be paying to see us, not the other way round.' Then she took a sip of the wine that had just been placed in front of her. She winced and then swallowed.

Hasina looked at her. 'Wine OK?' she asked.

Victoria forced a smile. 'I imagine it's all you have?'

Hasina nodded.

Victoria shrugged and took another sip. 'Well, then I suppose my palate will be forced to adjust.'

I smiled at Hasina and then took a big gulp of rum.

Victoria looked down her nose at me and shook her head.

'It's for the mosquitoes,' I explained.

She laughed. 'As a justification for alcoholism, that is one of your best.'

'Oh, shut up,' I said. 'You'll sink a bottle of that faux

Chablis by the main course so don't come down all high and mighty on me.'

She frowned. 'High and mighty?'

I nodded. 'Yes, with your stylised swimwear and your silly high heels, you're no better than anyone else.'

She sat back in her seat. 'I'm better than you,' she said.

I raised my eyebrows and took another glug. 'Oh really?'

'Yes,' she said, stony-faced. 'I never cheated on my husband.'

The muscles in my neck tensed. I went to reply but nothing came out. I looked down at the table and stared at a knot in the wood.

Victoria continued. 'You made a vow.'

I noticed how the shades of oak blended into one another.

'He's your husband.'

I ran my hand along the grain.

'How can you be so selfish?' She paused and took another sip of wine. 'What is wrong with you?' she said.

I shrugged my shoulders. 'I don't know,' I said.

Her lips tightened and her face flushed. 'How can you be so apathetic?'

I took another gulp of rum. 'I'm not apathetic, Victoria,' I said, still gripping the glass. 'I'm just torn.'

She let out a haughty laugh. 'Torn? You're not Natalie Imbruglia, for heaven's sake.' Then she glared at me. 'I'm so fucking angry with you right now, Ellie.'

'Clearly,' I said, slamming the glass back down on the table. 'So you came here to tell me I'm a shit wife?'

She shook her head.

'Seems like it,' I said. 'Well, you wasted your time, because I already know that. Besides,' I said, picking up my glass again, 'Nick's hardly been Mr Fidelity has he? You're the one who told me about his thing with Jenna.'

She sat back. 'Er, no I didn't.'

I sat back too, mimicking her. 'Er, yes you did.'

She shook her head and let out a sharp sigh. 'I simply re-marked that he was spending a lot of time with her.'

'Yes, so much time she had to sleep in his bed. Or, more accurately, our bed.'

'I didn't mean they were having an affair.'

'Well, what did you mean?'

'That you should be aware they were spending time to-gether.'

'Why?'

She raised her eyebrows. 'Why do you think?'

I raised my eyebrows back at her.

She stared at me for a moment and then held up her hands. 'It was to entice you back.'

I frowned.

She continued. 'To get you away from—'

'Dominic?' I asked.

She stared at me and sighed. 'Are you aware that you smile every time you talk about him?'

I stopped smiling and reached for my drink.

'You're in love with him, aren't you?'

I took a sip. 'What do you mean?'

She looked me in the eye. 'You. Love. Dominic. Don't you?'

I glanced out into the darkness. 'I'm not sure I under-stand what love is any more.'

She rolled her eyes. 'Trust you to say something obtuse like that.'

'It's not obtuse.'

She forced a laugh. 'Let me spell it out for you then: if love is wanting to shag someone's brains out and be with them all the time, then you love Dominic.'

'I love Nick,' I said.

'If you loved Nick, why did you leave him in New York to go gallivanting around the globe and taking naked baths with Dominic?'

I grimaced. 'Naked baths?'

She sniffed. 'Matthew told me.'

I glared at her.

'He was concerned.'

I sighed. 'It was a spring and there was a professor in there too.'

She snorted. 'Oh, in that case it's perfectly acceptable.'

I shook my head. 'Look. We kissed. We both knew it was wrong. But that's it. It's done now.'

Victoria took a sip of wine, without breaking eye contact.

'I wish I could believe you,' she said.

'You can,' I said, downing the last of my drink. 'You have to.'

Chapter 27

At 5 a.m. Victoria woke me up with a prod to my arm. I opened one eye to see she was clad in full safari kit.

'Come on,' she said.

I rubbed my eyes against the bright sunlight. 'Come on? Where?'

'Hasina said the witch doctor called. His advisor is collecting us in ten minutes.' She pulled off my blanket.

'Why didn't you wake me?' I asked.

'I just did,' she said with a smirk. 'Now get your rum-soaked self out of bed.'

I stood under the open shower and let the cold water pour over my head.

Victoria peered around and looked me up and down as though considering a purchase.

'You've put on weight,' she said, cocking her head. 'It's not a total disaster, but you need to do something to sort that tummy out.'

I stepped out and pushed past her to grab a towel.

She nodded downwards. 'And I know we're doing the back to nature thing, but there's really no excuse for that.'

I rolled my eyes. 'At least it's supporting evidence that nothing happened with Dominic,' I said.

She shrugged her shoulders. 'Hurry up,' she said, throwing my clothes on the bed. 'We're going to be late.'

We walked round the front of the lodge to see a Jeep parked. There was a man wearing a zebra-print shirt in the driver's seat. He turned to us and smiled.

'Good morning,' he said in a strong Swahili accent. 'My name is Jengo.'

Victoria stood by the passenger door as though waiting for it to open by itself. 'Good morning, driver,' she said.

He smiled and nodded at the door handle. 'It won't bite,' he said and then chuckled.

Victoria sniffed and then pulled the handle down roughly. Just as she was about to pull herself up into the seat, she suddenly jumped back and screamed.

'What the hell is that?' she said stepping back further.

I peered in.

'Matilda,' he said. 'She's Dr Menzi's advisor.'

Victoria shook her head quickly as though trying to clear her vision. 'He has a pet warthog?'

Jengo leaned back to pat the warthog's head. Matilda shuffled forwards and eyed Victoria. 'See, she likes you,' he said. 'Now please get in.'

When it became apparent that Victoria had no intention of testing Matilda's affection for her, I climbed into the Jeep first. Victoria reluctantly followed, then sat as squashed up

to the passenger door as she could. Matilda rested her head
on my lap and stared at Victoria, who occasionally snuffled
her nose and grunted.

While he drove us to an undisclosed location, Jengo prepped
us for our meeting by explaining Dr Menzi's eccentricities,
or at least those beyond seeking counsel from a pet warthog.

'He doesn't like to be interrupted when he is speaking,'
Jengo began. 'He is a man of few words.' Jengo raised his
hands to the sky. 'But the words he chooses are powerful.
They can grant us life, like the rains, we say in Swahili.'

I nodded, relieved that his hands were now back on the
wheel.

Victoria rolled her eyes, then shot a sideways glance at
Matilda, who was still staring at her. Victoria smoothed
down her ponytail.

Jengo leaned back and patted Matilda on the head. Then
he glanced at Victoria. 'She senses your doubt,' he said.

Victoria sighed. 'She's a hog. She probably senses the
undigested breakfast in my stomach.'

Jengo chuckled. 'You have much to learn,' he said.

Victoria let out an impatient sigh. 'So what research has
this doctor done? How is he an expert on love?'

Jengo chucked again. 'He is no expert,' he said. 'He is
a vehicle.'

'A what?' she mouthed at me.

'A vessel, I mean. He is a vessel for wisdom.' He threw his
hands to the sky again. 'It is passed through him to others.'

Victoria screwed up her face. 'A vessel for tourist money,
more like.'

Soon after, Jengo screeched to a halt by a dusty copse.
'We are here,' he said, turning round to face us. 'One more

thing,' he said. 'You must remove your shirts. He likes bare breasts. It's a tribal honour.'

Victoria looked up from her phone with a pained expression. 'I don't think so,' she said, then pointed to me. 'Although this one doesn't mind getting her kit off.'

I glanced at Victoria and then at Jengo. He grinned, then started to laugh. 'I am joking,' he said. 'Like British humour, yes?'

I smirked. Matilda grunted.

Jengo jumped out of the Jeep, still smiling. 'Come on,' he said.

Victoria followed, smoothing the creases out of her safari suit. Matilda and I exited at the same time, almost becoming wedged in the footwell as we did. Matilda grunted and made a beeline for Victoria. Victoria sidestepped her a few times, then looked around for assistance.

Jengo ushered us through the trees and into a small clearing. There was a large tortoise and a cluster of mud huts. I looked around expecting to find an elderly man with a feathery headdress and bones coming out of his nose, but Jengo ushered us further along, past the mud huts to a large building with a high stone wall around the side. He pressed a button on some kind of entryphone system.

There were some exchanged mumblings in Swahili and then the door opened. We followed Jengo into a stunning marble courtyard, at the centre of which was a clear blue pool. Matilda trotted up to a daybed under a shady palm, hoisted herself up and then flopped down onto her side. Jengo walked through an archway and held out his arms.

'Dr Menzi,' he said. 'How are you, my friend?'

I peered around the pillar of the archway to see Jengo high-fiving a man resembling a cross between Snoop Dog and a

Roman gladiator. He was wearing furry loincloth, diamond-encrusted hoops in his ears and had a leopard skin draped over his shoulders. At the tail end of his brotherhood greeting, he caught sight of me watching. Victoria tightened her ponytail.

'Welcome,' he said, swaggering towards us. I half expected him to launch into a 50 Cent–style rap about his crib:

You can find me in the sun, bottle full of rum. I'm into big pigs. I ain't into making love.

'Come give me a hug,' he said, bypassing me and heading straight towards Matilda. She rolled off the sunlounger and trotted towards him before nuzzling his loincloth.

Victoria screwed up her nose.

Dr Menzi laughed. 'It's the fur she likes,' he said.

Victoria held her hand up as though to halt any further explanation.

He smiled. 'Can I get you any refreshments?' he asked.

I stood silent for a moment, wondering if we hadn't inadvertently wandered onto an Eddie Murphy film set.

'Diet Coke?' I asked, realising it was an odd request put to a Swahili witch doctor but at the same time thinking that, given the circumstances, it seemed entirely reasonable.

He smiled, then turned to Victoria.

She sat up. 'Don't suppose you have a Petit Chablis?'

He nodded. 'Is 2009 OK?'

She stared at him as he backed away smiling.

When he was out of sight, and after Jengo had made his way outside, or inside, I hadn't really noticed, Victoria pulled out her phone from one of the many pockets of her safari jacket and began tapping on the screen. After a moment, she stopped to read something and then looked up at me.

'Dr Menzi,' she said. 'YouTube phenomenon, reached over ten-million views in the first week.'

I laughed. 'Seriously?'

She scrolled down and read on, shaking her head. 'Self-schooled sensation Dr Menzi Mandla Muti, the only surviving relative of the late Shaman Nkanyezi, Kenya's most revered witch doctor, has been dubbed the unlikely saviour by a loyal and extensive online community of American college students.'

I sat down next to her and grabbed the phone. Just as I was reading about the college server crashing during millions of Napster-style frenzied downloads of Dr Menzi's self-improvement videos, I suddenly heard the clinking of ice cubes in a glass behind me. It made me jump so I dropped the phone. Victoria lunged down to grab it but not before Matilda had snuffled it with her snout.

I looked up at Dr Menzi, who was grinning.

'Drinks, ladies,' he said, placing the tray on a table and taking a seat on the lounger next to us. I caught Victoria eyeing his six-pack and nudged her in the ribs.

'So,' he said rubbing his hands together and looking at the pool. 'Fancy a dip?'

Victoria pulled down the hem of her jacket. 'No, thank you,' she said. 'We are here for answers.'

He raised his eyebrows. 'Ah,' he said. 'Now I understand why you're dressed like a Nazi.'

She narrowed her eyes. 'It's safari chic,' she said, then sniffed, 'which, considering the setting, is infinitely more appropriate than your Flintstone pimp ensemble.'

He laughed. 'If you say so, Miss Uppity.' Then he handed her the glass of wine from the tray. 'Although I doubt you'll find many of the big five in my landscaped courtyard.'

Victoria snatched the glass and took a sip. 'Oh, I don't know. It seems you're wearing two of them,' she said, 'and then there's that ghastly hog.' She gestured to Matilda, who was now sprawled at his feet.

Dr Menzi leaned over and scratched behind Matilda's ear. Matilda glanced up and then rested her head back down with a sigh. 'She's telling me you need my help.'

Victoria spluttered her second gulp of wine out of her mouth. 'Well, her porcine perception is clearly muddled,' she said. Then she pointed at me. 'Ellie is the one who needs your help.'

He turned to me and raised an eyebrow. 'You do?' he asked.

I nodded.

He glanced back to Victoria. 'Those who know they need help concern me less than those who don't.'

Victoria took another sip. 'You know nothing about me,' she said.

He looked up at the sky. The sun was slicing through the long leaves of the palm. 'I know you're married, recently separated. You have a daughter who you've failed to bond with because she is too much like you for you to love her. Your husband is a good man who made a mistake because he felt starved of love. You try to push people away because you think it stops you from getting hurt—' he looked back down and took Victoria's hand '—and after thirty-five years of life, you've failed to realise that letting people love you is the only way you will ever learn to love yourself.'

Victoria tensed. Then blinked. Then she blinked again. She looked at me. I shrugged my shoulders. Then she looked back at Dr Menzi.

'Utter nonsense,' she said, taking another glug of wine. 'You could have gleaned all that from my Facebook page.'

Dr Menzi leaned forward and removed the glass from her hand. 'When you care about yourself as much as you care for your friend,' he said, glancing at me, and then back at her. 'Only then will you begin to heal.'

Victoria snatched the glass back, downed the remainder of the wine, and then marched off, claiming she needed the bathroom.

Once she'd gone, I smiled at Dr Menzi. 'Thank you,' I said.

He raised his eyebrows. 'She didn't need me to tell her that, though, did she? You could have said it instead.'

I frowned.

He continued. 'You are less of a good friend than she.'

I sat up. 'What?'

He looked me in the eye. 'She is worried about you. And you are also worried about you. When did you stop putting other people's happiness before your own?'

My frown deepened. 'Excuse me,' I said, sitting up further. 'For your information, I've made a career out of helping people.'

He shrugged his shoulders. 'I wasn't questioning why you stopped putting other people's happiness before your own. I was simply asking when?'

I stared at him. 'When?'

He nodded. 'Yes. I imagine you'll find it will be at precisely the same time things started to go wrong for you.'

I looked down. Matilda was sleeping. Then I looked sideways at the pool: the breeze blew gentle ripples across the surface. I looked up at the sky. Instinctively, my eyelids scrunched up together. I took in a lungful of the hot dry air.

Eventually, I opened my eyes and looked at him.

He continued. 'We don't exist in isolation,' he said. 'Each of us has a responsibility to one another.' He paused to pat Matilda. 'It has been said that it takes a village to raise a child.' He opened his arms. 'And it takes a community to support a marriage.'

I stared at him. 'I've been trying to help people, I really have. But I don't know how.'

'You don't know how, or it doesn't suit you to know how?'

'Of course I want to know how. That's why I'm here.'

Matilda let out a loud grunt. At least I assumed it was a grunt until I smelled the air wafting around me.

I held my nose but Dr Menzi seemed unfazed.

He leaned forward and looked me in the eye. 'Have you considered that preoccupying oneself with the search for a cure is an excellent way to avoid treatment?'

And with that he stood up and walked off. Matilda followed.

Soon afterwards Jengo appeared with a film crew and a friendly reminder that our time with Dr Menzi was over. I tried to explain that my questioning was not yet concluded but he simply directed me to Dr Menzi's YouTube channel and suggested I message him there.

As I stood alone in the courtyard waiting for Victoria, I took another deep breath, wondering if I might inhale some wisdom, along with any lingering emissions from Matilda. I glanced up at the sky. Maybe now, as a sinner, I'd been blacklisted from any spiritual intervention, my mugshot on the karma hit list. I thought about Nick. I could almost see him shaking his head and agreeing with my diagnosis. Then I imagined Jenna, wearing a body-con dress and pouring him a glass of wine on a Manhattan terrace, saying, 'It's a shame your wife prioritised her self-interests over your relationship. Oh well, her loss,' before shaking loose her mermaid-like locks and pouting at Nick.

Soon after, Victoria stumbled out onto the courtyard with Dr Menzi.

'They have an '89 Burgundy in there,' she said with a hiccup. Then steadied herself on a pillar. 'And a Crozes-Hermitage.'

Just as Jengo was helping a resistant Victoria into the Jeep, Matilda nudged me on the leg with her snout and then looked back at Dr Menzi. He smiled and nodded.

'Yes, Matilda,' he said. 'I know.'

I frowned at him. 'Know what?'

He smiled, then walked towards me and put both hands on my stomach. 'You will be blessed,' he said, 'with three.'

I stepped back. I could hear Victoria laughing from the Jeep.

'I don't think so,' I said.

Dr Menzi glanced down at Matilda and then back at me and smiled.

'You'll see,' he said.

Back at the lodge, Victoria headed straight to the Jacuzzi pool with a couple of bottles of the Hasina's faux Chablis.

'Do you think I'm self-medicating?' she slurred, pouring a glass up to the rim.

I laughed. 'Of course,' I said, topping up my glass. 'But it's working nicely, isn't it?'

She giggled, pulling up the top of her gold Versace swim-suit, and took another glug.

I stared up at the sky. The sun was hovering above the

horizon as though it hadn't made its mind up which way to go. 'Do you think Dr Menzi was right?' I asked.

She snorted the wine out of her nose. 'About you being blessed with three children?'

I laughed. 'No, that was obviously bullshit. I mean the bit about me forgetting to help others.'

She looked down into the Jacuzzi foam. 'I didn't hear that bit. I was in the toilet.'

I laughed. 'No, you weren't. You were hiding behind the pillar, quaffing Dr Menzi's fine wine collection. Matilda was staring at you. She gave you away.'

She smirked. 'I was intrigued,' she said.

'So, do you think he was right?'

She scrunched up her nose. 'No,' she said. 'You helped me.'

I stared at her for a moment. 'Yes, I might have helped you five years ago. But what have I done since then? Ignore you because you had a bigger house than me and a perfect child and a perfect bottom. Because you had the life I wanted.'

She shook her head. 'Ellie, you had that life too.'

I laughed. 'What, a dilapidated house, a barren womb and a husband who would rather stay out every night than be with me?'

Victoria topped up my glass. 'Well, at least your husband could hold a conversation with you without sneering or making little digs about your imperfect personality. It was like Mike hated me by the end. My daughter doesn't think much of me either. It was only that scrap of a hound that showed me any affection.'

I saw a tear edging out the corner of her eye. She blinked it away proficiently.

'And you gave him away,' I said.

She sniffed. 'No point getting attached,' she said, taking another gulp.

I watched her, waiting for the realisation.

She tutted. 'Yes, Dr Dolittle Dre is probably right. But how am I supposed to change the habit of a lifetime?'

I leaned forward and pressed the button to start the Jacuzzi bubbles again. 'Dr Phil says you only have to do something twenty-one times for it to become a new habit.'

Victoria rolled her eyes. 'So Mike must have shagged that trollop twenty-one times then before he decided to leave me?'

I glanced up. 'He didn't leave you. You left him.'

'Yes, because he was shagging her.'

'Shagging? I thought he said they only had sex once. That's what you told me.'

'Only?' she said. 'Only? Am I supposed to be grateful?' She forced a laugh. 'Besides, it was more than that. I've yet to prove it, but I know it. They only ever admit to what they can't deny, don't they?'

I sighed. 'Men don't behave as a collective species,' I said.

'So you think it's OK? You think I should put up with that?'

I looked down at the bubbles. 'Of course not. But it's never black and white, is it?'

She tutted. 'Yes, it is. "Do not put your penis in another woman" is quite a clearly defined expectation in a marriage.'

I nodded. 'Yes,' I said. 'But what do you think Mike's expectations were of you?'

Her eyes widened. 'Whose side are you on?'

'Yours,' I said. 'I want you to be happy.'

She rolled her eyes. 'Well, let me hate him then. That's what I need to do right now.'

I stared at her for a moment, then topped up her glass. 'Fair enough,' I said. 'Mike is an arsehole.'

She shook her head. 'No, he's not an arsehole,' she said, chinking her glass with mine. 'He's worse than that. He's a...'

I laughed, before I realised she was serious, then I stopped and stared at her. Her expression had the hollowness of a psychopath. I lifted her glass to her mouth. She swallowed and then seemingly regained her composure.

'Do you think Nick is one too?' I asked.

She smirked and then her mouth spread into a full smile. She began to laugh, a wild, untempered, hyena-like yowl. It echoed into the blackness around us. She laughed and laughed as though exorcising a resistant demon. When she'd finished, she paused, took a long deep breath and then downed her wine.

'No,' she said. 'I don't.'

We sat silently, listening to the water bubble and foam. I imagined tiny ships bobbing up and down, desperate for the storm to pass.

'So when are you going to admit you had sex with Dominic?' she asked.

I shook my head. 'I didn't.'

She leaned forward, eyes narrowed. 'But you wanted to?'

I tried to look resolute, but all I could think about was Dominic's arms around me, his chest pressing against mine, his soft deep voice.

She stared at me some more. 'You know he's engaged, don't you?'

I turned to her, eyebrow raised.

'I did some research.'

I raised the other eyebrow as well.

'According to government records, he's been engaged to a Connie Bragwell for seven years. He tells people she's dead but she's not.'

I swallowed. 'You're serious?'

She waved her hand dismissively. 'It's not as bad as it sounds,' she said, taking another sip of champagne. 'According to NHS records, Connie's been in a vegetative state for six of those years, with no chance of recovery. So you can't really blame him.'

'Blame him for what?'

'Falling for you,' she said, topping up her champagne. 'Apparently he was driving the car when they crashed, so you can understand he has some issues about telling people.'

I swallowed again feeling like there was something in my throat I was failing to dislodge.

Victoria continued, oblivious. 'I also had my private investigator delve into his financial affairs. Very interesting. Apparently he's made more money than his grandfa—'

'Enough,' I said, narrowing my eyes. 'I don't want to hear any more.'

She cocked her head with a pained expression. 'You really are in love with him, aren't you?'

I looked up at the sky. The stars seemed to be popping out like hundreds of bright eyes opening to witness a great event. I felt sorry to disappoint them. 'If a nasal spray switched these feelings on,' I said, 'then maybe a nasal spray could switch them off.'

Victoria turned to me. 'Hah,' she said. 'If only it could be that simple.'

I looked up at the sky and smiled. 'I'm starting to think it might be,' I said.

She forced a laugh, then reached for the bottle.

That night, despite the vat of wine sloshing around my body, I barely slept. It seemed as though every noise was louder; every rustle, every scuttle, dragged me back to consciousness. Images of Nick, Dominic, the witch doctor, Victoria, poor Connie on a life support machine, even Matthew's lap dance with the PC Truncheon, all flicked through my mind like an amateur cartoon strip. It was though my brain was desperately trying to file recent experiences but was at a loss at how to categorise them. I forced an image of Dominic to the front of my mind. The details of his face seemed hazy. His eyes were clear and his smile I could recall, but the rest seemed to be blurred, like a watermarked photograph. I switched the image to one of Nick. I tried to make the face in my mind smile, but it looked so sad, and the background grey. I zoomed closer. I could see every line, every crease deeply etched in his skin. I watched a tear trickling down his cheek. I heard sobs in my mind. I covered my head with my pillow, trying to block out the image. I couldn't. It grew bigger and bigger until I felt stabs in my stomach and my muscles clenched. It felt as though I was drowning in some kind of abstract pain. I tried to breathe but I couldn't. I tried to cry out but was paralysed. My skin felt hot, prickly. I was sweating from every pore. But I felt cold, so cold. Suddenly the image of Nick's face morphed into mine, but the eyes grew black, the expression sinister. Horns erupted out of the side of the head, thick red blood spewed from the mouth. The mouth widened and widened until the jaw unhinged and split from the face. I felt sucked in, dragged down, I was falling. All I could see was red. All I could hear was a high-pitched scream.

'Ellie? Ellie, are you OK?'

I sat bolt upright in bed and looked around. The morning sun was so fierce, it took a moment to register Victoria standing over me in her white nightie.

'Are you OK?' she repeated.

I rubbed my eyes. 'I think so,' I said, looking around. 'Where are we?'

She put her palm against my forehead. 'Shit, Ellie. You've got a raging fever.'

I lay back down and pulled up the blanket. My teeth began to chatter.

'I'm freezing,' I said.

Victoria looked around. Her hand hovered over the glass of water next to my bed. Then she retracted it. 'I'll get you some Evian,' she said. 'Wait here.'

I smirked. I tried to whisper, *I'm not going anywhere*, but just as I pursed my lips, I felt my eyes roll back into their sockets.

Chapter 28

I woke to see Nick's face peering down at me. He looked annoyed.

He turned to Victoria, who was again decked out in safari gear.

'You got me all this way,' he said to her, 'and it was the bloody flu.'

She shrugged her shoulders. 'I thought it was dengue fever. That's what the symptom checker website implied.'

Nick rolled his eyes. 'Flu. Brilliant. What a waste of my time.'

I pulled myself up in bed. 'People die from flu, you know.'

He glanced back down at me. 'Yeah, some people also die from eating a peanut,' he said. 'You look fine to me.'

I scowled at him. 'I didn't ask you to come.'

'No,' he said, turning to Victoria, 'your melodramatic friend did.' He put his hand on his hip and affected a silly high-pitched voice. 'It's serious, Nick. It might be your last chance to make peace with each other. Ellie needs you.' He rolled his eyes again. 'All that for a head cold.'

'Flu,' Victoria interrupted.

'Whatever,' said Nick, glancing back down at me. 'I'm surprised Mr Muscle isn't here, mopping your brow with his giant cock.'

Victoria screwed up her face. 'That would be an odd thing to do.'

Nick huffed.

Victoria studied him for a moment as though she'd been presented with an unknown mammal for classification. Her expression implied she'd place him somewhere between baboon and rodent.

'You're being quite childish, Nick. Ellie has been very unwell.'

He shrugged his shoulders. 'Karma's a bitch, isn't it?'

I pulled myself further up. If I'd had enough strength I would've bopped him over the head with my Evian bottle.

'Why don't you just go back to New York then?' I said to him. 'I'm sure Jenna and her fifteen-inch waist are missing you.'

He turned to me with a forced smile. 'Because, my sweet, the next flight back to New York isn't until tomorrow morning.'

I narrowed my eyes. 'Oh, another night without her. How will you cope?'

He glared at me and shook his head.

Victoria clapped her hands. 'Right now, children,' she said. 'That's enough of that.' Then she walked towards me and sat down on the bed. 'We're all highly relieved that you're not dying of dengue fever,' she said. 'But you need to rest. I'll take Nick on safari or something to keep him entertained.' She turned back to Nick. 'That OK with you?' she asked.

He shrugged his shoulders. 'Sure,' he said, 'just as long as it's safe to leave Ellie. I mean, who knows, she might get stung by a bee while we're gone.'

I tutted and pulled the sheet back over my head. My muscles ached and my nerves twinged. I peered out from the sheet to see Victoria and Nick walk away. I wanted to call after him but I couldn't. It was hard to see against the raging rays of the sun, but just as I dropped my head back down into the pillow, I was certain I saw Nick glance back over his shoulder.

It was close to dusk by the time they returned, and driven insane with boredom, I'd managed to drag myself out of bed and into the Jacuzzi. My fever had broken and it felt good to soak my aching muscles in warm water.

I saw Nick's face first when they both walked around the corner. He burst out laughing.

'How's the patient?' he said. 'Can we get you some champers while you're in there?' Then he nudged Victoria in the ribs. 'Pop that one in symptom checker,' he said, laughing some more.

I rolled my eyes and turned away.

'Glad to see you're feeling better,' Victoria said to me, before scowling at Nick. Then she said something about nipping off to have a quick shower and left me and Nick in a sulky stand-off.

We both stared out over the plains. The sun was halfway behind the horizon. It seemed tonight it was clear which way it wanted to go. I glanced at Nick, then back out at the setting sun. There was a comforting certainty to nature.

Everyone had their roles. The crickets chirped at dusk, the panthers prowled at night. There were no deviations. It was simple. Instinct, not logic was the drive. I rested my head against the side of the Jacuzzi and wondered if we humans hadn't brought misery with our complexity.

I turned to Nick. 'I'm sorry,' I said.

He unfolded his arms and squatted down beside the Jacuzzi. 'For what?' he asked, his expression softening.

I looked at him, about to apologise for Victoria's hysteria-inducing misdiagnosis, but before I could stop myself I blurted it out. 'Everything,' I said.

Nick stared into the water, took a sharp breath and then slowly let it out again.

'You're not the only one to blame,' he said, dipping his toe into the water.

I nodded.

He jumped up and started pulling off his trousers. 'OK if I join you?' he asked.

When he pulled down his underpants, I tensed up, feeling slightly awkward.

He plopped in next to me, laughing. 'Relax,' he said, 'I'm not Dominic. I'm not trying to seduce you. I just don't want to get my pants wet.' Then he stared at me, as though trying to read my expression. 'Or maybe I should try some of his moves? Is that where I've been going wrong?'

I looked at him. The idea of seduction by someone so familiar seemed odd, almost incestuous. In fact, in the absence of the appropriate neurochemicals, the notion of seduction itself seemed borderline ludicrous. I shook my head.

'No,' I said.

We sat in silence for a few minutes, then eventually both turned to each other.

'I never slept with him,' I said.

Nick looked into my eyes, his shoulders lifting slightly. 'I know,' he said.

I stared at him, waiting for him to reciprocate, but instead he said nothing.

My heart beat faster, my throat tightened. 'And you?' I asked.

He pushed my hair back over my shoulder and looked into my eyes. 'You already know the answer,' he said.

He put his arm around me, and I smiled and leaned into him, but my muscles tensed again. Part of me was desperate for clarification about Jenna. I wanted to delve further, to know precisely what had gone on: what he had said, what she had said, what he had thought and why he had stopped trusting himself. However, I knew that any answers would most likely pose more questions. Besides, there was no reason for me to share every thought I'd had about Dominic. What good would that do? I took a breath. Then I took another. With each breath it felt as though, one by one, my muscles began to relax. My thoughts began to settle too, this time with some order. It may have been because of the residual fever but when I looked up at the sky, the stars seemed to be glowing brighter, as though trying to tell me the answers had been there for the taking all along.

I stared at them some more and thought about what I had learned.

The divorce lawyer had told me most marriages could be saved; Ernest of the Texan retreat had taught me that resistance is fear. Susan Willecox had told me that our drives are incompatible with our values; Professor Sheldon had taught me that love is simply a physiological response to chemicals. Jed Tandy thought each of us perceived love differently. Bore Gunnarsson had said love is nothing more than moments in time. Professor Takahashi had taught me that technology can enhance love and Dr Menzi had taught me that a marriage could not thrive in isolation.

I glanced back up at the stars again. I'd hoped that by searching for information and consulting the experts, I would be more empowered to help people. However, it wasn't until now, nearing the end of my research, that I realised the answers I'd found had only raised more questions.

I laughed again, though out loud this time, and Nick turned to me. I couldn't help but smile. I knew now that love wasn't something we could control. Its component parts might be easy to manipulate, but its essence, like the universe, was undefinable and ever-changing.

Mandi had once said that love was a choice. And for the most part, she was right. The hurt Nick and I had felt was the result of the choices we'd made, not the feelings we'd developed for others. I could have chosen to postpone my research with Dominic and go back home. And he could've chosen to work less 'closely' with Jenna. I closed my eyes and the light from the stars throbbed through my mind, until eventually it faded to nothing. Then I opened my eyes and turned back to Nick.

'I love you,' I said.

He pulled me towards him. 'I love you too, Ellie Rigby.'

We smiled at each other. It was as though each time we said the words, we had a deeper understanding of what they meant.

Victoria never made a reappearance. Although, at one point between when Nick and I moved from the Jacuzzi to the sofa, I saw a flash of designer khaki, and heard some rustling in the bushes.

The African planes had quietened down, but Nick and I were just waking up. We drank Hasina's house wine and talked until it was only us and the cicada beetles left standing. We talked about his job, we talked about my research, and we talked about the life we'd had together.

'Did you really feel railroaded?' I asked, when he'd explained again that he had never wanted to live in Clapham.

He nodded. 'You were so enthusiastic. I didn't have the heart to tell you I hated South West London.'

'How can you hate it?' I asked. 'It's beautiful.'

He laughed. 'Rows and rows of the same terrace houses. Each one with identical interiors. Everyone drives a Range Rover. All the women are blonde, did you notice that? It's weird.'

I shook my head. 'I can't believe you agreed to move there if you hated it.'

He laughed. 'And I can't believe you agreed to leave when you loved it so much.'

I slapped my hand against my forehead. 'Why didn't we just talk?'

Nick put his arm around me and pulled me towards him. 'Because, my little firecracker, neither of us was ready to listen.'

I looked up at him, at his brown eyes shining in the candlelight, and I thought about how much had changed. 'I'm ready to listen now,' I said.

He smiled and then took my hand and led me to the bed. 'You need to get some sleep,' he said with a smirk. 'Don't want a dengue fever relapse, now do we?'

Then he snuggled up next to me and wrapped his arms around my waist.

After a while I turned to face him. 'Come back with me,' I said.

He smiled. 'No,' he said. 'You come back with me.'

I laughed and then pulled him closer.

'Let's go back together,' I said.

Chapter 29

I walked along Cabot Square in Canary Wharf, holding my laptop case in one hand, and my phone to my ear with the other. I took a deep breath and lifted my face to the sun, trying not to let my contented mood be subdued by the exasperated sigh Matthew had just emitted down the line.

'Right, let's get this straight,' he said. 'You've abandoned your quest to save everyone else's marriage in order to save your own?'

'The two aren't mutually exclusive,' I said readjusting the waistband on my pencil skirt. It was feeling a little snug. 'Besides, I haven't abandoned it. I've cut it short and now I'm compiling the research.'

He sighed again. 'OK, whatever way you want to frame it. And now you and Nick are happily back together?'

'Yes.'

'And living in Shoreditch?'

'Yes.'

He laughed. 'I love that you're now up the road from me.

But seriously, Ellie, we've discussed this before. You shop at Debenhams. Shoreditch is no place for you.'

'The flat is nice. And Nick loves it.'

'And you?'

'I'll take North London over New York any day.'

He laughed. 'And Jenna is still firmly placed across the water?'

'Yes,' I said, 'where her and her man-trapping self can stay.'

'And Dominic?'

I cleared my throat.

'Where is Dominic, Ellie?'

I said nothing.

'Tell me he's been run over, or moved to Nebraska?'

'No,' I said. 'He's still in the London office.'

Matthew let out a long sigh.

'It's not as though I can tell him to quit his job and leave the country, is it?'

Matthew said nothing.

'Anyway, I haven't seen him yet. It's my first day back.'

Matthew sighed again.

'Look, there's nothing to worry about, it's all good. Nick and I are good. We're good.'

'Do you want to say good again just in case you're not quite convinced?'

I laughed. 'I am convinced. Don't worry.'

'That's what Lucy said the night before she first ran off with Smarmy Balls.'

I sighed. 'But she's back now and that's all that matters, so you need to stop mentioning it. Remember what your therapist said?'

'Fair point,' he said. 'Although technically my therapist

said I shouldn't keep mentioning it to Lucy. I can say what I like to you.'

I rolled my eyes. 'You've chosen to forgiven Lucy,' I said. 'So you have to stop mentioning it altogether. To yourself included. Or I'll get PC Schlong on your case again.'

'Do that,' he replied, 'and I'll tell everyone you had a threesome in an Icelandic spring.'

'It was an interview.'

He laughed. 'Perhaps. But I can be very convincing.'

Given Matthew's mood, I decided to wait for a better time to impart the rest of my news. 'Flat-warming party, tomorrow night. Be there, or—'

'Or get double-dipped in a spring?' he said.

Before I could think of a quick retort, he'd already hung up.

It had only been a few months since I'd last been in the London office, but as I walked through the glass doors, it felt like I was stepping back into a past life. I hovered by the reception desk for a moment, almost contemplating signing in for a visitor's pass.

Suddenly something very pink engulfed my field of vision. It was Mandi, wearing a luminous pencil dress with some sort of bump-enhancing cummerbund. Not that it needed any enhancing at this stage.

'Ellie, Ellie,' she squealed, bobbing up and down on the spot, 'you're back!' She clapped her hands above her head and began waddling around the office shouting, 'Ellie's back everyone! She's back!' as though I were Marco Polo returning with treasures from the Orient.

Staff began peering out of their offices and waving a polite welcome. I felt a bit conspicuous standing in the middle of the floor so I found a chair behind my old desk and sat down. Immediately, I noticed everything was different. My stacked files and piled-up notes had been replaced by two Apple screens. The usually cluttered surface was clear apart from a phone. I glanced at the screen save. It was a photo of Tokyo and there was a girl wearing an orange dress. My stomach flipped.

I looked up to see Dominic standing in front of me.

'Hello, Ellie,' he said. 'Do make yourself comfortable.'

I smiled. 'Well, it is my desk.'

He laughed. 'You can have it back if you like. I was only keeping the seat warm for you.'

I glanced up at him.

He smiled. 'It's good to have you back,' he said.

Suddenly, Mandi rushed across the office towards us. 'Ellie's back!' she screamed, reaching such a speed that I was concerned she intended to take flight. 'Isn't that great, Dominic!' She hugged Dominic, then launched herself at me, flinging her arms around my neck. She pulled back. 'I'm just so excited to have you back, Ellie. I want all the details of your research. Did you find the answers? Did you find them? Did you? Tell me you did!'

She pulled at my arms to drag me up from the chair. 'Come on,' she said. 'I've booked a meeting room. I want all the details.'

As I stood up, she and Dominic both looked down at my stomach.

Mandi covered her mouth with her hands and then stared at me.

'Oh wow, Ellie,' she said, hands still over her mouth. 'I didn't notice. Oh my. Are you? You are, aren't you? I mean, you're not just a bit fat? You're, you know, expecting?'

I nodded and smiled.

Dominic leaned against the desk. His smile widened but his eyes didn't crease. He went to say something.

Mandi interrupted, still grinning. 'How far gone are you? When's the due date? Have you had a scan yet? Are you going to find out the sex? Do you want a girl? I bet you want a girl, don't you? Sorry, I'm asking too many questions. I'm just so excited for you.'

'It's still early days,' I said. 'Only eleven weeks. I've got a scan next week.'

Mandi's brow furrowed and then she scrunched up her nose. 'That's a huge bump for eleven weeks. I wasn't even showing until fifteen.' Then she stood beside me to compare bumps. 'Are you sure you got your dates right?'

I nodded. 'Certain,' I said, recalling the only possibility beyond elves with a turkey baster and a sperm sample: the night we'd escaped the Texan ranch.

Mandi shook her head quickly. 'Well, in that case,' she said, leaning forward to rub my stomach, 'you must have a few in there!' She laughed and then went on to congratulate me and tell me how pleased she was, and that I must tell Nick how pleased she is for us both but while I heard the sounds coming out of her mouth and saw her lips moving at record speed, even for Mandi, all I could think about was what the witch doctor had said.

You will be blessed with three.

His words echoed around my head. Surely he hadn't meant all at once, had he?

Mandi began waving her hand in front of my face. 'Ellie? Are you in there?'

I shook my head quickly to clear my thoughts. 'Sorry,' I said. 'Yes?'

Mandi grinned. 'I was asking you if I could tell everyone yet? Please? Can I?' she said, clasping her hands together. 'Pretty please.'

I grinned. 'Why not,' I said, rubbing my stomach. 'I suppose it's no secret now anyway.'

She hugged me and then waddled off clapping and giggling.

I turned back to Dominic. He was looking down at the floor. He glanced up to meet my gaze.

'Congratulations,' he said, leaning forward and squeezing my shoulder. 'I'm genuinely pleased for you. I really am.'

I nodded. 'Thank you,' I said.

He rubbed his forehead and then laughed. 'I'd give you a hug but that wouldn't really be appropriate, would it?'

I shook my head. 'No,' I said.

He sat down on the desk, in front of me. 'I've got some news of my own,' he said.

I looked up.

'I'm relocating to the New York office.'

I smiled, suddenly feeling a little wobbly on my feet. 'That's good,' I said.

He nodded. 'Yes,' he said. 'A new start.'

'What about your fiancée?' I suddenly blurted out.

He stared at me for a moment, then nodded. 'If I've learned anything from this, Ellie,' he said, 'it's knowing when it's time to let go.'

His expression was composed but I could see the pain in his eyes. I wanted to jump up and hug him tightly. I wanted to tell him that it would all be OK and that he would find someone who could love him as he deserved to be loved, but when I went to speak, nothing came out.

He leaned forward and rested his hands on my shoulders. 'It's OK,' he said. 'It really is.'

I looked up at him and into his eyes, and I wondered why love had to come with so much suffering.

He stepped forward and kissed me on the head. It was a long, tender kiss, as though he were trying to send a message straight to my soul. 'And if it isn't,' he said, stepping back and exhaling a laugh, 'then there's always another lifetime to hold out for, isn't there?'

I laughed with him. 'Yes,' I said. 'And we'll have all the answers by then, won't we?'

He stopped laughing and stared at me. 'You already have the answers, Ellie,' he said. 'Just make sure you don't forget them, that's all.'

It might have taken me a long time to understand, but as I watched him walk away, I realised that he was right. I glanced down at my stomach and rubbed it gently, making a silent vow to pass the wisdom along.

To however many I might be blessed with.

But for now, it was time I found my way back to serving others before myself. I pulled out a notepad and pen from the top drawer and sat down. I thought of the people who could do with my help, the friends and clients I'd been neglecting, and I began to write a list: Victoria and Mike, Cassandra and Richard, Kerri and Freddie, Kat and Klive... The list went on, page after page. When I'd finished, I flicked back through all the way to the top and smiled.

In the number one slot, I'd written 'NICK' in shouty capitals. I smiled again and then underlined it three times.

I may not have discovered the secret to a successful marriage, but I was beginning to understand the secret to our marriage.

* * * * *

'High drama and lots of laughs'
—*Fabulous* magazine

Fed up with disastrous internet dates and conflicting advice from her friends, Ellie Rigby decides to take matters into her own hands. Instead of looking for a man for herself, she's going to start a dating agency where she can use her extensive experience in finding Mr Wrong to help others find their Mr Right.

Well, that is until a match with one of her clients, charming, infuriating Nick, has her questioning everything she's ever thought about love…

MILLS & BOON®

*A fast-paced, fun-packed rummage
through the ultimate dressing up box.*

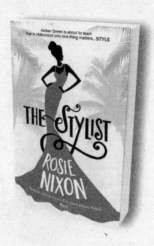

When fashion boutique worker Amber Green is
mistakenly offered a job as assistant to infamous,
jet-setting 'stylist to the stars' Mona Armstrong,
she hits the ground running, helping to style some
of Hollywood's hottest (and craziest) starlets. As
awards season spins into action Mona is in hot
demand and Amber's life turned upside down.
How will Amber keep her head?

And what the hell will everyone wear?

One Place. Many Stories

What do you do when you can't find any decent men? You date tried and trusted men, that's what — your friend's exes!

After a series of truly disastrous dating experiences, Marnie is trying something new — dating her friend's exes in an attempt to 'freecycle' love.

At least that's the plan. But through bad dates and good, Marnie and her three best friends Helen, Rosa and Ani begin to realise that while there are advantages to dating pre-screened men, there can also be some serious pitfalls to falling for your friend's ex!

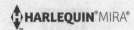

In the chaos of New York, true love
can be hard to find, even when it's
been right under your nose all along...

Love has never been a priority for garden designer
Frankie. After witnessing the fallout of her parents'
divorce, she's seen the devastation an overload of
emotion can cause. The only man she feels comfortable
with is her friend Matt – but that's strictly platonic.

But when Frankie and Matt are thrown into close
quarters working together on a beautiful roof garden
in Park Avenue… will the seeds of friendship grow
into something deeper?

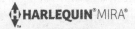

Bringing you the best voices in fiction
🐦 @Mira_booksUK

M453_SICP

**The ovens are pre-heating, the Prosecco is chilling…
and *The Sunshine and Biscotti Club* is
nearly ready to open its doors.**

But the guests have other things on their minds…

Libby: The Blogger

Life is Instagram-perfect for food blogger Libby…until she catches
her husband cheating just weeks before her Italian cooking club's
grand opening.

Evie: The Mum

Eve's marriage isn't working, but she's not dared admit it until now.
A trip to Italy to help Libby open The Sunshine and Biscotti Club
might be the perfect escape…

Jessica: In Love with her Best Friend

Jessica has thrown herself into her work to shut out the memory of
the man who never loved her back. The same man who's just turned
up in Tuscany…

**Welcome to Tuscany's newest baking school – where your
biscotti is served with a side of love, laughter and ice-cold
limoncello!**